BAR KOCHBA

From the Death Camp at Auschwitz
to the Battle for Jerusalem:
A Warrior's Journey

Ernest Weiss
and
Howard M. Cooper

PublishAmerica
Baltimore

© 2008 by Ernest Weiss and Howard M. Cooper.
All rights reserved. No part of this book may be reproduced, stored in a retrieval system or transmitted in any form or by any means without the prior written permission of the publishers, except by a reviewer who may quote brief passages in a review to be printed in a newspaper, magazine or journal.

First printing

This is a work of fiction. Names, characters, places, and incidents either are the product of the author's imagination or are used fictitiously. Any resemblance to actual persons, living or dead, events, or locales is entirely coincidental.

PublishAmerica has allowed this work to remain exactly as the author intended, verbatim, without editorial input.

ISBN: 1-60610-490-X
PUBLISHED BY PUBLISHAMERICA, LLLP
www.publishamerica.com
Baltimore

Printed in the United States of America

This book is dedicated by Ernest Weiss to:

My wife, Rachel

My children: Ilene, Edie, Sheila, Marilyn

And my grandchildren.

CHAPTER 1
Having to Run

The town numbered about 4000 souls. About 400 of them were Jewish. The Jewish souls and the non-Jewish souls kept themselves distinct. The crux of this distinction was not entirely physical since, fundamentally, they didn't actually believe in the same heaven. No one really knew for certain whether Jewish souls and non-Jewish souls were different; but in some indistinct way everyone knew that their physical bodies were very similar. There were certain assumed characteristics. Some Jews, for example, were swarthy, some were not. Some had brown eyes, others had green or blue. Some were relatively tall while others were relatively short. Their stomachs, livers, brains were the same as the internal organs of any other human being. Their hearts were characteristically the same. Shylock, in Shakespeare's *The Merchant of Venice* defends the general humanity of the Jew: "If you prick us do we not bleed?" The Jewish people both long to be the same and, at the same time long to be distinct. In our town, they were distinct. I remember the town I was born in. It was in Hungary, near the Czech border, in 1930.

I remember my early years with crystal clarity. It's ironic to use the word 'crystal' here because the town was so muddy and dull. Even so, it was everyday life for me and I knew nothing else. Our home was on the main street. The front portion was a cramped and tiny general store with little light and only a few paltry items. Behind it was the single small room where my family lived. The main street had perhaps 15 storefronts similar to ours. They were not brightly coloured and gay like they were in the city. They were made, as all the buildings in the town were made, out of stone. Our own house was made out of stone as well. It was 200 years old. I don't know how we came to live there. My father and mother were killed before I ever had a chance to ask.

The streets were makeshift, well trod and made of dirt. They were dusty or muddy in the spring and summer and frozen into ice in the winter, but that's another story. I remember asking my sister, "What if it was always winter?"

"Then we'd be cold all the time."

"Well, wouldn't we chop down all the trees and make a big bonfire in the centre of town to keep us all warm?" A child's imagination is avid.

"There aren't enough trees for that."

"But supposing there were." I pressed. "Would there be a Jewish side and a Goyshe side?" 'Goyshe' was our word for non-Jew.

"The Goyshe side would be hotter."

I got a little emotional. "But that's the point. We'd all be warmed by the same fire, even though we had different sides!"

"What's the point, Avrum?"

"Like the sun. The sun warms us the same way, all in the same way."

My sister stubbornly defended her position. "Not very much in the winter."

"That's the point. It's always winter in some ways."

She scowled. "In some ways it's sometimes summer too."

That was my clue to end the argument, so I deferred. "True. In some ways."

BAR KOCHBA

The reason I remember considering the differences between Jews and gentiles is because that difference was so imposing upon me from a very young age. I remember when I was six, I was just starting public school. I vividly remember it was public school because there were mostly Christian kids there. We were lined up to go into school, even though it was a long time ago I still remember. There was a Christian child, about my age, who said to me, "You are a dirty Jew!"

I didn't know what to reply. I said defensively, "I'm not dirty."

"Look at your stupid hair!" I wore long sidelocks that curled provocatively from my forehead and a black skullcap on top of my head. My sidelocks were dark and singular and they must have been tempting to jeer at to a gentile boy.

"These are my payas. Everybody has payas."

"Dirty Jew!" he said again. By that time the line had moved into the school and he had to shut up. He must have picked it up from his parents, which means, as the saying of that time went, that he must have 'picked it up from his mother's milk'. Jew hating was so popular among the non-Jewish population that it was a constant factor in all our affairs. I must point out that I only experienced this as it relates to boys. The boys and girls were seated in different classrooms. Perhaps the girls by nature are not bullish, like boys.

There were nine of us in my family, seven children and two adults. I recall, at about the age of 10, asking my mother why we were so many children:

"Because G-d wanted it that way."

This was not entirely satisfactory since my mother answered almost every question this way. "But did G-d want all of us?"

"Yes. All of you."

"Even me?" It was hard to feel special in a large family that barely had enough food.

My mother patted my head. "Yes, you too."

I was mollified, but had more questions. "Why are some children Jewish and some not?"

"To be a Jew is special, but it's also a great responsibility."

This was a difficult concept to understand. "What's 'kind of responsibility?"

"You have to love G-d very much because he made you a Jew."

This was also a common answer to many different questions. I dodged it by being clever. "How do I show that I love G-d?"

My mother was a sentinel for humour. That's why I liked her so much. "By being a good boy and not stealing food from the table."

I took the bait and ran with it. "But G-d put that food there!"

Her patience had run out and my initial question was about to become a parable. "Don't be clever. G-d put that food there for everybody, not for you to steal. When you take food that's not meant for you, you're stealing it from the rest."

"But what if I'm hungry."

"Remember the commandments. Thou shalt not steal."

I couldn't argue with my mother, she always had a commandment to call up for me. The reason I stole food was because I was always hungry. Like most of the other families in our community we were achingly poor. We worked, we were always busy, but we were almost desperately poor. There is an ugly myth that all Jews are rich. That just isn't so. In the cities there were rich Jews, but in the countryside where many lived they were not generally speaking rich at all. The thing was that the Jews were mostly merchants because they couldn't work with the non-Jews at most jobs or even on most farms. Sometimes they were not allowed to own land so that they couldn't farm. They often ran a business, and they sometimes became very effective at being businessmen. My family were in business of a sort, but we were poor.

We had the little store in the front room of our house, but the whole house consisted of only two rooms in total. The second room, which was in a rectangle of about 5 metres by 5 metres, was where we lived. Everything we did was done in that room. All nine of us slept together. I slept mostly in one bed with my father, though I sometimes had the happy privilege of sleeping on my own on a couch. Several children slept together in each of the other beds, all of which were set up around the walls. When we woke in the morning we would find ourselves all together in the same room. There was a wood stove. My mother would stoke it with firewood in the morning in winter. We dressed together, had a hot beverage that we called 'coffee'. It wasn't really coffee, to tell the truth. We couldn't afford coffee. It was, in translation from the German, 'artificial coffee', or 'ersatz', but it was hot.

Once I asked my father, "Are we poor?"

"What does it mean to be poor?", he replied.

The answer to this was very clear. My thoughts in those days were never far from my stomach. "Not to have enough to eat."

"I work very hard to get us enough to eat, but even if we don't have enough it doesn't mean we're poor."

"But doesn't not having enough mean that we're poor?"

He was emphatic. "No."

"What does it mean to be poor, then?"

My father would answer with a lesson if at all possible. "Not to have G-d. To be without G-d is the only kind of poverty."

My father was an optimist. Every day, rain or shine, snow sleet or hail he would get out on his bicycle and go around selling kosher wine. He was the agent for a local winery. But before he started to make his rounds, he would go to the synagogue to pray and study with the other men. There is a Jewish joke that is current but may apply here:

'In a particular region the waters of the local river were rising fast and a great flood was anticipated. Everyone left their homes for higher ground except one man. He said "G-d will protect me!" and he wouldn't budge. The flood came and the waters rose. The man was soon up to his neck in water. A boat came to rescue him, jump in, jump in!" the men called, but the lone man would not. "G-d will save me!" he said. Finally, the river rose so high that the only place safe was the rooftop. A helicopter came to save the man. "No!", he said. "G-d will save me!" Shortly after that the man drowned.

In Gan Eden, the man was stupefied. He hunted down the holiest angel and asked him why G-d didn't save him? The angel replied,

"G-d gave you a warning, but you wouldn't listen. G-d sent you a boat, but you wouldn't get in. G-d sent you a helicopter, but you refused it. What was G-d supposed to do, pick you up by the neck and haul you into heaven?"

My father didn't go so far, he was an intelligent and reasonable man. Despite what he said, in my understanding we were very, very poor. Much of my memory of my earliest years is related to my empty stomach. The reason for this is simple: I was hungry almost all the time because I didn't have enough to eat.

It's not a good thing to remember hunger so prolonged and so bitter as a child. It wipes out the space where a lot of other more meaningful and productive memories could go. Our food supply was extremely limited.

I can tell that although my family was very poor, they were occupied almost all the time. There may be a stereotype that poor people sit around all day, but this was not true of our family. From the crack of dawn til late at night, because of the poverty, they had to labour almost every waking hour. For example, they had to light the stove at maybe six o'clock in the morning. We had a cow and a couple of goats and some chickens which were kept in a separate room from where we slept, ate and lived. They had to be tended. The boys, from the age of about six, went with our father to the synagogue at around seven o'clock in the morning. Before going, we would have breakfast, always a bit of bread, never enough to satisfy our need. We had to go to school, even to Hebrew school in the summer when the public schools had stopped. My father went eventually to his job while my mother was busy at home cleaning and washing and cooking as well as looking after our little general store whenever there were customers. She was in the back room, but there was a bell rigged up in the front store to let her know when there was a customer. When all the children were in bed, she was still awake mending clothing. Whenever my father had spare time he went to the synagogue to study Torah.

Every week was the same routine. My mother would bake once a week, just before the Sabbath. She would roll out on a table an enormous bread, large enough to feed the family for the rest of the week. All week long she would cut off pieces for us until by the end of the week it was gone. The problem was that, enormous as this single bread was, it fell short of feeding us adequately for the entire seven days. Each meal she would cut off what seemed like a sliver to feed us with soup at dinner which, at noon time, was the major meal of the day. Part of our daily ritual was to try get more bread.

"My piece is smaller than Clara's slice. I need another piece."

"I'm sure your pieces are the same."

"But Clara's slice is so much bigger than mine. It's not fair!"

"You must be satisfied with your piece."

"Couldn't I have just a little bit more? No one will know."

"Really? First I give you a little bigger slice. Then the next one wants. Then the next. Soon its only Wednesday and the whole loaf is gone! What are we going to eat for the remaining few days? Then you'd be really hungry!"

"Just a little bit more!"

"You must learn to be satisfied with what you get."

Every day my stomach was empty, and it was often the case that my main concern was my mostly empty stomach. Except for the Sabbath! The sages call it 'the Bride', and welcome it into the home with great joy and much singing. No one can know the real beauty of the Sabbath who has not seen it come every Friday night as a wedding would come. In the synagogue the men sing holy songs with mouths round and joyous and with bowing from the waist in reverence and rapture. My father and brothers and I would rush home from synagogue to a warm room. My mother would have prepared a chicken that had been freshly slaughtered and that was prepared skilfully for us all. There were nine of us but a single chicken could scarcely feed so many mouths. She would stuff with bread every part of the chicken that could be stuffed; under the skin and in the neck. Even so, there was not enough food on Friday night to satisfy my need. The next day, Saturday, was the only time I was actually able to eat enough.

On Saturday my mother served a dish made of different kinds of beans and barley called 'tcholent'. On Friday afternoon she would prepare it in a huge pot. Then she would take the pot to the bakery where the baker would put it in the oven with the other pots of the other women. It would simmer into a savoury stew all night. The next day she would pick it up and bring it home at noon. She would say: "Now, you can eat as much as you like!" We would dive into that pot with a vengeance. She would happily encourage us to eat as much as possible because if there was any left it would go to waste. That was happiness; I felt full, satisfied and complete.

The Sabbath was actually the only time I had to play with my brothers and sisters like children often do. Most parents, it was the custom, went to sleep for a few hours on Saturday afternoon. This was a wonderful routine because not only did they get a rest from us and their normal hard work, but we got a rest from them and the rigorous demands placed also upon us. This period, on Saturday afternoons, also served an important creative function. Although I was blissfully unaware of it at the time, it was in these secret times that my brothers and sisters were probably conceived. Jewish law decreed that a man and wife could not share a bed. As mentioned, it was ordinarily the case that at night I shared a bed with my father.

Since I was the eldest, I had an unnatural privilege. I grew up with the uncomfortable reality of a kind of claustrophobia. We slept, ate, dressed, read and did everything you could do at home in one room. It contained everything we needed. There were beds around the wall and a table for preparing food and eating. There was a wood stove for cooking and keeping us warm. Most of what we did at home was welcome, with the exception of one thing. My mother gave birth to me and seven others there as well. I was too young to remember the child who came directly after me, but I remember the others. There was always a lot of commotion and activity.

"Father, why is mother crying? Is she hurt?", when the second child after me was being born. My younger sister was crying too.

My father was both very stern and at the same time very comforting. "You stay over there, in your bed. Don't you dare get out for anything and especially stay away from your mother."

"But she's crying so loud! Are we going to die?"

"No. Your mother is fine. It sounds like she's crying out of pain, maybe, but it's really out of joy. You're going to have a new baby to take care of. Here, take care of your sister."

We didn't have a doctor to deliver any of us. It was a midwife who took care of things. My mother cried out, and each time she cried it was like a thunderbolt crashing into my brain. For a long time I just sat on the bed with my hands over my ears and cried. My little sister Clara did the same. It seemed like it would go on forever until my mother's screams increased to an almost unbearable pitch. Then they stopped. I looked around from the bed. There was blood. Then I heard something that even at such a young age I knew was a good sound. The crying of my new born brother. I ventured quietly over to the other side of the room where the adults were surrounding the bed my mother lay on. My sister had crept beside me.

"What is it?" she said.

"A baby."

"Where did it come from?"

"I don't know."

"Why was mother crying?"

"I think she was praying to G-d to give us a baby."

"And G-d gave us one?"

"I think so."

My father came over to us. "Get back to bed and go to sleep. Mama's fine. Everything will be quiet now. You were good children. Now go back to bed and go to sleep."

We reluctantly went back to our side of the room. "I hope mama doesn't do that every night." my two year old sister said.

By the time I was 12 my mother had endured four more pregnancies. The first four were successful and slowly over the years I actually got somewhat used to the excruciatingly stressful births in the confines of that rather small room. By the time the fifth pregnancy came to its crisis there were seven of us children, two of them being very young. It was my task to maintain order among us.

"Mama will be fine but she's going to yell for a while. Just put your hands over your ears, and pretty soon you'll see a new brother or sister."

"Will it be a brother or a sister?" Ella wanted to know. "I don't want another brother. I want another sister."

"It doesn't matter what you want, it's what G-d gives us."

"G-d will only give us what's best." Clara said.

"Then why is Mama crying?", Edith, the second youngest, wanted to know.

"She's not crying, she's praying." Clara said. "G-d is making it sound like she's crying so that He knows she really wants a baby."

"She's had practice before and that's how we got Edith and Mordecai." Ella said.

"And the rest of us." Clara said.

But it was different this time. Mama cried like she did all the other times until it sounded like she would burst with crying. There was a final crescendo of sound and then there was silence. This silence was followed by something completely different, something horrible and unexpected. Mama let out a terrible wailing sound and this was followed by a mourning keen.

The child had been stillborn.

Mama wept and wept.

We didn't know what happened until days later. Finally, the truth broke for Clara and Bernie and Nicholas and me. The others were too young to know. Papa told them the baby had decided to stay in heaven.

We discussed it among ourselves.

"It was a baby, we know that." I said. "But it wasn't alive when it was born."

"Why would G-d give Mama a dead baby?" Clara wanted to know.

"Maybe it was such a good baby that G-d took it back."

"Maybe that's what happened. G-d liked the baby so much he took it back."

For us, the idea that G-d could do something that was bad was not conceivable. That child was the last that my mother conceived. We were to remain a family of nine until the war, when our ideas about life and death were put to a horrendous test.

We were quite serious about school, more than our Christian classmates. Our parents made certain of that. While our counterparts were doing chores we were still studying until late in the evening at Hebrew School. When we finished Hebrew School we went home and studied for an hour or two before going to bed. We were subjects of routine. Creativity was often lost in a broad but ongoing schedule.

It was particularly evident in the winter. Our winters were cold and there was a great deal of snow. We didn't have boots and the town was a deep bed of snow, by mid winter it was up to our knees. There was no snow removal of any kind in our town and in order to go anywhere you usually had to travel through the deep snow. The roads were dirt and there were no sidewalks. Horses, cows and other animals were all around. There were no vehicles except for sleighs drawn by horses. To keep us a bit dry and warm we used to wrap rags around our ankles and feet. When we left in the morning we would wrap dry rags, which had been left by the stove all night to dry, around our feet. Of course they would be wet all day. We wore leather shoes that would also be wet. At night, when we came home, we would take off the rags and put them by the stove and also our shoes. By the morning they were dry and the cycle would start anew.

Clothes were also subject to a kind of routine. Being the oldest, I was the only one to get new clothes once a year. These were then handed down from one offspring to the next. There were two sets of clothing for everyone, the ones we wore every day and the ones we wore to synagogue on the Sabbath. I would get a new coat every year to wear every day and a new Sabbath coat every second year. There was a great deal of jealousy and sibling rivalry to deal with.

"Why do I always get your old coat?" Miklos, my younger brother would say.

"Because you're younger and smaller."

"That's not a good enough reason. You never get patches and all I get are patches."

"What's the difference. A coat is a coat. As long as it keeps you warm!"

"It's easy for you to say. You have new clothes."

My mother spent most evenings mending socks and putting patches on our clothes. She was nimble and very good at it. Most of the time the patches were at least a close match to the original material. All of the

Jewish children wore patched clothing, so our family didn't stand out. There's a Philosophical question related to this topic that I learned later in life. It's not Jewish, it's Greek. It comes from Plato and is no secret. He says, "I had a sock, and it developed a hole. I patched up the hole. Soon there was another hole and I patched it also, but soon it had another hole and I had to patch that also. Eventually I patched the whole sock until there was none of the original sock left! The question is, was it the same sock, or a completely new one?"

It is, perhaps, the essence of things that actually endures. In the end, it didn't matter that our clothes were mended. Our parents cared for us as well as they were able and the love I felt for them then still remains. My brother died in the Holocaust with the rest of my family. Even his childish jealousy is something I remember tenaciously.

Hebrew school was harder than public school, if only because there were fewer students for the teacher to keep track of. We would go directly after public school and sit around a large table. We would read Hebrew and study the Torah till after dark. The teacher had a long bamboo pole. He would reach that pole around the table and smack anyone who wasn't paying attention. I remember that he wasn't always accurate. If he hit another student in the process, that was fine. He probably deserved it anyway.

In public school I was a good student. I remember one year, on a night when parents were invited to the school and the students competed in a quiz, I had the good fortune of making my father very proud. I won the prize for answering the most questions correctly. When we walked home together he was more familiar than usual.

"The second last question was the hardest."

"Yes. But I knew the answer anyway."

"Even the other Jewish boy didn't know the answer."

"I was surprised." I said, basking in the praise. "He's good at school."

"None of the goyim know the answers."

It always felt good to show up the goyim. "They never study."

My father looked at me with a light in his eye. "But they beat you up."

"They do, Papa."

"This time you beat them. That's good. You made our Jewish people proud."

"That's good."

"We don't beat people up, but we beat them at something. It's our brains that have given us survival, and G-d's will, not our muscles."

I wasn't so easy with this. I didn't think it was such a good thing. I secretly wanted muscles and I secretly wanted to beat them up too. This was a characteristic that became central later in life.

Anti-Semitism was such a part of our life that we could only escape it by staying in our part of town. Every day after school we were chased or beaten by bullies. The teacher's didn't stop it and they didn't care. It was the adults, after all, who created in the children these hatreds. One Sabbath day, when I happened to be alone with my father for a short time, I asked him why it was like this.

"In every generation it is like this." He said.

"But why? Why don't we learn to fight back?"

"You should not fight back unless the fate of the Jewish people is in danger."

"Isn't it in danger?"

"No, it's not. It's just uncomfortable, that's all, and we can put up with discomfort."

"Why do we have to put up with discomfort?" I complained. I couldn't understand why we couldn't fight back.

My father became quite serious. "You should know from Hebrew school that the Jews are a special people. We uphold the promise that G-d will bring the *Mosaiach* to redeem us and others as well. We have a responsibility to G-d and with that comes duty and obedience to G-d's will. We were slaves in Egypt and G-d delivered us. Why did G-d make the Egyptian's so cruel? So that we Jews would be more obedient and faithful. If G-d were less unyielding with us we would soon forget him and our purpose. If a poor student fails to answer any questions correctly we don't punish him, but if a good student misses even one question we punish him severely. That is the way it is with the Jew also. We wait through all the periods of the earth and rejoice at G-d's goodness at all times, ignoring and persevering through troubles and pain.

"Your bullies don't mean anything. They don't know what they are doing. They don't have our G-d to favour them the way he favours us and we are the ones whom He has chosen to be his people. They are hopeless and they do not share your history. You must run from these bullies, take a few blows if you have to, but know that all of Israel is behind you, that you are meek before them, not fearful. To be meek before your enemies is a blessing. To be belligerent and thoughtless is a curse."

I had to answer from my thoughts. "I'm not belligerent, but I'm tired of running from these bullies."

"Can you fight bullies all by yourself?"

"No." I conceded the point. "I need all of Israel behind me, I think."

"Maybe someday you will have all of Israel behind you. At least, maybe someday you won't have to run."

I had to be satisfied with that. It would be something, I thought. To have all of Israel behind me. I fantasized on that idea for a long time. I didn't know how real that could ever be.

CHAPTER 2
Deplorable

There is a term used by Jewish people to describe those who are non-Jews. That term is 'goyim'. Some people feel this is a derogatory word, but that is not actually so. The word is Hebrew and it is used in the Torah. It means 'nation', literally. G-d uses this term to refer to the Hebrews, meaning 'my nation', so more modern usage is not, in fact, derogatory; it is meant to confer nationhood on those who are not part of the Hebrew nation. It tends to imply that the Jews are one nation and everyone else is another nation.

In 1939 I was 11 years old. I didn't understand very well the idea of nations, I only knew too well that the other people in our town who were not Jewish were certainly different than us. What I didn't understand was why they hated us so much.

"Why do they hate us so much?" I asked my father once.

"I tell you the truth.", he replied. "They are jealous."

I laughed a huge laugh for an 11 year old. "Jealous! Of what? They have everything and we have nothing!"

"No.", he said. "It is the other way around. We have law, and they have none. To us, there are given 613 commandments, to them only a few. We have the word of G-d, the Torah. They do not. We have dietary laws to keep us clean and healthy. They eat anything that moves and they eat it with its own blood, in its own milk. And we have tradition. We go to synagogue, we go to the study house, we have our kosher clothes. But most of all, we have something they will always lack; the Sabbath. True, they hate us because we are different, and maybe that's all the reason they need. But, even though they may not know it in their own mind, they are jealous. That's why they hate us so much."

I listened to my father's words. I didn't understand them. I didn't think the others could be jealous of us, such a poor people. It was 1939. I had many lessons to learn. In 1939 Hungary was allied with Nazi Germany, but there was no German army in the country. Hungary was ruled by a dictator, Miklos Horthy, who was anti-Semitic but not to the extreme of the Nazis. So when the war began hardships descended on the Jews in great measure, but not so great as they would become. We had less and less and the conditions went from bad to worse to eventually terminal. Before 1942, life was hard. In 1942, it became deplorable. All Jewish men, from 21 to 50 were sent to forced labour camps to do work for the army, all of which were fighting at the Russian front. Very few ever returned.

In 1941 I was 13. It was my Bar Mitzvah year. Any of the men in our community who would normally have celebrated this event were there. Still, it was a dull affair, more ritualistic than anything else.

Shortly after the Bar Mitzvah my father did something that was, perhaps, the watershed of my young life, signalling the end of my economic dependence on my family. He took me, along with a valise containing what few clothes I had, to the train station. It was customary that when a boy became a man he was to leave the care of his parents and begin to fend for himself. My father gave me a train ticket and a solemn amount of money, about $5, and said in a customary way, "Now you are on your own."

I knew he would say that. "Do you mean forever?"

"I mean you are no longer a boy who needs to be taken care of by his mother and father. You are a man who must do his duty and accept his responsibilities."

"I will always be Jew."

"Don't worry." He said. "No one will ever let you forget you are a Jew."

The ticket was for a town some distance away where I was to begin study for a year in a *yeshiva*. A *yeshiva* is a study house, more advanced than the simple Hebrew School, also known as '*cheder*'. I arrived and there was no one at the station to meet me. The town was so much bigger than our town, I didn't know where to go. I waited about half an hour until another Jew came by, dressed in a black suit with sidelocks curling down from his temples. I asked him in Yiddish where the *yeshiva* was.

"Are you new?" he asked.

"Yes."

"Do you know how to be hungry?"

"G-d has been good to me in teaching me the more subtle end of hunger."

"G-d will be even better to you now, for sure. Come with me. I will take you to within a twenty minute walk to the *yeshiva*."

My initial task, upon arriving at the Yeshiva, was to go out into the Jewish area of town and knock on doors. I was to introduce myself to the household and request a favour. This was common practice, every Yeshiva did it and every student carried it out and every household knew it and accepted it without discrimination.

"My name is Avrum Benjamin. I'm from the *Yeshiva*."

"Yes, well, that's very nice."

"I wonder if you could do me the service of helping me with my studies."

"Very Good."

"I would like to receive food from you on Tuesdays in the Evening. Whatever you can manage."

"We don't have much, but I can certainly prepare an extra meal for you on Tuesdays."

"G-d bless you so much. You will be helping a poor Jewish boy."

"Say a blessing for my family, that's all I ask."

"Of course. I will not forget you."

Every Tuesday evening I went to that house for dinner. Every day of the week I went to a different house for lunch and dinner.

The *Yeshiva* was very organized and very strict. Our learning was taken extremely seriously. Each week we had to memorize four pages of fine print from the Talmud, a commentary on the Torah. Each week there was an exam on that section. One person would start to recite, and then the Rabbi would point to someone else who had to continue to recite from that point from memory. Every Saturday evening we had to also memorize both Torah and commentary. This was extremely difficult. The text was called the Gemmara. In a box in the centre of the page was the Talmud and surrounding it was more text in very fine print which was commentary. The centre box was in an older language, called Aramaic. Outside the box was Hebrew. We were awake at 5 A.M. and at the study house by 6:00 A.M. The great joy was the Sabbath, when we would sing and dance. Life was hard, but I was at least fairly well fed. Still the war was going on. News of atrocities in Germany reached my ears.

The student life of a *Yeshiva* boy was short lived for me. My father was sent to a work camp a year after I arrived at the *Yeshiva*. At fourteen I returned home to help support my family. For a short while I worked at a grocery, but the Germans took most of the agricultural produce and industry so that we were reduced to ration cards. My job ended and at the time there was virtually no other work. I talked to my mother: I was never to see my father again. "What are we going to do?" she wailed. "There are eight mouths to feed."

"I have to do something."

"What can you do?" she said ironically. "You can't just steal."

"I know some boys who do the opposite of steal. They get goods here, take them to Budapest and sell them there."

My mother gasped and grabbed me by the arm. "The Black Market? You want to work in the Black Market? It's very dangerous."

I countered seriously, "But so is starvation."

"It is punishable by death!" she cried. "I don't want you to be a criminal."

"Everyone is a criminal. It's the war."

It would be appropriate here to say a word about my father. He presumably died on the Russian front with many thousands of others. The rumours were that the German army stopped at Leningrad and also Stalingrad in the bitter cold of winter. It was said to be a 1000 day siege. The regular army was equipped with proper clothing, but the forced labourers were not. Most of them are said to have frozen to death. Most likely, this was also my father's fate.

With so much death, what can death mean? This is assuredly the question in any war. My father wasn't a soldier, he was actually a martyr, but it doesn't matter. He was a hero just the same. He died believing in something, you may not even call it Judaism. It was the principle of being an ordinary person; not a very rich person or successful person or even necessarily a scholarly person, but someone who lived a life with G-d at the centre.

The Black Market was, basically, a way of circumventing the ration system for people who could afford to pay extra for items, especially food and clothing which were allocated by the rationing system. Many people, especially Jewish people who couldn't find jobs at that time because they were very scarce, went to the Black Marketing system.

I have always been a bit of a loner and I have always followed my own way. With hesitation and with some fear I went into business on my own in the black market. Food was plentiful in farming villages, where I would buy it at a good price. Most of the food that these farmers produced had to be handed over to the Army, but they were always able to save some for entrepreneurs like myself. I took as much food as possible by train to Budapest to sell and used the money to buy clothes and other articles that weren't available in the town, especially manufactured goods, sugar and especially saccharine, which was highly valued. These articles I would again bring back with me and sell in town, buy food with the money and take it to Budapest. It was very dangerous. Black market dealings were highly illegal. If someone were caught, they would immediately be brutally beaten and taken to jail. There they stayed at the pleasure of the police, because Black Marketers were seldom tried in a court that was already corrupt. The police decided how long a person stayed in jail. However long it might be, it was not going to be pleasant.

Travelling to Budapest was dangerous. There were overhead racks in the car, and that's where we would put our Black Market goods. If a policeman came to inspect the racks, you simply didn't claim the items that were found. There were some anti-Semitic individuals who would point out to whom these articles belong, but that's an old story. The trip took six hours. Everyone was very anxious…there was a war going on and life was difficult. We Jews had a kind of password to identify each other. The word was "amcha", meaning "of your people". When someone used the word "amcha", you knew they were alright.

One afternoon I was sitting in a seat on the train just looking out the window. Two people came into the car. They looked around and noticed two seats next to mine. They were unusual, a boy and a girl about eighteen, because they were dressed like Jews. A Jewish boy and a Jewish girl of this age would rarely be seen travelling together. They came over to my seat, and spoke in Hungarian.

"Are these seats taken?" the girl asked.

"No."

"You don't mind then if we sit there?"

"No. Of course."

They loaded their backpacks on the rack, and I suspected they were Black Marketers. After they were seated the girl said to me, "Have you been travelling long?"

"About two hours."

"Going to Budapest?"

"Yes."

"So are we." There was a moment's silence.

"There are quite a few Jews travelling today", the girl said.

"For a weekday."

She then spoke in Yiddish. "You know the word Amcha?"

"Yes.", I replied.

"You know what it means?"

"Yes. It's just a word, nonetheless."

"Very good. We can enjoy each other's company on the trip, then?"

"Yes."

"My name is Lilian and my friend is Mordecai."

"Hello.", I said, relaxing a little. "My name is Avrum."

There was a moment of silent appraisal. Then Modecai spoke. He was quite tall and thin, with an almost aesthetic quality. Lilian was quite attractive, wearing her black hair tied up in braids and also quite tall for a girl.

"How is your family?" he asked. I was a bit startled.

"We get by. My father is at the front with the labour camp."

"With all the other Jewish men."

"That's right."

"The war is going badly for the Germans."

In a more cheery voice I said, "Is it?"

Mordecai smiled a wispy half smile. "Who really knows?"

There was another moment of silence. Then Lilian said the strangest thing.

"Would you like to leave Hungary?"

I actually laughed out loud. "I would actually like to fly to the moon and live there, but I can't."

Mordecai and Lilian laughed too. "Of course you are right." Then Lilian became more serious again. "But we are leaving."

"Leaving? Where are you going?"

"Anywhere. Into hiding if we have to. This is the Holocaust, soon it will arrive full force in Hungary and we are going to fight it or die fighting it."

"Holocaust? I don't know what you mean."

"You've heard word from Germany? Death Camps?"

"Only rumours."

"We know the rumours are true. We believe the rumours are true. We have news and we have talked to survivors."

"Where could you possibly go?"

"We're not sure yet."

"Why don't you let G-d take care of you, like the rest of us?"

Lilian's face went pale. It only made her pale good looks more evident. "There is no G-d." she said. "Not for us. Not anymore."

"G-d is impartial to the fate of our people." Mordecai said. The veins on his neck were tight. "I believe he wants us to fight for our survival, instead of turning dull eyed and passive towards him."

"But if you don't believe in G-d, what makes you a Jew?"

"You do. Other Jews do. Our own upbringing. Its not exactly true that we don't think G-d exists, but that he has set us a test which we must acknowledge and resist the wonton evil of this war. We are trying to go to Palestine."

"Are you married?"

"No." Mordecai said. "In this world where there is no truth what good is marriage."

"We love each other. That's a miracle in these times and reason enough.", Lilian added.

I paused on that. I had never met a couple who were in love and I had never met a couple, who were together but not married.

"You work on the Black Market, don't you?" Lilian said.

"What makes you think that?"

"Here." Mordecai said, writing down a number. "There are friends there. Go there, tell them you know us, and they will help you. Maybe we can even meet again."

"Why are you doing this? Maybe it will get you into trouble?"

Lilian and Mordecai both laughed out loud. "Believe me.", Mordecai said. "There's so much trouble in the world right now a little more probably wouldn't hurt us."

I sat then in what might be called stunned silence. Two young Jews, going underground, in love but not married, who didn't believe in G-d. This was unusual! What was also unusual was that I liked them. They had ideas, they had courage and they had integrity. The next few hours of the trip together were pleasing and exciting. We talked about the law, about the Torah, about the great teachers. Even Lilian knew many things a girl is not supposed to know anything about. They had a refreshing and lively insight. We parted at Budapest, and I was not to see them again, ever. A loss, because their impression remained with me for a very long time. I was too young to know, but these two young people supplied me with a role model that furnished me with insight many years later.

It was not their somewhat avant-garde presentation that remained so strong. They were actually so very different from other Jews in this regard that it was a leap of imagination for me to identify with them. It was, rather, the principle of resistance that struck me hard, the idea of somehow doing something decisive and real against the mindless brutality of the enemy, the possibility of dignity in a time of oppression. These young people knew something I had only guessed at. That G-d might look after those who chose to resist as well as those who chose to suffer without complaint. It was at that precise moment, significantly, that I began to think of myself as someone who could take action. Mordecai and Lilly only sat with me for a few minutes, but it was enough to shape my entire future.

In March, 1944 the Germans occupied Hungary without resistance although it had always been an ally. They did this for two reasons: For various reasons they did not trust the dictator Horthy to be loyal to the Germans and he had also bluntly refused to send the Jews to the death camps in Poland and Germany. Even though he was ferociously anti-Semitic he did not want to be remembered as a butcher of men, women and children. When the German's invaded Hungry their top priority was the extermination of the Jews. Even though they needed enormous facilities of rail, industry and manpower to feed the war effort they would give up most of what they needed to exterminate the Jews.

There were two kinds of policeman in Hungary. One was for big cities and the other was for rural areas. The big city police were pretty much like urban policemen anywhere. They were corrupt but you could reason with them. But the rural policemen were different. They were called peace officers and instead of carrying handguns they carried rifles with a bayonet at the end. On their head they wore a rooster feather. They were distinct because they didn't have to obey any law, they were extremely and ferociously anti-Semitic, absolutely brutal, mostly illiterate and they would beat up savagely anyone they pleased.

It was these peace officers that the Jewish communities were mostly very afraid of. There was no court of law or jury in these areas to speak of, although there was a magistrate, usually appointed by the state in each area, who was most often illiterate. These were the police who patrolled the railway until it arrived in Budapest, and these were the ones we dreaded even at home. When I was a kid we all feared these policemen because they always found excuses to fine us for things we hadn't done. In our village, for example, there was one man who was considered to be a thief. If anything was missing, mostly chickens or goats or the like, right away the policeman would go and find this guy, beat him up until he confessed (it didn't matter if he had actually stolen anything or not) and then they would send him to prison for a few months. When he got out everything would be fine until something else was stolen, and the whole cycle would start again.

Once, as I was in a train with Black Market goods in the rack above me, several of these Peace Officers came by. They found my goods on the rack and said to the car around me, "Who do these contraband goods belong to?" One anti-Semitic onlooker pointed to me and said, "They belong to him!" The Officers took me outside and beat me black and blue. I was a strong boy, good at sports, and I could take a beating, but in this case I had no choice but to confess. I thought my life was over, so I did a desperate thing. Before I was really badly hurt I took out some money, all that I had, and gave it to them. With a few parting kicks they let me off the hook. I continued to ride the train to the Black Market after that, but I always carried extra money to pay them off it they saw me. That only happened twice more. It cost a lot, but I was still able to put food on the table.

One time I bought some saccharine in Budapest. When I got home my mother tasted it and found that it was not saccharine but rather some other worthless powder. I lost quite a bit of money on that bad deal and my moral outrage was as outlandish as it was ironic. I had learned to be a good criminal, although the side of me that was still a *yeshiva* boy was also very strong. G-d didn't mind if you had to break the law to survive as long as you didn't hurt other people. The 'rules' of the Black Market were unwritten but they were rules nonetheless. To a boy of 15 the black and white of it seemed quite clear

CHAPTER 3
Five for Palestine

There are certain things children know instinctively. There are certain things they have to learn. Laughing is instinctive, so is crying. A child reacts to pleasure and pain with simple emotions. Play is instinctive. No one has to teach a child to play although they may have to teach them specific games. Play is the child's instrument for learning. Gratitude is an instinctive reaction to receiving unexpected rewards. By contrast, hate has to be learned. It is not an instinctive response to pain. It is a learned response to injustice. It may occur as a transitory or fleeting emotion, but if the injustice is constant or persistent it may become recurrent or even consistent. It may also become a feature of an abundant jealousy.

One day I was in the study hall in our town later than usual because I was reading a difficult and complex piece of the Talmud. It was essentially about the issue that we should love our enemies. The study hall was a rough building, but it was decorated, in contrast, with rich and ornate artifacts. The rabbi was reading also at the same time, and I asked him a question. The Rabbi seemed an ancient man because his hair and beard were grey though his eyes were a transparent blue. In those rheumy eyes were love and wisdom.

"Rabbi, I have a question." I said.

"You can ask me anything." His voice like soft music.

"If we don't hate our enemies, how are we supposed to feel about them?"

"You should feel love for them."

This seemed a curious answer. "Even though they cause us endless pain?"

"Yes."

"But aren't they evil?" I was querulous about this. It seemed very much to the point.

The Rabbi smiled wryly. "Perhaps, in a way."

"And shouldn't we hate evil?" My experiences on the Black Market had made me more bold than I should have been.

"Should we hate the cold wind when it makes us cold? Or the fire when it burns us? Are these things evil?" he said equally as bold.

"But the wind and the fire don't know what they are doing. They are natural."

"So are our enemies."

"But the wind and the fire don't know what they are doing." I repeated in earnest.

"Neither do our enemies."

"But they do. They know very well what they are doing. They don't have to persecute us."

"They do. They feel pain, they do not know the cause, they blame us. Why? Because we are different and seem to them not to suffer the way they do."

My father had used a similar argument to a similar question. I was not satisfied. "Why is that? We suffer too."

"Yes. Perhaps we do, perhaps we don't. But that's what they see."

I paused for a moment to process this idea. Then I said, "Should we love evil?" It was an irreverent question but I was pressed enough by circumstance to ask.

"You should be indifferent to it." The Rabbi tossed this answer off as if a fly had landed on his forehead.

"And the people who commit evil?"

He looked at me with a soft irony in his glance. "They are like innocent children who don't know any better. They have learned to love hate. They don't know any better."

"So how should we treat them when they beat us?" I had experienced enough physical pain to warrant an answer to this question.

"Like innocent children who don't know any better."

The rabbi seemed to have made his point here. Still, it appealed to me to press on. "What do we have that they hate so much?"

The old Talmudic sage looked up. His eyes seemed to become a bit hazy as he searched his mind. "In the simplest sense, we have love. That is what they lack and that we have. Where they have hate, we do not. And this makes us hateful to them. But, to be honest with you, they don't really care about that because they don't know it explicitly. We are, probably most of all, just a convenient target. We are scapegoats for their unhappiness and inadequacy. We are here in their country. It is not our country. We hope to meet sometime soon in Jerusalem. Until then, we persevere, until we can go home."

I didn't ask the Rabbi any further questions. To say we were innocent victims of persecution and prejudice would be transparent. We were Jews, we had been persecuted even before we were a nation. We understood that we were the chosen people and G-d tested us at every turn to keep us faithful. We were guilty of that and it conditioned us always. We had our own laws, and they were laws that kept us bound as a community. But we were innocent in the sense that even though we knew and to some degree understood that we were guilty of existing as a nation within other nations, and even though we considered those host communities as the ones who were actually alien, we were unaware of what was actually going on, at least to the extent of it. We were innocent of the intent of the progressively more and more serious persecutions and we were victims of our own insularity. We were innocent of the concept of genocide against us, let alone the systematic process of extermination it would take.

When the Germans attacked in 1944, they did so partly because even though Hungary was an ally of Germany and also contributed goods (they also confiscated agricultural and other produce) they had taken a distrust to the dictator Horthy. Perhaps they had intelligence that Horthy was preparing to withdraw troops from the Russian front but quite possibly the main motivation for the invasion was that the Germans wanted all the Jews to report for deportation. Although Horthy was a dedicated anti-Semite he couldn't bring himself to destroy the entire Jewish population. Prior to the war years the biggest industrialists were mostly Jews and they had probably contributed to his success personally and one of his sons was actually married to a Jewish girl.

Horthy ruled for 24 years. When the war started in 1941 the businesses and professions were abruptly closed to the Jewish people. If they had a government job they were dismissed and they were not permitted to practice medicine or any other profession. Ration cards were distributed to everyone for bread, sugar, clothing, everything. Jewish merchants were forbidden to sell anything that was rationed so that most merchants went out of business. The government had a list of all Jewish merchants who sold both retail and wholesale as well as manufacturing and they could not sell. This contributed to the impoverishment of most of the Jewish population. Not only did the Jewish people lose all this, they also suffered the loss of the head of the household. There were very few Jewish landlords. Most land in Hungary was owned by either the aristocracy or the church. There were some 'small landholders'. Horthy was able to go at least to this end.

We were aware of the fall of Horthy's regime, but not aware of what was to follow. The invasion of German troops brought my black market activities to an end. So I was home when the news finally came.

There was a great deal of excitement in the village one day shortly after the invasion. Everyone was gathering in a corner of our area. Everyone was talking together loudly. A man approached us. We knew him very well, he was the 'town crier', the man who made announcements in the town twice a day and beat upon a drum. This day was different. His message was desperate for us. We all fell into a hush. He spoke.

He cried out to us that there was a new law. Jewish people were to get out in front of their houses in the morning, to pack whatever they wanted but only that which they could carry on their backs and to leave the doors to their houses open. These were desperate instructions. Not only were we to leave our houses in the morning with whatever possessions we could carry, but we had to leave everything else we owned behind as well and leave the door opened. We were not totally blind to this intent. This was so that the population could take possession of the contents and the houses themselves.

After the announcement we stood around each other in stunned silence for a moment, then people started to talk. "They are only sending us to work camps", someone said. We will come back when the war is over."

"Carry blankets and bread." Another said. And still another, "They will take my Sabbath candlesticks."

My mother took us all home. She was struggling with panic. In quick steps she gathered food and blankets for all of us to carry. By this time it was getting dark. We sat on our beds and spoke in low voices. We whispered about where we were going…someplace where there would be food and shelter. My sister looked at me in the candlelight.

"What is happening, Avrum? Why is everybody so frightened?" she asked.

"The Germans are taking us away."

"I don't see any Germans."

"The Germans who are not here have ordered us away."

"But how can they do that if they're not here?" She was stubborn.

"They have ordered it done and the others are doing it."

"By what reason do they do it?"

"No reason. They do it because they want to do it."

She was childishly impatient. "That's no reason. There are lots of things I want to do, but I can't just go and do them just because I feel like it."

"This is different. The Germans can do anything they want to us."

She almost spoke aloud. "But why?"

"I don't know. They kill people who don't do what they want."

She crossed her arms and acquired the look of a spoiled little princess. "Then they are not good people. They are bad people and G-d will punish them."

I tried to quieten her. "G-d will not let anything bad happen to you. You are only a child."

BAR KOCHBA

She assumed the moral high road of certainty. "G-d will punish them. That's all I need to know. They can send me wherever they like, but G-d will punish them."

Slowly, we all drifted into sleep. I don't think any of us dreamed, at least not of the nightmare that was to come.

None of us talked very much when the morning came. We all had bundles of a few essentials to carry, even the youngest. As we left the doorway my mother looked back at our single room. Everything was left neatly behind. Nothing was forgotten. Whatever it was that had made this place a home was anything but the meagre furnishings. There were no pictures on the wall. Her children had been born here, her daily work had been done. I don't think she actually felt remorse or regret at leaving. I think she felt a loss and perhaps most of all an uncomfortable sense of foreboding.

Outside it was mild. We were not the first to come out, and as we looked down the road we could see every family, house by house, standing huddled before their homes bundled with provisions. There was almost no chatter, even among the youngest children. Everyone was waiting to be led away.

In the early morning the gendarmes came and escorted us all from in front of our homes to the synagogue. Poor as our homes were, we didn't leave them gladly. One family refused to budge when the gendarmes came to get them. We were not yet at the point of wonton violence. The mother and 5 children stood their ground, the mother demanded to see the document removing them from the town. My sister was afraid and enthralled by the conflict.

"We should all refuse to go. Why don't we?"

I had to play the role of pacifier with my sister because she didn't understand what was at stake. "It's not up to us to resist. It makes things worse. We fight injustice with justice. That's how it goes."

"I'm not going. I'm going to resist."

I admonished her. "They'll carry you."

"Yes, kicking and screaming!"

"Is that how you want to go?" I stared menacingly into her eyes.

"Why not! I don't have to act like a sheep going to slaughter!"

Her actions were getting dangerous. I knelt down in front of her and held her shoulders. "Nobody is going to slaughter. We're only being relocated."

"But to where? Can you tell me that?" Her expression was open and extremely serious for a 13 year old.

"No." I said without certainty. Then with a bit more tender understanding. "When the war is over we'll come back."

Her words were accusing rather than compliant. "With Papa? To a house we're leaving empty?"

There was no answer for her. I could only repeat what I believed my father might have said in the same situation. "Who knows? Just have faith."

Clara pulled away from my hands. At this time she was speaking specifically to me and our immediate life. "I don't spend my hours in the study hall, like you. I don't know all the ins and outs of G-d's ways. I only know this is not right. And it's not right that I do absolutely nothing while it happens."

My concern was also immediate. I knew of the dangers of this circumstance, whereas Clara did not. "Believe me...it's right. At this moment, it is right to suppress all else and just comply. There is no other best way. Resistance will only cause even more suffering."

"All right. For our mother's sake I won't make a fuss. But not because of what you say. Because I have so little choice."

The woman who had refused to move was still adamant. There was a small crowd of gendarmes around her until the Captain came. He talked to the woman for a few moments. She stood very tall, gathered up her children and her belongings and allowed herself to be led away. Even in this situation she had a great deal of dignity. She looked like a queen being taken prisoner by the enemy.

Eventually they came for everybody. When they came for us my sister hissed at the gendarme and said, in Yiddish, "You are only a dumb animal." Inside the synagogue they made a complete inspection of everything we were carrying. It was mostly food and perhaps one blanket or a comforter. We had to hand over any money or valuables and, to make sure everything was accounted for, they searched inside the lining of coats and jackets and any other place jewellery might be hidden. Then we went into the sanctuary where everyone settled, mostly on the floor, and waited. There must have been 300-400 people in the synagogue and no bathroom indoors. We had to use a back storeroom and the stench was unbelievable. We ate what we had, including some water we had taken with us. We slept there and ate and just waited about three or four days before they came and told us to start marching.

There were almost no incidents in the days we waited. The rabbi led us in prayer from time to time and of course in the morning, afternoon and evening services. There were almost no Germans in the village, but one drunken German soldier, a bureaucrat of some kind, wandered into the synagogue, and made a frightening scene.

He swaggered about the synagogue and finally noticed an attractive Jewish girl sitting with her family. He made a big fuss and said he "wanted her". A local member of council, who had the police under him, ordered the police to take him out of there. The man put his life on the line, which I never thought an Hungarian man would do for a Jew. While the drunken German was swaggering around the sanctuary my sister came to sit beside me. I was the oldest man she knew. She whispered, "What does he want."

"He wants to take advantage of a situation."

"He looks like an idiot."

"He is definitely an idiot. A big, ugly Nazi idiot."

"Why are they so proud to be idiots?"

It was the best question Clara asked that day. "They so often get what they want. There is no one here to stop them. They can do what they want."

"Are we cattle? Are we sheep?"

I was also exasperated, but I retained some objectivity. "We, at least are civilized people and we can endure. We have endured before and we will endure now."

Clara unconsciously crossed her arms. "I wish I could resist. If I can, I will resist."

I looked at Clara with honest surprise and some admiration. "That approach will get you killed and you won't have accomplished anything. Hold onto your anger, and in the end you'll have something to hand down to your children.

Even so, I must admit that I thought, but did not speak in words, the same thing

We had nothing to do but introspect and pass the hours in prayer and quiet discussion of the situation. It seemed like people were reliving their whole existence in the close confines of our little synagogue. The Rabbi was our leader. He initiated prayers at certain times, roamed the premises speaking to everyone in small groups and individually and speaking to us as a congregation periodically. Clara busied herself with taking care of her younger siblings while I spent hours sitting near my mother. We didn't talk very much to each other. There seemed to be so little to say after the first night. Other people came by occasionally to pass the time and at times my mother would wander a little also. By the end of the third day we were virtually established as a small, functioning community, sharing food and precious water.

After what seemed a lifetime we finally got the order to get up and take our belongings and we were marched down to the railway station where there were cattle cars waiting for us. We were loaded on board, but with so many people that no one could lie down although there was enough room for everyone to sit.

We were taken by this train to the provincial capital. All the trains from all the surrounding towns were brought to the provincial capital. There we were lodged in a ghetto.

The ghetto had been created by isolating the old Jewish quarter. There was no wall of either brick or barbed wire defining the ghetto. It was created by running one single piece of wire around the area and positioning police guards at certain spots. They were so sure of Jewish complacency that resistance was not a threat at that time. Even so, I don't think anyone ever escaped because there was nowhere to go. The non-Jewish people in our own town, for example, were standing and laughing when we were taken to the train. If anyone had tried to escape in that city they most certainly would have been quickly caught and turned in.

The houses in the ghetto area were all requisitioned and one room was allocated to every Jewish family and one kitchen for use by all the people in all the rooms. It didn't matter what the size of the family was. They had taken all the furniture away so we sat on the floor and ate whatever food we had left from home. There was no place to get food in the ghetto and no money to buy it anyway.

By sheer good luck we found an uncle, my father's brother, who we had never met but who had lived a town only 50 km away. No one had time or money to travel that distance in those days. My mother's mother lived only 30 km from our town but we only saw her once. That's how difficult it was to travel even a short distance. My uncle had hidden some money and he gave us some. That was very kind, but there was no place to buy anything. Even so, a little money might have come in handy later on.

Despite the fact that we were far from home and in a situation in which we did not know what our fate may be, it was a time of awakening for me because the strict ordinances for boys and girls set down by orthodox society were lifted somewhat and I actually had the chance to meet girls from all over. It was a very sad circumstance of course, but for a young boy it was kind of exciting also. Children don't grab the significance of some situations even when they are desperate. We were in the ghetto for 3 to 4 weeks and we thought we would be settled somewhere. The Germans were very clever and they gave it out that we were going to work camps. We completely believed them.

Out of the dozen or so young people my age there were five of us who became friends. We used to meet informally every evening in an alley behind an abandoned bakery. We were three boys and two girls. We told little stories about our towns and our families. The two girls were Greta and Chava. The boys were Victor and Stephan. We talked seriously once about the immediate past and our future.

"When the war is over, the Germans will let us go and return us to our towns. They are only doing this because of the war." Stephan said. He was a handsome boy with fine features and thick, curly dark hair. There was something fragile about him, as if you touched him in just the right place he would fall apart like a porcelain figurine.

"They are going to make slaves out of us, like the Egyptians did in Egypt." Greta had some Torah training from her Father and she knew some history. She was intelligent, intense and attractive. I had a secret infatuation with her, and we were in fact, though completely unspoken or even suggested, an invisible couple. I had never been in a situation like this with a girl before; it would have been impossible before the ghetto in my home town. I felt an affinity to her. Any thought of more than that would have been unbalanced. Still, fresh. strong emotions were being courted by these circumstances. Emotions that were, as they would be for any 16 year old boy, unfamiliar and confusing.

Chava had the most optimistic viewpoint. "The Germans are going to make us work, but they will pay us for it later. We will be trained to do many jobs and then we will be resettled, maybe in parts of Russia when the war is over." She was pretty, with curly red hair and little freckles accenting her nose. Her family had been closer to rich than any of ours. Her father had been a successful businessman before they sent him to the front. Her clothes were noticeable of higher quality than ours.

Victor had a good sense of humour. He took the relocation very seriously but he was able to make jokes about it much more easily than the rest of us. He wore his sidelocks tucked behind his ears, which looked a bit odd. "They're going to make us into soup and feed us to the army. I know the cook. His name is Adolf." Although his jokes were sometimes gruesome we laughed anyway, partly out of released tension and partly because we had never been, or thought to have ever been, in a situation where boys and girls hung out together so completely casually and with no supervision whatsoever from adults.

"The Germans will lose the war." I said. This brought gasps and the shaking of heads from the others of our group.

"And who is going to defeat them?" Greta asked with haughty certainty.

"G-d is going to defeat them." I said. "They will swim in their own evil and they will die. The Jews will be freed and go to Palestine." I was the only one who had worked the Black Market and had exposure to liberal Jewish thinking. I was as close to a Zionist as I could be without stepping firmly into that camp.

"Yes." said Stephan. "The sky will crack open and our enemies will be vanquished. That's what my Rabbi said, but almost no one believed him. Do you believe in miracles?"

"Yes!" I said. "I do. I don't think they always look like miracles, exactly, at least not at the time. Sometimes we have to wait to realize that a miracle has happened. But I think that they happen. Maybe the sky won't open, maybe it will. One thing is sure…if it does open and if lightning comes down, the Jews will be there to see it. Maybe not in our generation, but it will happen and we will be there."

There was a moment of silence. Greta looked up and said, "I would go to Palestine, if I could. I would do anything to have a Jewish homeland."

Chava, who was by far the most pampered of us, agreed. "I would go. I haven't seen my father in almost three years. We barely ate in the time since. The Hungarians hate us, the Germans persecute us and no one lends us a hand. I would go to Palestine."

"So would I." said Victor.

Stephan echoed "So would I. I would fight to go there, with whatever tools I had. I would go."

Greta stretched out her hand. "To Palestine!"

One by one we put our hands in a circle with hers. "To Palestine" we all agreed. For a moment we were free.

Eventually the order to move came and, again, we were loaded onto cattle cars. This time was worse because there were more of us and it was more disorderly and frightening. The loading was random and we weren't necessarily put with our families, but ours was lucky and we stayed together. My Grandmother kept saying "We're going to die! We're going to die!", but most of us thought she was just hysterical. The most frightening thing was that as we were boarded onto the cars, the Germans were hitting us with their rifles to hurry us up, especially the older people who were not as quick. They had only mercy on the old and infirm, their rifle butts came crashing down with bone chilling ferociousness on the heads and backs of their victims. This was causing a mild panic. People were screaming, children were crying. It was not only the noise that was frightening, with the guards screaming and people calling out or crying in pain and the piercing wail of the children. It was the sense of chaos and the crush of bodies being shoved into one another.

Just before we reached the opening to one car, my mother was pulled away from me in the crowd. I lunged towards her with an instinctive gesture and as I did so a rifle butt came, CRACK, hard into my shoulder. In an unconscious response I ducked below the guard's arm, grabbed my mother and pulled her back towards me. The guard couldn't reach me, but he smashed his rifle into my mother's back anyway. She cried out. It was the first time I had heard my mother hurt like that. It took all the wisdom I possessed as a 15 year old man to stop myself from striking back.

But that was a lesson for me. I couldn't strike back then, but I resolved, later, to remember that assault. We loaded onto the train, with chaos and pain and violence all around us. Neither my mother nor I were seriously hurt physically, but my resolve had been tested. I knew, in my heart, probably for the first time, that I had within me the spirit to resist. It lay dormant. If I lived, I vowed that I would let it work.

Once we were on the cars things were very bad. We had enough room to sit but not to lie down. We had one pail of water for 80 people. I was the person in charge of the water ration. This was a serious responsibility, since water was the most precious commodity we had. It was understood that I had to be both fair and ruthless. Water was life and we didn't know how long it would have to last.

I think they chose me to be in charge of the water because I seemed honest and strong. I don't know why people saw me this way, but it had happened before. I do not think of myself as a leader, but throughout my life people have turned to me when they need something important done. Not political or social things. They turn to me for physical action and sometimes protection. I was not a violent youth. I was not in any fights of retribution or any other kind. I was good at sports, but sports were not a big issue in our lives. It seemed that I had some kind of integrity that was, in a way, more a feature of my body than my mind. I didn't lead other's so much as I seemed to reassure them. A strange quality that was to figure strongly later.

At one end of the car a blanket was set up and that established a makeshift lavatory. Within minutes the inadequacy of the arrangement became apparent. There were very old and very young aboard the cattle car. Those who made it to the area used an open bucket. Many did not make it that far. Most women in that era did not wear underclothing and some simply urinated where they were. Babies could not be changed, and so after a while the car carried a sickening stench.

After what seemed a small lifetime we started a slow, agonizing movement down the track. As the train picked up speed our condition began to break down. It was very cold, but the heat of our bodies heaped close together made it better. Babies were crying and the sound of the tracks was not comforting. It only added to the sense of confusion, pain and distress. In the first hour after we started moving it seemed that hell had opened a window on our tightly wound little cattle car and let it's demons out.

I was sitting away from my mother, at the other end of the car, taking care of the water. I had to be very firm about the rationing and it didn't make me popular with some people. Being the eldest boy in a family of eight had driven into me a sense of responsibility that was possible a little beyond my years. We didn't talk very much. I had a brief conversation with my eldest sister before we left the ghetto. "Have you ever wished you weren't Jewish?", she asked.

"I've wished things could be different." I replied.

"Sometimes I want to know why we suffer so much.", she said.

"These people around us who are not Jewish suffer more." I replied. "They don't know right from wrong. They're like animals. They have no rational faculties. They act on impulse. They don't know G-d."

Clara asked the question that was on every Jewish lip. "But why does G-d cause us so much pain?"

I gave her the simplest of answers that I knew. We were in such a desperate situation that philosophy seemed utterly inappropriate. "He will reward us later. Now is the time to suffer and grow wise."

For the first time since we had been moved from our town, Clara expressed an idea that closed in on self-pity. "I'm only thirteen. I've got time to gain wisdom. I want to be happy."

This touched me quite deeply. I said fondly and emphatically, "Be happy. You're a good person and you'll be rewarded."

She was serious and tired. "But how do you know?"

It was like I was tucking her into bed although there was no bed, no bed covers. I wanted her to feel some sense of comfort. "After a long winter does spring ever fail to come? There is always spring. You cry now, but latter you will have a reason to laugh and you will feel better. All things change for the better. This life is winter. In the next life you will have pleasure and laugh."

After what seemed like eternity the train started. The cars lurched forward, the wheels began to roll very fast. We didn't know where we were going, we had almost no food and water and there was a gloomy mood of defeatism among us. To make matters just a little bit worse, there was a Polish Jewish man who had escaped from a camp who ended up in our cattle car. He said exactly what was going to happen. "You think you are going to work. Ha! They don't want you to work. They are going to kill you because they want to exterminate all the Jews! You aren't going to any work camp, you are going to a concentration camp, a death camp where all of you will be killed."

No one believed him; that the Germans would try to exterminate a whole population. He said to me, since I was young, "Lets jump out of the window and escape!" I said "First of all I have to stay and look after my family. And secondly, I don't believe a word you're saying."

One dark night he did jump out the window, probably at some point where the train slowed down. The train took about six days. I didn't know it at the time, but they were six days that would forever change my life.

CHAPTER 4
Two Lambs

Being on that train, in that car, was a very passive thing. It's true we were going somewhere. We were going somewhere, but we didn't know where. We had not purchased tickets, we had not planned the trip and with every jerk and pull of the train we were reminded that we were getting further and further from our home. Our homes. We had left them behind with almost every item and valuable memory behind. We knew that we would never go back to them. It was not only that our homes represented our only possessions. It was that they had been there, for most of us, for generations. We were being exiled, we knew that much.

People who don't know the truth often ask, "Didn't you do anything? Didn't you protest or fight back in any way?" They don't understand. We were poor people, steeped in law and tradition. We accepted our fate as G-d's will. Perhaps significantly, also, was that we truly didn't believe the rumours of mass murder or genocide. We thought, "This will get better." We waited, in some nearly palpable sense, to encounter reasonable and humane treatment.

Getting to the train and getting on were the worst part.

The first few hours were quiet and essentially civil. People settled into their spaces, mostly in small groups of two or three. People came to me for water, but I was very firm and didn't give out more than the ration. This made me both popular, for watching out for the interests of all, and very unpopular, for denying some individuals. There were some people sitting around me who were very encouraging. "Keep going!" they said. "You are guarding the gold on this train. Don't be weak!" I admit that at this point everyone seemed to be just a blur of faces, with no one face particularly distinguishable from another. After several hours I started to settle too.

I will never forget what happened then. It wasn't a big thing as things go, but it was a moment and a mental picture that changed my life. Someone came for water and I gave them some, then another face appeared, it seemed from below me, with a wan smile and the very pretty features of an angel. She said, in a voice that was confident and sweet, "You are very strong and fair. You're like Gabriel, the angel who guards the gates of Eden."

"The Cherubim are the angels that guard the gates of Eden."

"Oh. I was trying to create an introduction. I'm sorry. Can you give me a little bit of water, please?"

She was sitting almost beside me. "No, don't feel bad." I said, "I'm thinking of Rachael. She gave water to Jacob and to his camel too. That was a sign from G-d that she should be his wife." I gave her some water. She sipped it very slowly.

"I know that story very well, but I wouldn't go that far. Perhaps you are like Jacob, I don't know. But I don't think I'm at all like Rachael. She was very virtuous and beautiful. I'm not her." She looked about 15 years old. She was not a big girl but she was not petite either. There was something about her that was not frivolous; she seemed to be a whole person in this situation, not broken into pieces the way most of us were.

I didn't know whether to sit down again, because she was so close, but the circumstances transcended tradition. I had a bit of experience talking to women from the ghetto and, of course, from running on the Black Market, but I had never flirted before. It was the most crazy thing, being on this car, travelling on this train, to a future we couldn't know. I was about to engage in a first for me in my life. I actually believe that I was flirting. It was hard to start a conversation. She was good. She made it easy. She spoke first.

"What town are you from?"

I told her.

"Is it a nice place?"

"If you mean is it pleasant, I would have to say no. It's muddy in the summer and icy in the winter and it's a poor town. But for a Jew, it's home and even likeable."

"Is there a town square?"

"There are two town squares, one in front of the Town Hall for the Goyim and one in front of the synagogue for us. At the Town Hall there are four gas lights and on holidays people gather there to dance. At the synagogue we linger on the Sabbath to talk with each other."

"It's nice to linger on the Sabbath."

"It is."

"What do you talk about?"

"We talk about the war. We get some news from the papers from Budapest that are smuggled in, and there is hearsay. We talk about the Jews and what is happening with us. We knew what was happening in other towns before our town was deported but we weren't prepared to be brought to the ghetto and we didn't know that we would be transported to wherever we are going on this train."

I could see the light and the shadows from outside the car running like the ripples of a lake over her face. It made it seem like she was both more distant and, at the same time, more real to me. On the one hand, she was like a ghost, distant and unclear. On the other hand, she was so much a part of the car we shared I felt that I could touch her and it wouldn't be unusual. She said, "What do you expect they plan to do with us?"

"Take us to work camps and make us do labour for the war."

"Will the war go on much longer, do you think?"

"I don't know."

"Do you think Germany will win the war?"

"I don't know if 'win' is the appropriate word. I think they will triumph in some way but how can they take over all of Russia? There will be a peace, but it may not be an easy peace."

"What do you think will happen to the Jews?"

"I don't know. Perhaps they will settle us in work camps. I don't know."

"I think I know. They will make us into slaves."

"How can you know?"

"It's logical. They have already made our fathers and brothers into slaves. They will make the rest of us into slaves too. It must be their plan?"

"If they make us into slaves, the Mosaich will come, like Moses came to take us out of Egypt."

"Do you think the Mosaich will come in our generation? Do you think we will meet at the Western Wall?"

"Why not? We're persecuted, what better time?"

"Well, that would be something, I must say."

She smiled, and the light played along her face in such a way that for an instant I thought she must be from another world. I thought that because she seemed so very human, so down to earth that it was uncanny, almost supernatural. Someone came for water and I gave them some.

"What do you want to do when the war is over, if everything gets back to normal?" she asked pointedly.

"I want to be a rabbi."

"That's a worthwhile goal. Do you want to help people?"

"Yes, I want to help people. I want to teach and study Torah. I love to study Torah."

"Have you been to the *Yeshiva*?"

"Yes, until I had to come back to help my family"

"Were you able to help them?"

"Yes."

"How?"

"I had my ways."

"How. Did you find a way to work?"

"Sort of."

"Well you couldn't have had a job. Weren't you one more mouth to feed?"

"No. I helped them."

"How?"

"I worked away from home."

"In another village?"

"Sometimes."

"This is very mysterious. A young boy helps his family in this situation. How?"

"I can't tell you, but it helped."

"Maybe you'll tell me later? You've made me very curious. Was it illegal?"

"I can't tell you."

"Oh. You'll tell me later?"

"If were still travelling tomorrow, I'll tell you. I promise."

"I'm going to hold you to that promise."

There was an older man on the train who had a little slat to see through by the side of the car. Through the slat he could see the signs posted for the engineer telling him what country the train was in and how far the tracks had gone. This man would call out our location so that we would know where we were and guess where we were going. Just at that moment he called out, "We're still in Hungary." The girl and I looked at each other and a small smile passed over both our lips.

"What's your name?" she asked.

"Avrum. What's your name?"

"Miriam."

"Well. It's nice to know that much."

We didn't talk again for over an hour. The train stopped for half an hour at one point, but no soldiers came to our car. There was a lot of dust around and there was a baby crying most of the time. I saw that Miriam dozed off for a little while and when I saw that I closed my own eyes but didn't sleep. I had to guard the water and I was dedicated to my responsibilities. At that point Miriam was an oddity to me, a girl who knew something about the Torah and was not afraid to express her opinions. This alone was unusual. Even more unusual, for me, was that I had feelings for this girl that I could not describe. Her face made me feel warm. Her words sometimes made me feel like a needle was piercing the very centre of me. Perhaps it was the situation, being on this train, so bleak, so unpromising, so impersonal and so cruel. It was the last place I expected to find both beauty and meaning. In this dull, drab, miserable circumstance it was the last place I expected to find light.

The man who was watching the signs outside the car cried out, "We're still in Hungary! We're heading toward the Polish border."

Miriam sat up. She pushed her dark hair away from her face. "Avrum, why are we going towards Poland?"

"I don't know. Maybe they're taking us to Krakow, to a labour camp or to another ghetto?"

"Why would they do that?"

"I don't know. Why do they do anything with us? It's true we're Jews but we're only human beings."

"You know something? After all this, losing our fathers, having our homes and possessions taken away, being persecuted and sometimes even murdered and finally being put upon trains headed for a destination we don't even know, I still don't know why they hate us so much."

"In the Torah it says they rise up in every generation against us, but we prevail."

"But why?"

"The Torah also suggests that they are jealous of us because we have the Torah."

"You mean because we are the chosen people?"

"Yes."

"We were chosen for this, in our generation?"

"Perhaps. God says that we are the ones who maintain civilization, that without us there would be chaos."

"So why does He torture us?"

"So that we know how important we are. So that we know, from generation to generation, that we have a duty to uphold the word of G-d and protect his teachings."

"For this he has to persecute us?"

"So that we don't get lazy and complacent and forget. We are tested all the time to make our faith strong."

"What about the other peoples? Are they tested too?"

"Yes. They are tested so as not to rise up against us."

"This is very complicated and it sounds more like rationalization than like the truth. You are saying that we suffer because God favours us."

"Without suffering there is no growth. Imagine if God didn't give us reason to protect our faith? We would just be like everyone else. We wouldn't be special and we wouldn't be chosen."

"We'd just be happy and peaceful."

"No. We'd be restless and complacent."

"But we are complacent. We do whatever they want."

"Because we know G-d's will is for us to comply to his commands."

We paused for a moment in this discussion. It was not an easy discussion; it was hard to know what to say. Miriam asked difficult questions and my answers were far from perfect. A woman in a dark dress and with a dark scarf around her head came over to me to ask for water for her child of about 5 years old. I gave her some, but I had to tell her that she would have to make it last for a few hours since we didn't know how far we had to go. I figured that if the water lasted until the end of our trip, it would be a miracle. Miriam watched.

"Why does G-d torture that 5 year old?"

"G-d doesn't torture people. People torture other people."

"But G-d lets it happen."

"That's both the curse and the blessing of free will. It can go to good or it can go to bad. That's the question of evil."

Miriam looked perplexed. Her face, for a moment, lost its composure and fell into chaos.

After a moment, when her features fell back into beauty, she said, "This is all for nothing. Everything you say requires that there be a G-d to look for to explain everything, but its all rationalization and wishful thinking. I believe in G-d and I believe we are the chosen people, but I don't think we're supposed to be herded onto train cars like cattle and endure silently when our homes and families are murdered. This is not sensible, it's not even religion. In the Torah, the Jews learn not to be slaves and they fight for their freedom. You have to fight for freedom, not only pray for it."

This argument was often put forward, and I thought it was naïve. "Whom do you suggest we fight? Our neighbours who hate us because of our religion, or the Germans who hate us so much they take our fathers and brothers to die at the front and take away the property and belongings of the rest of us who are left behind? Who do we have to lead us to this freedom? Are we a nation within a nation, as in Egypt or Babylon? We're not. We exist as tiny villages in tiny villages with no army to fight for us. Who are we to fight against, to win freedom?"

"In Budapest it's different."

"I've been in Budapest."

"It's different."

"Its different but it's the same. The Jews mingle more with the Hungarians, learn from them, eventually assimilate and become just like them. Is this the freedom you advocate? The freedom to day after day, year after year become less like a Jew and more like an Hungarian?"

"In Budapest we had our culture, even in the thick of it. We had plays, music, cinema that was Jewish but that could be admired by the world."

"And the Torah?"

"But it is the Torah, it comes from the Torah, and the culture and traditions that have grown for centuries."

"You know Budapest?" I had to counter her argument.

"That's where I'm from. I was born there."

"But you were in the ghetto. I saw you in the ghetto."

"When my father was sent away my mother thought it was too dangerous for me in the city. We had relatives in the country and I was sent there. My father was a journalist for a Jewish Daily and she felt there might be reprisals over some of his work. My mother was a painter. The Nazi's hate intellectuals of any kind, especially artists and writers."

There was something very true and very shocking in what Miriam had just said. I had never met an artist; I don't think I even really knew what a painter was. "I feel very humble," I said. "My mother and father both worked hard just to put one loaf of bread each week on our table. Imagine, two people worked day and night to put one loaf of bread and some soup on the table for a family of nine."

I pointed at a woman sitting across the car next to a young child. "Look over there. See that woman? That's my mother. Everything she ever had in the world is gone. Her husband. Her meagre home. Even, now, her children? Do you want to know her freedom? That in the very worst of times she did not loose faith! She was a Jew, she did her duty, she suffered quietly and never gave up her belief in G-d. You can persecute her, you can murder her, but you can't hurt G-d. Even in that way, surely her life is eternal, and you can't say she didn't fight for that freedom."

Miriam looked a little broken. She reached out her hand to touch my arm. I don't think any girl who was not my sister had ever done anything like that before. It felt gentle and reassuring. "I'm sorry. I didn't mean it like that. I just don't think we should be led about like lambs."

"But that's what we are. That's what we look like to G-d. In a way, that's what we should be."

"There is also the Lion of Judah. G-d sees us like that too."

"Well, you are right. The Lion, right now is sleeping and in his sleep he is protecting the lamb."

Miriam laughed. "You are not so innocent."

I smiled. "Oh, but I am."

We both sat down in our own places with only a pocketful of sideways glances.

That night, as we ran through Poland and the rickety-rack of the cattle car made its rough music beneath us we sat next to each other on the floor. People were mostly lying down to sleep but they were squeezed up very close to one another. About two hours after dark Miriam shifted from beside me. She rested her back against mine and said, "Its cold, Avrum. Why shouldn't we try to be a little warmer?" I had never been so intimate with a woman who was not a member of my immediate family. I had never been with a woman who was so forthright and bold. I forgot where we might be going. I forgot that this was wrong. After a little while, it didn't seem to be wrong anymore. After a little while, it seemed to be just right. I could feel her breathing and her breathing was a part of me. After an hour or so I fell asleep.

CHAPTER 5
Love of Another

For two more days and nights we travelled, stopping occasionally for various reasons. Twice we took water. Three times we stopped at different cities along the route, twice for several hours. Everyone was suffering from hunger and dehydration. Children were crying constantly and this formed a background to our pain. One older woman was already dead in the car. A man had said Kadish for her and her daughter sat beside her corpse. It was cold, so she did not decompose too fast.

At the end of the second day the man who was watching the signs by the tracks became very excited. He jumped up and down and shouted, "We're entering Poland! Poland!". Everyone speculated about where we were going. "They're taking us to Krakow and then to work camps!", some said. A few voiced a different opinion. "We're going to Germany." Miriam's voice was quietly among them. "It doesn't make any sense to take us to Krakow.", she said. "Or to Warsaw. We know that the Jews there have mostly all been moved out already."

"How do you know?" I said.

"Because I met someone in the ghetto who had been in Budapest and he knew that the Jews in Poland were being shipped out."

"How did he know?"

BAR KOCHBA

"I don't know."

"Then it's only a rumour."

"Maybe so. But we don't know where we're going or what they're going to do with us."

"That's true, but it doesn't mean they're taking us to Germany."

"No."

At this point Miriam and I were very close. We were like old friends, except I had never really been close friends with a woman before. She seemed so close she was almost a part of me. No one, outside of my family, had ever felt like this before, and yet it wasn't like she was a part of my family. Still, she felt very close. I don't think I know what that feeling was.

Since the end of the third night we had done something unheard of. It was something I will never forget. Near the end of the third night, when every one else was asleep and it was still dark, while we were talking about little things because we couldn't sleep, she took my hand in hers. I had never felt anything like this before. It was like our hands had a direct connection to our hearts. It was like electricity ran between us on one thin wire. And it was very exciting. If anyone had seen us we would possibly have been reprimanded. Who could say? The situation was not normal and normal rules didn't necessarily apply. It was simply forbidden for a man and a woman to touch that way, although I had seen much more intimate gestures on the Black Market in Budapest. Even, sometimes, among the Jews.

From the end of that night I waited anxiously for night to fall so we could touch again. It was like being addicted to it. On the third night, after we had been in Poland for a day I did something unheard of and very bold. I gave her a brief little hug. I thought that was outrageous in itself, but she responded to it strongly. She turned around in her squatting position and threw her arms around me in an embrace.

The times were certainly not right. Our train was heading somewhere, to a destination we did not know, to a fate we did not know but which was bound to be full of suffering. We were full of suffering, hungry, thirsty, tired and dirty, persecuted to the very death. All our fathers were already gone, we didn't know if we would ever see them again.

But in this unstable and mournful state electricity ran up and down the hands and into the hearts of a young girl and boy. Why was that? We knew something about what we were headed for so how could such a thing be? That even in the darkest hours of human civilization, the laws of G-d could survive. That was the lesson for me and I think for Miriam too. We were not holding hands out of rebellion or to be sacrilegious. We were only giving a touch of humanity, possibly even divinity, to a very meaningful situation. We were expressing, in a tiny boxcar strewn with dirt and human beings, emotions that were actually bigger, greater, more powerful and compelling than the entire war effort of the Nazi's. Our adolescent gestures blasted the evil powers of the war to smithereens.

In the afternoon of the fourth day the train entered a tunnel. There were allied planes routinely crossing this area and perhaps the train needed to take shelter at this point. It stopped somewhere in the tunnel. There wasn't a glimmer of light in our car, it was utterly black. People talked in the dark about lighting a candle. There was a big discussion, partly to keep some kind of contact between us alive. Some wanted to light a candle. Other's said it would use up precious air. In the end, they lit one candle at the other end of the car.

Something happened I will never forget, through all the rest that was about to happen. While we were huddling together in the pitch black of the tunnel Miriam kissed me on the lips.

I'd never been kissed on the lips before. It was a feeling I cannot to this day describe, but it was like I had been asleep and this had finally woken me up. I kissed her back, letting my instincts be my instructor. When it was over we were both out of breath. We hugged, her head on my chest. "I love you.", she said. I held her closer than I had ever held anyone. "I love you, too." I said. Soon the train began moving again and in a few minutes it left the tunnel.

That was a turning point, not only in the train's long ride but also in my view of G-d. It was no mystery to me that even though I talked conservatively about religion I was slowly loosing faith in it. This kiss changed my understanding. G-d had made me in a certain way. Religion was not always the answer to every issue. I categorically trusted G-d but I was no longer sure I trusted all the interpretations of religion.

That night, when almost everyone was asleep and it was very dark, Miriam and I continued our embrace. Strangely, it seemed that this embrace was just part of a longer one that had started when she first touched my hand. We kissed deeply all through the night. In the morning we were exhausted.

"I don't want this to end." Miriam said. "I mean, I want the train to stop and let us go, but I don't want the kissing to stop."

"I feel the same way."

"This is like being married."

"I feel very strongly about you."

When night came we embraced again as soon as it got dark enough. But it was different than the night before. Miriam was very intense, very persistent.

She pulled me to her body with power and ease and we kissed and even touched passionately. Before I fully understood what was happening I was trying clumsily to loosen her clothes as if there was nothing that could be any more important in the whole world.

I had never imagined that I would have intercourse with anyone before my wife. The idea itself was unimaginable. But here we were, two people in a cattle car on a train in the middle of a World War, persecuted and driven from our homes, knowing not what might happen to us in the morning. We were adults, even at our young age, who might never see a normal life again, once this train reached its unknown destination. We were driven by extremes into a passion that might have played out differently in a sane world. At one point, just before I lost myself to emotions that were so strong, Miriam said in my ear:

"Avrum. I don't want to die without you. I don't want to die having never known love."

"Neither do I."

The logistics were impossible, and yet our bodies seemed to know what to do. People were sitting, though asleep, beside us and behind us. We were in a corner by a wall. We couldn't remain sitting, but the two of us, together, could stretch out against the wall. I didn't think about what we were doing. The sounds of the tracks, the stench of the cattle car and all the people on it, the anxiety of our future rose for a few moments like a dream around me. Then, as Miriam touched my face with her hands and her lips I felt only immense love and terrible urgency. I couldn't actually see Miriam in the dark, but I believed that I knew her more truly than I had ever known anything. I only felt one thing, but it was everything I had ever known. It was Miriam. I felt only love for Miriam. Her soft skin. Her wise and sweet demeanour. In the prison of that rail car there was this all powerful, all encompassing love for another human being.

We stretched out against the wall with Miriam's back against it. She had a large shawl which she spread over us both. We could not move to remove our clothes; we probably never would have thought of it. Miriam took my hand and pressed it to her breast. That touch, through the thin cloth of her bodice, was as if all the religion I had ever learned was rolled up into a tight ball and let loose to engulf me. Somehow, Miriam had lifted her long dress above her hips. I touched the bare skin of her thigh with absolute wonder. She reached her hand to my hips and then lower. I was in disbelief.

This wasn't merely eroticism. Love and death are often bedfellows. This was the affirmation of something utterly personal, completely universal and common and at the same time completely unique. I wasn't in love with lovemaking, although my emotions were on fire. It was Miriam especially, Miriam alone, who I loved this way. Who I would always love.

I thought I would explode too early, like a bomb. Somehow, I didn't. Miriam drew me into her, although awkwardly, like a moth to a fire, and I was totally consumed inside of her, burning like I had been engulfed by natural flames. We had to be silent, with bodies all around us. When my senses returned I was aware of Miriam's breathing but also of the rackety movement of the tracks and the sounds of pain and crying around me. I lay my head heavily on Miriam's chest. She pushed her skirt back into place. We were together like that for a long time. Eventually, someone came for water and I gave them some.

In the morning, an hour after the sun came up, the man who watched the stations looked around from his place by the door and called out. "We're coming into Auschwitz! We're coming into Auschwitz!" "There was a murmur throughout the car. We couldn't believe it. I turned to Miriam. Tears were flooding from her eyes.

CHAPTER 6
This Must Be Hell

There was a grey pall hanging over Auschwitz. We didn't know it at the time, but it was more than weather or a depressing atmosphere. It was caused by all the smoke pouring out of the crematorium 24 hours a day. Perhaps you can describe the smell of burning flesh but it's difficult to describe the effect it has on you. It simply makes you want to vomit. It was our nauseous stomachs and our burning eyes that warned that something even more terrible than we could have imagined was about to unfold. When the door to that cattle car finally slid open, and we could see the camp itself with its barbed wire and bare, structured, precise simplicity, and the uniformed guards so much like an army Satan could be proud of, I knew in a flash what was to come. I could deal with that, somehow, as a necessary reality of having already gone through so much.

There was something even more horrible. What consumed my passions and frightened me far more than death was the possibility that they would take Miriam away from me. We held onto each other like children, innocent and scared. Everybody who could stand was standing now. The train had come to a complete stop. There was a lot of noise from shouting voices outside the car and there was light breaking through the slats in the wall of the train. Miriam said:

"They'll separate us."

I was shaking. "I know."

"Whatever happens, we had this. This defies it all."

"I'll find you. We'll get through this and I'll find you."

"I know you will. I'll find you, too."

The doors to the car suddenly slid open. There were menacing soldiers shouting at us to move, move, move. We had to jump from the door of the car onto the concrete platform below. We were not allowed to bring anything with us from the car; no blankets, shawls, no extra clothing of any kind. As we came out of the car the soldiers cried out "Women here. Men here. Schnell! Schnell!". Miriam and I were holding each other's hand. We wouldn't let go. In an act of impossible defiance we stood like a ragged metaphor before the army at the foot of the car. Within moments the soldiers broke us apart by smashing their batons across our heads. I was beaten to the ground but Miriam was pulled away to the area where the women were. I rose quickly to my feet and ran to her again. She held me close for a moment and said, "Avram. They'll shoot you!". I felt the slam of the baton against my head and I was dragged away. They were the last words I heard her say. I couldn't go back a second time. They would shoot us both.

I felt an unfathomable rage at that moment, but it was incongruent to be angry in that situation, because if you acted out they would shoot you. My anger raged for a while. I shouted out. I was beaten. I cried out. I was beaten. It was worse than having no power. It was also a case of having absolutely no personal identity. As a Jew, I was not permitted to have any vestige of human dignity.

I lay on the platform, having been beaten into unconsciousness for a time, weeping with frustration. There was nothing I could do to be with

Miriam. I looked up at the smoke that hung over Auschwitz and something happened to me. My faith in G-d was shaken as if it were something separate that you could detach from yourself. How could there be a G-d while this was happening? And suddenly I saw myself lying on the concrete as if I were looking from above. Where was G-d? There was this. Slowly I got up. I knew one thing through all my body. I would survive. Somehow, I would have to survive, because it was the only thing that had meaning. I knew I loved Miriam. Everything else was a myth.

As I rose up from the platform it was as if a shroud had fallen over me. I was numb. I couldn't feel anything. I was able to hear and understand the orders, and obey, but I wasn't feeling a thing. I had been beaten. I knew I had to follow orders if I ever wanted to see Miriam again. I saw my mother being pushed into the line of women. I cried out to no avail, but it was the cry of a broken animal, not a human being. My mother, my staff, my only sweet angel was pushed away. I'll never forget how helpless I felt. In the future it would be that memory that would so often heat my thoughts.

The next two days were clear, because I had to have the will to obey. But they have only the shape of emotion associated with them.

As we came out of the cars and were separated into men and women, the clubs reined down all the time. As the two groups formed up, they were each divided further. An officer (they say is was Mengele himself, but I don't know for sure) culled the group. A gesture for one way; a gesture for another way. It seemed to be random but it wasn't. We learned later that one gesture meant to the barracks and life. Another gesture meant to the gas chambers and death. If we had known at the time what the gestures meant there would have been panic. I was sent to the good side; I was young and could work.

My uncle, his son and my brother were with me on the good side. "Your mother can work. She's not old. This is a work camp. She'll survive.", my uncle said.

"This is not a work camp. I don't know what kind of camp it is." I replied.

My uncle spoke. "They are going to make us work, one way or the other. They are not going to kill everybody."

"What then? First they work us until we can't work anymore and then they kill us."

"Have faith. We will survive." His words did not calm me.

"As G-d is my witness, He has brought us into hell."

"Do not question." He was not going to abandon faith. "He is with us and whatever happens He will never let you fall from his hand."

Those of us who had been chosen to work were taken to a large barracks with a row of platforms on either side. The platforms, they were like plain wooden bunks, held about ten men each, with the men lying flush to each other along the width. We were not allowed to speak or make any noise and we were not fed or watered. We were ordered to lie on the bunks. We stayed there all night.

Sleep, at this time, seemed something for the privileged. I lay in a stupor. Although I had been kept together with my brother, my uncle and his son, I could only think of Miriam and my mother. I thought they had probably killed my mother or were going to kill her. I dreamed that I cried out, but there actually was no sound.

When it got very dark the soldiers roused us. They lined us up in rows of 5, there were more than a hundred of us, with batons smashing into us freely and loud shouts of "Shnell! Shnell!" I had no time to think any further about anything. I only had time to obey orders. We were taken out into the open. The camp was lit up like daylight.

It was the first time I could actually see the camp. There were two rows of razor wire around the camp and a large fence around that. Before the razor wire was a single trip line. Anyone trying to escape would be shot by a guard in one of the strategic towers.

One man from our barracks did try to bolt. He made it to the razor wire. Then he was shot to death from several positions.

Then they told us to march. We didn't know where we were going.

We walked about 5 kilometres in the dark until we came to what looked like another camp. At the outside rim there was a sight that has never left my memory. A huge bonfire was blazing, as high and as wide as a large building. In the light of the tall flames there were figures, hundreds of them, it seemed. You could see that all of them were naked, and to see this number of naked people was startling. Men and women. They were screaming. By this time most of my senses had returned, and I was aware of what was going on around me. There was a man in line with me who I knew had been at Auschwitz for a while. I asked him what was going on.

He said, "The men and women are going to the showers. They'll be gassed to death there, and their bodies will be thrown into the ovens. The bonfire is for the babies. There are a lot of babies. They throw them directly into the fire. Alive. It's a means of saving resources through German efficiency."

I looked at that sight. The sound from the throats of the men and women was unforgettable. My mouth fell open, but my eyes looked up. I knew what I only suspected earlier. There could not be a G-d in the light of such human suffering. No man or woman deserved to die like this. No baby was guilty of anything bad, of any crime. The Germans were evil, yet they were supreme. Thousands and thousands of Jews were being killed. Nothing made sense. Order was gone. There was no sign of anything divine. There was no G-d that could justify this. I knew it, without rancour or even any extreme emotion.

G-d was a hoax, or he was indifferent to this. The possibility that this was part of G-d's plan and we would either understand or be rewarded later made no sense. Nothing could justify birth itself if in this universe so random a suffering could occur. This was not a rationale; it was simply a fact, like there being no life in a dead body. From that moment on I ceased to believe. I cast off my faith the way you would cast away a pair of old used shoes. I turned to my uncle and said:

"Now I know. There is no G-d."

He replied, "Remember Sinai when we were slaves. We suffered much, but G-d redeemed us and made us a nation. In every generation they rise up against us. This is horrible beyond understanding, but you must not try to understand. Only have faith. That is what will save you."

"In all my years of studying the Torah they never taught me this. That we would stand by helplessly again while they mercilessly burned our babies."

My uncle looked at my face for a moment. "You are beside yourself because you are helpless."

"Yes."

"G-d will give you strength, if you ask Him for it."

"I don't want to ask anything. He doesn't exist." I grit my teeth. Better to be an atheist with vision than a believer with blind faith.

When we were returned back to the camp itself we were led to a bunker, smaller than the one before. It had smaller bunks which could contain three men each. At that time we had still received no food or water.

Now that G-d was gone I had a lot to think about, and after the induction into Auschwitz there was some precious time to think. I felt a lot of anger deep inside. This, combined paradoxically with my love for Miriam, kept me going. A cold, hard determination began to grow inside of me. The workings of the world were strictly in human hands, and I had to take my stand if I wanted to survive. I understood that I had to act to bring about events. I couldn't wait anymore and expect G-d to do anything. This was a realization that was to effect my actions for very long to come.

I fell asleep briefly and woke up after a couple of hours. It was still dark. I thought that what I had seen the night before was a bad nightmare, because things that horrible couldn't happen in reality. My uncle was beside me in the bunk. His eyes were open. "I thought I saw a big fire." I said.

"No. The fire was real." I paused for a moment.

"This is hell, then."

"I don't know. Could hell be any worse?"

"What demons could conceive of such a place? How could G-d create human beings that would act in such a way?"

"G-d creates them but they choose their own path."

"I don't believe you. They are responsible for their own actions."

"They have chosen evil, even though most of them do not know it."

"Then G-d help the rest of us. I never did anything to deserve this."

"No. But it comes to us just the same. We are subject to the will of others. G-d help us and keep us from harm."

Barbers came in the morning and cut off every hair on our bodies. They missed nothing. We were told this was for sanitary reasons, but some said they also used it in mattresses. Our scalps were shaved except for a one inch strip left down the centre of our heads in a kind of groove.

We were taken to a building where we were told to remove all our clothing. Then we were pushed into a room where there were showers and we were washed clean by them. When we came out of the other side of the room we were given a uniform with large bands of black and white stripes on it. Both tops and bottoms. No socks, but wooden shoes with canvas uppers. The uniform was worn 24 hours a day, every day, all year round. There was no change of clothes and nothing warmer was ever issued. After receiving the uniform we again stood in line to receive a number. Some numbers were tattooed on a man's arm, some were only posted on their uniform. From that time on, we were not referred to by any name, only a number.

We later learned that this procedure was the same for the women: same uniform, same one inch stripe down the back of the head. They received no special articles of cleanliness for their menses. I thought of Miriam all the time.

Before dawn they lined us up 5 deep and they told us we must act in a military way. The Kappo's were in charge. We couldn't talk and we couldn't be slovenly. We had to stand at attention until told to do otherwise. After this kind of training the kappos beat those who were unable do it properly. Then they addressed us all, saying:

"Remember you are in a concentration camp. The only law here is Nazi law and we kappos or any of the S.S. can do anything we feel like to you, including killing you on the spot. There's nothing you can do about it, therefore you must obey all orders without question and you must have total discipline. Anybody who does not follow these rules will be beaten, even beaten to death, or shot by the S.S. You will never see your family again or your loved ones. Only the strongest and the best will be able to survive."

Then he made a sort of joke, one that I heard from Kappos and guards over and over again.

"The only way out of here is through those chimneys. Do you see those chimneys? Do you smell that smell? That's where all useless prisoners go. Your loved ones are just now being killed and gassed and burned to death. Therefore, you must be on total discipline, 24 hours a day."

There were perhaps a thousand of us.

Then another kappo said, "Any of you who have a trade, step forward. My younger brother was with me at the time as well as my uncle and his son. They were all standing next to me. My uncle and I had a moment to decide.

"What does it mean to volunteer in hell?" I asked.

"You are doing a favour to the devil." my uncle replied.

"What could they have us do?"

"Perhaps build a crematorium. Maybe a gas chamber."

"If we volunteer our skill and labour to this unspeakable horror we would have to be crazy."

We decided that we wouldn't volunteer for anything. My brother and my uncle's son were not so philosophical. They decided they would volunteer because they believed tradesmen would be treated better than the others. That's the last time I saw either of them. Wherever they went it must have been worse than for us in the end.

After the speech we were assembled in proper formation and told to march. They took us for a long march and at the end of it they gave us shovels to dig ditches. I believe there was really no purpose in digging the ditches, it was only so that we didn't lie idle. We had been in the camp less than two days. We worked digging ditches until it got dark at which time they marched us back to the barracks. We were all given a metal container and a spoon which we were to carry for the rest of our time in the camp.

In this container was poured some soup. It was made out of turnips and water. It was completely unpalatable. It tasted so awful that nobody could eat it. Little did we know it was all we would eat for another year. It was either that or we would eat nothing except a piece of bread that accompanied this soup. On the first day I refused to eat it. I only ate the piece of bread. It was the same kind of bread they gave the soldiers. I don't know how they baked it, but it was very hard and difficult to bite into.

This routine continued for about a week. Back breaking work that we were forced to endure. All this time we had to live with the smell of the crematorium. We slowly got used to it and we got slowly used to the discipline and in our minds we became resigned to the fact that we would never see our loved ones again. This was a great burden for everyone. It sapped our will and made the time drag on interminably.

For me, certainly, I missed my family, but especially I missed Miriam. In this dark time the love I had experienced with her was like a bright flame that could not extinguish. For a 15 year old boy this first love was as real and enduring as if it had lasted a lifetime, not only a few days. We believed we were going to end up like some of the inmates who were horribly emaciated, looking more like skeletons than human beings. We were told these people must have been in Auschwitz for a long time but they weren't going to be there for much longer. Every so often they would round up these poor people and take them to the gas chamber.

After about two weeks they gathered us all together, but not for a march to forced labour. Instead, we were marched to the rail line and loaded onto cars. They gave us half a bread, without water and arranged us in much the same conditions as the boxcar ride that had brought us here, but only men and boys, not mixed gender and families. This time we had enough room to lie down. We rode for about three days.

There was an S.S. soldier guarding us inside the car. At one point, when the train was stopped, a woman, possibly an associate of the S.S., came in and asked the guard in which direction the train was going. Apparently she was going in the same direction and she boarded the car.

It was a peculiar thing to see from the perspective of a Jewish prisoner, mostly starved to death and deprived of any rights. They were very friendly and it seemed that one thing led to another. She smiled. He touched her arm. Their voices got low. It is impossible to describe how disgusted I was; it seemed to make what had happened to Miriam and me a lurid joke. Once it got dark they decided to have sex on the floor of the car, but before they did the guard shouted, "Turn around and close your eyes. If you look over you'll be shot." Even so, we knew what they were up to. It was only fear that kept us from weeping or laughing out loud. The Nazis had no moral boundaries, and Hitler had told them to impregnate as many German women as they could to increase the numbers of the next generation of the super race. So the soldiers, both men and women, were under orders to procreate.

We arrived at a small concentration camp known as Gurlits. We were immediately called to an assembly where we had to line up perfectly, 200 prisoners to a square and there were four sides to the square. Five deep in a straight line facing outward. The head Kappo cried "Auchtung". We had to come to attention perfectly in unison or we were required to repeat it until all 800-1000 did it perfectly in one sound. Then they made a count. The Commandant oversaw the count until it was perfect, sometimes taking an hour. A kappo gave basically the same speech as before. By this time it was dark. We were told we were 'dismissed'. We were sent back, about 200 men to a barracks with three tiers of bunks. There was a mattress filled with straw, but no pillow. This time, each one of us got a single space to sleep in. We were directed to which bed was ours; perhaps since I was young I was assigned the top tier. We all lined up for a quarter of a bread and the turnip soup. These were starvation rations meant to keep us alive until we wasted to death or the war ended. Nevertheless, at this point we were happy to receive the turnip soup which, just a short time ago, we couldn't eat.

There were many miseries. Starvation is a slow but constant murderer. You feel as if some sort of evil parasite is working its way towards your bones. At first, all you want to do is eat; you want to feed this parasite which is eating at you. But eventually the focus shifts away from your mouth and you think only of your stomach. It's so small and empty you only want to put something in. You dream of black spaces at night. All day long, all through the night as you sleep, it conditions you to an empty ache. You're so hungry that at a certain point all you really want to do is cry like a baby, but you don't. You endure it as patiently as you can.

But as bad as the hunger was, there was something almost as bad. It wasn't on the inside, it was out. Little, dark, biting insects infested every part of us. Lice. They swarmed over everyone. So itchy, so ever present, so small and infectious. If the Devil had a curse to make a starving man suffer even further he would wish them lice. They were like the physical metaphor of all our suffering. Nothing we could do would make them go away.

Even so, we never stopped thinking of our loved ones, since that is what kept our identity alive.

"What do you think about most when your not thinking about your stomach?" I once asked my uncle.

"You'll laugh."

"I am incapable of humour." I replied.

"I think about being able to fly, like an angel. I think that whatever happens, when I die G-d may ask me what I want. I will answer, 'Thou, the creator of the worlds. I would like to fly like an angel.' And I see myself high up looking down on creation."

I smiled and clasped my hand on my uncle's shoulder. "You have accessed for me a corner of some emotion I didn't think I had."

"What do you think about?"

"I think about killing the men who have murdered my mother."

"With a machine gun?"

"With a knife."

Even though I talked about others, Miriam was foremost in my thoughts although I couldn't mention her to anyone. I tried a mental trick when possible. I imagined this had never happened and we were in the future living a happy life with each other and several children. I could almost always see her face, and I worked ceaselessly at remembering how it was without time and hunger wrecking my dream.

Any time someone got sick or fell out of the working discipline they were taken to a hospital, but this was almost surely a death sentence. Every couple of weeks those who were still there were taken back to Auschwitz and killed in the gas chamber. Therefore, if there was even a little life left in us we didn't want to be taken to the hospital or if we had to go to try to get out of there as soon as possible. The threat was always hanging over our heads.

There was a definite mood in the camp. It was total demoralization and hopelessness. This was not surprising. We had nothing to hope for. The SS and the Kappos told us over and over that there was no way out of the camp. We had to obey each and every order and we had to work extremely hard because if you slacked off they beat you up. You had to worry the most about getting sick. If you got sick, you were doomed. There was no 'bright side' to anything. There was no 'surprise' of extra food to be had, and our strength was always failing. There were no recreational activities. All we looked forward to all day at work was the night when we would eat. Since we only ate at night, we woke up hungry and we were hungry all day. We only looked forward to a little food and sleep.

For me, the dream of being somehow reunited with Miriam played over and over again in my mind, but I fell into depression nevertheless. Occasionally, the situation and the circumstances were too much for some people. They would run towards the trip wire surrounding the camp and were invariably shot by guards in the towers. It was the only way they had of committing suicide. No one in their right mind really thought escape was possible.

The routine was very stable. We were woken up at 5 A.M., no food or drink, and lined up in the Assembly Square. We were standing in perfect formation and we were counted. The assembly had to be absolutely perfect or they would keep us there lined up until they were satisfied. When the assembly was complete we would be marched out to do our work. This was hard labour and back-breaking tasks, digging ditches or breaking rocks. Hanging over us all the time was the immanent threat of being beaten. This could come swiftly and painfully. There was a 20 minute break at noon without food or water. We were marched back to the camp at nightfall. We were arranged again in an assembly. We were counted. If anyone collapsed during work they would be taken to the hospital. Very few of them ever returned.

Sometimes an inmate would escape. If the count was not correct we would suffer a further routine. If anyone was missing it was considered the fault of the commandant. When someone did try to escape, which was not often, our punishment was to be kept standing in the square without food for all night and we would have to do push-ups. If the inmate was not found we had to go back to work again right away without food or sleep. Mostly they were caught the next day or the day after. They could say good-bye to life because they were sent to the Gas chamber. Normally, when the count was correct, we were sent back to our barracks. We were fed the bread and turnip soup and went immediately to our bunks. This was the only time we had to talk to each other a bit.

At one point I fell ill with pneumonia. I had a high fever, so bad that when I lay down on my bunk, which was on the top tier, my shivers were so severe the whole three tiers shook. I had to be taken to the hospital, which in itself terrified me horribly. I lay there for a week before signing myself out. I beat the clock that time and was not taken to the gas chamber. Where I got the strength to do that I don't know. Perhaps the hope that I might somehow again see Miriam was stronger than pneumonia. Some part of me, in any case, wanted to live.

I was not alone in my barracks. My uncle was there, and we were close, luckily sleeping in adjacent bunks. There was a cousin, by a different uncle, and a few friends from my village. Altogether we were about 10. We gave each other support and generated faith among ourselves. My Uncle in particular had faith. We would sometimes talk about it, in whispers, in our bunks.

"Avrum," he would say, "you must believe that G-d is with you."

"Yes. He's going to hold my hand in the gas chamber."

"Yes. He will comfort you, even there."

"But it is He who has put me there!"

"No. It is the Nazi's who have put you there. It may seem impossible, but they are His children also."

"Can G-d create such evil children?"

"G-d does not play favourites. The Nazi's choose their fate. We, on the other hand, are in G-d's hands. We are so much better off, if only you could see it."

"I want to survive, but for my own reasons. I don't have the ear of G-d. He doesn't listen to my prayers. I only see men killing other men for reasons I don't understand, for reasons that may not even exist. The paradoxes of life are completely plain to me. The holiness and the sanctity of it are noticeably absent."

"Sometimes, when I am digging, I imagine that I am digging the foundations for the Temple in Jerusalem. I feel stronger."

"That's a good idea. I will try that too. Only instead of building the foundations for a Temple, I will imagine that I am putting up barricades to fight back against the Nazis."

"In any case, we will meet in Jerusalem."

"Alright. We will pray together in Jerusalem."

There were many in our barracks who were still religious. A few kept track of the Jewish calendar and they were aware when Rosh Hashanah and Yom Kippur arrived. We couldn't fast on the night of Yom Kippur since the only food we had came in the evening. But for Kol Nidre, the prayer for redemption, a rabbi who was among us led us in prayer. We were lucky. The Kappos, who were, after all, Jewish, didn't seem to mind. Perhaps in some way they thought the prayers might also be for them.

Although daily life and the struggle to survive was constant and ongoing for me in the camp, and any idea of life outside the camp was most often faint, the war was progressing. We didn't get much news, but rumour had it that the German's were being pushed back by the Russians and the Americans. I didn't know what to believe until early January,

1945. We could hear the Russian artillery getting closer and closer. This gave us some hope and for the first time there was an atmosphere almost of joyfulness.

The last thing the Germans wanted was for the inmates to fall into Russian hands. There were two reasons for this: First of all they didn't believe the war was over and they needed us to work. Secondly, they at no time gave up their mission to destroy the Jews and they wanted us all dead, not into the hands of the Allies.

They gave us individually a choice as the Russians advanced. We could stay in the camp or we could leave on a forced march. My uncle felt too weak to undergo a long march and he wanted to stay. I wanted to go, and I urged him to go also, because we knew the Germans would kill all of the inmates before they were near to being liberated. Nonetheless, my uncle fell back upon his faith and decided to stay back.

"They will certainly kill you." I said to him before leaving.

"In any case, I will be in G-d's hands."

I looked at him with my whole spirit and said something entirely out of character. "Do you know that I love you? That without you I don't think I would have survived to this point?"

"I'm made happy."

"G-d be with you." I said. "If there is a G-d, he must know that you are the very best of all possible Jews. You never complain, you always pray and hope."

"Thank you." He said plainly. "G-d knows your intentions and I believe He will address them. Because whether or not you believe in him, Avrum, He believes in you."

"Good bye Uncle."

"G-d be with you, Avrum"

BAR KOCHBA

They gave each one of us who were going to march one full loaf of bread. We were told that we could either eat it right away or ration it. The only intelligent thing to do was to ration it, but many couldn't wait and they ate their only ration for the whole march in one day. This was an unfortunate thing, for the march was destined to be a long one.

Because of troop movements and Allied reconnaissance we were marched mostly through the forest. I was not in the worst of shape, but many others were very weak to start. The SS walked behind the rear line of our marchers. Anyone who fell behind was immediately shot. The sound of a rifle echoed through the forest regularly. Each shot was so agonizing to me that I almost wished I was one of them. Some inmates allowed weaker ones to hold onto them. There was a sense of unity in this, that the stronger should look out as best they can for the weak. I helped several men since I could, but even so two fell behind. When I heard the shots I almost cried.

Every person had one blanket, the blanket they were initially issued. It was cold and there was snow on the ground. We slept on the ground and lay close to each other so the body of one could give warmth to the other. Somehow, most of us managed to survive. I think that if we hadn't undertaken this march as a compassionate group many more would have received a bullet.

A note about my uncle. The night we left, the guards in the tower were under orders to shoot everybody. They were supposed to use machineguns to shoot through the thin walls of all the barracks. Almost like in a fiction, in the moments that the guards were about to shoot through the walls of the barracks the Russians arrived and killed them all, saving the inmates at the last minute. Thus, my uncle was liberated 4 months before me. We later met up in Hungary, after the war.

We arrived in this huge camp, called Buchenwald, after 12 days march. We were overwhelmed by what we saw. I thought, in my head, I had finally arrived at the farthest reaches of hell and that I would never get out alive after seeing what I saw. I completely lost any belief, after witnessing what I saw, that I could possibly live any longer. We saw some of the inmates, dressed just like us, who were nothing but living skeletons. Practically no meat on some of the inmates. We saw dead people laying on the ground and sick people with nobody doing anything about them. The stench of death was so overwhelming that most of us vomited. The corpses were either bloody or covered with feces.

The first thing we were told to do, before even being given any accommodation, was to start picking up the bodies and taking them to an empty barracks, where they were piled like bricks on top of each other. They were all stiff. I could barely walk on my feet. First of all, we had just finished an incredibly long and difficult walk and secondly I was so overcome by the spectacle there that I was totally demoralized. I would say I was as close to insanity as I could possibly get, but I couldn't possibly avoid doing it because the kappos were there and they would deliver a violent beating to anyone who, even for an instant, gave sign of not being able to do it or, G-d forbid, refused to do it. After nine months in a concentration camp we had been conditioned to immediately obey orders, because if you didn't you were a dead man.

The last of my bread was gone now, and it was gone for everyone else as well. I had eaten only small pieces all along the march, maintaining a sort of discipline. In the camp itself we were waiting until evening while dealing with the corpses, and when night fell they put us through the regular counting. This was excruciating, since an accurate count after the march had to be made accounting for those who were missing. The hellish ordeal went on for hours. When they were through they gave us a little turnip soup and had us take over the barracks that had previously been used by the men who were now corpses. At this point we were allowed to get a few hours sleep.

We continued, the next morning, again without food or water, to collect the dead people. We also picked up some live people whom we took to a special barracks where there were several Jewish doctors. These men would decide whether it was worth saving these people in the hospital or sending them directly to the gas chambers. We still had to make an assembly every afternoon and evening. These were so fanatical that when the kappo said, "Hats Off!" all the hats had to hit all the thighs at precisely the same moment and make precisely one sound. If there were any discrepancies, the kappos would search with their clubs ready to see where the mistake had been made.

In terms of numbers, the image is fantastic. There were thousands of corpses. This was a very large camp, holding at least 20,000 inmates at a given time. The plan was to kill all the Jews anyway, so they culled the numbers by making the strongest work and discarding the rest. There was always a backlog. Trucks picked up the dead inmates, but there were always more than they could deal with. The biggest destroyer was dysentery which dehydrated the person and caused them to die. Anyone who got severe diarrhoea could expect to perish within a short time.

For myself, in the weakened condition that I was in, I tripped over a stone and hurt my thigh. I didn't pay much attention to it until it began to swell up to about the size of a grapefruit. Obviously this was an infection and there was no medication. I went to one of the Jewish camp doctors. He summoned four of the other inmates and had me held down on a bench and with a knife, an ordinary knife that wasn't very sharp, he cut open the wound and happened to get some rags and tie it up with them. And the beautiful part was, he saved my life! I was lucky because the doctor was willing to do that. I was young and in relatively good health compared to the other inmates who had come before me. He saw that I might be worthy of being saved.

Even so, every day I was getting weaker and weaker, and so was everybody else. We did the best we could at our task, which at this time became cutting down forests. We had, at one time, a small stove and we tried to cook the grass. Occasionally, the Germans would give us a piece of bread. It was reminiscent of an earlier event. In a previous camp, either out of total malice or perhaps misguided clemency, the Commandant decided to give us all a portion of sauerkraut from huge barrels he had obtained as well as a slice of bacon. For the first time in eight months we were able to eat as much as we wanted. Of course we all got sick. I remember being sick for three days and vomiting violently.

But now I was so weak that every day after work I decided that I would end it all, and so I stopped eating. The surest way of committing suicide was not to eat for three or four days. Lots of people just gave up. They couldn't take it any longer. A friend, who was a good friend, saw this happening and forced me to eat. It was a temporary insanity perhaps, because I got over it. In the camp, the idea that everyone was selfish and indifferent to each other is false. We were together in it all and we were a community as much as possible. The hunger, the hard labour, the lice, the constant nagging of the stomach and the beatings handed out by the kappos all contributed to the added hopelessness of it ever ending. People really just gave up and died without being sick. They died of hunger. Starvation. But we were a community. We knew who was going to stumble and fall and didn't ignore them.

BAR KOCHBA

The war ended on May 8, 1945. We heard the artillery. The bombing was so loud that the barracks shook, almost like a roller coaster. We weren't actually optimistic because, after all, this had happened before. From approximately 1000 people who arrived with me at Buchenwald, only a few hundred remained. But for those relatively few souls, liberation had arrived. American troops closed in on the camp.

CHAPTER 7
Liberation

On the morning of May 8, 1945 we were all woken up by a very strange event, or rather the absence of an event. There was no alarm to wake us. No shouts, no sirens, no kappos flogging us with sticks. Something was going on. We were very excited inmates. I'd never seen any of my friends as excited as they were on that particular morning, because we never thought anything good could happen to us and something, good or bad, was definitely going on. Some inmates noticed that earlier in the morning most of the guards had left their guard towers.

"What's happening?", we all wanted to know.

"What's going on!"

We couldn't understand what the situation was. We'd been disappointed in the past so many times, we were afraid to speculate. We all got out of the barracks and joined at the assembly place. We didn't see any S.S. on the watchtowers, so everyone was trying to figure out what was going on here. The repercussions were massive until one daring inmate, who somehow got hold of some wire cutters, very boldly and with everybody expectantly watching he began to cut away at the gate, which was all barbed wire.

Nothing happened. Nobody stopped him. At first he was alone, but soon other's joined him in tearing down the gate. Soon, inmates were on the other side. We couldn't believe it. It took a little while, with all of us standing on either side of the broken gate and no guards around anywhere, to think the unthinkable:

"Perhaps we are free?" my friend said to me. "Maybe we are free."

But we didn't dare believe it and we were in such a pathetic way of thinking we couldn't possibly accept any kind of emotional celebration.

"There are several thousand corpses still lying on the ground behind us. The idea of being 'free' is a relative one. Perhaps we are being allowed to escape."

However, after quite a number of inmates disappeared, having left the camp for G-d knows where, several of my friends and I crawled through a hole in the fence and to the outside of the camp. We were not brave, after being so long in captivity, but we were cautiously curious and emboldened. We began to walk away from the walls, in the open, with nobody stopping us. Our thinking wasn't noble; we had all been degraded to such a state that there were no philosophical elements to our thinking and we were mostly just poor degraded animals. There was one thing on everyone's mind: where could we get some food?

The air war wasn't over and we still saw planes fighting in the sky, it must have been the American against the Germans. The Germans' were given orders not to stop fighting until midnight on May 8, 1945. when the war would finally be thankfully over. This was still early in the morning of that day. Furthermore, as we kept walking, we saw trucks, full of German soldiers, driving furiously away from the camp, obviously caught in the camp and trying to get out of the vicinity. This time they were so busy escaping that they didn't shoot at us. This actually gave us courage to keep going and see if we could find some food. We didn't expect a parade and we didn't expect well wishers. The mundane truth was that food was the most demanding of our needs at that time, and the initial and immediate goal of our new found freedom was to find something to eat.

Several friends and I happened to have the luck to find a warehouse, probably belonging to the army. We approached it carefully.

"Over here!" Hershel said, "The door is wide open."

"There may be soldiers waiting inside." Isaac pointed out.

I was the most cautious as we huddled together to forge a plan. "One person go. Take a couple of stones to the door. Once he gets to the door, first call out. If no answer, then throw in the stones. If nothing happens, one by one we go inside and investigate."

My plan was accepted as tendered and I was elected to go first. I picked up a few stones and approached the door, as planned. When I reached the door I called out, "Is anybody there?" There was no answer. In my simple minded innocence I called out everything; "We're Jews." I cried. "We're from the camp. We don't want to do any harm. We're from the camp!"

No response, and it all seemed clear. I held my breath and stepped inside. There was warehouse machinery in the front section and just behind piles of cardboard boxes about 2 feet square. By the time I had approached the boxes Hershel had joined me. We looked them over. Isaac joined us.

"Lets open one." Isaac said provocatively.

Hershel and I agreed. We grabbed a lever and opened a box.

It was full of jars of mustard. We looked at each other, our tongues hanging out.

"We can eat mustard."

I opened a jar and tasted some. It was the first food I had tasted in 9 months that had flavour. I liked the taste, I didn't care what it was. We each took a jar and ate. It was good. It might as well have been steak and eggs to me. We each ate a lot of mustard before we were full.

The satisfaction of having a full stomach made us bold. We were like hungry wolves now, on the prowl for food. We kept walking for a while. In the near distance we saw a small frame house painted white. We stopped and went down on all fours like animals. For some reason we began whispering to each other.

Hershel said, "What if they have food?"

"We'll knock at the door and when they answer it we'll demand that they give us food!"

I contributed my part. "But what if they won't give it to us?" This caused us to pause for a moment and think. We were not ruffians. Before being in the camps we had all been religious students, and we had each been in the camps for at least two years. The oldest among us was 18. This kind of aggressive behaviour was completely uncommon, but we had been brutalized and that brutality had conditioned our minds.

"We'll knock them over the head!", said Isaac, who was the most radical of our three.

"Yes," Hershel said, "but with what?"

I was the most cautious and careful. "The war is ending. The Americans are here. We'll avoid violence and tell them that the Americans will replace the food they give to us."

We all agreed to that. We approached the house. With some stealth we peered in a front window. There was movement in the back room, likely a kitchen, but we couldn't see who was moving. For some reason I seemed to be in charge of this operation. I motioned with my hand that we should go to the rear door. We crept carefully around the small building. When we reached the back door I stood up and knocked three times. The other two stayed crouched down on either side.

A woman who must have been over 60 years of age came to the door. She was wearing a white apron. I didn't waste time. "We are Jews!" I said. "We have come from the camp. We are not going to hurt you. We just want food."

My German was rudimentary but effective. "We have been rationed. We have no food." She said.

My companions and I looked at each other. "Let us see." I demanded.

The woman let us in. It was clear she was shocked to see three men in such shape. I thought she let us in because she was scared. It occurred to me later that she actually let us in because she felt pity for us. Her husband came to the door at that moment. His face registered complete surprise and even horror. We asked if we could stay in their house and they agreed. They allowed us to stay in the basement because the fighting was still going on. At midnight, the German man came down to the basement and announced that the war was now officially over. He allowed us upstairs in his house and said, "I have a son who is a soldier. You can sleep on his bed." The bedroom was upstairs, which was fine, but the man decided to lock us in. That turned out to be a bad move. In the middle of the night all three of us got a bellyache from all the mustard we had eaten. There was no toilette in the room, and our need was absolute. We found the only solution possible. We hung our backsides out the window and did natures work.

It was terrible what happened. The next morning the German man saw it and gave us an awful tongue lashing, but in the late morning we saw scores of American trucks and armoured vehicles descending on the area. We followed them to the camp. The Americans couldn't believe what they saw inside; thousands of corpses and the nearly dead. We were able to communicate with some of the Jewish soldiers who spoke Yiddish. For someone who had never seen anything like Buchenwald it was an unbelievable spectacle.

The Americans brought truckloads of bread and other food and anyone could eat as much as they wanted for as long as they wanted, something we had not had the privilege to do for a very long time. But the American Army Doctors didn't know how dangerous it was to give such a quantity and quality of food to the emaciated inmates of the camp. Some of the foods, like chocolate and preserves in cans were too rich for us to digest. It made people very sick and some started to die from it. What the doctors should have done was lock us up and feed us gradually to bring us back to health. I guess we just looked so dreadfully hurt they wanted to remedy it immediately.

They called us 'walking skeletons'. After the mustard I watched my diet. I ate mostly bread and avoided the American tined meat called 'Spam', which was very fat. Many people ate that food and many, unfortunately died. Its one of the insane ironies of the war that a person can survive starvation in captivity only to die of overeating in freedom.

The American collected German citizens from the close area of the camp and made them dig big graves and made them start burying the dead, even though they all denied any knowledge of the camps themselves. This was an impossible claim, but intractable. The barracks were all cleaned and disinfected and American uniforms, including underwear, was distributed to the prisoners who were subject to a nauseating odour after living in the same clothes for so long. They burned the old uniforms and used DDT to get rid of the infernal lice which had plagued so many. They put in clean blankets. This process took several weeks, during which time Hershel, Isaac and I stayed with the German couple in their house. We were told to stay in the newly prepared barracks but not to do anything. We were told we could just stay there. They brought in good food regularly so that we should start to resemble some kind of a human being.

It took us a while to realize that we were human beings again. We were very, very grateful to these American soldiers and doctors and nurses who tried to make us whole again. It was not like a Hollywood film, with inmates jumping up and down with happiness. We were more animal-like. The basic needs came before everything, and the need was food. It was not an elation, it was more like going from one stage of life to another. "Before I was a slave, now I am a free man", did not strike us until later and it happened slowly.

In Buchenwald, which was liberated by the American forces, they were very nice to everybody and they checked anybody there. We were all ill but the seriously ill were taken to hospitals. They also brought truckloads of food, but that was a big mistake because people whose stomachs had shrunk and whose organs were damaged could not deal with it. They brought a lot of 'Spam', a fatty meat in a tin, and there were hundreds, perhaps thousands of people who died as a result. The Americans had never had to deal with this problem. I didn't eat much other than bread.

CHAPTER 8
A Bowl of Bean Soup

I learned this from Miriam while we were on the train:

Her family name was Spitz. She had an older sister named Rivka. They were modern Orthodox, which meant the two girls were not as carefully scrutinized as they would have been in an Orthodox home. When they were young they lived in a two bedroom apartment in Budapest. The father was a shoemaker who worked out of their home. The mother was wholesome and loving. Although they were not wealthy they were a very cultured family. When their father could afford it the girls were exposed to classical concerts and operas. Even so, like most children, the girls wanted more than they had.

"Can't we get a phonograph, Papa?" Miriam used to ask.

Her father would scold her. "Its not enough you go to live concerts when possible? A phonograph is very expensive; too expensive for us to afford. Also the records cost money. What would you rather have? Concerts and opera or a phonograph"

"You make it hard, Papa. I want both!"

"Well, you can't have both and a phonograph is not a priority. A phonograph is a luxury we can do without, but nothing can replace the experience of going to a concert. It's a luxury we can't do without."

Despite minor conflicts it was a happy life for Miriam and Rivka, who were very close. Rivka looked out for her younger sister with enthusiasm bordering on possessiveness. They went everywhere together. Although they were good at school they were not exceptional students. They had many friends and their social life was rich. Until the mother was diagnosed with cancer when Miriam was 10.

It was a terrible blow to the family. Miriam didn't really understand why her mother couldn't just go to bed for a while and kick it.

"Mama," she said, "You must get better soon. Go lie down! Then you won't feel so ill."

The mother would hug Miriam to her breast. "It will all be better in time." She said.

That was 1939. Miriam was in mourning for a time but eventually started going out again. The two girls liked to go to a park just by the Danube River and walk by the water and socialize. There was a strong anti-Semitic politic in Budapest, but Miriam and Rivka were fortunate enough, in this context, not to look obviously Jewish. Miriam was dark but Rivka had blonde hair and blue eyes. Of course, there were many young men who followed their every move. They didn't know the girls were Jewish and although they didn't hide the uncomfortable fact they didn't advertise it either.

One group of boys found out from a neighbour that Miriam was Jewish. One of them, who had been especially fond of Miriam, encountered her near the Danube shortly after he learned this news.

"Why are you Jewish?" he asked.

"What do you mean?" Miriam replied.

"Why don't you change?"

"I can't change. That's what I am" she said defiantly.

"No. You could change." He insisted. "You could be Catholic instead. Why are you Jewish?"

Miriam was startled. She bent her head to the side and looked into the boy's curious eyes. "I was born Jewish.' She said. "I was raised Jewish and I choose to be Jewish."

"I was born a Catholic, but you don't have to be. You can convert."

She was surprised. "How much do you know about Jews?", she asked.

"They're dirty, smelly, sneaky and they killed Christ. But you're not like that. You wouldn't kill anybody" He was entirely in earnest.

"Let me inform you. Jews believe in G-d. They are not dirty and smelly. They didn't kill Christ, that's just a story. Jews are like this. Like me. I'm a Jew and this is what I'm like. You either accept me or live with the consequences."

The boy looked at her. Lines crossed his face, too many for one so young. "Jew.", he said. "You may not be like the others and I've got nothing against you. But you're a Jew. You'll always be a Jew."

Miriam was hurt. She told Rivka. "Don't worry. It doesn't matter. We know the truth, they don't."

In 1942 the father was called up for forced labour. Miriam was 13 years old. He only had 2 days to take care of his affairs. It was a panic to see to it that the girls were taken care of. He sent a telegram to his wife's mother who lived in a smaller city named Patac.

"Unfortunately called up to forced labour. Do not know when will be return. Cannot leave girls by themselves. Request you accept young girls to your care."

The grandmother telegraphed back. "Sorry to hear of your misfortune. Will happily take care of girls in my home. Send them to me right away."

The girls left the next day in great haste. The trip from Budapest took six hours. When they arrived at Patac they ran to their grandmother's arms.

"Oh darlings, its so good to see you. I love you so much." She was a very warm and emotionally generous person with a light streak of possessiveness.

"Papa's gone away for awhile but not for a really long while." Miriam said. "He said to watch in the newspapers for the war to end."

Miriam and Rivka were somewhat displaced. They were essentially modern girls in a traditional environment. They lacked, for example, indoor plumbing, so they were not able to spend the time they were used to in the comfort of a fully equipped water closet. Instead of central heat they were faced with a wood stove and all the messy activities that came with it. They had no nice stores in which to buy fine clothes. The grandmother was a seamstress and she taught the girls how to sew and make dresses. This was a skill that could come in very handy. There was no opera or ballet. In the evenings, their grandmother did mending for rich people in the town. There were no paved roads, so the ground was muddy in summer. In winter, no one cleared the snow so it became very deep. They lacked high boots to keep them dry. This was extremely distracting especially because they were required to pick up and deliver garments for their grandmother to fix. There were no foods imported from other locations, such as vegetables and fruits, and the girl's meals were mostly potato or bean soups, except on the Sabbath. Their grandmother scrimped all week for Friday's meal.

One day about two months after they had arrived Miriam said to Rivka, "Give me your orange!"

Rivka replied, "Orange? Where would I get an orange?"

"From the orange seller in the market."

Rivka was shocked. "There's no orange seller in the market!", she said. "There isn't an orange in 20 kilometres of here!"

"Why not!", Miriam cried out, "Oh, I'd give anything for an orange. Why don't you have one?"

Rivka took Miriam's hand. "Wouldn't you much rather have a nice bowl of bean soup?"

Miriam held her head with both hands and moaned. "Oh, yes. Of course I would. Who needs an old orange anyway." They both laughed, but they felt somewhat miffed in spite of it.

Even so, the girls were good girls and not rebellious. They were largely content in Patac, but not as socially flirtatious as they were in Budapest. There was a Jewish community and they restricted themselves to it. Miriam was an avid reader. They waited daily for news of their father. Day after day they did not hear a thing.

The grandmother was very orthodox and didn't allow many of the things the girls were used too, like reading paperback romances. They would sneak them into their room anyway, when Grandma was asleep. She didn't allow them to mix with Gentiles at all. This was made more difficult since Grandma's business was making dresses for the aristocracy as well as small farmers. All in all, life in the village was primitive compared to the life the sister's led in Budapest.

Every day Miriam day-dreamed about her father returning from the front to rescue her and Rivka from this life of dullness and drudgery. Every night she went to bed disappointed.

"Papa will come soon, won't he?" She would ask her sister.

"Oh, yes!", Rivka would answer confidently, knowing otherwise.

"They can't keep him forever!"

"True."

There were no facilities to bathe in Grandma's house. The girls would go, once a month after their menses, to the ritual bath called the 'mikvah' to bathe thoroughly. Otherwise they sponge bathed regularly…but it was not like the shower they left behind in Budapest. They looked forward to the Sabbath meal. It contained both chicken and fish, since the Torah says both should be included in the meal. In the Shabbat afternoon the girls had some unsupervised time because the older people went to sleep. Then they could associate freely with the other ones their age and exercise at least some of the social skills they had been developing in Budapest. Miriam developed a few flirtations nonetheless.

"I want to kiss you." Her favourite boyfriend said boldly one day when they were alone in a field.

"You can kiss me here." She said coquettishly. "On the cheek."

The boy took a deep breath. He formed his lips and pressed them lightly to her cheek. "I'm very fond of you.", he said when it was over.

"Just because I let you kiss me doesn't mean you can say anything you want.", she replied.

"I'm not totally inexperienced now, I think. In 6 months I'll be sent to forced labour at the front. I can go knowing that I kissed the most beautiful, wonderful girl in Patac."

"I wish you didn't have to go. You're very brave about it and I like you very much."

"Then let me kiss you on the lips." He asked.

Miriam hesitated. "You deserve it.", she finally said simply, and she reached over and kissed him quickly. "Now you can know that someone cares."

This happened only once. Perhaps this encounter, and the general exercise of romance even on this scale, prepared Miriam for our lovemaking on the train. Certainly, she was more experienced and more ready than I at that time. The circumstances were so extreme they made the impossible happen.

Two years passed. They began to hear rumours of changes in Hungary, conflicts between the Germans and Horthy, the Hungarian leader. Although he is anti-Semitic he does not want to collect Jews for the concentration camps.

The Germans are so determined to bring about the destruction of the Jews that they decided to commit vital resources in men, machines, transportation and communication resources to make it happen. On March 19, 1944 they invade Hungary and eliminate Horthy. Within days the elite SS forces are in Hungary administrating the immediate deportation of the Jews to concentration camps.

Miriam, now 15 years old, is sent to Auschwitz on a train. The rest I have received from hearsay.

When Miriam was taken from the train and pulled away from Avrum she lost control of her emotions. She forgot Rivka, she forgot her grandmother. She tried to run to the line of men further down the platform and was beaten into unconsciousness by the kappos. She was dragged back to her own line, where she lay propped up by her sister on the ground, but she regained consciousness in time to see her beloved grandmother taken away also. She was hysterical with grief, and Rivka also, until the kappos began to beat them with their clubs. When they had finished both were crying but sober. After that Miriam never again showed any emotions of grief to anyone except her sister.

The women went through essentially the same experience as the men. Marched into a huge barracks, laid out in bunks 10 deep. Later came the most humiliating part. Barbers came in and cut off the hair all over their bodies, including private parts. A one inch strip was cut down the centre of their heads. Completely naked now and with no personal possessions of any kind left to them, they were taken to the showers and at the exit given the striped garments to wear. Finally they are returned to a normal barracks, 3 in a bunk, and given thin soup and a ¼ loaf or bread. Each portion was about 100 grams, enough to lightly cover their palm. After that they are commanded to go to bed. It's just dark.

Miriam is lying next to Rivka. They whisper together. Miriam said, "I'm so sore.". Rivka replied, "So am I. Where did they take grandmother?"

"I don't know." Miriam replied. "I miss my Avrum!"

"Why? He's only a boy you met on the train."

"But I love him, Rivka! He's the only boy I've ever loved!", Miriam responded.

"How can love survive in all this?", Rivka said.

"I promise you, it will survive."

Rivka paused for a moment. She knew her sister and how single minded she could be. "That's good.", she said. "If love can survive in this place we have hope. Don't let that love die, then. Make it always live inside of you."

They lay silent in the barracks, but all night long you could hear the sobs and the crying of the women as the grief of losing those they loved was realized.

Three days later, days of hard labour, the girls were separated with 200 others into a unit at roll call and marched directly to the train station. They were hurriedly herded onto cattle cars in extremely cramped quarters and taken away from Auschwitz towards Poland and another camp called

Majdanek. Auschwitz was especially a transfer point and a death camp. They were young and strong, they had been set apart to work.

When the train arrived and the inmates unloaded with the usual shouts and beatings, all 200 were marched to one barrack with a straw mattress and one blanket on the bunks. They were told to stay there until a bell tolled There was no accounting for the female kappos being any more kind than their male counterparts. The women kappos, were easily as mean as the men. They carried out their responsibilities tenaciously because the conditions were so luxurious. They got enough food to eat every day and sometimes a separate room. They, too, were always under scrutiny and they worked hard to please their masters.

After the roll call, which took, as usual, an excruciatingly long time, they were sent back to the barracks to eat soup and ¼ bread practically black, the same as given to soldiers but much less. The Germans, consistent with their love of efficiency and orderliness, didn't give containers to new prisoners. They had to scrounge for one, and a spoon. Miriam took control of this endeavour. She leapt around from bunk to bunk searching like a monkey, but she was triumphant. She returned to her sister with two metal bowls and two bent spoons.

"You are a perfect scrounger!", Rivka said.

"I know what I'm doing from Pesach when we have to search for the matzo."

"G-d has a plan for everything!", Rivka said.

"You see, everything will be fine. We will eat!"

The turnip soup was kept in large containers, like milk containers. At the top it was thin because all the bulk would settle at the bottom. Inmates tried to manipulate to get the bottom of the can. Miriam was expert at that. She used to find an excuse to look in at their bowls as other women came away with their soup. Then she would calculate mentally where in line the thickest soup would be.

"Can we come in here?" she would ask boldly or demurely as the occasion demanded. Sometimes there was an argument but it was rare. All the women knew what she was doing, but mostly they didn't mind. She was 15. They liked her. It was almost like play. There were some who were deadly serious about their food, but most were depressed and tragically miserable. They didn't all have sisters or family to be with.

"Sorry!" Rivka would say as she followed her sister. "You'll be better off in the end."

In fact, Rivka was always following Miriam to make things right. Miriam was relatively rambunctious compared to the other women. She had more energy and didn't seem to be as affected by the day to day routine. She was often in trouble for doing things that just stood out in the camp and she withstood with a certain pride her share of beatings. Rivka was her soul and anchor. She was actually cared for by some of the other women, like a mascot. The two were almost a comedy act, if such a thing were possible.

The thing was that Miriam was a natural leader, and that was perceived in some way even if not consciously acknowledged. She gave the other women some hope that life might still go on in some way.

Although Miriam and Rivka reported their trade as seamstress, they were sent out every day to cut trees. The worst job was in the latrines. The best job was in the kitchen where you might get the chance to take a bite out of a raw potato. That was considered a delicacy. Cutting trees was not the worst job. Miriam and Rivka actually liked it except for the beatings. One day they were cutting with a two person saw and Miriam broke some news to Rivka,

"I'm 10 days late for my menses." She said.

"It's no wonder. We're starving to death and beaten so often. It's just a natural thing."

"No, no. It's the second period I've missed."

They couldn't talk at that time any more. Later, when they were in the barracks, they spoke.

"Listen," Rivka said. "This is natural. Your menses may even stop completely. Mine is very erratic."

"Yes, but I am sick in the morning."

"So am I."

"No, it's not from what you think."

Rivka stopped and looked wide eyed. "Well, what's it from then? Miriam, you're a virgin aren't you?"

"Well, but, you see, that's just the thing." Miriam was abashed.

"Miriam!" Rivka almost cried out loud. "You are a virgin?"

"Avrum and I..."

"Yes?"

"While everyone was asleep on the train that very last night..."

"Oh no!" Rika cried.

"When we thought we'd perhaps never see each other again and we didn't know where we were going..."

"Miriam!" Rivka was almost beside herself.

"And I think I might be pregnant."

There was a pause as the two girls regarded each other.

"Mazel Tov." Rivka said without joy. "Couldn't you at least have been married first."

"There was no time for that."

"You're 16!" Rivka almost screamed

"I know."

"How can you be pregnant here? They'll kill you."

"Not if they don't find out." Miriam was emphatic.

"How will they not find out." Rivka was starting to feel anger and disgust.

"I don't know." Miriam said. "But I do know that I'll die trying."

Rivka suddenly felt a rush of affection for her sister. The other emotions passed. She threw her arms around Miriam's shoulders and hugged her. "I don't know either." She said. "But if G-d is with us, we will find a way."

In mid-July, three months after arrival in Majdanek an all important event started to happen. The sound of Russian artillery could be heard not so far away. Soon, the sound of it was closer and they could hear it all the time. Some bombs started to fall so close and were so loud that the barracks seemed to actually lift up from the impact.

There were thousands of inmates in the camp. They were all enlisted to build ditches around the camp to stop tanks made with stones and cement. It was very heavy work.

After labouring with this work for several days, Miriam confides to Rivka in the barracks, "I'm not well."

"What's wrong?" Rivka wanted to know.

"I just feel weak. I'm afraid I won't be able to do my work."

"You'll do it or you'll get beaten" Rivka, always down to earth, said.

"No. You don't understand. I'm afraid I might lose the baby."

There is silence for a moment. "You can't go to the hospital." Rivka said.

"No! They'll send me to the gas chamber if they know I'm pregnant and they'll send me to the gas chamber if I really am sick even it they don't find out I'm pregnant."

"You stick close to me, Miriam. Do the work you can and I'll cover for the rest."

For the first time in a long while Miriam forgot about herself and took a long, hard look at her sister. "You are more than a sister to me, Rivka. You are a gift from G-d."

Rivka smiled a gentle smile. "And you are the same to me."

The sister's plan worked, but they were saved from discovery anyway. A few days after that it was determined that the inmates of the camp were to go on a forced march out of the immediate area. Each person was given some bread and a blanket. Some ate the bread right away which was a sure sign that they would die on the march. Miriam and Rivka had made a Polish friend, which was not unusual because the camp was in Poland. Her name was Wanda and she was from Warsaw. But Miriam was set in her mind. She was sure she would not make it on the march. She gathered Rivka and Wanda together when there was a chance and said, "I'm not going to make it on the march. I want to make a plan for us to stay behind. If you want, you can stay with me. If not, I am prepared to go it alone."

The other two slowly agreed that they wanted to all go into this together. It was a good sign, since Wanda spoke Polish. Their wills were set. They would reach for freedom, one last time, or they would die searching for it.

CHAPTER 9
Bread

The three women huddled together in the few minutes before curfew that night, although if they had been seen together they would have been beaten almost to death. They whispered their plan in the dark. Miriam led the conspiracy.

"We must stay behind when all the others are taken away." Her voice was tense and quick,

"We may be thin, Miriam, but we are not yet invisible." Rivka was always critical of her sister's schemes.

"We have to hide." Miriam said in a throaty whisper.

"You suppose you can hide somewhere in this barracks?" Rivka said through the silence.

"There must be a way! I know it!" Miriam was determined.

Wanda looked up in the waning light. "Under the mattress." She said.

"What?" Rivka thought at first she was joking uncharacteristically.

"Under the mattress." She said again. "There are boards in the floor under the mattresses. Slats. Under the slats there's a small space, maybe just enough for a thin person to lie in."

The sisters were stunned. Rivka was cautiously curious but Miriam was excited. "We can hide there!" She almost spoke too loud. "Each of us under their own mattress!"

"You only have to lift two boards. They're nailed down but only loosely. I'll come with you now to pull them up. Together it should be easy." Wanda said with plain but muted enthusiasm.

"Fine." Said Rivka. "If the others ask what we're doing we can say we're looking for food."

"Let's do it." Miriam said.

One by one they went to each mattress. Miriam held the mattress up at the corner while the other two pulled up the boards. It wasn't hard. Each board was tacked down by two nails. A quick tug by the women brought the wood up. No one noticed what they were doing. In only a few minutes it was done. The space under the slats was only 6 inches, but enough for each of them to lie prone underneath the mattress. Although it would not be comfortable, it didn't matter. It would be their grave or it would be their passage to live. Just as they agreed on tactics and retreated to their own bunks, the kappo entered the small building. There would be no more talking. No more chance to talk.

They didn't sleep. Each one lay awake, eyes open, minds alert. They could hear the Russian guns in the near distance. Finally, around two o'clock in the morning, the night was broken. With a great noise of shouting and with the slapping of batons against wood the inmates were roused and herded out of the barracks into the night. The death march had begun. There was no time to loose. As the other inmates were beaten and rushed out of the barracks each of the three women lifted the boards beneath their mattress and lay down. Then they placed the board back in place above them. In a few minutes there was silence in the room. They remained inside their rough compartments, hidden from view.

The forced march was initiated so quickly that the guards had no time to take a count of the prisoners. Half an our after the others left they heard shots not far away. It was the Nazis shooting the patients who had been left behind in the hospital. The guards came back into the barracks only once to check for problems. They didn't find any. The women, so far, were undiscovered. For several hours there was a great deal of noise; shouting, many trucks moving, people running past the building. Like water running out of a cup everything outside slowly gave way to quiet. The women lay in their little tombs. Their plan was not to come out until the coast was completely clear. Just before dawn, Miriam took a chance. She left her place just long enough to confer briefly with the other women.

"We stay hidden until something happens." She said. The other's agreed.

They lay in hiding all day. They were hungry, but they were used to hunger. They were sore, but they were used to pain. The artillery seemed closer and closer. They could hear German voices periodically during the day, so they knew the Nazis were still around. At dusk there was a lot of commotion; again shouting, running, trucks moving but not as much as earlier. The last of the guards were leaving the camp. Then there was silence in the camp for several hours, punctuated by artillery fire and eventually rifle fire. Following that, there were more sounds and more voices, but different. There were shadows of men thrown into the barracks. Wanda got up from her space. She went to Miriam's place.

She whispered. "The voices." she said. "They're Russian."

So as not to endanger everyone, Wanda went alone to meet the Russians. She spoke the language a little bit. She quickly met a Russian soldier. He was about to shoot but he was stunned by how she looked. Head shaved. Clothes dirty and striped from top to bottom. Hair cropped short with a stripe shaved down the middle. Emaciated.

Wanda's Russian was not terribly strong. She didn't know what to say. The startled soldier cried. "Who are you, there!" Wanda replied. "I am here.", Meaning in the camp. "I am alive."

The soldier was far from satisfied, although Wanda's arms were in the air. "Where do you come from?" he wanted to know.

"This is a concentration camp. I am a prisoner here. There were hundreds of other prisoners and many German soldiers but they have gone now." She is being as clear as she can. "I was hiding when the other's left."

"Wait.", he replied. "I will get someone."

Soon an officer came. He spoke more quickly and with more authority than the soldier. "Who are you?" he asked. He had seen the ovens and knew something unusual had happened here.

"I am a prisoner."

"What went on here?" he wanted to know.

"Horror!" she cried.

He took her arm. "Come with me." He commanded her. She followed him. He took her to a building that used to be for the guards. There were Russian officers inside now. She was taken to the Russian General. His hair was dark and he had a slim build. An air of order and intensity showed in his voice and gestures. He looked at her with curiosity and mild shock. "Who are you?", he asked.

"A prisoner."

"Are you political?" He thought perhaps she was a communist.

"No. A Jew." She stammered a little.

"Were they all Jews here?" the General wanted to know.

"Most of us." she replied.

"That's interesting." He commented.

"Why?" she wanted to know.

"Because I am Jewish.", he said.

Wanda looked at him in disbelief. "Are we safe now? You won't hurt us?"

"We won't hurt you." he stated reassuringly.

"There are two more." she said.

Wanda returned to the barracks. She approached Miriam first and then Rivka. "They are Russians. They will help us, but be careful. Russian soldiers are not noted for their courtesy. It is still war. People can still be very brutal."

When they met the General he was quick but gracious. "I want to know what went on here. I want every detail you can give me." He was clearly taken by Rivka, and he spoke Yiddish. "You!" he said to her. "You have blond hair and your skin is very fair. Are you Polish?"

Rivka did not invite any enthusiasm. "No, I'm a Jew." She said. "Just a Jew." She had come to see that aspect as more personal than public.

"You look very thin." The General said. "Clearly you have been hungry. Do you want food?" he asked.

"Yes. Please.", Miriam replied for all of them.

"I will get you some."

"My sister needs medical attention." Rivka said with a tone almost of apology.

He looked at Miriam. She was obviously in pain. "I will get you a doctor as soon as possible. You understand that they are fully occupied in the field."

Miriam looked at him simply. "I'm alright. A little food will help."

The three women were given chairs to sit on first, then taken to another building that was empty.

They experienced, for the first time, a feeling that there might be some safety for them. "Is it over?" Miriam wanted to know, though in some way she was being ironic. They all knew that there was still enormous danger.

"Perhaps the worst is over." Wanda replied. "Its hard to know. The war is still going on. We will still have to survive. Not all the Russians are gentleman or generals. He likes you, Rivka."

Rivka was not impressed. "A woman is a woman in wartime. I'll probably never see him again."

At that moment a soldier came in with bread. Their eyes went wide. Rivka said, "Our troubles are not over. But I don't care. All I prayed for, while lying under the floorboards, was a chance to survive long enough to see my sister again and some bread. Now I can die happy."

"No one's going to die. Eat.", Wanda said. It was almost morning.

Wanda felt more affection for her two comrades than she would ever admit. That morning, as they sat in the shelter of the Red Army drinking coffee for the first time in a very long time there was a moment of calm. Something had to be established between them all in this bubble of peace. Without them, she would have been one among the many on the death march. Possibly, she would not even have made it that far. Her history with the Nazis was more dangerous and dark than theirs. She had lost two children. She had replaced them in her affections as her children.

The sisters focussed on Wanda, who had helped so greatly in saving their lives. They knew so little about her. For a while, there was silence between them. The two sisters looked at each other carefully out of the corner of their eyes. Finally, Miriam spoke up.

"We know you are from Poland." Miriam began. "But where in Poland are you from.?"

Wanda held her mug tightly. "From Wasaw." She said quietly.

The girls looked at each other meaningfully. "You were in the ghetto?" Rivka inquired.

After a brief pause Wanda replied. "Yes. I was in the ghetto."

Everyone knew that there had been trouble in the ghetto, that almost no one survived, although very few knew the true story. There were rumours that the Jews had resisted the Nazis, and that the action had been called an uprising by some.

Miriam asked curiously, "Were you deported before the trouble?."

"No. I was not deported before the revolt. I was a member of the uprising."

The girls again looked briefly at each other, then back at Wanda. Rivka said simply, "Yet here you are. I thought no one survived."

Wanda looked down. "No. Some survived. Most did not."

Miriam, ever clumsy with her curiosity, asked "How?".

Wanda looked at her as if through a ghost. She looked at Rivka also and said plainly. "I will tell you what happened in the Warsaw ghetto, not because I want to but because people must know. Because you are Jews and Jews especially must know. History must know.

"We did not go to the slaughter easily. It started after the first deportations, in the Summer of '42, when word reached us about what was happening to the people who were deported. Rumours abounded that there were death camps at Treblinka and Majdanick, but we weren't sure that everyone was killed. Then letters came to our leaders from people in the camps that were seemingly ordinary but which were actually impeded with code. They told of the truth, that the deportees from our ghetto were going to be exterminated. This motivated many people.

"There were politicos among us, mostly socialists who knew about organization. They had worked in Jewish and Polish factories even before the war, organizing workers and generating awareness. They talked to people, families, explaining that the best way to escape was to resist and convincing others that a unified resistance was needed. These people were convinced that although most of the people in the ghetto would not be part of a fighting group, almost all could support it. They formed an organization called the 'Jewish Fighting Organization' and many people joined. This was during the summer and Fall of '42 when the deportations were at their height. I didn't join at that time, but my husband did. I had two young children to take care of, and I wasn't very political. The Nazis would come to a random address at any time during the day or night and take everybody. Those without proper identification were taken first, then the rest. "

Rivka asked, "Did you have guns?"

Wanda smiled. "At that time we didn't. We were still getting organized. When the deportations stopped in September, for reasons we didn't know, a large number of people did join this group and others. Everyone knew that the deportations were not over, that they would start again before long and that all of us were destined for the camps and certain death. The groups that formed were necessary in order to maintain any hope to survive. There were various factions, all of which maintained an orientation to resistance, most of which were linked to Polish Underground outside the ghetto.

"At that time about 300,000 of us had been deported. Those of us who were left were mostly young people who could fight, about 60,000 of us. I still didn't join at that time, because of my children, but my husband was gone most of the time. They were preparing for a return of the Nazis. Arms were collected and distributed. Members were trained in the use of arms and combat. We were constantly aware that the Germans could resume the deportations at any time. We were all tense and excited, though the actual number of fighters was small. They prepared. They anticipated. Finally, it happened in January."

Miriam wanted to know. "How did you expect to resist without larger numbers?"

"We didn't care. We had some hope, that was what mattered, and the fact that were together in spirit. We knew we would be sent to our deaths in any case, so resistance was our remedy to despair. My husband was gone every day. We never talked about what he did, but he was usually in a heightened state of controlled confidence and excitement.

We had some guns and grenades by January, 1943. At that time the Germans began to enter into the ghetto again in order to begin a new wave of violence, but our fighters were ready for them. Armed resistors appeared in the street and confronted the soldiers. They surprised the Germans, but the soldiers were much better armed and they fought back very quickly."

"That was the first time that the Jews in Poland had offered organized resistance against deportation. When the Nazis came up Mila Street we attacked. It was a bloodbath. We were vastly out numbered and outgunned. I was watching from a building. It was horrible to watch people you knew and loved falling in the street, but it was inspiring at the same time to watch Jews fight back so hard and with such courage. They fought to the end, only a handful escaped. When the bullets ran out they fought with clubs and boards and finally their bare hands and fingernails. Most of our brave fighters fell upon the German troops tooth and nail, using hands, feet, teeth and elbows. Almost all of the Jewish unit were killed, but their deaths were not in vain. The clash had been instigated by a group from the Fighting Organization under the command of Mordecai

Anilewicz. My husband escaped, not out of cowardice but because of the children."

Miriam was anticipating the end of the story. "Was that the end of it? Did you then escape the ghetto?"

"You could not easily escape the Ghetto. And where would you go? Jews were not popular in Warsaw and the Germans made it worthwhile to turn them in. Several of our fighters escaped at one time to the woods outside of Warsaw. They were betrayed and the Germans hunted then down and killed them.

"It was similar in Budapest.", Rivka said. "There was enormous anti-Semitism. If it wasn't already there, the Nazis created it."

"Even so, after that initial battle between the ghetto fighters and the Germans they put a halt to their attempts at deporting the community for a short period. That gave us unexpected but critically needed time to rethink our purpose and plan our strategy.

"After the January attack several things started to happen. Everyone was sure after the attack that the deportations meant certain death. The leaders talked to everyone, and before long it was unanimous. The entire ghetto was united in a spirit of resistance. But there was a difference now that we all knew the truth. Whereas before there were about 100 armed fighters, now there were several hundred more. Everyone had the same feeling; resistance could stop the Nazis from liquidating the ghetto. For the first time we truly believed that only resistance could prevent our certain deaths. We strongly believed that it was more than a political show; we thought it was the only approach that could save our lives and the lives of our children. And even if not, everyone was determined to put up a good fight and die trying. It was a new kind of collective will. Finally, after years of persecution, we Jews were united in fact and in principle. We would fight back with a will."

Miriam cut in. "That must have been something to see."

Miriam looked down. "It was inspirational, yes. The leaders were tireless, effective and efficient. They smuggled in as many guns as possible from outside, mostly handguns, and they smuggled in grenades but not many. Mostly they taught us how to make small bombs out of gasoline, ethanol and a glass bottle. We made hundreds of these. From January until April of 1943 we prepared. Even so, it was not an easy decision to accept armed resistance. It was not actually in my nature to participate in violence. In the end, it was not only the reality of certain death either way that made up my mind; it was the mood of the ghetto, the rising conviction and energy that persuaded me to join the resistance. It was care for my children that convinced me to actually join the fighters.

"For the first time in my life I realized completely that utterly personal decisions had to be made even in the face of giant events. I carried a gun, a pistol, that I used in several of the attacks.

"We were organized in units, each with its own leader and we were prepared for attack from February on, at all times. Our strategy was to avoid direct battle with the Germans, but rather to attack them from the cover of buildings and from the rooftops. From the sufferings of hell they forged the weapons of resistance and battle. Also, we took up positions in bunkers prepared in basements all over the ghetto so that we could hold out for an extended period of time even if we were cut off from one another. Several families would usually occupy a bunker. My husband and I and our two children were in a basement with two other families. We were in a unit commanded by a man named Berek. He showed us how to jump from roof to roof to escape. We prepared each day for the Germans to return.

"What a remarkable thing." Rivka said. "I knew we Jews could do it if we tried."

"The Germans came back into the ghetto at 6:00 A.M. on April 19th. We were ready for them with guns and the bombs I mentioned, Molotov Cocktails. The first of the German soldiers were forced to retreat. We did not attack them head on, like before. We attacked them from buildings and rooftops. In subsequent attacks, the Nazis found that they could not confront us directly. Although we lost fighters, we had succeeded in turning them back at this point. The Germans were surprised and outraged at our resistance. They removed the current head of the unit with a new officer named Stroop. He determined a new approach to cleaning out the ghetto. He would go from building to building and burn them."

"But that would be so costly!" Miriam cried out.

"It sounds like typical German strategy." said Rivka.

"We were unaware of what was actually going on until it was more clear. Our fighters resisted at every opportunity. The Germans didn't only burn a building at a time; they burned entire blocks of buildings at a time. People were forced out of their bunkers firing only the small handguns they had. Many died in the fires rather than succumb. After a short time, our ghetto was a bonfire.

'There were countless acts of bravery and courage. I was in a fighting unit different than my husband's. In the last attack we were able to make, our leader Berek fell on the street, critically wounded. We were going to drag him to safety when he cried out 'Keep fighting! Your weapons are necessary!'". Then he took his revolver and thrust it into his mouth and pulled the trigger. He wanted to make sure his revolver was used again.

"From mid-April until mid-May we resisted, suffered and fought. At one time I was with a small group in a bunker that was under attack. There was only one entrance that the Germans could use, a break in the wall about a meter wide. They were there, getting closer to firing into the space when a young boy, David, thrust his whole body into the crack and shouted; "Go, go! I'll hold them off!". The Germans fired, but David's body blocked their way. We were able to flee to another rooftop.

"We were starving, also. We were just skeletons with sub-machineguns. By early May there were only a few hundred of us left. My husband and I and our two children had survived, and one of the leaders, Marat, had arranged for us to find haven with a Polish family outside the ghetto. We were to escape be way of an underground sewer that ran into the ghetto from the city. We found the entrance with help from a man named Abrasha. The pipe was 28" wide. There were shots close by.

"My husband tried to go first. He was a large boned man, but as genial and self-effacing as any hero. He tried to go first but could not fit into the tunnel. The shots came closer and we knew it would not be long before the Germans would be able to see us. My husband turned to me. He put his hands on my shoulders. "You must go! I'll be fine, Abrasha will take care of me. Go!". I urged my children to go first. I turned around to say goodbye to my husband. He was gone. I have not seen him since."

"I'm sorry." said Rivka.

"That sewer was so foul." Wanda said with disgust dripping off her tongue. "It's a miracle we got to the end. We emerged on a small street in the city of Warsaw. There was no one waiting for us and the street was empty. There we were, the three of us, soaked to the skin and stinking. A man came along on his bicycle, thank God he was honest. 'You are Jews?', he asked. 'Yes.' I replied. I told him the address we had been given. 'Its just around the corner.' He said. We found it in a few minutes, knocked at the door. A middle aged woman took us in. 'You must go to the attic.' She instructed us. We went up. Half an hour later the Nazis arrived. Our journey was over. Our resistance had failed."

"No, no!" cried Miriam. Rivka said, "Your resistance was perfect! You showed the Germans and the whole world the courage and determination of Jews everywhere. Think of the future, Wanda! Your acts will be the inspiration of a nation."

"Even so, we were finally betrayed. The Nazis took the three of us to the train station where we were sent to Auschwitz. On the train platform in the camp my children were torn away from me, all of us kicking and screaming. I was beaten with the end of a gun but I would have kept fighting if I didn't think they would make my children suffer more for it. My precious beauties."

"Be strong." Rivka said kindly. "You have suffered a terrible loss."

Wanda frowned. "I still have hope that I will see my husband."

There was silence as the story sank in to all of their hearts. At that moment a Russian soldier came through the door. In his arms were a number of army blankets. He was respectful and polite,

"You are requested to return to your barracks for the night. You will be safe there. No one will be in the barracks but you. Here. Take these blankets. Soon someone will bring you army clothes." He noticed Miriam looking longingly at her bread. "You can take the food with you.", he said reassuringly.

The women walked to the building that had been their residence for what seemed like forever. As they approached the barracks Rivka almost stumbled. It was as if chains were falling away from her body; as if scales were falling away from her eyes. The building looked different, It looked peaceful. That building had always looked indifferent. Now, there was something almost human about it.

The same feeling came over all three of them. Even before their minds could grasp it, their bodies were aware and reacting. They had been liberated. They were free. They were protected. It wasn't joy they felt. It was an extreme weariness, right through to their very souls. They reached the barracks. It seemed to be both a short walk and it seemed, at the same time, to be a very long way. When they arrived, without any talk to speak of, they crawled into a bunk. All of the bunks were free but that didn't mean anything to them. Wanda went to her old bunk. Without really thinking about it, Miriam and Rivka crawled in beside her. They curled up together and fell into a deep sleep. They dreamed a single dream. A single candle burned carefully in the dark. It's light was delicate, but bright.

CHAPTER 10
Resistance Recounted

When the women awoke to the light of day they could hear Russian soldiers conducting their activities outside the barracks. On a bench below their bunk were army pants and shirts. Also some bread and other rations. Miriam was hungry but also a bit queasy. She was the first one awake. She disengaged herself from the other two sleepers and lifted herself out of the bunk, which was on the second tier. She looked at the food with some interest but the anxiety in her stomach was very strong. She thought she was going to throw up. She made her way to the back of the barracks where she vomited. She sat down. She was weak and tired even though she had just woken up.

Wanda woke up a few minutes later. She saw the food and the clothing on the bench, but that was, for the moment, a distraction. She heard moaning coming from the rear of the barracks. Miriam was sitting on the floor of the building, holding her stomach, rocking back and forth and moaning. She went to her instantly.

"What's wrong?", she said. "You are in pain?"

Miriam grimaced. "A little bit. It's not too bad."

Wanda looked serious. "I'm sure you're moaning and holding your middle out of the happiness that we have some food." She was making a joke but she was very concerned.

"I threw up." She gestured with her chin.

"I see." Wanda said. "That's what you think of Russian army rations?"

Miriam laughed. "Don't tell the General."

"He'll have you court marshalled."

They both laughed. They were actually happy, despite Miriam's condition, for the first time in a very long while. It was the first time in three years that they had at least a thin sense of safety. It felt so good to enjoy, for a moment, a brief experience of spontaneous joy.

Rivka also awoke at that time and within a few seconds joined them. "What's wrong?"

She asked anxiously.

Wanda replied. "Miriam vomited. There's pain in her stomach."

"What kind of pain?", Rivka wanted to know.

Miriam tried to cover it up. "It's probably cramps from the food."

"And you threw up?", she pressed.

Miriam gestured with her fingers. "Just a little, tiny bit."

Rivka looked at Wanda. They both looked worried. "I'm going to talk to the general, if we see him again. A doctor should look at her.", Rivka said.

Miriam didn't protest. Normally she would have avoided this concern over her health. But it was not her own condition she was worried about. She was worried about Avrum's baby.

In the camp there were quite a few soldiers visibly running from one place to another, but to the women it seemed deserted. They didn't leave the barracks because it was not easy for Miriam to walk any great distance. Within an hour a soldier came to them. He looked them over carefully and then gestured at Rivka.

"Please come with me.", he said. "The General would like to see you."

Rivka looked surprised. It had been a long time since seeing an officer didn't mean trouble. She squeezed Miriam's hand. "I'm going to get help for us.", she whispered.

When she reached the office they had been in last night the General was reading a map. He looked up and smiled at her. It was a welcome and relatively comforting smile.

"You received some food and rest?", he asked.

"Yes. Thank you."

"I've called in a doctor to look at your sister. He should be here some time today."

Rivka was cautiously relieved. "Oh. Thank you very much."

The General turned to a more serious approach. "I would like you to tell me what went on here. Give me details. What we have found up to now is very telling, but I need to know the details."

Miriam swallowed almost painfully. She began to talk. The words had meaning because someone from the outside wanted to listen. She listened to herself speak as though she were a little girl in high school explaining an injustice to her teacher. Somehow, it seemed so small. In a big war, where horror is everywhere, horror like hers seemed almost commonplace.

But she had, in the face of her immediate sense of reality lost perspective because she had just been set free. The General, who had seen a great deal of pain, was, in fact, horrified. The scale of this treachery was so intense that he found himself riveted to Rivka's description. The ovens, the gas chambers, the starvation and violence were terrible. But the fact that was becoming to clear to him as Rivka spoke, that this was a full out attempt at murdering a whole civilization without any thought of their own humanity or the humanity of their victims. He knew before he arrived that the camps existed. He didn't know that they were practicing genocide.

Rivka spoke for about an hour. The General asked questions while she spoke, but not too many. At the end he asked her to clarify a few details. He was gracious. He carefully thanked her. "You have done an important thing.", he said.

When she got back to the barracks Wanda and Miriam were sitting on a bottom bunk, quietly talking. She told them a doctor was coming. Two hours later he arrived. Because of the trouble moving Miriam he examined her at the back of the building. When he had finished they both joined the other two.

He was a Major who had been conscripted. His hair was brown and he was verging on tall. His face was worn and tired for a man hovering around the mid-thirties. He spoke to all three together. "It's plain to see that you are all suffering from extreme malnutrition." They all nodded. "You must not eat rich foods until your stomachs can get used to it, and don't eat too much of anything at all. You need to get your strength. Your internal organs have been hurt and they need to get better." All three of the women shook their heads in agreement. He turned to Miriam. She was just a little older than the daughter he had left back home.

You have been badly affected by starvation. You told me about how you had to lift heavy rocks and other materials for very long periods of time with no food or water. This has caused problems, and I believe your liver is damaged, although probably not so severely that it can't recover. But there is another factor that appears possible." He paused for a moment and looked directly at Miriam. "I think you are pregnant."

Miriam looked a bit abashed. "I think so too.", she said quietly.

"You are very young. But the combination of these two conditions is difficult. I would like you to think about the options for you. You are not too far along in your pregnancy to have options. I'm going to arrange for you to go into the hospital in Lublin, but it will take a few days. I'll be back then."

He was about to leave, when he turned back. "Who was here?" he asked the women. Rivka replied, "Mostly Jews."

"That's what I heard. It's a pitiful thing, this camp. Like you, I feel a terrible anguish. I am also Jewish.", he affirmed, and he turned around and walked away.

In the period between that meeting and the arrival of transportation for Miriam there was anxiety in the air. Rivka and Wanda were worried about Miriam. On the second day Rivka spoke to Miriam quietly while Wanda was out in the camp. "Everything will be fine," she said, "after the abortion."

Miriam replied calmly, "What abortion?"

Rivka had that look of controlled concern in her eye. "You're going to the hospital where they will administer an abortion." There could be no doubt of this in her mind.

Miriam shook her head and lightly laughed. "Don't be silly. I'm not having an abortion. I'm just going to have some treatment."

"Miriam,", Rivka said in a matter of fact voice. "Your health is in danger. You need to give up what you're carrying."

"Not so!" said her sister. "I'm carrying my husband's child. I'm not going to give that up."

Rivka was becoming angry. "You can't call that boy your 'husband'. You're only 16 and you are not married to him."

Miriam swung her head gently in a gesture of understanding. "I may be 16, but I'm not a slut. I have a mind of my own and I have a life that belongs to me. It was war. We were in love. No one can take that away."

Rivka was nearing exasperation. "Alright. You don't need to justify being pregnant. I agree. But be reasonable. It IS a war. It's not over yet. You're not strong enough to carry a baby. You need to think about that. The whole world is still in pieces and it's going to take a long time to put it all back together. How will you take care of a child when it's born? Where will you take care of it. Your whole life is at stake. You must give up the pregnancy."

With an emphatic grip on her sister's arm Miriam expressed her strength and determination. No.", she said. "This baby is life itself. It was conceived in the darkest time. It is my loved one's child. Under no circumstances will I kill it, in the light of so much killing everywhere."

Rivka backed down. She knew this was not the time or place to find reason. "We're all shaken, Miriam. We all need time to put ourselves back together." She kissed her younger sister gently on the forehead and pulled her head to her chest in a gesture of love. There was no arguing at this point. Rivka knew she had to convince Miriam to terminate the pregnancy. She didn't know how yet.

Three days later the Major came back with two paramedics and a small army truck. "The city is recovering from a state of near chaos.", he stated. "The hospital is organizing slowly. There is a bed for you, Miriam, but the facilities are not good. There are shortages of everything. I will be your treating physician."

The other two women sat in the back of the truck with Miriam as they drove to St. Mary's Hospital in Lublin. The camp was just outside the central area of the city, on the other side of the hospital. The city was full of military vehicles and personnel, but there were signs of the citizens regaining some normalcy. They passed small groups of individuals working on preparing shops to operate, and merchants in open air markets selling vegetables and meat, clothing and fabric. There was an atmosphere of cautious expectation. Here the immediate reality of the war was essentially over, but there was still a great deal of fear. Instead of being occupied by the Germans they were now occupied by the Russians. Even though individual lives may not have been in such immediate danger no one really knew what to expect. The Communists were at one and the same time their liberators as well as their potentially new oppressor.

The paramedics carried Miriam from the truck to the hospital in a stretcher. The Major led them to the second floor in an area that had not suffered too much damage. There Miriam was placed on a hospital bed in a room with two other women. Her sister and her friend stood by as the Major spoke to her.

"I'm going to arrange an operating room for your treatment." He said to her.

"What treatment?" Miriam inquired. There was a muted urgency in her voice.

The Major looked back at the two women. "The procedure that will help to make you well."

Miriam looked directly at the Major. "You can do any procedure that you like but you cannot in any way hurt the baby." She sat up to be able to look the physician in the eye.

The major wet his lips. He again looked at Miriam's companions for support. "The baby is not the issue here. Your health is the issue. You can have another baby. You cannot have another life."

"I won't have an abortion.", Miriam insisted.

"But it's absolutely necessary.", the doctor said.

Miriam spoke with an emphasis that was controlled but strong. "What do you think I am living for? This war has made my existence a sham. So much hate, so much violence, so much destruction. In all of this one boy made me feel something good, something real and something positive. The only result is that I can have his baby. That is the only result I care about."

The Major came close to Miriam. He spoke softly. "Miriam, what do you think the chances are of this baby surviving?"

Miriam shook her head but remained firm. "I don't know but I'm still young."

"Your internal organs, including your womb, are damaged." he said. "The pregnancy will demand all the strength you have and it will be difficult for your general health to resume."

"I will survive." Miriam stated.

"You may survive, but the chances of both you and the baby surviving are in doubt. The baby could easily die even if you don't have the abortion. If you don't have the abortion the chances are both you and the baby could be lost."

Miriam fought back. "I won't kill this baby! If I die I will die carrying it! I don't want anything in this world but my baby, and for my loved one to come back to be with me. I refuse to have an abortion. You can't change my mind."

The doctor had seen what war could do. "I could force you to have an abortion for medical reasons but that would be unjust. You carry your baby to term," he said "with all the power you have, but I hope your sister and friend can eventually change your mind.

"The facilities here are not very good and I don't think they can treat you fully. Still, it's the best we can do at the moment. You must stay in the hospital. He looked at Rivka and Wanda. "I'll try and arrange with the General for accommodation for you."

BAR KOCHBA

He said a quick goodbye and left. When he had gone Rivka and Wanda were left alone with Miriam, who was still wearing the army clothes. The hospital was overflowing with wounded soldiers and civilians who had been hurt in the advancing offensive. The rooms were filled to overflowing and the corridors were lined with patients. It was well known that Miriam was an immediate protégé of General Kahani, who was the interim governor of Lublin and the whole region surrounding it. No one in the hospital wanted to cause any slight to the General, who was at that moment the most powerful commander in the area. But no one was happy either about a foreign girl of 16, pregnant, taking up space and using up precious resources. The fact that she was a Jew was almost maddening to most workers at the hospital. There was constant talk in the hall of how to avoid dealing with Miriam. Short of simply ignoring her, which wasn't entirely possible because of her status, some nurses refused to give her food. Even though the Russians had liberated the city from the Germans, which was a most desirable thing, they were regarded with both suspicion and hatred. When Rivka had waited several hours for Miriam to receive some food at the usual hour, she approached a nurse who was on duty. "If you want better service," she said, with an emphasis on 'service' "you'd better go to Budapest." The mood in the hospital was angry.

General Grigori Kahani had enormous responsibility in the area. He was a commander of the Red Army and had some concern for military strategy, but he was also the General who was in charge of civil affairs in this part of Poland as it was wrestled from the Nazi's. He was the Russian's emissary for political control. His main task was political. He was meant to make certain not only that order be established and maintained but also that the groundwork was laid for a communist occupation.

In his military entourage was a woman with special privilege. She was a Captain, but her major function was to provide a needed companionship to General Kahani. This task was not only public. It was intimate as well. Although Kahani was a family man, with a wife and three children at home, he needed a confidant. The Captain added some insight to Kahani's decision-making on the field. Without that he could lose an important perspective needed to both govern the country and contribute to the war.

When General Kahani met with his consort after meeting Miriam, Wanda and Rivka at the camp he was distant and distracted. "Are you surprised that they were killing Jews?" the Captain asked, trying not to be too insensitive?

The General grumbled. "No, I'm not surprised they were killing Jews. I'm surprised at the system they used to do it and the specific Jews they killed."

The captain, who was dark haired, full figured, elegant, looked at Kahani's hard set features. "Everyone knew they wanted to destroy the Jews. Why is it a shock." She was attempting to lessen the event.

"Killing, I am used to. Mass murder I am not."

"Really." She said. "Why not?"

Kahani sat down. "How far will it go?" he said almost to himself.

"Can you imagine more horror?" the Capitan asked.

"Yes." The General replied.

"Then you must be prepared for it. It will happen. You will see it. It is your responsibility to see that it is judged and dealt with and that it never happens again."

The General looked at her face. "I can't believe the depravity we human beings are capable of."

The Captain smiled gently. "…and the compassion they can display.", she said.

Kahani smiled back.

For the first few days that Miriam was in the hospital Rivka and Wanda walked every morning from the camp to the city to be with her, a distance of four kilometres. It was late July, 1944 and it was not a difficult walk. They stayed with Miriam most of the day, wandering out of the hospital periodically to get fresh air. On the third morning General Kahani appeared at the barrack. He was at the camp to inspect it one more time.

He was in a serious mood but informal. "Are you comfortable in the barracks?" he asked genially.

Wanda answered with a nod and a look at Wanda. "Yes."

"Nevertheless, the camp is under scrutiny and its not safe. I've arranged for you to stay in an apartment in Lublin. Also to get you some fresh clothes."

"Thank you." Rivka said sincerely. "You are very kind."

"You can go there now. The Captain at the headquarters in Lublin will give you the address."

Once the two women found the apartment and settled in roughly, they went to visit Miriam. Now they were so close to the hospital they could come and go more frequently. Also, they could participate more in the life of the small city. They bought food at the open market, having been given some Russian currency by the Captain at headquarters. Such luxury and such pleasure had been absent in their lives for a long time.

"How good it is to buy a common turnip!" Wanda said to Miriam one day. "Whoever would have though such a simple thing could bring such happiness?"

The Major came to visit Miriam every other day. Although he was concerned with her as his patient he looked forward to seeing the other women also. Especially Wanda. They used to go for walks outside the hospital.

"Do you miss Warsaw?", he asked one day.

"Yes and no." she replied.

"Pardon me. The war has made me insensitive."

Wanda gestured with her hands. "Not at all! The war has made me brutal."

"A doctor should be used to suffering. You should not."

"Why not?"

"War is not usual." His expression was matter of fact.

"Isn't it?", Wanda intoned. "I don't know any more."

"I think I know. It is not normal. Peace is normal. As a soldier I have to know that. As a physician I have to practice it."

Miriam let a smile cross her lips. "Look at Miriam. She found love in it."

"Yes", the Major replied. " A love that has survived. Of course, she's sixteen. She has a certain privilege."

Wanda looked at him with insight. "That isn't the point is it, really? A lucky child always knows love. Miriam refuses to let her love be less important than anything else in her life. That's an affirmation of something, a challenge and even a triumph."

They stopped on the walk and looked at each other amiably. "We're lucky to survive this long, aren't we?" the Major said.

Wanda looked down. "Lucky." She said simply.

The Major's hand touched her arm. She thought, "I am so thin and ugly!", but deep inside her being a part of her that had withered with disuse and in response to years of meticulously premeditated hate began to shift.

CHAPTER 11
Portrait

The Major was a sensitive man, in fact he was a bit of a romantic. In Russia he had liked to sketch portraits. He had collected quite a number of them. When the war started he began a project of drawing faces of wounded soldiers. It went on for a short time and then it stopped. He had wanted to catch the inner strength and humanity of the wounded but he soon discovered that it was too difficult. The inner qualities were there, but he was unable to capture it. Instead, his portraits became a record of pain. Personal, intimate and inexcusable pain. He burned what portraits he had in 1941. Now it was August, 1944. He had been assigned to the hospital in Lublin. He felt something he had not felt in almost four years; he almost felt roots.

He checked in on Miriam every day, and almost every day Wanda and Rivka were with her. Miriam's condition was very serious. She was only able to survive because she had been kept in bed most of the time and received some treatment. The Major had respect for Miriam, and he understood her position. He had no respect for her choice. As a physician he believed she was committing suicide and he felt that in the midst of so much death her refusal to terminate the pregnancy was madness. Still, he recognized Miriam's symbolic decision as meaningful.

Several weeks after Miriam had entered the hospital Wanda was alone with her in her room. He and Wanda had talked many times. They had been to dinner at the army barracks set up outside the city. They were friends, as much as that was possible in the circumstances. Miriam was asleep when he arrived.

"Uri," Wanda said. "You are here early."

"The General has given me a free day. He can't give me a leave although I have been with the Front for a long time. He said I should do what is essential but he released me from wearing my uniform for the day. I tell you, though I feel ridiculous."

Wanda smiled. She was wearing a long burgundy dress and white blouse. It was not stylish but it was clean. Wanda was at the upper end of average height. Her hair was growing out from the shaved state it had been in at liberation and was dark blond. Her face was almost soft and it shone with highlights of compassion. It was a countenance that touched a note in the Major's makeup. In itself it wasn't cosmetically beautiful but it had deep emotional resonance.

"There is a concert for the soldiers just off the base at seven o'clock this evening. Why don't you come with me?"

Wanda's face became concerned for a moment. "I'm not a soldier."

The Major looked at her seriously. "Aren't you?"

"No."

"You don't carry a gun. Perhaps you no longer wear a uniform. Do you think that's all there is to being a soldier?"

"Isn't it?" she said.

"No, its more. You know you are very welcome to this concert You and your friends are very welcome."

The concern on Wanda's face lightened. "Alright. I'll meet you there."

BAR KOCHBA

Wanda and Miriam had been set up in a small apartment near the centre of Lublin. They were able to get simple clothing and basic food. The major also had an apartment near the hospital. He was allowed that because he was administering the hospital. It was temporary. He knew that he would be moving out and back to the front before long. When he met Wanda for the concert she was wearing a blue dress that looked nearly new. Uri thought she looked almost vulnerable. It was not her dress that made the impression. This was the first social occasion she had been to since the war started. She was carrying a lot of history. After the concert, which was really a show verging on vaudeville, they walked towards the city centre.

"Nice to hear music!" Uri said.

"Yes. Nice to see men simply enjoying themselves. But nicest of all was the laughter. That was the real show for me. Maybe the world will go on?"

"I have something like coffee at my apartment. Would you come over for a cup? It's not far." Uri said.

"Sure." Wanda replied.

"I have a favour to ask of you." Uri said quietly.

"Yes? What is it?"

"I'd like to draw your portrait in charcoal. I've done it very often before."

"Why me?"

"I want to remember you. And you have a quality of both strength and softness I'd like to try to capture. I think our generation is unusual, and I perceive that uniqueness in you."

Wanda was slightly flattered despite herself. She recognized that she was still vulnerable to gentle sentiments. And she realized Uri's need to see human qualities and express kind emotions.

"Yes." She said agreeably. "I'd like to come to your apartment.

In his one room were some neatly stacked papers and reports, a small table with two chairs and a simply made bed. In one corner was a gas hotplate and a coffee pot. Uri put on some water. They chatted about Miriam and Rivka while the water boiled, and about progress in the hospital. When the black coffee-like substance was made they sat opposite each other at the small table.

Uri had never revealed anything about himself to Wanda. She wanted to know more about him. "Do you hear anything from your family?" she asked.

"From my wife. The last time I heard from her was two years ago. She's in Moscow with our son."

"How old is he?"

"He's eight."

"Does he know he's Jewish"

Uri almost laughed. "Does he know? Such things are not spoken of in Moscow. He knows he's Jewish, but it's not a central part of what he knows. To him it's an almost secret part."

"Is it also a secret part for you?"

"Not so much secret as practically redundant. We're all something. My son will have a bar mitzvah…a secret bar mitzvah. After that it will be up to him to know how important being a Jew will be for him. My wife is Jewish and the grandparents are Jewish. He will know enough."

Wanda was satisfied with Uri's understanding, but she was curious about something else. "Tell me. Honestly. There's no one here but me. Are you a communist?"

The Major laughed out loud. "But we are all communists! We are all comrades! We are the sons and daughters of the revolution!"

Wanda pressed further. "I know that. But what does it mean to you?"

"I am a child of the revolution, like I say. The revolution is like my father. I may disagree with my father. At times I may dislike him, I may even hate him at times. But he is always my father and I cannot disown him."

Wanda demurred. "I am a Jewish child. I cannot forget that."

Uri reached across the table and took Wanda's hand. She squeezed it back. "We all must belong to something or someone. We all need to believe in something. Look at Miriam. She has an implacable faith. I do not. I believe in medicine. In any case we are only human and cannot know anything that is absolutely true. All we can do is believe, and that belief in itself is what makes us real."

Wanda wondered what she believed in. "It's not Judaism that is the whole truth for me. It is the existence of a people that we must fight for, and the right for principles of decency to exist."

Uri wanted to close this conversation. It was becoming maudlin. He also wanted to reach Wanda in more than a merely philosophical way. "Do you think decency can ever exist again in this world?" he said. "Or love, for that matter."

Wanda smiled wanly. "Oh, love can exist! Of that I know. But to express it! That's the question."

Uri got out of his seat. He was not smiling. His face was gentle and intense at the same time. As he approached Wanda she rose out of her seat also. He advanced on her and instinctively she raised her arms in front of her. He embraced her whole body, her arms folded between them. She was not really pushing him away as much as she was making a gesture of self-defence. At first she resisted his kiss, but only tentatively and only for a moment. Then they folded into each other like clouds of vapour.

Throughout the rest of the summer Wanda and the Major were understood by everyone to be intimate although they tried to be careful not display their liaison publicly. What showed was not a sexuality. It was rather a familiar intimacy that was clear. They were obviously like good friends.

Miriam's health was slowly but steadily deteriorating. The baby was due in January. At the end of August the General invited Wanda and Rivka to join him for dinner one night. Uri was also invited as well as the General's adjunct, Mira. They were housed in an elegant building that used to be owned by a local Jewish family. It was preserved almost intact although much of the furniture had been looted. Now it was a beautiful shell with more functional furniture. The general had gotten hold of an army cook to prepare a meal. It was served by a local teen aged girl.

Dinner talk was low and polite at first. Mira picked up the pace as they were into the main course. "Rivka? How do you come to speak Yiddish so well?"

Rivka put down her knife and fork. "My mother spoke it quite often to us when we were young and we spoke it with our friends sometimes at school. It was common among Jewish youth. We were given lessons at one time."

"Do you think you will speak it again when the war ends?", Mira asked.

"Yes, I expect to. It links us together."

Wanda spoke up. "We are going to need a lot to link us together. More than just Yiddish."

The four Russians at the table began to speak all at once. The General prevailed. "In Russia we must work steadily and seriously to maintain our culture. The arts, the letters, the language."

Rivka spoke up. "What about the religion.?"

There was a pause. Uri spoke first. "There is no religion in Russia. We believe in each other. We believe in common goals and universal realities. Religion is superstition. It takes responsibility for all things and deposits them in a fairy tale."

"God is not a fairy tale." Rivka replied. "If you can't believe in God, what is there left to believe in?"

Mira spoke up. She was a tall, elegant woman in her early thirties with a strong emotional undercurrent poised against her cool exterior. "Rivka. What makes you think that God exists? Is it the mountains and lakes? You know they have scientific explanations. The clouds are made of gases, not anything more spiritual. The sun, we know, is a star. We've known since the 15th century that the earth is not the centre of the universe. What makes you think that God exists?"

Rivka hesitated for a brief moment. "I can't really answer your question. Knowing God is not something you learn through reason. It's something you feel."

The General cut in. "Not something you know through reason, but something you feel? Rivka, do you expect to live your life through your feelings? If I ran my command through feeling, do you think we could possibly fight our way through this war?"

Wanda spoke up. "You can believe in God and not give up reason. This war is an example. We have seen the horror of what people can do to each other, but if we don't have faith that that will change, hope in the future, how could we go on? Even if we believe in God not so much as a deity as we believe in him as a principle. Things will get better. They will always get better."

Uri interjected. "Faith is one of those issues that blinds us to the real question. There is no doubt that faith is important to the human mind, but it can lead us into trouble just the same. Too much faith can make you silly, you believe in foolish things, like God will do anything for you if you pray. The individual must take responsibility for what they do. They must not rationalize in the name of faith. If a farmer had faith that rain would come and it didn't come he would lose his crop. Science is much more dependable."

Mira had the final say before the conversation turned towards something different. No one wanted to pursue this topic any further. "Its necessary and good to have faith that things will get better, but it is faith in humanity that is needed. There are many truths in the world and many emotions. A balance is necessary to achieve progress."

In November Uri was sent to the Front. The separation was very hard on Wanda. Shortly after he left she and Rivka were walking back from the hospital. Wanda was walking very erect, so quickly that Rivka could not keep up with her. "Hey, Wanda!" she called out. "Don't be in such a hurry!"

Wanda stopped dead in her tracks. "I'm sorry," she said. "I didn't realize I was walking so quickly." She bent over a little and put her hands on her thighs. She looked into Wanda's eyes. "How can I live?" she said. She started to cry.

"We live because that is what we have to do. That is our goal. It is amorphous. There is no reason but to live for what we cannot know in the future. Miriam's baby. The world that it can help to make better."

"What if that baby is never born?"

Rivka was irate. "Don't ask questions that we can't answer! Wanda, the worst has happened. It can only get better, maybe not all at once, but slowly step by step. Even if Miriam's baby doesn't make it, we have seen her courage. There is no more! To die with dignity is to justify it all. How much truth can you absorb?"

Wanda was bent over with her head in her hands. She began pacing in a small circle around Rivka like she were lost in a very small space. "So much loss! So much loss!" she repeated over and over.

Finally she fell gently on Rivka's chest. "Oh, Rivka!" she moaned. "I'm so torn! I had love! There was love! In all this, there was that! Why should I care that it's gone?"

"It's not gone." Rivka said calmly. "You will always remember it."

Wanda started to cry and then, in the middle of it, she began to laugh. "Love was here! It exists. All is not lost!"

"Exactly." Rivka said. "You can love. It exists. No matter what they may strip away from us."

The paradoxes and the truth of all this was too much for Wanda. She feel to her knees in the empty street and wept without restraint. Rivka stood beside with her left hand touching the hair on the top of her head and looking directly at the sky. They formed a beautiful tableau in the waning sunlight.

On December 28, 1944 Miriam went into labour. Rivka and Wanda by her side until she went into the delivery room. Her resolve was very strong. "I have been waiting for this moment so long." She said. "It seems like I've been waiting all my life."

As 2:20 in the morning, the doctor came to Rivka and Wanda in the waiting room. "It's a girl." He said. "She's healthy and normal. The mother needs rest. It was hard on her. With time, she should recover some of her strength. She's a true fighter. Congratulations."

The two women turned to each other with large smiles on their faces. They spontaneously embraced each other with exuberant joy. They beat each other's back and made incoherent sounds of unrestrained happiness.

"Miriam wants to call her Leah.", Rivka said. "Please God she should have a good life."

CHAPTER 12
Hope Child

After the birth of Leah things became more complicated for the three women. Miriam's medical condition improved somewhat, but the damage to her internal organs was severe and she was in a weakened condition. Although she was able to breastfeed and was able to stand up and take a few steps, she had to lay down or sit down much of the time. This left care of the baby in Rivka and Wanda's hands much often, since the nursing staff was very busy and not able to care for her.

Rivka was tireless in looking after Leah. Once she had the baby in her arms she almost never let her down.

"It's a shame you can't nurse her.", Miriam said to her one time.

"I could hold her forever!" Rivka replied boldly.

"She is beautiful, isn't she?" Miriam asked simply.

"Leah lights up the room!" Rivka exclaimed.

"No she doesn't." Wanda cut in. "She lights up the universe."

Wanda was a constant companion, spending almost as much time at the hospital as Rivka. They were both aglow with the presence of this new life. The darkness of the war was still a foreboding aspect all around them, but the birth of this bright hope was a strong agent for renewal and change.

Leah was born in late December. In mid-January, 1945, Budapest was liberated by the Russians. When the news reached Miriam and Rivka they were ecstatic. They shouted out loud. They did a short dance of victory. They wept with both joy and sorrow.

"We must go back!", Miriam said.

"People we know must be there!", Rivka stated.

"It won't be the same."

"No. It will be different."

Miriam confirmed her feelings. "We have to go. It is the only place we ever belonged. It is the only place we ever called home."

Wanda, who had been sitting quietly in a corner, suddenly seemed visible. "Of course you will come with us?", Miriam said.

Wanda looked down. "I don't have a home, I think. Warsaw cannot be home. I have no one left in my family. Where else should I go?"

War, suffering, death, even birth. Wanda had been through all this with Rivka and Miriam. They could not imagine that they would have survived without her guidance, her knowledge and, of course, her wit. Rivka looked directly into Wanda's eyes. "You are family to us. You always will be. Come to Hungary; we don't know what we will find there. There are thousands of people without homes. We will find our way together."

It was not an easy thing to travel across Europe at this time. There were no scheduled trains, no passenger trains to speak of. The women relied upon the General to help them arrange transportation. When the approached him with their wish to go to Budapest he was reluctant.

"It's dangerous. Three women, one barely able to travel, and a newborn child. Do you realize how difficult that will be?"

Rivka spoke. "Budapest is our home. We belong there. There will be people who survived who were part of our community. They will help us to establish ourselves. We have nowhere else to go! If not Budapest, then where shall we live?"

"Why don't you wait for awhile? You're not in bad shape here in Lublin. You know, Budapest is not in my jurisdiction. I won't be able to look out for you"

Rivka reasoned hard. "Your assistance has been so very essential to us, and we are very grateful, perhaps more grateful than we are able to accurately express. We are refugees and we need to go home. If we wait to go back everything will be done. Now, all the survivors are going back to re-establish their lives. We need to be part of that initial process of rebuilding a community. We don't want to miss the chance to be a part of a beginning. We want to begin to build our lives."

The General pondered for a moment. "I can't hold you here. I don't want to. Give it a few weeks and I will help you. By then, supply lines should be rebuilt and travel will be less difficult."

The wait was well worth it. Both Miriam and the baby got a little stronger. Also, their mental preparedness was improved. Their stay in Lublin was more pointed and focussed. It was no longer a place where they were being housed indefinitely; it was a place they were preparing to leave. The city seemed more hospitable now that they had a larger purpose. Miriam and Rivka made plans. They hoped to get their apartment back since they heard that the Russians were returning lost property to the Jews. They talked about walking in the park again.

When the General came through for them, he came through completely. They were given a berth on a troop train heading into Hungary and arriving at Budapest. They had documents from the General giving them safe passage as well as a letter for one of the commanders in Budapest requesting that he look out for them. They saw the General only once before leaving. "Shalom Aleichem.", he said to them. "Keep your wits about you. Be strong and be hard. You have a great deal to fight for."

Travelling with Miriam was less difficult than they thought it might have been at first. She never complained. She held Leah most of the time and fed her whenever necessary. The baby was relatively quiet throughout the trip. None of the soldiers travelling on the train bothered them except once when Wanda made her way to a forward car. The sight of an attractive woman on a troop train excited the men and they made some remarks. No one expected any less. The women were thankful there was not more.

When they arrived in Budapest their excitement was contained. The train station was overrun with Russian soldiers embarking and disembarking. There was a feeing of place for the sisters. Their mouths fell open. Some of the landmarks were in ruins but some remained. Without realizing it both Miriam's and Rivka's mouths hung open. They slowly looked at each other.

"I feel a sense of home," said Miriam. "Don't you?"

Rivka answered with a measured tone, "I feel familiarity." She said. "I don't know yet whether I feel a sense of home."

After getting oriented the first thing they did was deliver the letter to the local commander. He was very gracious but didn't spend any time with them. Then they went immediately to Rivka and Miriam's old apartment. There was a man and woman living there who would not acknowledge the women's assertion that this had been their home. At first the couple were arrogant and then they were abusive. Rivka could see that all their furniture was there and she knew that the apartment still belonged to them. There was some shouting and some very nasty gestures.

While Miriam and Wanda stayed in a warm café near the apartment, Rivka went back to the office of the commander. He dispatched two soldiers to go back with her and carry out the law. When they arrived, the military men took over. They made it clear the occupants were there illegally and that they were to vacate at once. With much complaint the man and woman complied. They were only caretakers for a ring of criminals who were selling property and items left behind by the Jews. When the apartment was vacant Rivka went for Miriam, Wanda and Leah. They settled in with a sense of nostalgia they had not felt in several years. Rivka went to the kitchen and sat down at a little table. They had eaten their breakfasts there when they were small. Rivka was very strong, but this moment was too much for her. Slowly she began to cry. She was venting pain built up over a very long time. The loss of faith. The loss of her father. She cried a little more. Then she wept. This only lasted a few moments. Then it was gone, and she felt better.

Miriam went to her bedroom. She sat on the brightly coloured comforter covering the bed. She missed her Papa, but she had as much love around her as she needed at the time.

Once they had settled in things developed in ways they had not anticipated. As spring approached their fortunes began to fall apart. There was a great deal of anti-Semitism in Budapest and with it came many bad memories for Rivka and Miriam. They began to see that post-war Europe was not to be the ideal place to settle and to raise a child. They had help from an American aid organization called JOINT. This organization helped survivors in every way possible. They met people there. Many of them planned to go to Palestine. There were discussions held in both formal and informal settings about the necessity of a Jewish homeland. One day in early March Rivka and Wanda had a decisive conversation with an Hungarian woman who had decided to go. Her name was Devorah. She was energetic, lively, determined.

"They still hate us here in Europe, even more so because they think we have caused them shame in the eyes of the world. Where are we supposed to go?"

Rivka responded. "The Russians will not even let us practice our religion." She was concerned about the Jewish faith as well as culture.

Devorah continued. "We have nothing of our own. Our communities are no more. Our livelihoods have been ruined. Truly, this is the time to bring the Diaspora to a close. We need to regroup. We need, more than ever, to ensure and protect our Jewish faith, heritage and culture. Now, when all of us are refugees, we must create a true refuge in a Jewish state in Palestine."

Wanda broke in. "How can we go to Palestine? The British control it and they won't allow us in."

"We will change their minds." Devorah said. "With persistence and determination we will make them see that Israel is the Jewish homeland must be the Jewish state. They allow some of us in, a few at a time. We will make the world see that the future of civilization depends upon our own nation in Israel. The British will have to let it go."

Although Rivka was sympathetic to Devorah's words she was concerned about pragmatics. "It's a desert." she said. "How are we supposed to live there?"

"There are modern methods of agriculture that can be used there. And I ask you, Rivka. How are you going to survive here? Is there anything for you in the ashes that were Europe?"

The task of building a life in Budapest was daunting to all three women. They had the apartment but with the communists in control there was no telling how they would keep it. There was a consensus that they were not planning to leave Hungary after the war. Agents whose task it was to bring survivors to Palestine fought for the hearts and minds of Jewish men and women. One such agent, an emissary for a political group in Palestine, paid particular attention to the three women. He wanted them to go to Frankfurt to join a kibbutz in order to prepare to emigrate to Palestine. After a few weeks of discussion, the women were compelled to agree. The association with the arguments and the closeness to the passion of the Jewish community that had roughly formed in Budapest made the possibility of devoting themselves to a purpose like this very strong. The thought of starting a new life in Eretz Israel was very attractive, but Rivka and Wanda were broken. They conceded that the purpose was good, but they were not entirely convinced it was a perfect thing. Miriam, on the other hand, was very ill. She was extremely interested in going to Palestine in principal, but at the same time she had a reluctance on account of the physical safety of her daughter

The overriding factor was that in the largest case the women were refugees and had no where else to go. The possibility of staying in Budapest became more and more evasive as the days wore on. There were reports of pogroms in Poland. There was the emerging spectre of communist control of Hungary. There was the enormous fact of the Holocaust itself and all it meant to the women. They had to leave, almost by default. Although their conviction about Israel was sincere there was an underlying theme of residual pain and doubt.

In late April they left for Frankfurt. Crossing the zones was very difficult, but the emissary made it much easier. The Russians took every precaution to prevent people from leaving the communist zone. The women had to wait at the station for a proper train; there was no

BAR KOCHBA

passenger train schedule and travelling on a passenger train was not possible if you planned on passing the border. They waited for a freight train going through to Austria and were able to find a place to sit in it. The emissary was with them.

The trip was uncomfortable and anxious. Miriam was clearly uncomfortable, suffering and in paid. At the checkpoint the emissary left them to deal with the crossing. He had fake documents for the women. They had to wait a long time. It was very hard to cross, it could go either way and the three women were very tense. The baby cried and Miriam put her to her breast

Finally, after they were sure they would be turned back, soldier came to look at them. The emissary was with him. He looked through their few possessions. He observed the scene of the three women and a baby. He moved away from the car, but in the dim light Wanda could see him receiving some money from the emissary. He left. The emissary rejoined them. About an hour later the train pulled out from the border and slowly made its way into American occupied territory. Everything on the American side was easier and once they were passed the checkpoints they weren't bothered anymore. They arrived in Vienna a few hours later. They were in the American Zone now. They were cautiously excited and relieved. They really didn't know exactly what to expect from the Americans. The rumours were that they were human.

It was clear, when they arrived piecemeal in Vienna, that Miriam was loosing strength and she had to go into a hospital in Vienna. Travelling was not good for her, but they still had further to go to get to Frankfurt where they would stay on a kibbutz created as a link between Palestine and Europe. The Jews were allowed to bring 1000 people per month into Israel and most of them came from kibbutz like this. After three weeks in Vienna they took a train to Frankfurt. Miriam was very ill.

Before even going to the kibbutz, which was located in an unused military base just outside the city, Rivka and Wanda took Miriam to an American hospital in town. They stayed with her overnight. In the morning an American Army Jewish chaplain came to see them. He was young, dark haired but pale. Despite his youth there was compassion and knowledge in his face.

"There is a Jewish patient in here?", he asked gingerly in English. When he saw the confused look on their faces he repeated himself in Yiddish. That got a verbal response.

"My sister." Rivka said. She was holding Leah.

"What's her name?"

"Her name is Miriam."

"And this is your daughter?", he asked quietly.

"No. Its her daughter."

He looked concerned. "So you're the aunt?"

"Yes.", Rivka replied.

He was very pleasant and easy to like. "A gorgeous family. Two aunts?" he asked, indicating Wanda. She replied, "No. Just a friend."

"I'm the religious soldier. My name is Asher Teperman. How is the patient?"

Miriam rose to the occasion. "Miriam.", she said quietly. "I don't want you to say kaddish yet." Kaddish is the prayer for the departed.

Asher laughed. "I'm going to say a morning prayer. Its very hopeful."

Asher said the prayer while the women looked down towards the ground. Rivka couldn't see it, but his gaze unwillingly drifted towards her. When it was finished everyone looked up and smiled. "I'll be back around dinner time." He shook their hands and left.

Asher became a constant visitor over the next few days, while Miriam was still able to care for Leah. He was a *Yeshiva* boy' from upstate New

York who administered as a Conservative Rabbi while practicing as a Modern Orthodox. He had found that the Jewish soldiers were alienated by too much religious practice although many of them thought about G-d some of the time. Asher never imposed religion upon the soldiers. He thought of himself as a receptacle, sometimes a cup which was never empty from which the men could drink. Much of the time he only had to offer his confidence and friendship; that was often more important even than prayer. For Rivka, Wanda and Miriam he was very welcome. Asher didn't know very much about Auschwitz. The Americans were still in the dark about the details of the Holocaust, but he had met with some survivors so he wasn't completely naive. The week after his first visit he arrived in the afternoon while Wanda was out and Miriam was sleeping.

"You were in Auschwitz?" Asher inquired.

"Yes."

"Do you want to talk about it?"

Rivka was holding Leah while she slept. "No. But I have a question for you? See this little child? This little baby is a child of love. Why do people choose to hate so strongly?"

"They hate because they don't know their own true natures. That's simple minded, maybe, but hate isn't really complex, is it? It's a base, uncivilized, brutal emotion."

"I've often heard that it isn't easy to be a Jew. I know how true it is." Rivka held Leah very close.

"Would you have it any other way, being a Jew I mean?"

Rivka shook her head. "No. I am nothing if not a Jew."

Asher concurred. "Being a Jew is a gift, but it is also a responsibility. Would it be worth being a Jew if there wasn't a challenge in it also?"

Rivka changed to a another topic. "Is it different in America?"

"Different?" Asher said quizzically. "Superficially, perhaps, but mostly no. Except that there is a freshness in America, a hopefulness, and a conviction that as a nation we are on the right track."

"There is no place for us in Europe. That's why we are going to Palestine. To build a home that has a future." Rivka was a bit wistful.

"Is that what you really want?" Asher sensed there was more to Rivka than this. She laughed lightly.

"I'm not very political, I'm afraid. I want a safe home for my sister, my niece, my friend and I."

"You're not exactly romantic, either. You're a pragmatist."

"And you?" Rivka enquired.

Asher smiled. "I am a romantic. I want to get married and serve a congregation." He paused for a moment "Are you interested in that?"

Rivka held back a tight smile. "Oh, yes. But where, when and with who?"

"There are men who see genuine power and beauty in a woman like you. A wise, experienced and spiritual woman. One may be closer than you think." He was looking directly at Rivka's eyes. She looked down demurely.

"Well." She said almost wistfully. "They say there is no such thing as coincidence."

The following week Miriam took a turn for the worse. She was very weak. Within a few days her kidneys ceased functioning. Rivka and Wanda were with her day and night. Leah was cared for right in the hospital. She was off Miriam's breast and on formula.

On the fourth night after being admitted Miriam was in a great deal of pain. They were giving her morphine but it didn't completely work. She was still clearly in some pain. About 2 A.M. she spoke to Rivka. Wanda was in the corridor with Leah, both of them asleep. Leah was in a bassinette supplied by the nurses. Wanda was sitting up in a chair.

"You should go." Miriam said. "I'll be fine."

"It's alright. I want to stay." Rivka replied.

"You are too good to me. I don't deserve such a wonderful sister."

"Just so you know, Miriam, I can say the same thing. Thank God we have each other."

Miriam took Rivka's hand. They were like that for a long while. At 5:15 in the morning Rivka went out of the room to get some water. When she came back Miriam had passed on.

When Rivka found her sister lifeless in that bed a shock like a gunshot wound struck at her heart. She shouted "NO." out loud and fell to her knees beside Miriam's body. Two nurses came running. Rivka sobbed out loud, crying "No! No! Not my sister! Not my sister!". She was hysterical with grief. She had lost control. The loss of all she had loved her whole life was gone. She wept and cried at the side of Miriam's bed.

All the pain and death of the war wound her up and wouldn't let her go. She clung to her sister's side for three hours. Wanda was able to take her away after that, and she calmed down a little.

The Kibbutz arranged a funeral for Miriam the next day. She was buried in a Jewish cemetery near Frankfurt. Asher Teperman was the Rabbi. Almost everyone from the Kibbutz was there.

Rivka was virtually inconsolable, but there was some comfort. Wanda didn't say a great deal but she was solidly there for Rivka, always at her side. The 'shiva', the seven day mourning period, was located in a comfortable room at the kibbutz. Different people came by in a constant stream, but there was one person that stood out in relief. That was Asher. He came by for a few hours every day to comfort Rivka. He always seemed to create the right mood. He was funny at times, he was serious and straight at other times. At first, Rivka didn't show that she especially noticed him, but after a day or two she acknowledged that his presence was valued. If anything could cheer Rivka, it was Asher's good will and gentle humour.

When the shiva was over Asher was there for Rivka, saying prayers in the last hour of the sitting. He left her alone after sunset but returned to see her later the next afternoon.

"How do you feel?" he asked.

Rivka replied, "I feel a great absence. I'm completely drained and empty, as if the sun had been torn out of sky."

Asher nodded. "It's not only a sister that has been lost, is it? You are grieving for the war."

Rivka looked confused. "You know, Asher, it really is mostly for my sister. I didn't start the war, I'm not going to grieve for it. I just don't know how I'm going to face the future."

Asher looked down at the ground. "Maybe I could help?", he said.

Tears welled up in Rivka's eyes. He was so kind. "Oh, Asher. I wish you could."

"Well, Maybe I can. Rivka, we haven't known each other very long and yet I seem to know a lot about you. Still, you are so strong and a mystery to me."

Rivka looked at him with a simple, plain smile. "And what does that mean?"

Asher had a lump in his throat. He had been through the war and seen much. Now, sitting with a woman he thought he might love, he was nervous. "You could come to America with me."

"What?"

"We'll adopt Leah, get married here in Europe, and go back to America."

"You're serious?" Rivka was between tears and laughter.

"If it please G-d, I've never met anyone else I've ever wanted to marry."

Rivka adopted a stern look, but her emotions were jumpy. "You'll give me time to think about this?"

"Yes, of course. Think about it."

They talked a bit more about the pragmatics of this. Rivka waited two days before giving Asher a reply.

"Asher," she said. "I've given it a great deal of thought. I believe you are sincere about adopting Leah. I think you are a good rabbi, earnest and caring." She stumbled over her words. "I would like to marry you, if you still want me to."

The arrangements were drawn out but they went fairly smoothly. Asher and Rivka were expected to be married in a military ceremony in May, 1945 but they weren't expected to return to the United States until some time later. They would have a second Jewish wedding back in Rochester, New York. Rivka would be considered a war bride and would be able to follow Asher back to Rochester after the war. She was very concerned about Wanda.

"You should come to America also." Rivka told her.

"I have no connection as a refugee. I don't know anybody there. I'll go to Palestine and I will help to build a nation and I will build a home."

"If you wait, Asher and I will send for you."

Wanda smiled. "If that is in the cards, we shall see."

In May the war in Europe officially came to a close. For the whole world there was a renewal of hope. Miriam was an unfortunate victim.

Rivka would find a home. Wanda would move on to a hopeful new destiny. And the little girl, Leah, a daughter of love and destruction, would grow in a new world of promise and love. What circumstances would shape her future? The forces of darkness were receding. Light was beginning to shine again.

CHAPTER 13
Destiny on a Full Stomach

When the Americans liberated us they were shocked by our condition. This confirmed our idea that if the Allies knew about the concentration camps they would have done something to help us. For our part we were so brutalized by our experience that we did not recognize them as a force for good, we only recognized them as agents of change. After all, an army is always an army, or so we thought. At first we did not reach out to the Americans as liberators because we were exclusively concerned with our own survival. Like children who have been abused we were suspicious even of the hands that helped us. It took several weeks before we were able to relate to the American presence as benign and even helpful.

On reflection its possible to consider the actual effect the camps had on us up to the point at which we were liberated and continuing after that. Perhaps the largest casualty was trust. There were different levels of loss of trust; trust in nations, trust in individuals, trust in G-d. We had been betrayed by entire nations. We had been persecuted to the extent of genocide. This last reality is very hard to realize while it is ongoing. The sheer horror of the genocide machine is so large that it defies interpretation. It is so immediate that it hits every level of existence; your self, your family, your community, your faith. It was this element that most affected the rest of my life. I could have overcome a personal attack by rationalizing it in some way. I could have assimilated a political attack as having some reason behind it. But genocide as practiced by whole nations had no reason and could not be answered philosophically. It was a palpable and irreducible reality that called for immense resolve to approach. For me, it became a rationale to respond to this puzzle as a Jew to something indigenous. We, as Jews, had to take action to protect ourselves. No measures were too radical to protect our nation; no philosophy was too extreme to ensure our survival.

Trust in G-d at the moment of liberation was not a generalized truth. It was very specific and personal. For every one of us who survived there were scores of others who had died. This was hard enough to process without the knowledge that they died for only one reason; that they were Jews. No one can see their little children die, or see a small brother or sister killed, without doubting G-d. The single issue that one had to deal with was G-d's will. If G-d was all-powerful He must have wilfully allowed the Jews to be killed. This was something that required almost superhuman insight to comprehend. Isaac, Hershel and I talked about it the night we were first liberated after having sufficient food for the first time in almost two years.

"G-d lives in a full belly." Isaac said irreverently. "Now that I've eaten a little food I feel more religious."

Hershel was miffed. "G-d is there for you even more when you are hungry,"

"How so?" Isaac inquired.

"When you need G-d the most he reaches out to you."

"Really? Did he reach out to your mother and the rest of your family when they were thrown into the gas chamber?"

"You can't question whether he does or not. You can't know his will." Herschel was trying to articulate a complicated idea. "G-d is not your servant. You can't presume to know why he does what he does. You can only accept what comes to you with humility and faith."

"I hate to doubt even you, let alone G-d Himself, but did you ever consider that what you are saying might be superstitious drivel. What evidence do you have?"

Herschel was getting excited. "My evidence is the world, the Torah and the experience of every sentient being that G-d exists in every atom of existence, whether hungry or not."

I spoke up at this point to try to smooth out the conflict. "G-d doesn't show himself in any condition and if he does we call it a miracle. The three of us are alive. We're friends. Isn't that miracle enough? The Messiah will come at the right time. We will celebrate next year in Jerusalem, G-d willing. I think you have to take control of your life whether you believe G-d controls it directly or not."

"If you want Him, He is there. I looked to Him every day and He made me feel better." Hershel maintained.

Isaac responded. "The reality is that Faith is real. What G-d may do we can only guess at."

I replied, "We all know that the worst of possible worlds happened around us. We experienced an unthinkable injustice. Now, we will see if that can be replaced. We know that G-d will not do it for us unless we take actions to do it for ourselves."

We were not the only inmates to roam the countryside searching for food after the camp was initially liberated. Few stayed behind the barbed wire to see what would happen after the guards fled and left everyone behind. Certainly, there were many too weak to flee, but most of the rest of us exercised our freedom to look for food. Like Hershel, Isaac and myself they approached farmhouses and other dwellings where they might find food. There was not much reason to this adventure since the Americans brought plenty of supplies with them, but reason was not a plentiful commodity among us. We had been starved and beaten for years and resembled demented animals.

Hershel, Isaac and I asked roughly if we could stay at the house of the older German couple after the first night. They agreed cautiously. The Americans had made it clear that all the inmates would eventually come back to the camp to stay, after they had cleaned it up and prepared it for reasonable comfort. In the interim we needed help.

Immediately after the war ended on May 8, 1945 the Americans started to bring order to the German countryside. Even so, it was not entirely easy to get food. Isaac was not satisfied that the German couple we were staying with were doing all they could to get food for us. He urged us to ask for more. Since I was the spokesperson I went to the woman and asked for more food.

"Down the road there is a farm where they have many chickens. Go get some chickens, bring them to me, and I will cook them" She said. That was good news for me.

We went down the road and, sure enough, came to a farm with many chickens in the yard. There was no one there to hinder us.

Catching the chickens was not so easy for us, but within a short time and with a great deal of clamour we each had one noisy chicken which we held proudly. Isaac held his bird tightly as it tried to escape from his grasp. With feathers flying and much cackling he said, "Now, Avrum, you kill it!"

Suffering had made me tender. I thought about how I would kill the chicken but I couldn't bring myself to do it. "I don't know how to kill it." I proclaimed. I turned to Hershel. "You kill it." I demanded.

Hershel looked at his chicken. "I don't know how. You kill it, Isaac."

Isaac's eyes went wide and he paled. "No, I don't want to kill it. I don't know how."

There we were, three young men who had been exposed to unthinkable cruelty and mass murder. None of them could find the cruelty to kill a chicken.

We left the birds behind and returned to our residence. I told the woman we couldn't kill the chickens. She smiled the first really kind smile I had seen upon her face. "Bring the chickens to me. My husband will kill them and I will cook them for you."

We did as she asked and that night had our first foul in several years. Afterwards, we talked in our room. "This couple are kind." Hershel said. Before the war he wanted to be a Rabbi. During internment his faith was challenged. Now, slowly, it was coming back.

"They owe it to the Jews." Isaac said. "We are Jews. Therefore they owe it to us."

My own feelings were more neutral. I believed I had seen what G-d could do and what He could allow to happen. I had a new respect for human will and what humans were capable of, G-d or no G-d. "They are doing what they have to do.' I said. "Not because it is good or bad, but because it is right."

I was beginning to see, at this point in my journey, that it didn't matter who was victim and who was oppressor. What mattered was that you did what was necessary to do to obtain that which was right. To enact G-d's law a person had to act. There was no merit in acting innocent or playing dead. If there was evil, you had to destroy it. If there was good, you had to protect it.

A few weeks later the Americans told everyone to return to the camp. It had been entirely made ready for human life. At first, the Americans gathered the local German population to come to the camp to bury the dead and disinfect the whole camp from the bunks to the latrines. They brought in fresh mattresses and prepared a supply of American army uniforms died black to clothe the former inmates. They brought some kind of order out of chaos. The kitchen and the hospital were also prepared to keep the inmates alive and make the environment as normal as possible. All of this was accomplished before any plan of what to actually do with former inmates was revealed. Everyone eventually received medical examinations and were divided into two groups and told to be very careful about what they ate; fatty foods and raw potatoes, which former inmates might find, were especially cautioned against.

We were physically comfortable in this environment, but a lingering question hung over our heads. Who, in our families, had been left alive and how would we find them? Also, now that the war was over, what would we do? This was especially difficult to know for the Jews because there was immense doubt as to weather we would be able to establish some kind of life in our former homes given the realities of the Holocaust. We didn't talk about any of this a great deal, but it did come up explicitly from time to time. Once, after a few inmates left the camp to travel to their old homes, Hershel, Isaac and I had a specific conversation.

"Do you expect they will receive a warm welcome at home?" Hershel asked rhetorically.

"Their possessions will have been sold and they probably will not be able to get their homes back." Isaac replied.

"I have seven brothers and sisters." I said. "I wonder if any of them are left alive. Otherwise, there's not much reason to go back. My town is just another kind of prison."

News came up every day regarding resettlement of refugees, which we slowly and reluctantly acknowledged included us. Word reached us that Zionists were recruiting people for Palestine, but the British were very strongly discouraging immigration of the Jews. The American government, because of its prejudices, decided not to let any of the former inmates into America. Although the inmates were free to go at any time, most of them were in no shape to go anywhere. They mostly just took one day at a time. In a short time, all the inmates under 18 were separated from the others. They were considered to be 'orphans' and determined to be the 'most important group'.

Around that time the French Government decided to allow 450 children under 18 to a rehabilitation camp in France and the British decided to let 1000 persons who were below 18 and considered 'orphans' into Britain. They also determined that 250 orphans could go to Palestine. Those who remained in the camps mostly went back home.

The greatest push for Zionism came from a very assimilated Hungarian Jew named Theordore Hertzell. He was a reporter for a prestigious Austrian Newspaper approximately around 1890. At that time a trial occurred which became known as the "Dreyfuss Affair". Dryfuss was a military Captain who was accused of being a spy for the Germans. The accusations later turned out to be false, but there was a trial in which the anti-Semitic population of Paris showed their hatred. They shouted "Kill the Jew", "Convict him!", "Jews are spies" and provoked hatred towards the Jews in general.

Hertzel realized his own Jewishness because of this acrimony and began to furiously and very publicly promote the idea of a homeland for the Jews. Around 1900 he called together all Zionist Jews from around the world to a Zionist Congress' in Basil, Switzerland. This in itself was a strong, positive act, and he also visited leaders of many countries to help to establish a Jewish homeland.

Hertzel died quite young. When WWII was ending there were only about 600 Jews living in Palestine. When Ben Gurion proclaimed on May 15, 1948 the creation of the state of Israel there were only about 600,000 Jewish people there.

Once they heard about 250 orphans being allowed to immigrate to Palestine, the Jewish agencies who had assumed responsibility for organizing immigration sent emissaries to get them together. These agencies, who would inevitably become the government of Israel, knew there would eventually have to be a war in order to establish the Jewish state. They considered these orphans to be the potentially most valuable fighters. These individuals, who were powerful and intelligent speakers, needed to convince orphans that both their responsibility and their future was in the creation of the State of Israel. In accomplishing this task they were not always scrupulously honest.

One of these fiery orators came to Buchenwald. There were quite a few young Jews there to hear him when he spoke. At that time, a few months after liberation, my frame of mind was both disturbed and angry. I was angry about the past and uncertain about the future, which created for me an underlying mood of anxiety and inaction. I wanted to fight back, now that I was gaining strength, but I didn't know who to strike back against. So, when this speaker arrived to talk about Jews and their future, I was willing to give him my attention.

He stared off by trying to make us feel at ease. He congratulated us on our good fortune in surviving the camps and lamented the death of our people, our families and friends. He said he knew we were concerned about the future. "Look around you." He said. "What do you see? Is this your homeland, where you are surrounded by others like yourself who make you welcome and share with you a culture, a purpose, a people?" He touched the centre of every one of us in that place. He went on:

"What you see around you is smouldering hatred, a poisoned legacy of bigotry and anti-Semitism. The fires of war have not burned generations of unyielding prejudice out of the character of Europe. They have, rather, fuelled the furnaces of insane jealousy and murderous animosities. There are reports of pogroms even now in parts of Poland.

"Do you think that you can go home again to the life you once led here in Europe? I am telling you that you cannot. How can you live beside your neighbour knowing that they cheered when you and your loved ones were driven without mercy from your homes to the infamous railway cars that carried you to these hellish camps? Do you remember how your local police, people you may have known, beat you and your loved ones and laughed. How could you begin to raise a family knowing of this murderous potential and intent right beside you at all times. The one, your neighbour and countryman, who jeered at your beloved mother as she was taken to her fate. Could you live beside him peacefully now, knowing of her unnatural murder, knowing he would gladly do it all again to your own wife and children?

"Do you think you can go back to meet family or friends in the warmth of your home? Do not dare to think so, because your friends and family are dead and you cannot live anywhere here with warmth and simple companionship. You will know, in every hour and in every act, that no place is safe for a Jew without a homeland and that homeland is in Israel.

"Without hesitation you should desire to come to Palestine where you can help create a state for the Jewish people where there will be justice.

Come to create 'Israel' and you will not be slaves or put into concentration camps. You will each have a gun to defend yourself. Here is the truth; you will be the first soldiers of a Jewish army in the last 2000 years. Do you want to choose to return to an anti-Semitic country where you have been oppressed for 1000 years or would you rather live in a free country where you can defend yourself and your family for the future?"

He spoke further about the kind of country we might wish to create in Israel and the benefit of being the very first to establish a new land. Finally, he closed his argument with an appeal: "You cannot turn away from the past and equally so you must not turn away from the future. The future is struggle, but also reward. The future is pain, but also accomplishment. The future is hard work, but also the fruits of your labour. The future is Israel, a state for the Jewish people. History will know your aim and history will mark your choosing. Choose to come to Israel. Your destiny is there."

After this speech I found myself in a kind of daze for several hours. It was as if that orator had reached inside and grabbed my heart. Hershel, Isaac and I went for short walk and talked about it. Hershel didn't want to leave Europe. "How does anyone know who's alive or not at this point. I know my mother is dead. I saw her led off in a line from which no one ever returned. But other members of my family could have survived."

Isaac spoke. "There isn't any possibility of a State of Israel being established in Palestine. What's going to happen to all the Arabs? You think they will just lie down and play dead? Or maybe they will voluntarily leave all their homes behind, put up banners saying "Welcome, Jewish friends" and move to…where? Where are they going to go? You think the rest of the world will take them in? The whole idea is absurd!"

I countered. "This is not the point. We can't establish a State of Israel if we start off undermining our intent. Our first job is to make a case. Our first job is to be there."

"Be there!" Isaac was outraged. "How are you going to be there when the British bar the door!" Isaac was doing more than playing Devil's Disciple. He was also rationalizing his own fears.

I responded. "At least some of this has to be done on faith. We have to believe this can be done."

"Oh!" said Isaac. "You need to believe that G-d Himself wants the Jews to take Palestine? You think G-d is going to reward the Jews for the destruction and murder in the camps, as compensation? You think now that G-d has tested us he's going to give us Israel?"

Hershel broke in. "G-d knows what we want. Peace. And a chance to worship Him again as Jews. So some of us stay here, in order to keep the faith, not to break it."

I had to address Isaac's question. "Faith is more than believing you know what G-d wants. It's also knowing that you sometimes have to fight for what's right, even if only you think so. Remember when the Jews came out of the desert and sent spies into Canaan? They were punished by G-d because they were afraid and decided not to fight. It's like that now, isn't it? We know what's right, once again a homeland for the Jews and again in Canaan. Again there are a people there and again we need faith to make it happen. Faith is the essential motivation. The rest is history." I hadn't said that much in a coherent whole in a long time.

"I have faith that there is a place for Jews in Europe." Hershel said. "The people will respect that we suffered and make room for us."

Isaac laughed. "Sure. A place underground. You can share all the underground you like."

CHAPTER 14
Only Ghosts

All the next day I stayed alone. In the morning I got a pass to leave the camp and I walked through the war torn region. There were American soldiers everywhere and small groups of Germans surveying the devastation and clearly making plans for reconstruction. The countryside showed symbols of both disaster and strength. I thought about my future for the first time in several years. Now that I was no longer a prisoner, what was I to do?

The speaker from Palestine was right. The future in Europe for those of us who survived the camps was not rosy. There would be suspicion, jealousy and hatred in every corner. My entire family had been wiped out. If I left, I would be leaving with a clean slate.

Palestine seemed so far away, yet emotionally it seemed so near! To be a pioneer in a new country seemed to be an irresistible endeavour. The tug of patriotism notwithstanding, the call of a deep purpose, the creation of Israel, was very compelling. I asked myself over and over again what I would be leaving behind. The answer was always 'ghosts…only ghosts'.

When I returned to the barracks shortly before dinnertime I was a man who had something he had not had when he left. Purpose. A slow burning, smouldering purpose. I sat down to eat with Isaac and Hershel.

"Did you hear the news today?" Isaac announced. "They don't know exactly how many Jews were killed but they estimate more than three million!"

"How many Jews were in Europe before the war?" Hershel asked.

"I don't remember ever hearing a number." Isaac replied.

"Well, take that total and subtract a handful and you'll have the body count."

"There must be three thousand in this camp." Isaac estimated. "Its one of the biggest camps."

"I wouldn't be surprised of the number of dead was much higher. There must have been three million Jews in Germany alone." Hershel thought.

There was a short pause in the conversation. Isaac finally said, "Going back to my town is going to be very lonely. Maybe there will be one or two other survivors, I'd be surprised at more than that."

"Hardly a community." Hershel added. "Where will you get kosher food? And if you don't keep kosher, what's going to keep you apart from the rest of the people? You won't have a synagogue, or a congregation to be part of. You won't even have a 'minion' for saying prayers."

Isaac went on. "There will only be a few people for Sabbath dinner. Maybe you'll even have to prepare it yourself. There won't be many Jewish girls to get married to. You'll live alone, in a little house in the middle of an empty community."

"Could this be what G-d has in store for us after saving us from the ovens?" The two boys were having some fun with this line of thought, but there was meaning to it too. Isaac looked over at Avrum who was listening and eating quietly.

"And you!" he cried out. "You are going to Israel! To be a pioneer!"

Avrum looked up. "I am going to Israel." He said.

"He is going to Israel to show G-d almighty that a miracles can light up the desert."

Avrum looked at him from his corner of the long table. "That's right. G-d has saved our lives for some reason. I'm going to Israel to find it."

"I will pray for you!" Isaac declared.

"And I will pray for you." Avrum said. "May you find what you need from the Almighty."

"After what G-d has given me whatever else I receive can only be a blessing."

The next morning Avrum went to the building where the Jewish Agency had an office. It was only a day since the speech and there was a line of young men in front of the door waiting to sign up for Israel. Behind him was a boy of about 16 years old who looked familiar. Avrum tried to place him but it was difficult. There were so many faces he had seen. Avrum turned around and smiled. The boy smiled back with a bright shiny face. "Shalom." He said. Avrum replied "Shalom"

"You are signing up to go to Israel", Avrum asked.

"Yes. I want to be a part of it."

"So do I. There's a future there." Avrum stated.

"Just to be Jewish again. That's all I ask." He was sincere.

"Just to be Jewish in our own country."

"That's it! To build a nation that is new. To be a part of that would be a great blessing."

Suddenly, Avrum remembered where he had seen him. "You used to work in the same field as me, didn't you? I think I remember you."

"Perhaps."

"I remember once, about two months before liberation I watched you being beaten in that field by several kappos. You were beaten unconscious."

The boy winced. "Yes. I remember that. I woke up in the infirmary."

"What did you do?"

The boy thought for a moment. Then he remembered. "One of the kappos was yelling at an inmate. The man was doing all he could and seemed close to collapse. Without thinking I called out to the kappo, 'You are too cruel! You can't be so cruel! G-d will punish you for it." He didn't like that. They fell upon me with their sticks."

"You were brave.", Avrum said.

"It was not bravery that prompted me to call out. I was not prepared to withstand any more injustice and savagery."

"Do you believe it will be like heaven in Eretz Israel? The Arabs are there."

"I don't know. I hope that whatever I do it is in the sense of being a Jew. If I act like a Jew nothing can be wrong. I believe that." He knew why he was signing up.

"What's your name?" Avrum asked.

"Dov. And yours?"

"Avrum. Where are you from?"

"A town in Eastern Poland. You sound like you're from Hungary."

"Yes. A few hours by train from Budapest."

We talked on while the line crept forward about some of the details of our mutual interests. Finally my turn came up at the door. I was let into a small office with a long table and several chairs. There were three people behind the table which was piled with office paraphernalia and many file folders. The used ones were in boxes on the floor while the unused ones were on a corner of the table.

A heavily built man with deep brown eyes and brown hair gestured at me to come to the table. He had a look of keen interest on his face. I sat down in front of him.

"You want to go to Israel?" he said. It was an almost rhetorical question.

"Very much." I said.

"Let me ask you." He inquired seriously. "Why do you want to go to Israel?"

I didn't hesitate. "My family are all dead. I have nothing to hold me here. After all that has happened I am still a Jew. I believe my fate is in Israel. I want to help to build a state, so that Jews can have a home for themselves and be safe from persecution."

"What do you want to accomplish in Eretz Israel?"

I was less sure about this question than I would have liked. "There may be a place for me there. I'm young and I want to be a part of it. I want to be a part of the future. I want to help to make sure that Jews can take care of their own. I want to help to make sure that what happened here can never happen again."

"Are you willing to work closely with others on a kibbutz? It's hard work!"

My mood was becoming stronger and I was willing to speak out. "I am not afraid of hard work. My life has not been easy, even before the war. I believe in Israel. I believe that we will have to fight to build it. I am not afraid to build and I am not afraid to fight and I am not afraid to die, at this time, to reclaim my right to live a free man."

The man was interested. "You're not afraid to die to make the state of Israel?"

"No. I'm not afraid."

"That's good. But are you willing to live in a state that is always in a struggle?"

My voice rose in pitch despite my wish to stay calm. "I will live for Israel, I will fight for Israel and I will die for Israel."

The man looked at me appraisingly. "You have a lot of passion. You seem to know what you want. I promise you…life in Palestine will challenge even your deepest resources." He paused for a moment. "You have to sign those papers." He indicated another person holding some papers in front of him at one end of the desk. "We will do a check on your background which will take a few days. You will go immediately to the infirmary for a medical and from there you will get whatever things you have and go to the special barracks set aside for the youths going to Israel. You will be notified of any events as they arise.

"Thank you for your cooperation here. You have made a difficult decision, a decision that will undoubtedly change your whole life. This is an important opportunity, an important first step. I wish you G-d Bless."

After that it was all paperwork and the medical. The war had made checking our backgrounds very difficult if not impossible. We were considered orphans and refugees, so processing could be quite quick. I was in my new bunker before the evening meal.

That night, the first night that many of the youths who had signed up to go to Palestine were together as a group, a discussion broke out among the former camp inmates. We were all under eighteen and we were very excited. Few of us actually knew very much about Palestine, although many of us had heard stories about the Zionist groups and we all knew something about the Jewish Agency. None of us had been given the time to think very much about what we were doing. We were running on sheer emotion, although there were a few moderate voices.

A tall, lanky boy expressed the common view. "We're pioneers. We're going to build a new country with our bare hands. We're going to create nothing short of a miracle."

We all looked pretty much the same. Our hair, which had been shaved, was slowly growing in so there was stubble. We were all very thin, although some boys were beginning to fill out a bit. What differentiated us mostly was our bone structure. Another boy responded. "Do you think this job is going to be easy? We have to fight the British and we have to deal with the Arabs. Do you think we can just walk into someone else's land and call it our own?"

The first boy shot back with certainty, "There will be enormous resistance, but if we are persistent and strong we will succeed. We must hold tight to the given idea that we will succeed."

Another boy leapt in to the conversation. "The State of Israel will emerge like a flower from the desert."

Still another said, "We will win with peace and with right on our side. We will pray every day and G-d will deliver the land to us."

Another speaker made a plea. "I am not a fighter by nature. I want to farm and live a peaceful life. If I have to fight for my homeland I will fight, but I'm not a fighter by nature. I'm not going to Palestine to make war. I'm going to make fields and groves of orange trees."

The first boy countered. "How can you say you are not a fighter? You survived the camps, didn't you? You didn't die in them. That indicates a desire to live, and in these camps you have to fight to survive."

"But I didn't have to kill to survive. I left that to the kappos.", the other pointed out. The two of them were becoming less friendly.

"Look! We know from Jewish history that some are meant to fight and others are meant to study and pray. It takes both types to maintain a civilization. You will pray. I will fight. That is the way it normally is. But when it comes to establishing the State of Israel, you will fight and pray because we are going to need every hand we have."

"I know that's true.", his counterpart said. "I'm just saying that I'm not going to Israel with the intention of committing violence. I am going with the intention of being a farmer and claiming that which is mine."

"In Israel every man and woman will be a soldier. Maybe they will be farmers first and soldiers second, but they will be a soldier."

A new voice was heard, a boy with a sweet face and blue eyes. It was Dov, the fellow I had talked to earlier. He drew attention because he had a strong, steady voice. "You are wrong. In Israel we will be Jews first and everything else second. We believe in peace, that's what being a Jew means. We will believe in peace, most of us, until the final moment that it flickers and fails. Then we will fight when we have to. We will be soldiers reluctantly and at the last. We will not do anything to offend G-d."

Someone else spoke up. "You think G-d cares? How can you think he cares after this war?"

The blue-eyed boy responded, "Many are dead but we are alive. There is purpose in this even though we don't know it. I believe we will make a State in Israel, but I believe that it will be G-d's hand that guides us, not our desire to make war."

The final voice expressed my own feelings quite closely. I left the barracks at that moment and went outside. I stood by the door, in the cool night, and breathed deeply. Something was happening. I don't deny that it was hope, but it was also something even stronger. Being able to come and go. Wearing clean clothes. Not smelling horrible and being covered with lice. I was experiencing something I never thought I would experience again. It was freedom, the ability to live decently and even make life altering decisions. I had my freedom back again. Freedom to pray. Despite myself, something happened that had not happened in all this time. Tears welled up in my eyes and I started to cry. Soon, there were great sobs but they didn't last long. After, I felt purged. I wiped my face and I smiled. Life had come back to claim me. I felt like a survivor.

A short time later I experienced a similar moment. I was on the boat heading toward Haifa with a living cargo of 250 Jewish youths. The sense of this voyage was both exhilarating and serious. We all knew this was a journey that would condition the rest of our lives, so the mood was restrained. For the brief voyage most of us kept to the makeshift cabin hung with hammocks that had been created for us out of what had previously been the hold of this freighter. It had been purchased for this trip by the Jewish Agency who had also taken care of our passports and other papers. It was not an easy task to get the vote, visas, provisions etc since nobody really rushed to help the Jews at this time. An agent from the Jewish Agency was on the boat which was alive with the energy of 250 teenage boys. The boat was crowded but the agent tried to keep us busy singing Israeli songs and telling stories about Israel. Everyone was excited and joyful, especially so since the agent brought with him not only a record player with recordings of all kinds of Israeli music but also a small ensemble of Israeli youths, boys and girls whose purpose was to help enrapture the young people on the boat. These healthy and outgoing teenagers mingled with the larger group answering questions and sharing stories about their experiences and Israeli history.

On the first night out we had a kind of 'pep rally' to introduce us to the pleasures we would encounter when we reached Israel. First, we listened to recorded music, both folk and inspirational. Then the young Israelis got up and danced a number of folk dances accompanied by their own musical instruments eventually organizing us into little groups and making us dance. If someone had suggested only a few months before that we would be on a ship headed to Palestine dancing with other boys and girls at this time we would have scoffed. But here we were, with music and dance and food and a clear purpose. Despite my sombre mood and darker thoughts I found myself swept up in the happiness of the event.

After we were exhausted by the dancing, laughing and breathing hard, they asked us to sit down again and listen. We all brought our seats into a large circle and surrounded the Israeli youths. The emissary said that now was the time for us to ask questions. Slowly we began to query the youths, with simple questions at first and then more probing.

"Will we live in the desert?" one of us wanted to know.

The youths laughed. "I suppose most of you think that Israel is one big desert." An Israeli girl answered. "We have a saying, 'The deserts will bloom". You will live on a kibbutz which is agricultural. You will irrigate the land and plant many trees. You will be very creative and hard working and you will soon see the desert turned into beautiful fields and orchards."

"What will it be like on a kibbutz?" another one of us asked.

"A kibbutz is a special community created to give you the best of life. You will live and work with other Jews, making a society based on equality and justice."

Other questions were met with similar answers of glowing accounts. By the end of the evening I knew a great deal more than I had before. But I was not satisfied. What I had heard was largely propaganda to make us happy, but I knew the truth, for me at least, would be less simple. I was going to Israel to build a nation. I knew that would not be easy. I did not think singing songs and dancing would convince the British to let go of Palestine. I did not think farms in the desert, no matter how politically advanced, would compel the Arabs to give up their lands. I was thinking of Miriam all of the time we were dancing. I had not forgotten her even now. How I longed to be dancing with her, going to Palestine with her. It was not so much that I was lonely, it was more a case of having lost someone who I could never replace.

It was evening, our second day out. Most of the boys were in the hold singing patriotic songs. A few were on deck but they were scattered in small groups around the other side of the ship. I was standing alone by the rail on the deck and looking down at the rushing water. The sky was clear and there was a bright quarter moon hung in the sky. I felt moved. The sea air, the rushing water, the romantic sky. I bowed my head, which seemed a natural thing to do. Then I did something I had not done in several years. I started to pray.

I prayed in Hebrew and I prayed only for myself. I did not say known prayers or any Psalms. This was the first moment in a string of unspeakably horrific moments that I was not angry at G-d. The world was beautiful right here, and I was heading toward a new life. Perhaps I could put the old one behind me. It was a meaningful moment for me. I said:

"Terrible things happened here on Earth, L-rd. War, murder, genocide and perhaps worse. Whether Your hand was in it or not I don't know. Terrible things happen in the Torah also, but always there is a reason and always there is an end. I have survived, somehow, every attempt to kill me. Perhaps your hand is in that too? Really, I don't know. Here I am alive and heading toward Palestine. I still believe in You and even, perhaps, feel that I know you a little better.

"The past is done, now I am heading to Palestine. I have to say some things to you now so that you know that I know what they mean. I was a child when the war started. Now I am the next best thing to a man.

"My father, my mother, by brothers and sisters went to their deaths innocently. Also Miriam, who I miss very much. They had committed no crime except to be Jewish and I am not ashamed of their deaths because I know that they were noble. I will not let my people be persecuted again. You know me here, I am not a violent man. I love peace, the family, faith, but I will not stand by and let blind aggression destroy Jews any more. I swear that I will fight back, with real and honest weapons to preserve my people. I will fight to create a State of Israel because that is what I believe we must do to survive. I believe, above all else, those who died did so in a cause of freedom, that You have brought me here to this ship in this night to create a place where Jews can live as you meant them to. I believe I am doing Thy Will. I pray that I am right and that if I am wrong You will show me another way.

"We must establish a homeland. You will show us the way. I have no desires but to do Thy will, to possibly know Thy will and to live the life you would create for me. I know you are there. I want to serve you. Make me Your servant. I have no other desire. L-rd, help us to build a homeland in Israel."

Two days later we approached Haifa. It was mid-afternoon when we could finally see the shape of the buildings on the coastline. I was transfixed. My emotions were so aroused that I could only identify them as an intense excitement borne from elation. For me, it was as if this ship had transported us to paradise and what I perceived was the firmament itself. I was struck by memories of being very young in the study house at the *Yeshiva*. This arrival in Palestine meant more to me than I could have imagined, because it challenged the terrible humiliation and pain of the camps by its very promise and hope. A homeland for the Jews meant freedom to me, and freedom meant life itself. All of this was stirring in me as we came into the port.

There was a surprise waiting for us at the dock, something no one had anticipated. We were, apparently, the first boatload of survivors to land legally in Palestine, and the incredible fact that we were also youths and orphans turned out to be a heady combination. The Jewish Agency had gone all out to greet us with as much pomp and pageantry as possible. Waiting at dockside was a welcoming crowd of about 10,000 well-wishers drawn from the local communities. Dov was standing next to me. "Do you feel like a hero?" he asked me lightly.

I laughed with good humour but also abashedly. "No. Not at all. I feel hurt and broken."

"I think some part of building a country must be putting on a good show." Dov said.

I chuckled and looked out over the water. "'Come to Israel and join the party!"

Dov laughed. "No one ever said it was an easy life here. We must represent a new beginning for Israelis. The Holocaust is over. The survivors are coming to help establish a nation. It's important to celebrate happy occasions, like the Sabbath and Yom Kippur. So we seem special today. Tomorrow it will be forgotten and w e will be a part of the crowd."

There were banners welcoming us and there was a brass band playing Zionist and Israeli songs. It was very colourful and extremely lively. Music. Cheers. Flags waving. It was totally unexpected but at the same time extremely welcome.

Even so, as looked at this celebration from the deck of this makeshift liner I was not moved to feel flattered. I had learned humility in the camps and I was not about to loose the memory of murder and hatred at the first sign of celebration. With that firmly in mind there was still something important to this dockside spectacle. We were welcome not only because we were the first boatload of Holocaust survivors to arrive in Israel but because we were all so young. Israel cried out for young people who could take up leadership positions sometime in the future. We represented the promise of good luck to people who foresaw a ferocious struggle ahead. What I saw was the creation of a moment that I would probably never forget. It was the seed of a nation that would inevitably prevail. I saw a demonstration of hope for a future.

As we came down the gangplank to dry land the band played the Hatikva. I was towards the end of the line of 250 youths disembarking from the ship. It was a slow moving group and my anticipation of touching holy ground grew as it came closer. Finally, after what seemed to be a long time, I came to the last step before touching soil. I set foot upon what I believed would be the future State of Israel. Without thought, without artifice I fell to my knees. I would never be at this point in time again. I bent forward and kissed the ground.

For a moment, I was surrounded by silence in the middle of a great desert. There were no well-wishers, there was no brass band, there were no youths and there was no ship. Just me, my relationship to infinity and G-d. and this sacred earth. This only lasted an instant but it would remain with me for my entire life. I was a new person in a new homeland. When the vision vanished I heard the cheers of the crowd. Reality had caught up with me. Someone laughed and gave me an orange. Someone else reached out and put a skullcap on my head. I confess it felt unbelievable wonderful. At that point in time not only had all my dreams come true, but all the potential for my future dreams as well. I couldn't have been happier or more blessed. I thought of Miriam. How I wished we were together.

David Ben Gurion, the head of the Jewish Agency, led the celebration. He was a mesmerizing speaker and he took this opportunity to tell us all about our destiny. "You young people are the future of Israel. Having survived the worst atrocities imaginable you have made your way here to Israel. Never again will Jews live in a 'galut'; a place in which they are not welcome. You represent the potency of the Jewish people, the resilience and the promise. You are the generation who will bear the pain but never without purpose, never without meaning, never without just cause. You are our soldiers in the army of righteousness. You are truly are children of great worth and you are exceptionally welcome."

There was a reception later at a ballroom where we were presented with proper clothing including khakis and shoes which we all put on immediately. In the temporary structure built just for the purpose dignitaries and guests gathered. The agency brought in a marching band who prayed Hebrew nationalistic songs. The very top people of the Jewish Agency, including Ben Gourion and other founders, the leaders of various Kibbutz and 'Halotzim', meaning the pioneers, were present.

There was an enormous amount of excitement and hurried activity, all on a scale I had never before been exposed to. We were hastily arranged into rows at one end of the large space. I didn't know what was going on, but the massive gloom that had accompanied me for two years mostly fell away, if only entirely for the moment. Dov and I were next to each other and we were both smiling very broadly. "Do you know what a movie star is?" he said.

"I think so."

"Well! Get ready to be famous!"

All of our 250 survivors marched past the stands where the dignitaries were seated to the Hymn of the Haganah and the Pal Mach. Cheers rose up in the audience when this march happened. We waved broadly as we marched. I must confess. I had never been happy in this way before in my life. I had never in my life been paid this much attention. What kept my spirits in check was a constant ache. Miriam was not here. I wanted her here so badly. The cheers were so loud. I was nearly moved to tears, so compelling was my joy in the moment and my loss from the past.

We were finally, after the excitement of the march, settled in chairs facing the stand. There are speakers from each political party: the Herot on the Right, which I leaned had been established by Jabotinsky; the Betar; the religious party, represented by a Rabbi, called the Mizraheh and the Aguda,;on the left the Brodr and Shomer Hatzair. Also the Mapai, the main party, left of centre led by David Ben Gurion, who gave a second speech especially welcoming us to the life of the kibbutz and encouraging our participation in the full political and cultural life of the land. He ended his speech with these words:

"Now you are Israelis. You must not look back on persecution and pain. You must look forward to the joy of building a nation and the hard work of establishing a future. You live in a democracy. You are Jews and you have rights that are positive and real. Participate in everything you can…farming, collective work, politics. You are invited to examine the political and social process and join in as seems fit. You are going to be an essential part of our life from now on. God bless you and make you strong. God bless Israel."

When the speeches had ended we were led to an area at the back of the ballroom to enjoy some food. Since it was just after the war there were shortages of some things, but the Jewish Agency set up a table for us with sandwiches and fruit. There were signs saying "This is the fruit/vegetable of the land of milk and honey". There was actually milk and honey on the table to represent that this is a holy land.

When the meal was finished a large number of youths we brought to the area. Even though we were now dressed very much alike, there were obvious differences. These young people were tanned and healthy, vibrant and energetic. Our group was more pale, serious and awkward. You have to see it to really understand it; what prolonged starvation, beatings, the murder of your family and friends can do to you. It's not only physical. It takes a while to recover and I don't think any of us had fully recovered yet.

The Israeli youths were very outgoing and friendly. They circulated talking to all of us in small groups or individually. I hung back a little, listening to conversations from the sidelines and not being too vocal. It wasn't that I was shy. It was that I so wanted to observe at this time. And it was something else. I missed Miriam. She had become an invisible companion to me for a long time and I experienced a hollow feeling sometimes without her.

As I was standing at the rear of a group that was talking about living on a kibbutz, a dark haired girl dressed in khakis and a light shirt approached me. "Are you enjoying the day?", she asked.

"Oh yes! Its very wonderful. It's all so massive! Leaving Europe only three days ago. Arriving here in the Holy Land. And now, this celebration! Tell me. Is everyday so exciting here?"

She laughed. "Its pretty exciting. Life on a kibbutz is full of adventure and surprises. You always have things to do. You belong to a group You always have friends."

"It seems very political. Is that so?" I asked carefully, knowing it might be a sensitive question.

She smiled simply. "Well, we're establishing a nation in the middle of two antagonistic powers. Politics is very important and extremely real and immediate."

At this point in time something unusual was happening to me. I was loosing inhibitions. My natural disposition was contemplative but oriented to action at the same time. Now, I felt very much in control of my appearance. I felt strong but not aggressive. I was able to ask probing questions.

"How do you go about building a nation in a land occupied by two armies?" I asked.

"You find out from others what the options are a join in. You don't try to do it all on your own."

I laughed. "What makes you think I would do anything on my own? What could I possibly do?"

She looked at the ground. "I'm sure you wouldn't do anything on your own." She looked up and smiled. She had an impish smile and simple good looks. She was thin and her clothes actually flattered her figure as much as that was possible. She looked about 16.

"My name is Avrum. What's yours?"

"Orly." She said.

"Thank you for the advice. I do know that I need it."

"Where are you from?" Orly asked.

"A little place in Hungry."

"My grandparents lived in Hungary." She said excitedly.

"Really? Maybe they knew my grandparents?"

"That would be an incredible coincidence. But possibly we can discuss it further."

"How so?" I asked.

"I live on the Dafna Kibbutz, the same one you are going to." There was a trace of anticipation in her eye.

"I look forward to that. Maybe you can be my political guide?" I suggested.

"Oh, yes!" she laughed. "I'm an inspired teacher."

After Orly left things wrapped up quite quickly. Without waiting for nightfall, we were placed on busses headed for the Dafna Kibbutz where we were going to live. During the two hour ride I gazed out the window with intent. The land was flat. The air was dry. My emotions started to settle down. I felt different than I had before. I felt less agitated, less anxious, less perplexed. There was something new in my being that was working itself through my system. I was home. For the very first time in my life I felt a sense of place. It was unmistakable. I was home.

CHAPTER 15
The Firelight

When our busses arrived at the kibbutz it was dark, but the buildings surrounding the enclave of the farm were lit up like a menorah. As we pulled in we could see it; acres of fields strung with lights for almost as far as the eye could see. The structures we could see from the bus were simple frame buildings, all of them painted white. The largest was in the centre of a large square. As we descended the busses about two dozen people, mostly young, thronged around to greet us. They were very excited but very polite and as we met each one there was a kiss or a handshake. This was a more intimate welcome than we had enjoyed at the harbour in Haifa. These people were going to be our extended family. They greeted us like long lost journeymen coming home.

We were taken to the large building immediately after leaving the busses and discovered that it was the dining hall. Inside it was lit with bright lights. There were many long tables and chairs in rows, but at the back of one end there were a series of tables spread with all kinds of fruits and vegetables prepared to eat. There were oranges, apples, melons and peaches. There were cucumbers and cooked squash, tomatoes and potato salads, hummus and tahina. There were flatbreads and loaves of bread. It was all produce of the kibbutz laid out for our arrival both as a lesson and as a meal. We descended cautiously on this feast largely for its own sake. Everything looked so delicious we had to give it our best.

About an hour after we arrived, when we had easily finished our meal, we were called outside by our hosts. We were led a short distance down a wide path. As we walked, we could hear voices and music from the distance, and as we drew close we could see the source. A huge bonfire was crackling in the centre of a large clearing, and around it there were musicians playing and many people dancing. As we came into view people opened up their circle. They took us by the hand and led us into the midst of the dancers. It was magic and it was joy. It took a few moments to understand and to warm up to something that was, after all, so alien to us. I escaped from the throng to stand a little on the sidelines, as did some of the others. Beside me was Dov, whose eyes were wide and excited.

"Is this all real?" he asked, laughing. "Has God really answered my prayers?"

"I don't know what to say." I responded. "Is it possible that the camps were a dream and that we've finally reached reality."

A lithe figure came out of the shadows like a ghost. She ran before me, came to within a hairsbreadth of me, and took my hand. She was laughing with good humour and excitement. "You must come! Dance! This is your day! You must grab it!"

It was Orly, the girl I had met at the affair in Haifa. She pulled on my arm and I pulled her back. I was not going to be led quite so easily. It was still hard for me to throw my heart into celebrating, not only because it did not come naturally to me but also because I was less than 24 hours off of a boat from Europe. The horror of the camps, and even what came before, had not gone yet. I was a *Yeshiva* boy, from a poverty struck home.

BAR KOCHBA

It was hard to change in a moment and the truth was that I didn't want to forget. Still, with all the events of the day, with the greetings and good wishes of so many people, with the dancing and this hypnotic, blazing fire, I was more willing to change.

Orly tugged gently on my arm. "You are now in Palestine. Come on, I'll teach you how to dance!" I smiled wryly. I remembered Miriam and I knew she would want this for me. "I know how to dance." I said. "Teach me how love it."

And I danced. At the end of that day, by the light of the fire, in the heart of Israel I danced. I danced for all that had been and I danced for what would come. I danced in a circle with all the rest, singing, shouting. We were all Jews and we were all here. The future seemed to beckon in the firelight.

We were awakened at 5 o'clock in the morning. After a lingering breakfast we were taken on a tour of the kibbutz. It was a world of wonders. We saw the barns with row upon row of dairy cattle. We saw the shed where equipment was repaired. There were several hundred chickens in wire coops. We wandered through seemingly endless fields of grain and corn and other crops.

Where the fields ended, the orchards began. Acres of orange and grapefruit trees, all in neat rows. There were groves of olive trees as well as date trees. We reached the vineyards and the massive sheds where wine was made and bottled for sale. We had gone in a very wide circle and soon returned back at the village. We were shown the workshops where clothes were made and shoes repaired.

All of this impressed me greatly. I couldn't help comparing it to the village I had grown up in back home. The scale here was completely different, as was the way of life. Here, everything was done in a spirit of co-operation and fellowship. In Hungary there had been suspicion and hatred. In Hungary, we lived in a tiny, crowded shelter which was barely a refuge from an unhappy life. Here, there was joy and pride and seemingly endless space. Here we were all Jews sharing a dream of the future. I was massively impressed, and I determined that I would do everything in my power to work towards the realization of this dream, a dream that was not merely physical or material but spiritual as well.

We reached the village about an hour before lunch and were given time to wander. Dov and I began to explore the site. There were more buildings than initially appeared. At one edge of the compound there was a long, low series of buildings. We could hear something unmistakable; the sound of children. We looked at each other.

"Children!" Dov said "That's what we missed. Children!"

"I didn't think there would be children here, but of course, that must be so."

We followed the noise, turned a corner around a small building and saw them. Several dozen children playing in a playground. There were several adults minding them. We approached the area and one of the women came to join us. She was full figured, almost plush, and she wore the khaki pants and shirt that were most common.

"You are from the orphans, right" she said warmly. Dov and I both nodded. "Are you being treated well?" Her voice was inquisitive but not prying.

Dov answered. "If we were treated any better we would float up in the air. I'm so full of delicious food, and lunch is in half an hour."

She laughed. "You are a very special group! Soon enough you will become one of us. My name is Illana."

We nodded and told her our names. Dov pointed to the children. "Are these the children of families in the Kibbutz?"

The young woman responded. "Yes, they are all children of our members. The older children are over there in the school." She pointed at a building down the way. "The teenaged children go to school there too, but they also work on the kibbutz." She indicated a structure just behind the school. "That's the dormitory where they stay."

Dov and I looked at each other. "A dormitory? Don't they stay with their parents?"

Illana shook her head. "The children live together in a dormitory. Each group works and plays together. We believe that children should be independent but related to the community's social life."

I was a bit confused. "What about the parents?" I asked. "Don't they want to raise their children themselves?"

Illana smiled simply. "The parents see their children often, at least once a day. But the attachment is also to the group."

Dov looked uncomfortable with this idea. "Do they grow up well adjusted?" he asked.

Illana nodded her head. "Our experience is that as long as they get plenty of love, they do very well. I can tell you first hand, because I am one of them! I grew up on this kibbutz. And my daughter is over there, playing."

I was struck dumb, because this was something entirely new to me. "Is this in the Torah?", I asked.

Illana looked a little shocked. "I don't know." She said. "No one has ever asked me that before. Is it important?"

It was my turn to smile. "They say everything is in the Torah, Illana. And what isn't, we don't need to know."

She laughed lightly. "My daughter will grow up knowing not only that her parents love her very much, but also that she is a part of a community. Who's to say that isn't a better way to grow up, or that it isn't blessed."

I looked over at her little girl playing in the playground. She looked happy. "I guess if you are building a new world there are going to be great changes. Thanks for enlightening me."

Dov and I moved on. He had a large grin on his face. "Happy?" I asked. He looked at me with a glow all about his face.

"This is heaven to me." He said.

I couldn't help but smile too. "You don't miss Europe any more?"

He let out a groan. "Europe is Europe." He said wryly. "Can you call the war, the Holocaust, civilization? How did you live in Europe before the war? Was it beautiful?"

"We were a family of nine living on nothing at all in one room. I was always hungry even before the camps."

Dov grimaced. "I was a little better off. I lived in Krakow and we had enough to eat. But even then the persecution was terrible. When the Germans arrived we suffered even more pain. It was almost impossible to live a decent life."

I agreed. "It's only our first few days. It will become common before too long. But this place is truly remarkable. It's an oasis, literally, in the desert. "

Dov raised his arms over his head and shook his fists with joy. "This is the new reality, Avrum! Everybody working together for the common good, for a common goal."

We were eighteen years old and we were prone to excitement. I raised my arms also and shouted at the sky, "Blessed art Thou, who has created the kibbutz in the land of Israel!"

We laughed with pleasure and kicked the dirt beneath our feet. "Can I tell you something, Dov?" I said ruefully.

"Of course!" he replied.

"I like the kibbutz very much. I'm not sure I really understand it yet. But, to tell the truth, I don't really want to be a farmer."

Dov gently answered. "You don't have to be a farmer, Avrum. Not every Jew wants to be a farmer. But the kibbutz is a model for Israeli society. The common good, the forward looking social structure. Even the new morality?

"What is the new morality?" I asked.

"Simple!" Dov responded. "Love your fellow like yourself."

I looked at him with a clear eye. "This may be so, but we are not Israel yet. Perhaps our neighbour doesn't perfectly love us back?."

For the first month we didn't work like others in the Kibbutz. Instead of working most of the day we had Hebrew classes and classes in the history of Zionism and the holy land. It was a wonderful time for all of us, enjoying the best that the kibbutz had to offer without being completely drained. I learned a great deal during our classes, mostly this: The land we were living on was not Israel. It belonged to the British and the Palestinians. Progress in achieving the State of Israel was slow and ineffective. I was numb with the knowledge of this condition. We were not so much, as people were fond of saying, 'children of the dream'. We were children of hope and delusion. Although I was young I knew that the kibbutz itself, perfect as it was in so many ways, had to be protected. I longed for a door to open that could lead me to an answer to this knowledge.

Though our days we filled with learning and good feelings, our nights were mostly spent by the bonfire, singing and dancing until late. Everyone who was single lived in dormitories, while the married couples lived in similar structures but with separate apartments. Everyone ate together in the dining hall. After dinner there were always meetings to attend. The kibbutz was based upon socialist principals. Everyone who lived here had the same, essentially. There were no rich and poor people. The philosophy was to serve the community, which was democratic. Consequently, there were meetings to keep the kibbutz running all the time, although the tasks were all broken up into committees. We attended a few meetings just to be exposed to them, but more often we were free to join with other young people like ourselves.

I was sitting by the bonfire one night in the first week we arrived when Orly, the girl I had met in Haifa and again on my first night here, came and stood before me.

"Are you getting used to things?" she asked gingerly.

I smiled up at her. "I'm completely numb!" I said.

She displayed a mock frown. "Well that's not very good. It means you can't feel anything!"

I laughed quietly. "I mean emotionally numb. I'm so excited I don't know exactly what to think."

She sat down beside me. "Think about what could be. Think about how you can play a part."

"That's good. I definitely want to play a part. I think there are many different parts that could be played. Can I play them all?"

She gently punched my arm. "Not all at the same time! Maybe in sequence?"

I was not really used to touching a girl, but impulsively I softly punched her arm back. "I want to be a Jew first and foremost. I think in some ways that is what this is all about." At that moment something broke inside of me. I thought of Miriam. I felt a longing for her that was almost desperate but somehow for something unattainable. I smiled at the girl beside me. I felt remorse for Miriam, but definitely interest in Orly at the same time. She was lithe and tanned. Her face was active, her eyes dark and bright. She was not Miriam, and Miriam had been like no other could ever be.

Secretly, I had been living a fantasy life with Miriam while in the camps. I had toyed, in my imagination, with every possible event we could have shared together. I had imagined walking out of that train car into a married life. Now, that act of imagination was competing with the reality of a new life, a renewed life. Miriam would always be a part of me, I knew that for a fact. But reality also needed a chance. It hurt me to admit that, but it was true.

"Hey Avrum! Where did you go? I was sitting right beside you but you went somewhere else!"

I apologized. "No, no. I'm here and I want to talk with you. What do you do here on the kibbutz?"

We were sitting on a stone shelf. She hugged her legs giving her a cozy look in the light of the flickering flames. "I work in the garage, learning to fix machinery."

"That's wonderful!" I almost shouted. "What made you choose that?"

She hugged her legs even more. "I've always loved mechanical things. When it came time for me to take my place I tried a few jobs and eventually felt most happy with the machines. A committee had to vote on it. When I approached them I was so nervous! But they liked the idea. It was not only sensible but also a philosophical choice. A female mechanic seemed perfect, and here I am."

"That's nice." I said. "Everyone gets a good deal." I felt awkward. I didn't know what I wanted to do. My most serious work had been selling on the black market.

Orly said. "Why don't you like to dance, Avrum?"

"Oh!" I replied. "I'm just not used to it."

She stood up and pulled me by the arm. "Come on and dance!" she said. "Don't be a humbug! Let yourself go a little bit!"

I let her pull me up. "Why not? But if I trip up, don't blame me! I got pulled into it."

Orly became a regular companion. We met casually a few times at the bonfire nights and then we started meeting purposefully. I thought of her as a good friend. Then, one night after we had been seeing each other for several weeks it changed. She had me dancing a lot and I did enjoy it. I confess that even though I liked it I felt it was frivolous; this was likely a holdover from my *Yeshiva* days. After getting exhausted we sat down on the edge of light cast by the fire.

"You've come a long way!" she said breathlessly.

"Many miles!" I joked.

She took my hand. "Oh, Avrum! Don't you think we're good together?"

I was abashed by the sudden intimacy. "Well, yes. We have fun."

"No. I mean good together as people." She had never been this kind of serious.

"I think you're wonderful!" I intoned. "You're beautiful, you're strong and you're intelligent."

"I mean, do you feel something."

"Yes. Definitely friendship."

She laughed haltingly. "You foolish man! Something even more than friendship."

At this point I was catching on and I began to pull her leg. "You mean there's something more than friendship?"

We were starting to get somewhere. "Yes, you social idiot!"

I was teasing her now. "You mean like brother and sister?"

Then she jumped on me raining down soft blows with her flailing arms. "I mean like more than sister and brother!" she said, and in a moment she was kissing my mouth and hitting me gently at the same time until I kissed back and it was all turned into an embrace. "I want you for my love partner." She whispered.

I didn't consider the consequences of this, only the rewards. "Where do I sign?" I said. She took me by the arm and led me to the dark fields. That night was so beautiful I can never forget it. We were more than friends after that. We spent a lot of time together. Even so, it was clear that we were not a couple. Our relationship was physical, but it lacked a romantic commitment. It was clear neither of us wanted that, and eventually the physical part did end although we remained close.

Although the first month on the kibbutz was a very happy time for me, I was unsettled. I liked the kibbutz but I was restless already. I knew I wanted to do something to make Israel live and the kibbutz was too pastoral and even idyllic. It was definitely worth protecting, but I believed that more directed attacks had to be made on the British and Arab resistance. I was consumed by a fire that was called Israel and it burned in me all the time.

Dov and I were walking through the kibbutz one day about a month after we arrived. He broached a subject that I thought was not at all evident.

"You're restless, aren't you Avrum? You don't want to stay on the kibbutz."

I replied evasively. "Is there anything outside of the kibbutz?" I asked.

"Yes. There are many possibilities. People are coming to talk to the survivors soon."

"A lot of talk I imagine."

"Maybe. But what do you want?"

I looked at him blankly. "I want the passion of Israel to fuel my deeds. I want the fire of those deeds to ignite the whole of this land in the spirit of victory."

Dov looked doubtfully at me. "Avrum, you're 18 years old. Take a little time."

"These years have been nothing but a lesson. Didn't the war teach you anything?"

Dov looked down at the ground. "Yes. To hate war and to always be against it. To be against violence and persecution of any kind."

I smiled cheerfully at my friend. "You are wonderful! You come through the camps with a gentle knowing. You have peace in your heart, but I have fire in my veins and I must act."

"Israel cannot be built upon the bones of others. We will win it through persistence and peace. God will give us the land. We can't wrestle it from his grip and try to take it ourselves."

I differed strongly, but restrained me emotions to make my point. "God will not deliver anything to us unless we fight for it ourselves. Even in the Torah we had to fight for the land of milk and honey, shed our blood to achieve it. We were punished for refusing to do that at first. I'm not saying your way is wrong, Dov. We Jews need both heart and soul, those who pray and those who act. Equally, both are necessary and important."

Dov looked darkly at my eyes. "I don't like violence, Avrum. I've had too much of it. I know your heart is full of love and meaning. We are both warriors, you of action and me of peace. We are all Jews. Nothing can go wrong."

People came to the camp to talk to us over the next few weeks from the different political factions. I went to hear every speaker. The left were too idealistic. The right were to materialistic. The centre was too inactive. The Haganah, the informal 'standing army' made sense, and they were the most interesting group to me until I heard from the last group. There was no schedule for them. One night, news was spread by word of mouth that a secret group were in the kibbutz. We should go to the dining hall right away to hear them. I went with several other boys, through a guard who checked us out as we entered. There were other guards around the hall. They all had guns. The hall filled slowly. When it was filled a man came out from the shadows of a doorway. Someone told me his name was Menachim Begin. Someone else said his group was called the 'Irgun'. He waited a moment for quiet, then he spoke in a clear but husky voice.

"You young men and women have something very rare for the Jewish people. Its something incredible and its something deep and meaningful. Its something you can fight for and its something you must win. You are the first generation in 2000 years to know that you can see the land of Israel open like a flower in the desert of Sinai. You can see Jews from all over the world return to a homeland once again, a homeland made possible by unselfish devotion and untiring effort. You people specifically have the happy good fortune to be among the few who will open up a great frontier, one that had been promised for the Jews for two millennia. But I have one message for you that you must not forget: With Fire and Blood the holy Temple was destroyed and with fire and blood the holy Temple will be redeemed!'. We have to commit our bodies, our souls, our complete and entire will to the creation of the State of Israel! By all means possible! We must not hesitate and we must not weaken. We must act, intelligently and urgently!"

"Why are you so lucky? The delusion that the land of Israel would fall into our hands like fruit falling from a tree has reached an end. The Holocaust was a breaking point, but some of us knew even before this that the time had come to act. You have been forged from the fires of hatred and brutality into instruments of freedom and change. Here you are, without families, without parents, without possessions testifying to the case that only Jews will ever save or shelter other Jews. You testify to the fact that Eretz Yisroel is a reality, not just an abstract idea. What action will you take to protect and extend the reality? Will you fight? Will you commit yourselves accomplishing this end, or will you choose to allow fate to take a turn at determining Israel's destiny without a push from its children?

"History has shown that without struggle freedom never comes. You must fight for what you believe in. There are British interests here; they must be met. There are Arab interests here. They must be dealt with. Without hate or rancour we must ceaselessly approach our goal, knowing that it alone is unchanging and absolute. Our individual and collective acts must be exclusively directed to that goal. We will create the State of Israel right here and right now. Nothing short of this approach will bring freedom.

"Without an absolute will our people will seem weak. Look at the actions of the brave fighters in the ghetto at Warsaw. They knew that resistance was the honest way to go. Yes, they perished, but they died with purpose and with glory and they gave the gift of hope to us all. Without establishing the State of Israel the Jewish people will wilt like the flowers of an uprooted tree. You cannot win through discussion and you cannot win through negotiation. You can only win through strategic action and consistent effort. You can only win by taking up arms. Your actions must be utterly clear and entirely effective.

"The Jewish people are traditionally warriors. Let us be warriors again! You have the responsibility to rise up and make history. In your time the future for the entire Jewish people will be played out. This is no transient notion or passing phase. Will you sit by the border of commitment and look on as your brothers and sisters act? Or will you leap like heroes to the call of your very generation and take part? This is the individual challenge you young people face. Who will you join in this struggle? Will it be for Israel and the future, or will it be for the passive acceptance of the past? I urge you to choose action and the meaningful path of planned resistance. Hold the reality of your history high. Don't allow reality to pass you by."

Without waiting for applause he was gone in an instant. I stood in that hall in some shock. This man had revealed my deepest hope. There was a group that expressed what I felt, it appeared. I wandered out of the dining hall in a daze. I sat by the empty pit that was sometimes the bonfire we danced around. Now, the bonfire was inside of me. I burned with a restrained excitement. Something to live for! Something to die for! I knew there was a future. I would learn more about the Irgun, what they did and what they stood for. My will was strong and directed.

CHAPTER 16
The Promise

I didn't rush headlong into my search for information on the Irgun. There were several reasons for exercising restraint. First of all, they were an illegal, underground organization and asking questions might seem either reckless or stupid. Secondly, I didn't want to raise any suspicion about my intentions. I only knew about the organization what I heard from their leader at the speech. I had no idea how to contact them, but I knew that for me contacting them would be a matter of life or death.

Two days after the speech Dov and I were cleaning out a corner of the dairy barn. We volunteered for the job since both of us had a acquired a taste for physical work. It was early in the morning when we started and the sun rose shortly after we began. The light was rather dim at first, but after a while we could see the sun shine through the cracks in the metal walls of the barn. The sound of the cows as they shifted and mooed in the stalls and the odour of them in our noses made the experience a pleasant one. For me, growing up in a mostly pastoral setting it was somewhat nostalgic and made me think of a life that I had all but forgotten. We worked hard for an hour and half, then sat down on some stools to have a rest.

"You know something?" I said, though it was a bit unusual for me to start a casual conversation.

"What?", Dov replied.

"This reminds me of home." I said.

Dov was interested but non committal. "Did you look after the cow shed?"

I laughed. "We had a cow. One cow. It stayed in a room just behind the room we lived in. It was part of our house. Two rooms, one for our family of nine and one for the chickens and the cow. The house smelled something like this; not as strong but similar. Everyday I had to clean up after the cow."

"How wonderful for you." Dov said sarcastically, but he kept up the conversation. "We lived in an apartment. Just us, no livestock. The whole building was Jewish, which was very nice. This kibbutz is like heaven for me. It's so different to what I was used to, and after the camps…it just seems like heaven!"

"For me, not so much." I volunteered. "It's beautiful, but to tell you the truth I don't feel so useful. It's not that I don't like the work. It's that I want to do more to help make Israel a reality. I want to help make it happen."

Dov was a bit defensive. "How could you be doing more to make it happen than being here doing this? This is the soul of Israel, right here! This kibbutz is what will make Israel a country, if anything will."

The last thing I wanted to do was offend or alienate my best friend. Dov was the most important person to me in the kibbutz, and I steered clear of causing an argument. "You're right." I said, and I patted his back. "This kibbutz is the soul of Israel. And it is a piece of heaven. But there are other's for whom Israel is an ideal they oppose with passion, with guns and with power. They must be dealt with before this beautiful dream can become a reality."

Dov looked at me with concern. "Haven't you had enough violence in your life to know that brutality only creates more brutality?"

I responded with caution. "But haven't you also learned that oppression is only overturned by force, that it will never surrender without action?"

"Well, what kind of action do you mean? If you mean violent action, then I say no! In the end, it will only lead to more violence. Organized, persistent, intelligent resistance is much more effective."

"Yes." I relied steadily. "But organized, persistent, intelligent opposition is needed also. The war didn't end through happy thoughts, it ended when the allies forcefully defeated the enemy. The Germans didn't hand over the third Reich willingly. They fought right up to Berlin."

Dov was becoming a bit emotional. "This is not the same as Europe. It's not the same circumstances and its not the same situation. The British will hand over Israel to the Jews in time and the Arabs will integrate with us. That's the way it must be!"

I brought up the issue that was mostly on my mind. "You heard the man speak. Do you remember his words: 'By fire and blood was the temple taken from us, and by fire and blood it will be returned.'. We've waited 2000 years for Israel to be a reality."

Dov looked down. "You liked what the Irgun had to say, didn't you?"

My voice was steady and low. "They made some points."

"If you join them you are joining the extreme."

"Who said I was joining anybody?"

Dov smiled one of his wise and rueful smiles. "You will act on what you feel. I know you that well." He touched my shoulder and broke into a good natured grin. "Act upon that shovel like it was the answer to your prayers, and we'll be done this job in no time!"

I was happy Dov ended the conversation at that time and in that way. He was a kind and sincere person. "Right!" I said. We didn't say any more until the stall was clean.

When I was walking with Orly a day later the same conversation came up. Our hands were joined when we were far enough away from the buildings not to be seen, but that kind of thing was not common among youth. That night by the bonfire, when she took me to the dark fields, was not completely what it may have appeared. Sex between young people was not encouraged on the kibbutz, which had an implicit religious aspect despite its rather left leaning political approach. When we were in the fields that night we kissed a little, but mostly Orly talked about the Kibbutz, the people on it, the ideas it cherished and promoted. After that we saw quite a bit of each other but we didn't do a lot of kissing. Everybody would know and it wouldn't seem right. Although we were young we were expected to act responsibly.

On this day I was very absent minded, and Orly could tell there was something going on. The truth was that I could hear her speaking, I could see her lips moving, but I didn't hear a word. She let go of my hand, stopped in her tracks and faced me directly in the eye. "Would you like to hear me sing the 'hatikvah', or should I just continue talking to a wall?"

I replied in spirit. "Orly I'd love to hear you sing the national anthem but wouldn't you rather just hum a few bars?"

Orly was not impressed. "Avrum what's going on with you? There's something on your mind besides this kibbutz. Maybe the past, maybe the future, but you're not here."

It was true that when I was with Orly I was most often with Miriam as well. I couldn't forget her, and I didn't want to. I used to play a game of seeing her face, I would imagine different angles of it. Miriam was a person who represented freedom, beauty, innocence and true love for me. I went over the time we had together over and over again in my mind. Perhaps that's why I didn't take Orly as seriously as she expected. Although she was attractive and interesting she couldn't compete with my memories of Miriam.

"Do you think the kibbutz is the soul of Israel?" I asked soberly.

"Definitely." She replied.

"So do I" I was only partly lying. There was a moment's silence as we turned around and walked on. Eventually Orly spoke.

"You don't like the kibbutz, do you?" This was a simple question but it implied a great deal.

"I do like it a great deal."

Orly pressed further. "You like it a great deal, it is the soul of Israel, but the first chance you get you'll leave."

I absorbed the shock of this blunt statement and then spoke softly. "My deepest wish is to be a good Jew." I said. "Next comes everything else."

Orly wasn't moved. "Even so, you're heart's not here. I only hope it's in the right place. Be careful, Avrum. You can follow your heart but it can also play tricks on you. Every Jew knows that."

It was clear to me my intentions were more obvious than I would have liked. I couldn't stop thinking of the Irgun and of what Menachin Begin had said to us. All of my past life had been burned away in the camps. All that was left was that I was a Jew, which was itself a jeopardy at certain times, and that the safety of our people was utterly essential. I had no other identity because what Dov and Orly had said was true. After a number of weeks I still didn't feel that the kibbutz was the answer for me. My thinking and my feelings were so strongly drawn to action. Something inside of me demanded that I become a soldier. I had to risk my life in this struggle; anything else was meaningless.

I worried and lost sleep for the next few days, unsure of what to do while knowing in my heart and soul what I wanted. At the end of that period I felt I had to act. I decided to talk to the leader of the kibbutz, and I walked in to see him in his office. His secretary greeted me warmly although we had never met.

"You're a survivor, aren't you?" she said.

"Yes." I replied simply.

"Everything going well?"

"Yes. Very well, but I'd like to see Chiam Samovich." I felt very small at that moment. I wasn't sure that what I had to say was really important.

The secretary smiled genuinely. She was quite young, maybe in her mid-twenties. She was dressed in the standard Khakis but had a blue and white handkerchief tied around her neck. It was the only affectation of business, "He's busy right now. Can you come back in, say, 2 hours? I'll make an appointment for you."

I also smiled, to show that my intentions were friendly. "Sure." I said. "I'll come back."

It was always clear to me that I wasn't yet nineteen and that I appeared as a teenager. I didn't feel like that most of the time, and on the kibbutz it was never important. I felt older, more mature. Whatever fire of youthfulness I ever had had been burned out by extreme poverty before the camps and extreme suffering in the camps. My actual age didn't matter to me because, for one thing, I was in the process of being reborn although I didn't explicitly know it and for another thing I had already experienced the equivalent of two lifetimes and was in the process of beginning a third.

It was mid afternoon and, since we had not yet been assigned our own stations I had time to myself before the appointment. I didn't have a watch so I had to guess two hours. The kibbutz didn't really run by the clock although there was one on the wall of several of the buildings. Almost no one wore a watch because they really didn't want to be reminded of the time. The kibbutz was a hard working but abnormally happy place. People liked their work and engaged in it unselfconsciously and even with joy. There was an open atmosphere of dedicated harmony and an unusual sense of quiet harmony. While I was waiting for that two hours to pass I realized something that had not been obvious before, that the kibbutz was the immediate opposite to Buchenwald. Now, here at Dafna, there were people working together with joy and purpose whereas in the camp there was only slave labour and complete destructiveness. In Dafna, there was friendship and trust. In the camp there was pain and struggle. Dafna represented life, from the marvellous agriculture to the married couples and the children. The camps represented death, nothing more. I sat by the orchard, watching the workers go about their jobs, and I realized this. But I also realized that this was thought to be the 'soul of Israel'. In order for this mystery to thrive it had to be protected and in order to protected it urgently needed a State. This couple of moments of simple reflection acted as a catalyst for my deeper ideas. I knew for certain now that they were right.

When I went back to the kibbutz office Chiam's secretary smiled at me warmly. Her lips were red because she was wearing lipstick, a completely uncharacteristic kibbutz convention though somehow appropriate for her. "Avrum. Hello!" she said in a half amiable half businesslike way. "Just sit down for a minute." She went into the office for a minute and came back swiftly. A minute or two later Chiam Samovich came through his door. He was tall, over 6 feet, and dark, like most of the members of the

Kibbutz. He was ruggedly handsome with a strong nose and modest chin. What was unusual about him were his eyes, which were a translucent green. He put out his arm in greeting as though taking me by the shoulder even though I wasn't there.

"Avrum! Come in!" he said. I stood up next to him, I was just as tall, and the arm that had been hugging the invisible air rested firmly around my shoulder. We went into his office.

"Is everything alright?" he asked.

"Yes, but I wanted to talk to you." I wanted to appear firm.

"You have my full attention." He said.

So there would be no mistake about my seriousness I came to the point. "I want to leave the kibbutz."

Chiam paused for just a moment. "You're not happy with it?"

"I'm very happy. It's a beautiful place, but I want to do more for Israel." My naivety was apparent.

"You want to do more for Israel than live and work on a Kibbutz?" His face was bright but his eyes clouded just a little.

"That's right."

"How do you want to do this?"

"I don't know." I said, evading the question. "I want to do everything necessary to fight for Israel."

Chiam looked concerned. "Do you intend to do this alone off the kibbutz?"

"No." I didn't know how much of my desire to reveal. "I have to be a part of a group of people who also want to do whatever necessary to make the State of Israel a reality."

Chiam's concern deepened. "Even if that means doing things that are extreme and dangerous?"

"I think that without danger little progress is made. I believe you have to fight fire with fire."

The director frowned. "And blood with blood?"

I didn't answer. Chiam sat down on the corner of his desk, "You are a survivor, Avrum, and you probably know more about life and death, at your age, than I do. Probably more about violence too. I agree with you, in part. It will take all kinds of efforts to bring to reality the State of Israel."

"I believe that's true." I said.

"But you don't have to leave the kibbutz to find a cause. Every person in Palestine, especially Jews, needs a place to live and a livelihood. You want to find your friends. Wait, and before long they will find you."

This actually made sense to me. I was doing what I could to find the Irgun. Chiam Samovich would not lead me on, I sensed that very clearly.

Chiam said, "You don't have to leave the kibbutz right now. You are not only welcome here, Avrum, you are needed. In fact, I already know a little about you from some others. We have chosen a place for you for work."

I was uncharacteristically excited about this. "Can you tell me what it is?" I asked.

"Yes. We think you would be a valuable member of our security force. With 5000 people here surrounded by unfriendly elements we need full time security. The kibbutz is quite large physically and patrols are essential. Do you think that would be a good place for you?"

I thought it would be all right because it would give me time to think. "Yes." I said firmly but without revealing too much excitement. "That might be a good place for me."

We talked a little about details. Chiam asked me about my family as a means of kindness, and I left. I had gotten more than I expected, which made me satisfied. I learned something, too. I learned to trust the people who cared about you to do the best they can. People in authority can be wrong but trust has a place as well.

Over the next two weeks I did nothing more about the Irgun but yearn. It seemed unwise to mention anything about them to anyone on the kibbutz, even in the most indirect way, since I didn't wish to arouse suspicions. I understood that membership was not a matter for public knowledge, and I accepted Chiam's implication that I should wait. A few days after seeing him Shalom Belzen approached me in the dining hall. He was the head of the security team. He was pleasant but businesslike.

"Chiam has told me that you are interested in joining us in security. Is that so?" he asked in a somewhat formal tone.

"I'm interested in giving it a try."

His swarthy skin turned a shade darker as he questioned me further. "Have you ever used a rifle?"

"No, we didn't use them much in my town in Europe although, truthfully, I wish we had."

Shalom's eyes narrowed. "You think a gun will be useful here?"

I looked down. "The last thing I really want to do is shoot anyone. I believe in peaceful coexistence. My entire family were killed in the war; I would have done anything to save them, but I was 15 and we were not a violent family. We would never have thought of arming ourselves."

"And you regret that?" Shalom looked directly in the eyes. I responded in kind.

"The persecution of the Jews in Europe was an incredible catastrophe. Not only for the Jews but for the whole world. Sometimes I imagine how different it would have been if we had defended ourselves."

"Like the Warsaw Ghetto?" he asked darkly.

"Yes. Like the Warsaw Ghetto."

"Of course," he said, "there were no survivors"

I said softly, "Their courage survives and their deeds."

"Do you think the situation here is different?" Shalom was narrowing his approach.

"No. Not different. Except you are offering me a rifle, which I didn't have before. The fact that I don't want to use it does not eliminate the reality that I will if I must."

At this point Shalom defused the conversation. "We mostly patrol the boundary. Often there is no fence or physical boundary, we check around the edge of the fields and orchards. We patrol 24 hours a day, so some shifts run all night. Can you start tomorrow morning?"

I was decisive in response. "Sure. I'm reliable."

Shalom smiled kindly. "See you then." He said. He shook my hand briefly and walked away. I sat down. This was an exciting moment since I felt that I had been placed perfectly. I'm not proud of it, but I was excited that I would learn to use a gun. If I looked deeply enough into my soul I would have to confess that I was also excited that I might have a need to use it.

The first 10 days on security went by quickly. I was trained on using a rifle and a handgun which seemed, to my surprise, almost natural. I was a good shot with the rifle butt almost uncanny with the handgun. Within a few days I was on the perimeter with a partner. Then I was on my own.

It was wonderful to be on the beautiful earth of Israel, alone, walking with dedication and purpose with, I confess, a gun. This would have shocked me in Europe, but here it seemed to be natural. Before the war, when I was a *Yeshiva* boy, the idea of me standing to my full 6'2" in light clothing, in the warmth of the Mediterranean sun, strong and free protecting my people in Israel, would have been unthinkable. It had been three years since I had been in the death camps. It was amazing that this new reality, so completely different, so much the opposite, should have happened to me. On the third day out on my own the contrast was too much for me. I had to thank G-d. In the shade of an orange tree, at the outer edge of an orchard I fell to my knees and prayed. I thanked the almighty for making me a new man, perhaps a soldier, willing to die for the freedom of his people.

When I rose up from my knees there were two men beside me, dressed in casual suits. They were serious looking but even more than that they were clear and decisive in their words. "Avrum?" they asked.

"Yes." I replied with a question in my tone.

"Come with us." There was nothing but sureness in their voices, but no hint of threat.

"But why?" I asked. "I'm on duty!"

"Just come. Don't ask questions."

I could have resisted more than I did. Somehow I decided just to do what they wanted, not for fear of my safety but for a need to know where they were taking me. They had a car parked nearby. Before I got in they blindfolded me. I confess that I was a bit frightened, but I didn't show it. We drove for over an hour. I was taken from the car with the blindfold still around my eyes and we climbed some stairs. We entered a room, I could tell because the quality of air changed. They removed the blindfold at that time.

I was in a room with flowered wallpaper in yellow and blue. There was simple furniture arranged like a living room, except there was a large desk facing the centre. Behind the desk sat a middle aged balding man in a khaki shirt and brown slacks. He wore wire rim glasses which softened his features and made him look kindly.

He gestured with one hand, "Sit down, Avrum. You are in no danger."

Without speaking I did as he suggested. He offered me a cigarette. I said no.

"You have nothing to fear." He said. "We do not have any intention of harming you. He looked at me appraisingly. "You have expressed some interest in working toward a Jewish state. Is that so?"

I hesitated for a moment before speaking. This situation was completely unusual and in most ways appeared hostile. "Every Jew hopes for a Jewish homeland."

"Perhaps that's true. But there are many others who oppose it."

I remained silent. He went on.

"You come from a family of 9. All of them perished in the Holocaust."

He called it the 'Holocaust'. That was a new term for me.

"You went to a *Yeshiva*, but had to leave to help your family. You worked on the Black Market. You were sent to Buchenwald. You survived somehow. You immigrated to Palestine three months ago. You are almost 19 years of age."

I was shocked inside that he knew so much, but I tried not to show it. I still said nothing.

"You should talk to us. We are not against you."

I asked pointedly, "Who are you?"

The man stood up from his chair behind the desk. "We are people who want peace more than anything in Israel. We are perhaps the people who want it even more than most others. But we are not willing to wait. We are, perhaps, impatient. Are you impatient?"

I thought of what to say. I chose discretion. "No. I'm not impatient."

He looked more serious. "Be honest with us. We are your friends, we are Jews, and we will not hurt you."

I made no response.

"Talk to me, Avrum. Despite what may appear I am your friend. If what I know about you is true I may be your only friend. I may be the one to actually give you what you want. Talk to me."

I had one thing to say. "Who are you."

The man looked at the others. He looked at me squarely. "We are from the Irgun."

I was surprised and, inside, I felt a wave of warm blood wash through my veins. "How do I know?" I said.

"You know. In you heart and soul you know."

"With blood and fire the Holy Temple was destroyed." I said.

"With blood and fire it will be redeemed." The man replied. "Are you willing to do whatever is necessary to redeem Israel?" I remained silent. "Are you willing to shed your own blood; possibly the blood of others?" Again, I held my peace.

The man was silent for a moment. Then he turned to the others. "Take him back. He doesn't belong here."

Without thinking I rose to my feet and waved my arms. "No! No! I want to fight for Israel. I'm willing to die for it. I'll do anything!"

The man with the glasses gestured to the other two. He looked at me over the lenses. "Sit down." He said. "It's not easy to say a thing like that. Do you mean it?"

I was desperate not to be sent back without expressing my desire for justice. "Yes. I believe Israel must be redeemed."

"How do you think this should be done?"

"With strength and purpose." I replied.

"Do you like violence?" This was a leading question.

"I was an inmate in the camps. I hate violence. But I learned something in the camps. To love justice even more."

The man looked surprised. "That's good! You know a little about the Irgun. Do you think we are a violent group?"

I didn't know what to say. "I don't think of you as violent, because that indicates blind, mindless aggression. I think of you as strategic."

The man looked deeply into my face. "We are soldiers. We are soldiers for a cause. Do you think of yourself as a soldier?

"Yes. I want to be a soldier in this war"

"How much?"

"More than my life!"

He smiled a half-smile. "Will you swear to that?"

I was only certain that what I was saying was in some way sensible. At this point I wasn't really sure that I wasn't a bit confused. "Yes! I swear that I would do everything possible to work towards a State of Israel!" If this was the Irgun, unconsciously at least I knew that I would do anything to be a part of them.

The man sat down. "You are a smart, earnest young man. You will be taken directly from here to another place. You will not be going back to the kibbutz, but no one will miss you because they will think you are somewhere else."

He paused, then spoke more slowly. "Being a member of the Irgun is a grave responsibility. We are an organization of trust and discipline. You are going now to learn discipline and trust will follow. We are highly organized. You will learn what that means. Go now, and may G-d speed."

The two other men guided me by my elbows. I had lost my fear. I was thinking, rather, of Miriam. I imagined how she would look as she watched me being led away. "Avrum." I heard her say. "I'm proud of you!" Even though I had been alone for some time, I still needed to at least imagine certainty. In some sense, what I was doing I was doing for her.

CHAPTER 17
The Cost

Six days after returning to the kibbutz, as I was picking up my weapon at the security office, the head of operations spoke to me in a low voice. "Be at the third post on your watch at seven o'clock this evening." When he spoke those words I felt a strange calm come over me. The wheels were turning; the organization was intact. Years of longing to act for justice were going to come to an end. I was going to my first assignment.

As I engaged my responsibilities at my post many thoughts flashed past my consciousness. For some reason I remembered working on the Black Market, travelling by train into Budapest to sell food. I remembered the friends I had made, and how the world of secular Judaism had been revealed to me. Now, even though I was not overtly religious, I was possibly more of a Jew than ever before. The camps had done more than harden me; they had transformed me into a fighter who stood for the right of the Jewish people to dignity, freedom, life itself. I admit that I was nervous. I had never hurt anyone before and I was afraid I would stand down at the last minute. I fought those thoughts bravely. I would only do what had to be done. I would never cross the line into random butchery.

At seven o'clock in the evening I was at the third post. Immediately a car came up with a driver and passenger I had not seen before. The rear door opened and the passenger motioned me to get in. I had my rifle with me. He took it away from me. "You'll get it back when you return", he said. We drove away travelling south at a legal speed. "I am Simon." He said after several minutes had passed. "You will be known as Weitz. We're going to a town in Samaria, an Arab town, where there are known to be several men we want. Two nights ago a synagogue was burned to the ground nearby and a woman was killed by gunfire. These men belong to the Muslim Brotherhood, an Arab group advocating terrorism who want no Jews at all in Palestine. They are well armed and ruthless.

"We are going to approach two locations simultaneously, each one about a kilometre from the other. There is a third location being approached in another town. We don't want to kill these people; we want to bring them in for interrogation if possible. It might not be possible. We will be with a group of three attacking the house of the group leader." He paused for emphasis. "They probably expect a retaliation so they will be armed and prepared. We do have some element of surprise, however. They don't know when we will appear."

The remainder of the ride was quiet. Within two hours the driver turned off the lights and turned off the road. We soon arrived at a site outside a small town. Simon motioned for me to get out of the car and he got out himself. In a moment a young man stepped out of the dark beside the site. This man was of average height and well built. He shook my hand. "Uri." He said. He went back into the dark and emerged with three revolvers. He went back a second time and came back with two sten guns. Sten guns are automatic and carry a large clip. As well as these weapons we had Arab headpieces.

We started to walk. We could see the lights of the town in the near distance. Our weapons were concealed under our loose clothes, the sten guns held in cloth sacks sometimes carried be Arab men. 'Uri' took the lead, guiding us to the right house. It stood alone at the end of an unlit road. There was a man armed with an automatic rifle standing guard outside. This was not going to be an elegant mission. The deed that preceded it called for retaliation, not compromise. Simon motioned for the three of us to spread out. I took a position to the far right of the building. I only had a revolver. It was understood that I would back up the rear.

As soon as we were in position Simon fired on the guard with his revolver. The shot was good, the Arab guard fell to the ground with a bullet to the heart. Within seconds a firefight broke out from inside the house. I guessed there were two others inside armed with automatic weapons. In a few minutes it was over. The two Arabs were dead. 'Uri' was hit in the hand. Simon began to approach the target with 'Uri' close behind, holding the wounded hand to his side. I followed, checking behind to see if anyone else was coming. Miraculously, although there were people standing back watching, no one came forward; there were no other armed terrorists in this town.

When I reached the front door and saw the results of our attack I confess that I was a bit surprised. The two armed men were lying on the floor covered in blood. The house was full of broken glass and riddled with bullet holes. Even though I had been assaulted with the most sickening violence which had been executed against the Jews I had never seen violence carried out by Jews. There was screaming in the back room. 'Uri' and I went back. A woman was protecting three children with her arms; two of them were screaming. On the floor was a man, apparently her husband, who was wounded in the upper thigh. Simon looked in and indicated that this was the man we wanted. Uri and I took him under the arms and started to carry him out. Just as we crossed out of the front door another man came from the left with a gun. Without thinking I called out in Arabic "Go back!". He didn't listen. I lowered my gun and shot him. Then we took the wounded prisoner out of the town with no one following. The car was ready. We threw our captive into the back seat and the driver took off.

The prisoner was co-operative because it was clear that we would shoot him if he resisted. We bound his hand with cord that had been placed in the car and gagged his mouth with a cloth that Uri had. Then we tied a tourniquet to his leg. In about an hour we stopped at a house that was isolated from an urban area and took the Arab inside. It was a very ordinary house to all appearances and there were several men and women inside. We left the man there, and 'Uri' as well. Simon took me back to the car almost immediately, where the driver was waiting. "We're taking you home." Simon said.

As the car reached a major route Simon told me, "You did well.". I let out a breath of air. "What will happen to him?"

"We'll ask him a few questions. Then we'll take him back."

They dropped me off exactly where they picked me up and gave me back my own rifle. The energy of the evening began to lift and I felt both drained and shaky. It had been my first assignment. I had killed a man. That was a first. It had happened so fast I didn't have time to think about it. It was not relief that I felt. The actuality of the night's event seemed very real and concrete. I felt sorrow. I never wanted to kill, even in the camps. In the camps, it was evil itself that was the enemy; here it was simply other human beings. I knew that I would have to kill again, and it lay like a painful burden in my soul. What made the burden so heavy was that there was no other way. I was fighting for my people.

That burden was real but it was also unavoidable given the way I had chosen. I fully believed that it was the only way. Every soldier must face the same conscience. To survive it must be borne like armour. It is a protection against random slaughter.

I had only two days to think over the raid on the Arab house before I received another message to meet someone at a different spot than the last one at a certain time. I was not nervous this time. Certainly, I was not bloodthirsty. When I joined the Irgun I knew what I would have to do but I understood that we were at war, that the survival of my people was at stake. It was clear that the world was not ready to accept Jews from the Holocaust. It was clear that no one would stand up for us and that we would be judged and persecuted wherever we went, forever, if we didn't accept that we had to take matters into our own hands. Israel was the only place we could take a stand. It was not hatred of the Arabs or the British that motivated anyone I knew; it was, rather, an implicit understanding of the political and religious realities. I believed without a shadow of doubt that this action was what G-d planned, that we had to win back our homeland through trial and test, with fire and blood. This was a mandate. It was not an act of terror.

When the car picked me up at the appointed time and place there were three other men in the vehicle. One of them was Simon. He greeted me with a warm handshake and patted my back briefly. Simon was a man who was larger than he actually looked. He was built like a steamship, you couldn't imagine anything getting in his way. His fine dark brown hair was thinning but he gave the impression of being well groomed. His jaw suggested strength rather than expressing it, in fact it was slightly receding. He was a man who appeared competent more than dangerous, particularly on account of his dark green eyes which softened an otherwise hardened look. One thing I had noted about Simon during the first assignment; he could move like a giselle when he wanted to.

En Route Simon explained the details of our run. Five Arabs had attacked a kibbutz in the Golan region two nights before, killing three kibbutzim. We knew they belonged to the Muslim Brotherhood and we knew where they were staying. As in the earlier operation these men were expecting a strike, but unlike the other operation they were on a farm, not in a town. Although we lacked a complete element of surprise we had something useful; a grenade launcher. It would serve mostly as a distraction but that might give us a bit of an edge.

We left the car several miles from the destination and went in on foot. There were two guards outside the one story house. Fortunately, they didn't see us. When the four of us were in position, one of our men fired the grenade into the door of the structure. The explosion blew out the wooden frame and wounded both guards. They lay on the ground moaning.

We immediately attacked. I had a sten gun, as did all our men. It was not a well planned manoeuvre, unlike the earlier operation. Three men were inside the house. Two emerged, shooting sub-machine guns, before we reached the door. One of our fighters went down. Without thinking about what I was doing, seeing only the desperate situation, I cut down the Arab on the left with a short burst. Simon wounded the other, and had to stop over his torso to fire a fatal shot. In that instant, I saw the third enemy leaning up against the back wall with a sub-machine gun ready to shoot. Instead of firing at once I leapt at Simon and dropped him down flat. At the same time I fired a burst at the shooter, catching him in the stomach and chest. Two Arabs came from the fields, one on each side of the house. Simon, who was still low on the ground, took out the one on the right. A single shot slammed into the wall beside my head. I turned around and fired instinctively with my revolver. The shot hit the other Arab and he fell with a bullet in his chest.

It was over in less than two minutes. One of our men was down and five Arabs were dead. I had to shoot my last target in the head to be sure he was dead. We left the two Arabs hit by the grenade without killing them. It didn't impress me. It was a bloodbath. I felt no glory or even victory. I felt no hint of vengeance, no feeling of revenge. I only felt pain and sorrow. Now I was an experienced killer. I wondered if that was what I had wanted.

On the way back our wounded soldier was very brave. The bullet had smashed his collar bone but had missed his lungs and spine. Simon reached over, once we had put some distance between us and the farmhouse, and grabbed me by the neck. "Good!", he said emphatically. "You did very good!"

I didn't feel that I had done 'good'. I knew very well that it had to be done, that I had sworn an oath to do just that and more, that I had done, in some sense, my duty and maybe more. But it wasn't 'good'. It was awful. It was something that, at this time in history, a Jew had to do, nevertheless I could not say I was proud.

Two days later I was summoned to an address in Tel Aviv. This time I had to get there on my own. I took a bus from a road near the kibbutz. On the trip I tried to think about Miriam; what we would be doing now, but it was not easy. My mind kept falling back upon how to assemble guns, the proper way of handling explosives and the men I had killed. Although my mind was active my emotions were steady and calm. I don't know why that was so, except perhaps that I was becoming a more professional soldier.

The address I finally reached was a two story brick building just outside the docks area. There was a woman inside waiting. I had a password that had been given me earlier to respond with to a cue. She smiled broadly and said, "Are you here to greet the speaker?" 'greet' was the cue. I responded, "Yes. I missed the last session." 'Session' was the password. There were two meetings going on, one upstairs and one on the ground floor. "Go upstairs, please.", the woman said quietly, and I went up.

There was a room at the top of the stairs and two rooms further down the hall. The first two rooms were empty. The door on the third room was closed. I had been told to knock on a closed door in a clear pattern of three knocks. I did so. The door opened a crack and a man peered through. "Weitz", I said. The man let me in.

There were seven men sitting on straight back chairs around the perimeter of the room. Two more came shortly after I arrived. There was nothing very notable about the men. They were all dressed in casual clothes, as was I. There were no excessively large men, and perhaps the only common look was that all were athletic looking. There was some pleasant chatting among some of the group until a third man knocked, entered the room and took a place at the front of the room. Everyone stopped talking immediately. It could have been a university seminar.

"You are going to blow up a rail line at the moment a train runs over it." He said. The rest was detail. We would head out separately in a truck and two cars. All weapons and explosives would be in the truck. The train would pass over the line at 11:24 P.M. It would be carrying ammunition and explosives as well as some troops. We were to destroy the ammunition and explosives. It was vitally important that they not reach Jerusalem and it would be virtually impossible to salvage them for ourselves.

BAR KOCHBA

I was instructed to go with two other men, neither of which I knew. They both shook my hand. One was called Gabe. He was my height, light skinned and had sandy brown hair. The other was Rosen. He was two inches shorter but very muscular. His hair was black but his skin was light. He had a very cheerful smile.

The three of us went together in one of the cars, none of us actually speaking a word except the occasional bit of small talk between us so that no one would be suspicious of four men sitting still and silent in an automobile. I didn't really want to talk anyway. It seemed very important to stay focused on our task.

After driving for an hour out of Tel Aviv we turned off the main road and travelled another half and hour, first on dirt roads and then on tracks through some bush. We stopped at a spot that was hidden by a bluff. We got out of the car and the driver pointed west. "Go that way for about 2 kilometres where you will see the tracks. There is a sign at the tracks that says 'Switch 4 kilometres. Stay back from the tracks, behind a low hill. The others will meet you there." We each nodded and headed west.

The walk didn't take long. We reached sight of the tracks but couldn't see the sign at first. We moved a bit, slowly, to the west and finally saw it after a few minutes. We could see the outline of the little hill and we went to it. The three others were waiting for us. Their job was to plant the explosives by the tracks and rig up the detonator. Our job was protection. Each of us was armed with a sten gun we brought from the car. There was no doubt that we would need to use it.

When everything was done and the wires double checked we knew we still had about 32 minutes to wait. Very quietly we went over the plan. Then we waited silently. At 31 minutes into our wait we saw the light at the head of the train appear from the west. We kept our heads low. The fellow operating the detonator watched the train very carefully. When the engine was just at the marker, he pushed the grip. There was a flash of light, a ear shattering explosion and a deafening boom.

The train was six cars long. The engine crashed off the rails making an enormous sound because of the grinding and buckling cars. The whole train, in one long, snake like motion, leapt off the tracks and turned over. Before the cars hit the ground we were at the front cars, which was were the soldiers were. We didn't know how many there would be. We didn't want to kill them if that was possible. None of us knew how possible that would be.

The cars carrying troops were directly behind the engine, lying almost on their side. The first soldiers emerged with their guns ready. I shouted "Drop your weapon!" to the first man. He fired at me and I fired back. I hit him in the chest with two bullets. Before the first shots I was nervous. After that I was braced by calm and a sense of competence, like in playing a competitive game. I only saw what I had to do and I did it without thinking of anything else. The second man came out of the rail car. He aimed his hand gun at Rosen. I shot him in the upper chest. More British soldiers emerged from different windows, all of them armed. We shouted, over and over again, "Drop your weapons!" but they wouldn't do it. Eight soldiers came out of the train car. We kept firing as they appeared. It was a slaughter. Six were killed and two were wounded. When the gunfire had stopped I went into the train car looking for British soldiers who might be holding back. There was only one man in the car. His legs were pinned under a broken seat. I approached him loudly, with my gun going first, shouting. "Don't move! Put your hands in the air! Don't move!" His hands went up into the air. "Don't shoot!" He shouted. "Don't shoot! My legs are broken."

I didn't shoot. Gabe had followed me into the car when he heard the shouting. We lifted the seat that was on top of the soldier and lifted him outside with the other wounded men.

The three of us pulled them away from the tracks because we knew the ammunitions and explosives were about to go up. The soldier I was dragging was conscious. He asked me, "What do you want?"

I replied "Freedom for Israel."

"I can't give you that." He said

"Oh!" I said. "I think you can."

At that moment the train went up. There were three massive explosions and when they were over the entire train was a wreck on fire. We surveyed the damage; everything had been destroyed. Immediately, we left the scene, knowing that it wouldn't take long for the British to arrive. None of us were injured; it happened so fast that the British soldiers didn't have a chance to respond effectively. At the car the driver was ready and we took off right away. We didn't talk. The ride back to Tel Aviv seemed very short. They let me off in the city.

If anything was going to convince me that we were in a war, this assignment is the one that did it. On the way back to the kibbutz, on the bus, I kept feeling anger. 'Why didn't the British listen when I shouted to put down their weapons? Why did they make us shoot them?' This tack brought to another. 'Why are the British persecuting the Jews? What are they doing here anyway? They block our way, they prevent us from achieving our birthright. They make us kill them!"

There was something wrong with my logic, but what was even more significant is that I didn't take the blame, this time, for murdering other men. It wasn't the political reality that I was rationalizing; it was the emotional one. I had to kill. That was a part of my job. I was doing, in my own experience, what every soldier does. I was rationalizing. I was making sense out of something that was insensible. I was becoming a fighter.

Two days later the wedding of Orly and Aaron took place. The whole kibbutz was there to celebrate in the outdoor meeting place. Tents were set up to cover the food and drink areas. There were cheeses; chala, white and rye breads; potato, chick pea and tabouli salads; houmous and tahini; falafels and pita buns; fruits and fresh vegetables. There was home made wine and beer. Orly was dressed in a white cotton blouse and long taupe dress. She wore a garland of white flowers on her head. Aaron was dressed in a blousy beige shirt and white pants.

We didn't actually have a rabbi on the kibbutz. You'd think that with nearly 2000 Jews there would be a rabbi, but the organization was secular and we had to bring someone in from outside. Since they were married on a Saturday, the Rabbi conducted a partial service for us. We listened and prayed with him. I was brief. At the end Orly and Aaron stepped under the chuppa. Orly walked around her betrothed 8 times and at the end Aaron shattered the glass under his heal and like music the assembled kibutzniks let loose the cheers and blessings of all. There were two guitar players and a clarinettist to mark the ceremony and to their accompaniment the wedding couple left the temporary shelter of the canopy and walked back into the known world. Everyone was smiling and laughing together. I was standing with Dov. We were both clapping and smiling at the lovely couple.

I knew that it could have been me in the groom's place, not because I would have been chosen at any time over Aaron, who I believed fully was completely loved by Orly, but because I was in that place for a while early on. I was a wounded soul, an exotic creature who was little known.

BAR KOCHBA

Dov turned to me and put his hand on my shoulder. "Are you feeling absolute joy or a trace of sorrow?" he asked.

I smiled with complete certainty. "Do you need to ask? I have nothing but utter and complete joy in my heart."

Dov laughed loudly. "Then let's eat! Before there's nothing left!"

"You go stuff yourself." I replied. "I want to hear the music for a while before I eat."

The truth was that I was a bit sad, not because of Orly and Aaron, who were a perfect couple and for whom I had nothing but good wishes. I was thinking about Miriam and the emotions I felt about her. She was so much in my heart. She was, in fact, what kept me going. Two days ago I had killed several men. When the Rabbi said the blessings for the Sabbath I wondered if I deserved to say them too? I believed completely in the necessity for the Jewish homeland. I knew it was the only hope to keep our people alive, that without the State of Israel we would not survive.

I knew that without ferocious and structured opposition the British would never leave Palestine and I knew the Arabs would never give it up either. There were bold and clear statements in the Torah that we must fight to gain our land, that no amount of diplomacy would get it for us without violence. Still, a large part of me was with the Yehiva, studying Torah and begging for my supper. Part of me was in the concentration camp thankful for my thin soup and struggling only to survive. I was committed to what I did, fully. The fact that it was uncharacteristic of the person I used to be was irrelevant. The biggest part of me was the man I had become: a killer but for the preservation of all. I accepted it as a responsibility. I accepted it as a role, although I had just seen twenty years of age.

But I wondered what Miriam would say? Would she support my choices? She was my real conscience in all of this. I imagined her words:

"Do you know reality from illusion" I heard her say.

"Do you mean the illusion of a State of Israel or the reality of the death camps? Didn't our families really die?"

"Yes, they did. That is a reality."

"The British want us to forget that it happened. To let it go on in the rest of the world. To let it go on here, by the Arabs."

She might then ask, "Is it an illusion that a country can be created out of armed struggle?"

I would say, "That is mostly the only way they are formed."

"Do you fight for a reality or an illusion?"

I would respond, "I'm fighting for a reality, the only reality I know. If we don't fight in an armed struggle for Israel, if I stand by and watch the reality fade, I will be supporting the illusion; that we can win without strategy and attack. My family were killed. My nation was subjected to mass murder, calculated and specific. The realness of that fact eliminates all others. They murdered us. That made me a murderer, though G-d help me for believing it. I am, at least, a soldier in a meaningful army. At least I don't kill randomly. I kill only other soldiers and not, though it may sound redundant, because I hate them. Only because I must in the wake of battle. Only for a cause which is the only thing I can see as real."

Miriam might look at me with tired eyes. "You are a soldier in a meaningful army, then. What more do you want to know?"

The wedding party was joyous. Music was happy and many people were dancing together under the gorgeous sky. They danced in a circle, with arms linked and feet lifting in rhythm. As I was getting some beer for myself I felt a hand on my shoulder. I turned around. I saw Orly smiling at me.

"Why don't you dance?" she said happily.

I smiled. "Perhaps I will. Later." I took her hand. "Mazel Tov to you, Orly. You know how to pick the best."

She laughed. "I think so! Do you think he's handsome?"

I shook my head in mock disbelief. "No. Not even a little bit. But that's alright, because I'm not married to him"

She slapped my shoulder. "He's gorgeous! Say you're happy for me!"

I took both her shoulders in my hands and brought he forehead towards me. I kissed her gently and quickly. "Orly, you can't imagine how happy I am for you. You can't imagine how much happiness and success I wish for you and Aaron."

She stood for a brief moment in silence as she smiled pleasantly at me. "And what about Avrum?" She said. "Is there a wish I can make for you?"

I laughed. "You can wish that I don't possess two left feet instead of one as we dance together!" She grabbed my arm and pulled me into the circle of friends.

Later, when the celebration was dying down I sat outside the dwindling circle of dancers in the quiet of my own space. I looked at the dancers and at the tables of leftover food and drink. I was happy outside, but I hid the feelings that were in my heart. I would go on a mission soon enough, I knew. The part of me that was here, the social part, was very much in contrast to the part of me that would fight within the next few days. I would fight and I would kill, perhaps even be killed myself. That was not necessarily how it should be, but it was my complete conviction that it was as it had to be. Were these two parts compatible? I actually didn't know. Could I be a soldier one day, and a kibbutznik the next?

The strange thing was that these separate parts were both real. I was a fighter for the state of Israel but I was also a Jew living in the Kibbutz. These two parts were not incompatible. There was nothing to rationalize;

they were consistent. Instead of falling apart, as I felt I might do, I was becoming more integrated. There was no doubt that I hated what I had to do as a member of the Irgun outright, only because it involved killing. Even so, I believed fully that it had to be done, and that it was my essential duty to my own understanding that I had to do it myself. I couldn't simply leave it up to someone else. As evening fell, and as the music played, I thought of Orly and Aaron. I felt it my responsibility that I had chosen to protect their choices as well as my own.

I wondered if I would ever stand beneath the 'chuppa' with anyone? I did want eventually to get married, but now I could not think of it. My heart was fully engaged. I was a fellow of Israel. My personal life would have to wait.

CHAPTER 18
The Night of the Airfields

There was a brief pause in operations before I was called away for another mission. It was not a relaxed period because I knew I would be summoned at any moment. I stood at my security post every night for three nights and had plenty of time to think. It was mostly dark. There really wasn't much on my mind, but my emotions were in a turmoil at first. I had rationalized what I was doing fully, and I completely believed in the cause. But my feelings had not caught up to my thinking process and I felt a kind of agitation. I think it was guilt. Although I handled a gun quite well I had not yet come to an agreement with what I did with it.

On the third night, when I came around to the western gate, I saw something I didn't understand at first. The gate was closed but there was something wrong that I couldn't quite see. My instincts were sharp and they engaged completely. I pushed the gate. It swung open with a sharp squeak. Without thinking I ran down the long road to the kibbutz. There were men, women and children sleeping at its end. I ran very fast, and in a matter of seconds saw five shapes ahead of me in the shadows. I called out "Hey!". Three of them turned around. They didn't wear the headdresses of Arabs, but they opened fire on me. I fired back and my training kicked in. I hit one in the chest. I hit another in the stomach.

Three were left. We had all taken cover in the orchard beside the road. One of the Arabs took a position close to the road behind a tree. He was the cover for the other two, who were making their way tree by tree towards the kibbutz. The cover fired at me from behind his tree. Although I couldn't see him in the dark I could see the flash from his gun. This gave me an advantage because I realized that he didn't know where I was. With instant timing I darted across the road to his side of the orchard, while he kept firing at where I had been. Now I could see his fire and I knew the probable position of his body. It was of ultimate importance that I shoot perfectly with my first shot. If I missed, he would know where I was and pin me down. My rifle was an Enfield and I had only a few rounds left. I saw his fire. I guessed he was on my side of the tree. I fired twice and hit him once in the shoulder and once in the head. I had aimed a bit high.

Suddenly the alarm went off in the kibbutz and the floodlights came on. I could hear shouting and other sounds coming from the enclave. The other two Arabs were somewhere east in the orchard. I heard someone running towards me. I could hear their breath, but I didn't know if it was one of the Arabs or someone from the Kibbutz, so I waited. Part of our equipment was a short knife, not meant as a weapon but as a tool along the long fence. I knew I could not fire at the man without knowing who he was. I drew the knife. As he ran by I leaped up and out of my cover and ran my arm around his neck. He swore in Arabic. Without thought I plunged the knife into his heart. He moaned and I let him drop to the ground.

At that moment there were shots from the kibbutz and shouting as well. Lights quickly approached where I was and Hebrew voices called out, "Stop where you are." A light struck me in a moment. I was caught standing over the body of a bloody corpse with my knife in my hand.

Word soon spread of what had gone on. Before the kibbutzniks had found me they had already shot the other intruder. Voices spoke of what I had done; foiled the attack, killed four men, one with a knife, and saved the lives of innocent people. After I was found I had to explain what had happened especially to Security and most of that was done while still standing in the orchard. I didn't feel much like talking and I didn't feel any pride. I had acted instinctually mostly but my instincts were quite well trained. When I saw the face of the man I had killed with the knife it didn't occur to me that he was about my age. My instincts were sharp even in this; that he was the enemy and I didn't consider anything else. When I came into the circle of light around the kibbutz I was walking slowly. A small crowd of people calmly gathered around me as I walked. Someone reached out and touched my arm gently as if I had done something special. Then everyone was talking at once, shaking my hand, saying thanks. They wanted to talk me down from my emotional high. I didn't think I was special. I only thought that I had been well trained.

A few days later I received a message to be at a certain location at a certain time and to wait for a certain car. I was picked up by the three men who seemed at this point to be part of my cell, Simon, Rosen and Gabe. Simon smoked a cigarette as he described our mission. "We are attacking an airfield. Our objective is to destroy the runways and blow up planes. This is a joint operation; there will be other cells carrying out other operations. Our specific task is to guard the entrance. It won't be easy. We expect that if we don't move fast enough reinforcements might arrive."

He described our weapons and our strategy. "Apparently we are getting a reputation. We have been good in the field, so that's where we are going to be placed. Other cells are best with tactics. They're the ones who will carry out that part of this mission."

Gabe smiled. "Well, at least we're good at something."

Simon grinned back. "We're a young group. I'm not ashamed of our effectiveness."

Rosen spoke quickly. "Don't boast about it. You'll bring bad luck."

"Right.", Simon replied. "We shouldn't boast. We're the hammer. The only thing we need care about is hitting the nail."

The airfield was modest but strategic. It was not terribly well guarded. The plan was that we would approach the guardhouse on foot, attack and draw fire away from the runway. The other cells would then attack the hangars and the runway having cut holes in the fence surrounding them. Cars would appear at the cut fence and at the guardhouse so that we could escape. The entire process planed to take no more than five minutes. Timing was essential: it would take only seven minutes for more British troops to arrive. The airfield wasn't entirely isolated, it was on the outskirts of an Arab town. This allowed our car to wait close to the gate, and it allowed us to approach on foot, dressed in Arab garb, without arousing an alarm.

At exactly 9:15 P.M. we approached the gate. There was one British soldier on guard. Rosen went up to him and addressed him in Arabic, showing him some forged papers. The guard didn't know any Arabic; he thought it was a local. Abruptly Simon came up out of the shadows pointing a handgun at the guard's head. "Get down on the ground quickly,' he said. "or I'll blow your brains out."

The guard got down. That was a good thing. I was left with him at the gate while Simon, Gabe and Rosen went into the one story building that was adjacent. A moment later there were shots and a moment after that there were explosions on the runways and the hangars. Things seemed to be on schedule although from my vantage point it was difficult to know exactly what was going on. Then, suddenly, all hell broke loose. Two jeeps with British soldiers appeared just outside the gate. They must have been close by and heard the explosions. They could see me, dressed in Arab clothes, standing by the guardhouse with a gun. They shouted at me. I fired back and retreated to the rear of the guardhouse. They opened fire and I was sure I was a dead man.

But I was lucky. I stumbled on the curb and tripped, so that the British thought I had been hit. They drove by very fast, one vehicle going toward the hangars and the other toward the low building. The soldier I was guarding ran there also. I fired at him but missed.

Gunfire was coming from the low building. I ran to it and found my friends fighting on two fronts, each on either side as they made their way out of the doorway. I joined them and fired at the left, outside the building. I had a sten gun and a revolver. With the sten gun I was able to strafe the outside soldiers and wound one of them. But the soldiers on the inside had an advantage because they had taken good cover. With horror I saw Rosen go down, hit in the leg. None of us could get to him and it looked like we would have to leave him there. Gabe and Simon tried to retreat through the door, but the outside soldiers pinned them down. I fired at one and was lucky, I hit him in the shoulder, but the other two turned on me. I saw Gabe shoot back. He cried out loudly, hit in the arm, but he didn't fall. Simon looked over, but as he did he was struck in the neck by a bullet. I grabbed him under the arm and pulled him away while Gabe covered us both. I was able to drag him toward the guardhouse, and I could see that he was bleeding badly. All of a sudden the car appeared, not at the guardhouse but right next to Simon and I. The driver opened the door and reached toward Simon to lift him in. Gabe came around the corner of the building firing his sten gun at the British soldiers. I saw him as he approached the car.

I looked back towards him and saw the soldiers coming around the corner. I called out for him to run "I'll cover you!" I cried. But at that moment the world ended. I felt the most powerful punch I have ever felt in my life hit me in the left shoulder. Everything then went black.

CHAPTER 19
"What Does He See in Me..."

There were a lot of marriage proposals as the war came to an end. They represented a universal longing for renewal. In response to so much hate that had devastated Europe, love began to make a very strong comeback. After Asher proposed to her Rivka returned to the room she shared with Wanda and the baby in the old army barracks on the kibbutz. Wanda was sitting in a straight-backed chair feeding Leah with a bottle. Rivka sat down on the bed. "You look perplexed." Wanda said. "That's not like you."

"Oh." Rivka said. Then she smiled slightly. "I'll tell you the strangest thing. Asher wants to marry me." There was disbelief in her voice. "Can you imagine that?"

Wanda laughed in a hearty, good-natured way. "Uh, well, yes, actually. I can imagine that very well. You are a beautiful and fine woman, although I know you would be the last one to admit it, even if you thought it was true."

"How can you say that!" Rivka cried out with utter conviction "I'm a complete mess! I have nothing in the world, no family left, no possessions. I have a baby to take care of. What does he see in me?"

"I don't know." Wanda responded. "Could it be your charm?" Both women laughed lightly. It wasn't exactly a funny occasion but each of them felt a little giddy despite it. "You've certainly gone through a great deal of suffering, but like our entire generation you have been put through the flames. All that remains is what really counts, and that is what Asher sees. Courage. Strength. Wisdom, perhaps? Asher is a smart man and he sees you as you are. Clearly, he wants you as you are."

Rivka shook her head. Her hair, which was beginning to grow long again, brushed past her cheek. "Miriam has been gone such a short time!"

Wanda stood up and put the baby back in her basket. She stepped over to Rivka and put her head on her shoulder. "But she would be so happy." Wanda said. Rivka began to cry. She gulped the air in heavy sobs. "I'm so happy and so sad.", she said, "all at the same time."

Wanda rocked her friend gently. "That's the best way." She quietly said.

The wedding was set for the end of September, 1945. Word got out somehow (it was hard to keep such a secret on the kibbutz), that Rivka and Asher were going to get married. They were both extremely well liked in the camp because of their caring and friendly natures. Soon after the engagement they were both separately invited to come to the base for a specific purpose, and they were both brought by different people who were secretly guides. They were both bought through a back door of the dining room into a room where they thought they had met by accident. Each of them thought they were there on personal business, but when they left the room and went into the dining area it was decorated with red and white streamers, there was Yiddish music playing from the portable record player and there was a crowd of people standing and talking. When the engaged couple entered the room everyone turned towards them and shouted out loud. Mazel tov! Mazel tov! Congratulations!

Both Asher and Rivka smiled with both joy and embarrassment. Everyone in the camp was invited to the party. Someone handed the baby to Rivka, who held her close and tight against her chest. The dancing started. Asher laughed and joined in a circle doing a *hora*. It snaked in and around the happy hall. Within a very short time everyone was drunk, both with alcohol and with dancing. The dining hall literally shook with stamping feet and the shouts of joyous celebration. These people hadn't let loose in a very long time and the engagement of two of their own brought the house down.

After a few hours the celebration began to wind down. Amid many 'good nights' Rivka and Asher left the hall, leaving Leah for Wanda to take care of. The newly engaged couple got into Asher's army Jeep. Before starting it Asher turned to Rivka. "Everyone is very happy for us, but I can see that you are not so happy, deep inside." He touched her cheek gently. "Why?"

Rivka blushed slightly and looked down. "We're going to be a married couple, complete with a little baby. I have everything I want, more than I need. Yet still, the ravages of the war are not over. Our people have been persecuted and slaughtered throughout Europe. Israel is only a dream." She paused, not for effect but to let the fact sink in. "Miriam is gone."

Asher looked at her with calm and understanding. "You don't feel you have the right to be happy?"

Rivka looked up. "Yes. This celebration is fitting but the occasion is wrong."

Asher frowned. "You don't want to be married to me?"

Rivka spoke quickly to correct that view. "Oh, yes, I want to be married to you. Out of everything that's happened, marrying you is the one thing that does actually make sense. Asher, you're wrong, I'm very happy inside for what we are to each other. But there is still, so fresh, such misery and death that I can't free myself from it to love you completely. That makes me sad, and that's what you are seeing."

Asher thought for a moment. "We are going to have a wedding in Rochester, G-d willing. Do you want to wait to start married life?"

Rivka took Asher's hand. "No, Asher, that's not it either. I love you, I don't want to wait to prove that. I just want you to know. When the war is truly behind us, when the deaths have been mourned I will be a happier being. If I seem distant from you now, just know that it is not because of us, and that it will pass and I will come round. I will be your pillar and your rock."

"And I to you, the same. I will be your staff." Asher said.

The first unselfconscious smile since the evening began passed over Rivka's lips. "Let's go." She said. "It's our night to enjoy." Asher started the jeep and they drove into Frankfurt.

In a short while there was another major reason for celebration. The war with Japan ended in August, 1945. Although not so meaningful in Europe as the surrender of Germany on May 8, it did mark a final end to World War II. It was an extremely gratifying and victorious day for the Americans. In Frankfurt the troops went wild, and on the kibbutz a raucous and spontaneous pandemonium broke out. The whole camp converged on the dining hall, which couldn't contain them all, and they spilled out onto the areas outside. Several groups of musicians spontaneously formed at various places and they played song after song. People danced, people hugged and kissed one another. People sang. Off to the sides people sat down and cried.

Rivka came with Leah and Wanda while Asher went to the U.S. base to be with the men. For him, there was whiskey and beer. The soldiers also had music, and they sang popular songs and danced round and round. Asher found his friend David with a group of Jewish servicemen singing Yiddish and American songs. He joined in. He put his arms around the arms of others and danced wildly. He drank whiskey until he was dizzy, a behaviour that was uncharacteristic for him. After two hours of the revels he took himself apart from the group and sat back in his Jeep. David came over to join him. "There'll never be another night like this!" he said. "This night will never come again."

"That's why I'm not drinking any more. I want to be able to remember it."

David laughed a little drunkenly. He was a graduate of a Southern Seminary school and a rabbi as well. He was outgoing and funny and had a definite talent for getting along with people. "Now you will be able to say to your children, 'Kids, in the Great War I was a Chaplin and in the end we had whiskey and peace. G-d willing, we will have peace forever. And you can thank G-d that you have been born in America, where freedom from persecution is the way of life we fought for!"

The two rabbi's put their arms around each other's neck and shook themselves together. "This will never happen again!" Asher said with conviction. "We must work and we must pray! This will never happen again!"

Rivka and Wanda, at their camp, also had beer and wine. They also sang and danced. They also got a little drunk. Most of the people at the camp would be going to Palestine. About midway through the evening they all burst into a spontaneous version of the Israeli anthem, *Ha Tikva*. They sang it over and over for at least 20 minutes, standing, some with arms outstretched. When it was over one of the rabbi's in the camp shouted out the first words of the *Kadish*, the prayer for the departed. All fell silent as they said the prayer in unison. When it was over the bands held off for a few minutes while individuals spoke to each other quietly. Wanda turned to Rivka. "We are survivors, Rivka, and life will go on. Maybe it will never be the same, but it will go on."

Rivka looked at her friend with open eyes. "If not for you, I don't think I would have survived."

Wanda shook her head. "The same is true of me. I had nothing to live for before I met you and Miriam. And now there's Leah, a child of hope."

"I wonder if her father is still alive?"

"Can't you search for him?" Wanda suggested.

"I don't know? Maybe. Maybe he survived." The music started up again.

"You know what?" Wanda said to her, grabbing her arm firmly with her hand. "Tonight is not a night to think about death. The war is over, finally all over, let's celebrate our life. We're alive, let's be selfish for a few hours. We're alive! Thank G-d for this miracle, and let's hope we can be worthy." She held up the cup she had been holding in her hand. "*L'Chiam!*" She cried, in a clear, strong voice. "To Life!"

Someone heard her. They echoed her. "*L'Chiam!*" they called out. And within seconds all around the hall people cried out "*L'Chiam*" and hugged each other. Then the music took over once again and the dancing moved on towards a frenzy.

The wedding took place quietly in September. Rivka and Asher stood before a Jewish Army Chaplin, who was a close friend of Asher, in a small room off the main dining area of the Kibbutz in Frankfurt. He conducted the brief marriage ceremony. Asher put a plain gold ring on Rivka's finger and then she put one on his finger also. They kissed very briefly but sincerely. Wanda was a witness with David, a friend of Asher's from the field. They signed the marriage papers; the entire event only took twenty minutes. The wedding celebrations were relatively simple and low-key; everyone on the Kibbutz was invited for refreshments and dancing once again in the dining hall and a number of Asher's closest friends from the army base came also. For the first few hours the newlyweds didn't spend much time together, they were so busy talking to friends. But as the night wore on they were quietly and discretely urged together by the increasingly helpful guests. At first, there were cautious glances between them from opposite ends of the hall. Then, as they were drawn closer together their hands furtively touched at their side. Finally, David broke the ice by clinking his glass loudly with a spoon and calling for attention. "To a couple who affirm the rule of love in the universe!", he said. "And to their undying commitment to order and sense in life!" Asher and Rivka both blushed lightly. Quickly and tentatively they smiled, but their wedding kiss, though brief, was deep and pure. Now, as a couple, they made their way to the door and to Asher's Jeep. When they got there they sat still and quiet for a moment.

"I'm very happy." Asher said. "I want you to know..." he stumbled over his words, "that I never hoped for this night to be any more perfect."

Rivka actually giggled nervously. "Let's not talk too much. Just start the engine and get on with it."

Asher had rented a small apartment for them just outside Frankfurt in a pleasant suburban area. It had a living and dining area, a modest bedroom and a small, adjacent room for Leah. It was furnished comfortably with stuffed chairs, a burgundy sofa, a lovely old dining table and chairs and a big wrought iron bed in the bedroom covered by an ivory feather comforter with a paisley design on it in white. Rivka had not seen the place before. As they approached the front door, Rivka behind, Asher turned to her abruptly and said quickly, "An old American custom!" Without hesitation, in one swift motion, to the complete surprise of his bride, he took her up in his arms and carried her through the doorway. Rivka was almost giddy with nervousness. She clung to his arms. Without putting her down, Asher kissed her deeply on the lips. Rivka was not the submissive damsel talked about in fairy tales. She responded to this kiss slowly at first, then more forcefully and with growing conviction. Asher put her down, so that she was standing on the ground. They broke for air, just for a moment, and quickly their lips met again to repeat the act. Rivka had never kissed anyone like this before, but Asher had more experience. He lightly nuzzled his tongue into Rivka's mouth and swept it over her teeth, seeking out her soft and sensitive tongue. Rivka responded with unselfconscious passion. She had not known what this would be like and despite herself and her seemingly practical nature she moaned softly and almost swooned. This was the first kiss. They soon melted together onto their knees on the floor. Asher placed his hand around Rivka's neck and stroked it. Carefully, but with strength and powerful grace, he slid his hand to her breast and summoned the excited skin to action. Rivka was swept into a virtual reverie she never thought imaginable and never really wanted, but quickly she overcame the waves of sensation and pressed back with her own fire. She kissed Asher's face and neck over and over. Asher cooled down enough to unhook her dress and lift it meaningfully over her head. What he saw amazed him. Rivka was so beautiful that he gasped out loud. More like the soldier that he was than the Rabbi this night, he carried his wife to the bedroom. He dropped his loved one like a bomb close to going off and reached to his neck to undo his tie.

When they had done everything for each other that they dared, when the sweat had ceased to spread a shining glow over their bodies, when the emotions and bright new sensations had been spent, they lay together like bodies washed up naked on the beach. "Oh, Asher!", Rivka said. "I didn't know it was like this!"

"You think I knew?" Asher laughed. "I was improvising too."

In the afternoon, after another momentous improvisation, Rivka went to the kibbutz to pick up her baby. When she got back home with Leah, Asher was still sleeping. She looked at him lying in the sheets with his face towards her. She liked his face; it was simple and strong. The irony of the reality that morning was powerful, and she never forgot it. The war was over. Her husband was lying in their bed and her sister's baby was gurgling in her carriage. So much to be thankful for, to G-d, and yet so high a price to pay for it. Is it possible to accept personal happiness in the midst of suffering and pain? She didn't know for sure, but she felt that it was out of this circumstance, a husband, a wife, children, a home, a purpose, that goodness grew and flourished. It was desire for this circumstance and the creation of it that would ensure peace in the future, and that without this possibility and the realization of it evil would always grow.

Asher woke up while Rivka was thinking. "Shalom!" he said. "Welcome back to our humble home." Rivka felt enormous affection for him, but characteristically she didn't immediately show it. Instead she said, "Do you think it is coincidence that I am married to a rabbi?"

Asher smiled. "I hope marrying me is not a coincidence! I hope there was something about me that wasn't random. Maybe you like my nose? My hair cut? Perhaps you're attracted to my teeth, which used to have braces?"

Rivka laughed lightly despite herself. "I think it was the ears that really convinced me." She did bend down and kiss his lips gently. "But the mouth was the big surprise."

She had a question in mind. "As a rabbi, what do you think is the most important thing about being a Jew?"

Asher acted stunned for moment. "That's an interesting question. I've actually thought about it a little bit. I used to think it was worship, the means and ways of worship. I don't think so any more."

"What do you think now?" Rivka asked. Her forehead was furrowed on this question.

"I think it's values." Asher replied simply. "I think Jewish values are the most important thing."

Leah was curious. "Thousands upon thousands of Jews went to their deaths without resistance. Is that an example of Jewish values at work?"

Asher nodded vigorously. "Yes, yes, I really think so. They proved that they were truly civilized and peaceful in G-d's eyes. They went to their deaths as victims and martyrs with some kind of faith. They proved who they were in G-d's eyes. The Nazi's proved they were just murderers. G-d will be the judge of both."

Rivka wanted more on this idea. "So Jewish values won, even though so many died to prove it?"

"Yes." Asher said. "It's a gruesome truth, but I believe it is a truth, maybe not the whole truth. The values of the civilized world, including the values of the Jews, won. That's the final outcome."

"And us?" Rivka asked. "Are we a part of that outcome?"

"Definitely." Asher said as he got out of bed. "There is no question that we are part of that outcome. We are the secret weapon!"

When Asher met Rivka he wrote a letter to his parents in Rochester, N.Y. as he did every few weeks, telling them a little bit about her. As their relationship developed he continued to write, but not about her. He left that out because he didn't want them to pursue that relationship to any conclusion. His feeling was that he neither wanted to get their hopes up nor to confuse them about what was happening to him while the war was going on.

Now that peace had come, and he was married to Rivka, he sent them a letter.

Dearest Mom and Dad,

Jubilation! The war in Europe has finally come to an end. I have thought about what to say about this, but I have failed. I will, therefore, say no more about the war at this time. Instead, I will tell you about 'Peace'. The men and women here are a changed lot. Always hopeful, even in the worst circumstances, the light in their eyes which seemed shielded in the past, shines brightly now as they work and play. There is purpose in their step and, perhaps, joy in their hearts. Also, something important! Compassion for those who have suffered and care for them.

Regarding the Jewish community here, I believe you know something from my previous letters and perhaps from news reports. Our people suffered persecution beyond belief, and I don't want to tell you more than that at this time. Perhaps I will write you later in a separate letter. All I can say is that there were concentration camps and many were killed. Many survived, but are badly traumatized. You should know that I will be needed here for what might be a long time. Our people have to be cared for and resettled, many please G-d in America.

There is some news that I must tell you about myself, and I must also apologize for not informing you about it sooner. I had my reasons for remaining silent. A few months ago I wrote to you about a young Jewish woman named Rivka and her sister's baby, Leah. I mentioned that she had been in the concentration camps and had managed to cross Europe to arrive here in Germany. She is an extraordinary person; strong, intelligent, beautiful. That last part is the part that, although it may be superficial, caused me some trouble. I'll make a long story short and tell you that we became friends and soon I fell in love with her. You must know that in the setting of this war, even as we hoped for an end, honest and true emotions stood out very boldly. When you are in a situation where the reality of chaos is all around you, when you see death and pain all around you, you don't linger over important decisions. It doesn't seem right. I must tell you now, I asked her to be my wife, we married just over a month ago.

Although this may seem capricious, I need you to know that it is most considered and real. Rivka is unique, I am extremely blessed to know her and almost ecstatic that she is my wife. Not only that, but she is the caretaker of a wonderful and Oh so precious baby girl who, I must tell you, also stole my heart. It was so hard for her to care for the baby alone, even with a very loving and capable friend to help her, that our marriage seemed to be a good idea in every way. Now, as the wife of an Army Chaplin, she gets all the material needs she has met. Pragmatism may not be a reason for marriage but these circumstances are extreme. It didn't hurt for us to think life might be a little easier for her with a partner.

So, since our last correspondence you have acquired a daughter and a granddaughter. Surprised? You know that G-d does create miracles, even for someone as simple as myself! I think you will be very, very happy with Rivka as your daughter-in-law. She is tough, pragmatic, but also loving and kind. Wonderful combination, I think you will find. The news I hear from headquarters is that I will likely be here for at least a year, but the immanent danger is most likely past now. At this time, I am performing the tasks of a rabbi, much needed, more and more.

I love you both very much and will write again soon.

One more thing! Please keep this news secret. It's especially necessary to keep news of the baby out of circulation. Her future depends on it.

Once again, all my love.

Your loving son,

Asher

Asher showed this letter to Rivka before sending it. "There going to be very surprised!" she said.

"Well, yes. I hope they understand."

"What?" Rivka asked. "That you married secretly in Europe?"

"No. That I love you!"

Rivka laughed. "Oh, come now? There must have been someone at home for you! The rabbi's son, in a small place."

Asher blushed and stammered a bit. "Uh, well, there was someone I had been writing. You know, far from home in a bad situation you turn to someone." Rivka knew he was minimizing this relationship but didn't press it any further. Asher did volunteer one more thing though. "We were dating, but we weren't even close to marriage. We weren't even close to being engaged."

Rivka couldn't resist one little pun. "But you were close at times, I'm sure."

Asher blushed again, but laughed also. "It was before I was ordained and we just held hands."

After six weeks, during which there was much activity for both Asher and Rivka, they received a letter back from Asher's parents.

Dear Asher and Rivka,

> News that the war is over reached us weeks before your letter, but it was such a relief to hear from you that we tore the letter open, so fast that we almost ripped it in two. G-d has been so good to us here, we prayed for you every day. We are getting reports all the time now about the concentration camps. The newspapers are full stories. They say hundreds of thousands of Jewish people may have died. We don't know what to do, don't know what to think about helping the survivors. We've held events to collect money, clothing, food and blankets. We expect to see survivors arrive in Rochester sometime soon.
>
> It would be wrong to say we weren't surprised to learn that you are married now, but it would also be wrong to say that we are not completely happy! Asher, you went away a promising young boy and you are coming back a man. We are sure you made this decision in the best interests of you and your new wife, and we are terribly excited about the baby! We both agree that you were absolutely right to get

married when you did and that you were being the one thing that a mature individual has to be: responsible. We don't believe the other possibility, that you were being irresponsible. That wouldn't be you.

Tell Rivka that we look forward so much to meeting her and the baby, Leah. We really can't believe that we are going to be grandparents!

Let us know when you are coming home as soon as you know. We want to get ready. We haven't told anyone about your marriage or about Leah and we won't unless you tell us differently. Asher, we miss you very, very much and can't wait to see you again.

Once again, our love to Rivka,

All our love,

Mom and Dad.

A few days after receiving this letter, Asher was having a drink with his friend David. Asher was saying that European Jews were different from American Jews.

"I don't think so." David said. "They are pretty much the same. European Jews just have a slightly deeper culture."

"No, American Jews are American first, Jews second, even though they don't always say that. When someone asks you what you are, do say 'American' or 'Jewish'?"

David looked a bit startled. "I dunno. I guess I say 'American'"

"My wife doesn't say 'Hungarian'. Hungary is the place where her family was killed and where there was persecution. She's still a Jew, though, even after suffering for it. The refugees we see? Don't they say they're Jews even if they come from a certain country?"

"So, is this a good thing?" David wanted to know. "A Jew is a Jew is a Jew, no matter where they come from. That's what Hitler said and this is what happened."

"But even now the survivors still are Jews. They've lost everything and sometimes everyone, but they are still Jews. Just look at how many want to go to Palestine!"

"Yes, that may be so, but there are plenty of reasons for that. It's not only because they're Jews."

"O.k. That may be so, but it's mostly because they are Jews that they want to build a homeland." Asher was trying to make a point but was wandering a little.

"So how are American Jews different?" David wanted to know.

"They believe in their country."

"Do they?"

"Yes, they do. They are free to be Jews in their own country and that makes them different. Not better, but different." Asher was getting warm.

"You think a Hitler couldn't happen in America?" David challenged him.

"Right! I don't think a Hitler could have happened in America. The people wouldn't go along with it."

David looked into his beer. He said softly, "Well, my friend, I think you should look closer. America is a complex place."

Asher was startled. He was seeing things in a very positive way because his own situation was happy at this moment. He had never thought about the trials of being a Jew until he came to Europe. He was trying to rationalize the deeper meanings of the slaughter in the camps. "America is certainly complex." He agreed. "But the people there are free and they value freedom more than anything."

David looked at Asher's clouded face. "Not to worry!" he said, and put his hand on Asher's arm. "G-d is in the Heavens. He doesn't care if you are American of not, He knows you very well."

Asher smiled down at the table. "Why did so many have to die?" he said. "I don't understand it."

David tried to enlighten him. "The Jews carry G-d and civilized culture on their backs!" He said. "Hitler couldn't dominate Europe with them in it. And they were scapegoats. Hate was necessary and the people needed someone to hate. The Jews were convenient."

Asher shook his head. "From the point of view of an American rabbi that's easy to say. The refugee's we see don't seem to feel they carry the weight of civilization. Do you feel that way?"

"Well, I carry the Torah with me and I uphold it."

Asher conceded this point. "We're the 'chosen people'. Perhaps we have to suffer to make us strong."

David smiled. "Don't think it's the end of our suffering. We have more to come."

They picked up their beer and drank a sip. "To American Jewry!" Asher said. "May they practice the Torah in peace."

"And to European Jewry!" David replied. "May their suffering not be in vain."

CHAPTER 20
In America

Because Asher was commissioned somewhat late in the war his tour of duty extended for a year after peace arrived. There were many American troops stationed in Germany to help establish and protect the increasingly hostile border with Stalin's Communist Russia, soon dubbed the Iron Curtain by Churchill, and the Jewish soldiers needed pastoral care like any others. Asher held services every Friday night and Saturday morning; he helped those individuals who had suffered in action to resolve their affairs. Rivka was kept very busy with helping on the kibbutz and with taking care of Leah.

In May of 1946, Asher received word that he was to be shipped back to New York where he would be decommissioned. He and Rivka were excited, but Rivka was also, despite what she knew was an important change, a bit apprehensive. The move to the U.S. represented a massive life-altering move for her. Leah, now more than one year old, was an easy and delightful baby. Uncharacteristically blond and light skinned, she gurgled, laughed and even babbled cheerfully much of the time. She was easily playful. When she cried it was usually clear that something specific was wrong. She was not a temperamental baby; she was good natured and adorable. Even so, a baby is demanding and Rivka could only hope that a prolonged sea journey on a crowded ship would not be too taxing on any of them.

When the time came to embark upon the freighter that had been converted into a troop carrier by the military, Rivka and Asher spent the last night in Europe tucked in their little apartment amidst their few packed bags and familiar furniture that would be left behind. They lay in bed beside each other looking up at the ceiling at first. All the bureaucratic affairs had been taken care of over the previous year and they were given approval to travel to New York together with Leah, although they would be on separate decks.

"You know, Rivka, I have been extremely blessed here. I've learned so much about humanity."

Rivka continued to look up. "You're a fine Rabbi." She said. "You give the men just the right amount of inspiration."

Asher looked surprised in a way that was typical of him in this kind of situation. Quizzical, as if he didn't deserve the compliment. "What makes you say that?"

"Oh, sometimes they talk to me after service at the synagogue on Saturday. They're not specific about it, but I can see it means a lot to them."

"Any Rabbi would do the same!" Asher pursed his lips. Rivka turned towards him and he also turned to face her.

"Any Rabbi might do the same, my dear, but you bring something rare. A ray of spiritual hope; a feeling of destiny in meeting with G-d. There is something extraordinary about you. You really care about who they are and what they want and how they are going to get there. You are not only religious. You are an humanitarian."

Asher reached out and touched her face with his fingers. "I don't like to think of myself as special in these circumstances." He said with quiet strength. "Who am I, after all, in the scope of these events? I say my prayers. I try to maintain faith and hope. So many went to a much harsher fate without a hand to comfort them."

"You feel privileged?" Rivka asked solemnly.

"Yes, I think I do. I don't feel I deserve anything special for what I do, believe me. I sometimes wish I were the smallest beetle under some rock to receive what I really deserve from G-d. I'm only a ministering agent of assistance, perhaps at best, not a ministering angel at all."

"You must be happy with both the good and the bad, so you've often told me, and treat them just the same."

Asher looked at his wife with light in his eye. "I'm going to ordain you right here and now if you're not careful."

They laughed together. Asher kissed Rivka's lips gently but for a long time. "You are more than I deserve, Rivka. I have to be good and strong to deserve you."

"Don't be ridiculous!" Riva cried. "I'm a crank and you know it!"

"You can be touchy at times, that's true, but for good reason. Leah is like that too."

Rivka's eyes looked down. "When we reach New York I will be even tempered and bright."

Asher smiled. "We've been in love, here in this apartment, for a year. Let's forget about America for this night, and just thank G-d for the love part."

In an hour they fell brilliantly asleep.

The freighter looked pretty rough. It was an old ship and from the dock it showed no signs of luxury. The hull was painted battleship grey. There was no evidence of the military having put forth much effort to create any amenities for the troops. For the travellers that was difficult to deal with in itself, but surprisingly it didn't command a great deal of Rivka's attention. Wanda came to the docks also to see them off.

If it was terribly difficult for Rivka to leave Miriam behind as well as everything she had know in her whole life, saying goodbye to Wanda was an act of total loss. As she prepared to line up to board the ship Wanda stood right behind her. Wanda was more than just a friend and she was more than a companion; she was a symbol of defiance in the face of darkness, of strength in the face of adversity and of hope in a time of complete despair. She had survived the Warsaw ghetto uprising, she had guided her adopted friends, the two sisters, and she had made seemingly insurmountable pain and loss more tolerable. At this last moment, while they were standing before the boat that would take Rivka away, she stood calmly and proudly beside Rivka, not speaking, not wavering. There was a genuine, heartfelt smile on her lips.

Not so with Rivka, who was normally stoic and straightforward. When she turned to say farewell to her friend her emotions were almost twisted. "I can't say goodbye." She said. "It's just not in me."

Wanda put her arms loosely around Rivka's neck. "Let me say it for you. Your new life is bound to be better, please G-d. You have made the right choices. Now, go with faith and hope."

Despite her effort to be even and calm, Rivka broke into sobs. Tears flowed over her cheeks. "We'll send for you when we arrive. You can come to America and join us!"

"I'm going to Israel first. I believe that is where I should go. We'll keep in touch. I know your address in Rochester."

They kissed each other on the cheek and held each other in a tight embrace. Then they let go. Rivka, Asher and the baby Leah joined the line to board the ship. Wanda melted into the crowded dock, waving and blowing kisses with the crowd.

The journey across the Atlantic was hard. Men and women were separated in different parts of the hold. Sleeping accommodations were rough; the men had hammocks three high slung from pipes while the women had double bunk beds with thin mattresses. Passengers could go up to the deck, but there were only rudimentary comforts. Soon after they left port Asher became seasick, but it passed after a day. The women helped Rivka with the baby, who was quite good considering the circumstances. Three days out they encountered bad weather. In the hold of the ship it was very frightening. Still, it only lasted a day and then they had smooth sailing. The entire trip, which lasted seven days, made the transition to a new world more real to Rivka, because it tended to erase all doubt that a change was taking place and that she was going to a new land. For Asher, similarly, the ocean journey confirmed that Europe was behind him. When they reached New York City they were standing on the deck, with Leah in Rivka's arms, gazing with something like awe at the skyline. They looked like refugees arriving in America, like so many had looked before them. It had been arranged that Asher's parents would meet them at the docks.

Asher's parents had written that they would make the trip from Rochester to New York City to pick them up when they arrived. They might not have done that if Asher were coming home alone. The fact that he was coming home with a bride and a daughter made them happy and excited. They were so very relieved that their son had not been hurt in the war that they wanted him to know how much they cared about him. Also, they secretly wanted to spend some time with Rivka before introducing her to the congregation at home. She had learned quite a bit of English in the year she spent in Frankfurt, so she would be able to communicate with the family quite well.

BAR KOCHBA

As the ship was pulled into the dock by the tugboats, Asher's parents were waiting with other relatives of the passengers. Asher and Wanda were standing on the deck just behind a railing scanning the crowd for Asher's mother and father. He saw them first. With enormous excitement he grabbed Rivka by the arm and shook it so hard she had to break free. "There they are! There they are!" he shouted, and pointed to their place on the dock. There was so much noise no one could hear him cry out, "Mom! Dad! Over here! Over here!"

Somehow people's vision adapts to a complex scene. Asher's parents caught sight of their son as the ship was about to be tied to the pier. In a while, Rivka was able to follow her husband's lead and discover his two wildly waving parents among the faces below. "That's them, the woman in the green hat beside the man wearing a yarmulke and a dark jacket and tie. See?" Rivka saw them when Asher pointed out the yarmulke. There was only one man in the crowd wearing one.

Rivka waved somewhat tentatively when she could identify them. She was nervous. Not only was she coming to a brand new land, she was also many miles from all that she had known. Despite the fact that she was with her husband, at this moment she felt alone. Would they like her? Would she like them? She hugged Miriam's baby girl close to her bosom. "We're here." She said softly to Leah. "There's no turning back."

It took almost two hours for the passengers to disembark from the ship. Asher, Rivka and Leah descended the gangplank together, Asher literally bouncing ahead. His mother and father were waiting at the bottom. Without hesitation Asher threw himself into his mother's arms, picked her up in a strong embrace saying over and over "Mom! Mom!". Then he turned to his father and clasped his hand before hugging him to his chest. In Hebrew his father said, "'He who has saved one life, it is like saving the universe.' You have brought two young people to us as well as returning safely yourself. You are a fine person and a good man."

Rivka was standing behind Asher holding Leah. There was a tense but happy smile on her lips. They were almost exactly like she had expected them to be since Asher had described very well in some detail. She wasn't able to think very much because the moment was so emotional. She simply stood her ground, waiting her turn.

As soon as Asher had said his quick and warm greetings he turned immediately to Rivka and the baby. There was an image created quite clearly at this second of Rivka standing in a brown dress holding the baby alone in relief against the grey ship. Mrs. Teperman was the first to move. She couldn't hug Rivka because she was holding the baby so she grasped her by the right hand and almost bowed. "Rivka, yes?"

Rivka let her smile be more relaxed. "Yes.", she said. The woman before her had a quiet beauty about her. She was elegant in a way Rivka had never exactly seen before. Somehow plain and at the same time sophisticated. She thought, for the first time in a while, of her own mother, who had also been beautiful. She was reminded in this encounter that she had no family left, except Leah. It wasn't explicit knowledge. It was an undercurrent that played beneath the surface.

"Let me welcome you to America, Rivka," Asher's mother said, "and to a life we all hope so deeply will be wonderful for you. You and your daughter are so very welcome, and we want you to know that we are as happy as two people can be to have you as a daughter"

Rivka heard these words and felt a great swell of joy rise from the base of her spine. She felt like a queen being greeted at dockside. She didn't think she knew just what to say. "Thank you, Mrs. Teperman. You make me feel at home."

BAR KOCHBA

Asher's father also shook Reva's hand and expressed to her his joy at the marriage and her arrival back to them. "We have rooms at the Sheraton. We've booked them for two days so you can have a chance to see New York City. Then we'll drive to Rochester and get you three settled in."

It was odd that at this specific time no one knew quite what to say to each other. As they turned to leave the dock Mrs. Teperman said to Rivka, "Would you mind if I carried the baby for a while. Its been a long time since I was a young mother."

Rivka laughed lightly, mostly because she was nervous. "Of course not! It would be a pleasure!"

Mrs. Teperman took Leah carefully in her arms. She smiled brightly at the little girl, touched her cheek with her finger. "Little Leah!" she said. "G-d grant you the happiness you deserve."

As a family now the five of them made their way through the rest and headed for the hotel.

Their rooms were on the same floor but not adjacent. It was now late afternoon and they were all preparing to go out for dinner early in the evening. In the privacy of their room, the senior Mr. and Mrs. Teperman let the excitement of seeing their son safely back on American soil and meeting his new bride and child slowly fall away. Mrs. Teperman sat before a mirror and brushed her hair. Mr. Teperman stood behind her with a bottle of Coke in his hand. "Well," he said evenly, "what do you think?"

Mrs. Teperman stopped bushing and turned to him. "Oh, Samuel!" she said. "Don't you think she's beautiful?"

"Yes." He said positively. "She is certainly beautiful. Nice features. Lovely figure."

"No, No!" Mrs. Teperman protested. "I mean, yes, she is physically nice looking. But she seems both humble and wise."

"And how can you know that, Rachel, after only a few minutes together? Are you a magician?"

"Of course not. I'm going on first impressions at this point. But she showed real grace…she didn't have to be so gracious. She showed humility in meeting us for the first time and to me that indicates wisdom."

"Who knows what she went through over there. Asher wrote that she had been in a concentration camp but he didn't say anything else about it. You've seen the pictures. Horrible conditions. She survived. Somehow, that must be a miracle."

"The miracle is that she is going to be a part of our family, a part of our community." Rachel said pensively. "I have to tell you, Samuel, I couldn't be happier. We have a blessing in bringing Rivka into our family, not only because she has survived a terrible ordeal but because she's so perfect for Asher, and a committed Jew. She has worldly, down to earth quality that I don't often see in our girls. She almost shines with it."

Samuel was not so easy to project qualities onto a woman he hardly knew, but he had also been impressed by Rivka. "She does seem polite, possible even humble. And she is beautiful in a solid, down-to-earth kind of way. Asher seems very much at home with her; that's got to be important."

Rachel turned her attention towards her son. "Is it the same Asher who went away, Samuel?"

Mr. Teperman pursed his lips much the way Asher did when he was thinking about a personal question. "He's fundamentally the same and fundamentally different." As a Rabbi, Samuel could be very allegorical.

"Well, that covers all the possibilities!" Rachel laughed.

"Do you know the parable of Socrates' sock?"

"I do not." Rachel said with some good humour. She really wanted to talk about their son. She was used to discussions with Samuel that played out in their own time and she secretly enjoyed it much more than she would ever let Samuel know.

"Socrates said he had a favourite sock that developed a hole in the toe. He darned the sock but it soon developed another hole in a different place. He darned that also, then the sock developed another hole and then another. He continued to darn all the holes until the entire sock had been darned all over. He then asked this question: is this sock, which has nothing of the original left, the same sock?"

Rachel laughed out loud. "Oh, my goodness! What is the answer?"

"It's not so much the answer that counts here, Rachel, it's the question. Is the sock the 'essence' of sock or the 'substance' of sock?"

"Interesting, in a way. Which one is it, Samuel?" She was a bit annoyed although she knew her husband well enough to expect some resolution to this issue.

"Rachel, Asher is the same in essence. He hasn't changed from that young man with fine qualities that we loved and honoured. But he's certainly been through many trying and difficult experiences and they probably made holes in him and they've been mended, but he's not entirely the same as he was before he went to war."

Rachel was alarmed. "You think he's been hurt?"

Samuel took care in describing what he thought. "Not irreparably damaged, no! I don't think so. He's been deepened and seasoned by experience, that's all. It's a good thing, Rachel, don't you think?

Rachel thought briefly. "Yes." She said definitively. "He's more sure of himself, maybe even more mature. He doesn't appear to be hurt, although you can see that on his wife. She carries a weight. I see that."

Samuel stroked his greying beard thoughtfully. "They make a fine couple, I feel that."

"Yes," Rachel said quietly, "We can certainly give thanks for that."

Samuel went out to smoke in the lobby while Rachel continued brushing her hair.

Down the hall, Rivka and Asher were lying on a double bed resting from their journey. "They're not too bad, are they?" Asher asked while holding Rivka's hand to his chest.

"No. Quite the opposite. They are pleasant and charming."

"Are they what you expected?"

Rivka was a bit temperamental. "You know, Asher, I didn't marry you for your parents' sake. I married you selfishly, for you and for me. Even if your parents didn't like me I would go on living."

"Why shouldn't they like you, Rivka?"

She closed her eyes demurely. "I'm not what you would call a debutante." She said.

Asher moved even closer to her. His face was close to her. "You are so much more than a debutante! You have beauty and strength and courage and kindness."

Rivka looked at him blandly. "You must have rehearsed that in front of the mirror!"

"No. I did rehearse it though. In my heart, where I keep my thoughts about you mostly private. Look, Rivka, you don't have to like my parents as your own or accept them as like your own. You do need to give them a chance. Don't be afraid of happiness, its growing all around you. I can see it."

Rivka's mouth broke into a soft smile despite her effort to remain aloof from randomly happy thoughts. She let out a simple laugh. "Alright.

I'll give them all the chances in the world. I'll give this country all the chances possible. I will try, as you say, to let myself be happy."

Asher looked satisfied. "You make me love you all the time."

Rivka looked into his face. "Alright." She said. "You can love me all you like." She kissed him hard on the mouth.

"But first you must let me feed the baby!" She leapt out of bed and went to the crib where Leah was lying.

CHAPTER 21
Closing in on Happiness

The drive to Rochester seemed longer to Rivka than the four hours it actually took. Although Asher and his parents talked animatedly much of the time, sometimes with laughter and high spirits, Rivka wasn't able to follow many of the parts of the conversation that were in English. She understood enough to understand that most of it was gossip about people they knew, other American rabbis, news of Israel. For part of the conversation they spoke Yiddish so that Rivka would not be excluded. She appreciated that, because the drive was long, but actually preferred it when they spoke English. The steady, constant movement of the car and the drone of the engine soothed her, and she was thrown into a pensive mood as she looked out the window at the scenery as they passed by.

She was, in fact, dumbstruck by what she observed. New York City had seemed unreal to her. She had never seen lights like that, or buildings so high or so many people hurrying along the crowded streets. Then, as they drove out of Manhattan, the sheer size of the city as it sprawled for miles around the outskirts. The width of the highway was impressive as was the size of the cars as well. But after they left the city of New York, as she played quietly with Leah and gazed out the window, it was something else that struck her over and over again. It was room. Everything seemed to be surrounded by its own particular space. As they passed through smaller towns the buildings stood separately from each other, more independently than in Europe. The roads were wider, there were large lots for parking large cars, there even seemed to be more sky. It was not more beautiful than Europe, in fact there was a practical kind of plainness about the scenery. It seemed more new, more simple, everything looked useful in the small cities. But in the countryside, as they passed the farms, that changed. The fields were large and even expansive. The fields sprawled like massive quilts away from either side of the road.

When they arrived in the suburbs of Rochester the mood in the car changed. Asher and his parents became quiet and there was an air of expectancy in the vehicle. Asher's mouth was tight and he almost held his breath as they passed into the hometown of his birth.

"It hasn't changed." He said evenly to his mother. "I've seen so many cities in ruins I kind of expected things to be different here too."

"They're not." His mother replied. "It's the same old town as when you went away."

"You'll stay in your old room, Asher". Mr. Teperman said. "We haven't changed a thing, you'll see. If you don't mind, Rivka will sleep in the guest room until the wedding. It's more for the community than anything else. It wouldn't really seem like a wedding to them if you were already living together."

Asher's mother turned to her and spoke in Yiddish. "No one knows that the baby is adopted. I know that you wanted it that way. They know Leah is almost a year old, but they think you were married almost two years ago."

Rivka looked at her eyes steadily. "Thank you."

"After the wedding everyone will forget the timing of everything. They will only remember the wedding here, in Rochester."

"Yes." Said Rivka. "It's not for us. It's for Leah."

"I know", the older woman said quietly. "It's hard for a young girl to think she's adopted."

Ten minutes more and they arrived at a two story suburban house on a small suburban street. The house was surrounded by a rather large front lawn with a big oak tree in the middle. There were bushes by the front of the house, green and lush, and blue, pink and purple flowers before them like a blanket. In the centre of the right wall there was a trellis grown over with red roses. The house itself was white with deep blue trim around the windows and on the shutters. To Rivka it seemed both simple and beautiful. She had been in places that were too desolate and inhuman to describe. She could remember, only when she cast her mind back and even then only when she felt secure and safe, the apartment in Budapest she and Miriam grew up in, and the last real joy she had known. Now, as she got out of the car with Leah close by, she felt the same kind of feeling she could remember only from that time. It wasn't only the house. It was the drive, the ever advancing feeling of security she had felt coming off the boat in New York, being in the hotel room with it's dark colours and rich textures, eating at a nice restaurant and eventually getting to know Asher's parents. Now that the drive was at an end, she knew her feelings about his parents. They were kind and caring, serious about life but confident also. They were not afraid. They were funny when they wanted to be. And they were in love. They were in love with each other and they were in love with their community. They were also in love with their faith in a way that was different than Europe They were expansive about it, more open about it. They were free. That was a big joy for Rivka, something she could never have expected or even imagined.

But there was something else, in addition to all these things, that complimented and, perhaps, even encompassed it. It was the single thing that, in her ever vigilant and pragmatic mind, was crucially important. They were a family. They gave out every sign of being a family. That's what Rivka thought when she stood by the lawn, at the side of the old tree, with the Tepermans and her daughter at her side. Things might be good. They just might be better.

But the largest surprise was the welcome offered by Asher's community. Within hours of arriving the house was full of people. The first to arrive were neighbours who had seen the car drive up and Asher get out. The doorbell rang and a couple from down the street greeted Asher with shaking hands and flashing smiles and great sounds of happiness and pride. A few minutes later the doorbell rang again and another group arrived. Soon the living room was almost full and the front door was wide open. People just kept coming. Some brought whiskey, some brought beer, before long it was a large, loud party all over the house. A group of men and women surrounded Asher, who was trying to take it all in without getting giddy. Rivka was in a corner of the living room with Mrs. Teperman, also surrounded by people. She was fighting the impending experience of being overwhelmed, but from Asher's perspective on the other side of the room Rivka looked like she was holding her own. She bore a tense smile at first but that soon transformed into a more relaxed expression of gratitude and, eventually, simple composure. She couldn't understand all the English, couldn't respond verbally to much of it. Still, she remained very alert and focused in what could have been a very confusing circumstance. After three hours of this, she knew enough to fundamentally relax. She began to laugh at jokes she understood, to allow her English to flow a bit more, to respond to individuals with care and attention and to the group with good natured aplomb. By the end, just around dinner time, Asher regarded her in a new light as he watched her deal so regally with his friends and neighbours. She looked like a queen; a young queen with a big future.

One event stuck out in her mind. There had been a moment, around 3:30, when a lull occurred in the throng around her. She had a window of peace around her. Suddenly, there was a woman facing her with a drink in her hand. She was pretty, like most of the young women she had met that afternoon, but there was something different about her from all the others. Rivka couldn't quite figure it out. It wasn't exactly physical, it was something else. Spiritual, perhaps, or even psychological. It was in the way she stood, slightly bent on one hip, slightly provocative. Her lips were full and cherry red with dark lipstick, and yet they seemed entirely natural, not fake or painted. Her hair was unusual for her counterparts who Rivka had met so far. It wasn't pinned up like the others. It was dark and loose around her shoulders, curled up slightly but not stiff at the ends. The dress she wore was simply cut, unlike the others who wore suits or more expensive, more conventional skirts and blouses. Her smile, as she spoke to Rivka, was genuine but somehow suggestive. The first impression she had made upon Rivka was clear; this woman was provocative and even bohemian.

She said, in a husky voice that reminded Rivka of Miriam, "Congratulations, the future Mrs. Teperman."

Rivka looked almost gently in her eyes. "Thank you. Please, my name is Rivka."

"Rivka, then. I want to welcome you to America. I'm Aly." She held up a drink to Rivka, just below her chin. "I thought you might like one, I saw that your glass was empty." She flashed a smile that was both full and cute.

Rivka took the glass politely. It was rye and ginger ale. "Thank you." Rivka stumbled over the next phrase. "Ah, the smell is good. Like a spice.

I don't often drink strong beverages." She raised the glass. "This I will like!"

"I'm an old friend of Asher." Aly said. "We go back almost to childhood."

"You must know him very well." Rivka replied.

Aly laughed and looked at her with tilt of her head. "Better than most!", she said. "He wrote me that you were coming. He said that you were getting married right away."

"Oh." Said Rivka, polite and noncommittal but with interest.

"It was so good to hear from him. Although he wrote fairly often we always worried. The letter about your marriage was a complete surprise, but a good one. I was surprised to get the letter. That was just over a year ago, in June."

At first Rivka didn't catch on to the implication.

"You must have been pregnant then."

Rivka stopped short of a sip of her drink. "I beg your pardon, please."

Aly looked at Rivka's face as it flushed. "That's ok, it's nothing." She didn't seem embarrassed, but a shadow of remorse passed over Aly's soft features. "I hope it was easy being pregnant."

Rivka relaxed a little. She laughed good naturedly. "Yes. It was very easy, thank you."

Aly looked down. "That's good. Asher will make a wonderful father, I think."

"Yes." Rivka replied. "I think so."

"So do I." The pretty young woman said. She looked at Rivka with a quite secretive smile. "I've always thought so."

Then some other people came towards them and Rivka and Aly were interrupted. In a few seconds Aly was gone. Apparently, she left the party. Rivka didn't see her again that day.

Later at night, when they were alone for a few minutes in the kitchen before going to bed in their separate rooms, Asher said, "You did really well. You did more than hold your own, you shone!"

Rivka laughed with a high sound that was tinged with joy. "You think I held my own? I've never been so popular!"

"You know, the wife of a Conservative Rabbi is a very special person. She keeps things sparking and at the same time she keeps things steady."

Rivka felt, for the first time in their relationship, that Asher was projecting onto her a role she had only thought about in pieces. "The wife of a Rabbi!" she replied plainly. "This is something hard for me to understand. I knew, in Europe, that this role might come but I think it was different in Budapest. The wife of the rabbi was just a woman."

Asher smiled and took her hand. "I married a woman who, for me, was 'just a woman'. That's why I loved her, because she was special that way. Here, I'm rather afraid, that woman is special in a certain way. She's a model in the congregation. She has a certain place."

Rivka fell just short of scolding him, although somewhat in jest. "You never told me that. I never knew you had some expectations."

Asher squeezed her hand. "If you don't want it, Rivka, we won't do it. I'll teach instead. I'll be a High School teacher. I'm qualified for that."

"And would that satisfy you?"

Although Asher shook his head it didn't look convincing to Rivka. "We're together on this. Whatever you want I must consider."

Rivka shook his arm vigorously and smiled. "You be whatever you want, my dear one. I will be a Conservative Rabbi's wife with joy, not only because I love you but because it is G-d's will. He made you a Rabbi. You are a wonderful, skilful rabbi. I'm your wife. I will follow you and I will be your friend."

"You cheer me, Rivka, as always."

"But don't think I'm not an equal partner in this relationship!" Her tone dropped to sotto voice. "I want more children, Asher! That's where you must do your part."

"I promise, darling. If there's anything I can do to make that happen I will." He drew her hand, and with it her shoulders towards him. They kissed lightly.

"A Rabbi's wife needs children and Leah is lonely, Asher. After the wedding, we can try."

At that moment Mrs. Teperman came into the kitchen with a handful of bottles from the other room. "Oh!" she said. "I didn't know you were here! Would you like a drink? There's some whiskey left."

In her own kitchen, three blocks away, Aly was sipping at a glass of sweet wine. She'd drunk more alcohol this day than she normally would. Two of the young men who were both friends and suitors had called but she told them both that she wanted to stay in. Her mother and father were out. She was alone in the house. Her chin was in her hand. For a moment, she made a move as if to leave the table, but for some reason she hesitated, then moved back again. A few moments later she made the same start, with more conviction, and that time she did move.

She went upstairs to her room, reached up into the rear of the closet, moved some shoes and boxes out of the way latched onto a square, tin cookie box. She took it downstairs.

At the kitchen table she opened the container. There was a collection of letters in it, most of them handwritten in the same even hand on thin blue air mail paper. Except one, which was in a small white envelope. They were all from Europe, mostly Germany, and they were all from Asher.

From the time they were in junior school she and Asher had been friends. At first, until they were fifteen, they had been distant friends, part of the same crowd. Their friendship had been real but indirect and unfocussed. In grade nine they started hanging around each other more because they were both interested in drama. They were in a play together. They started to talk more. They had a single sense of humour. They liked each other. They were friends.

In grade ten they were inseparable. It was love, but it seemed utterly innocent of sexuality and completely platonic. At sixteen most Jewish boys and girls in suburban Rochester listened to their parents. They believed that sex was for marriage, but they were still curious. There was kissing and petting but intercourse was only for the most daring, freethinking or stupid.

In their senior years Aly and Asher drifted away somewhat because both of them were dating other people, but their affection was still strong. They got together about once a week and just talked. About drama. About religion. About themselves.

Directly after graduating Asher went away to a Hebrew University while Aly enrolled at NYU. Aly was marginally content but distracted and lonely. When Asher came to visit her in the middle of the second semester she literally jumped up and down, her pony tail bobbing eagerly. They talked in her room until early in the morning, when Asher lay down on a sleeping bag on the floor. They talked more, until dawn. Aly felt something she had not felt before. She was warm and tingly all over. She was happy. It was the first time she perceived that since arriving at the university.

Asher worked at a camp in the summer in the country while Aly took a job in a clothing store. They met only once in late August, then they both went back to their separate schools. But something had happened to both of them in exactly the same way at exactly the same time. They wrote long letters to each other. This time, when Asher came to her campus in November, Aly met him at the bus. She was wearing a long dress that clung to her shape. When he reached her side, she threw her arms around him. "I'm so glad you're here!" she trilled in her husky voice. Then she said, in a louder voice so it wouldn't seem too intimate, "You know I love you!" But the kiss, the first on the lips, was not loud. It was sensuous and deep.

That night, they kissed and touched in a new way. They kept most of their clothes on, but in the morning they both lay asleep together on the floor on the sleeping bag. Aly loved Asher, but she felt more that they were soul mates, destined to be friends forever, than a couple headed possibly to the alter. It wasn't that she didn't want to marry Asher. It was that it would have seemed redundant. They saw each other often during the next two years. Everyone knew they were going out, including their parents who didn't disapprove. They kissed and hugged in private, but never to completion.

Their relationship became more intimate, not only physically but also, perhaps even more so, emotionally. They had been dating for a long time. They were very secure and very close, but that wasn't all. They knew, though probably not consciously, that the relationship was wearing down in some way and that they were each feeling more platonic. Rather than reducing the physical intimacy this ongoing development made it more frequent and intense. Perhaps they knew that this was the key to the waning romance between them. Perhaps they wanted to deny it was waning at all by practicing more serious intimacy. Perhaps it was mostly because they were now in their twenties and could expect more.

Whatever the reason, they began pushing the boundaries further and further, about as far as a rabbinical student could dare to go.

Just before the end of their respective third year they went as far as they had ever gone. Aly's smooth and bare breasts felt more beautiful to Asher than anything he had ever imagined. She reached down to his phallus, stroked it gently. She had never felt anything quite like it before. She began to pump it, completely fixed by how strong it felt and how good it was to feel it's weight in her hand. They were both very excited. She pulled the pulsating organ out of Asher's underwear and examined it with her eyes. She was fixated on its colour, its shape and size. Asher was moaning quietly. She put her hand fully around the head and squeezed. Asher cried out. A tiny squirt of liquid escaped. It lubricated the head and the shaft. Aly slid her hand over the whole shape, fascinated by the throbbing shaft. She pumped, up and down until Asher was moaning softly over and over again until the sound reached a fever pitch. Suddenly, the throbbing caught, just for a split second, and was replaced by a violent spasm. Smokey thick liquid leapt out of the hole at the top of Asher's penis. It covered her hand with warmth. She removed her hand. Asher was breathing heavy. She was deeply pleased.

When Asher received his orders everyone was very concerned and encouraging. He and Aly were both back in the suburb of Rochester for the few weeks before he had to report. Asher had been ordained at that time. He was utterly serious about his commitment, but he was concerned about Aly. They had not been intimate over the months since the dorm because both Aly and Asher had been drawn in different ways: Asher felt an obligation to observe the laws of his faith while Aly knew that she didn't want to be the wife of a rabbi. Aly was drawn towards the Arts. She was a good painter and an accomplished sculptor. She wanted to go in that direction.

BAR KOCHBA

In the week before he was scheduled to leave, she had met Asher at his parent's house. They went for a walk along the suburban streets. They didn't hold hands.

"I'll come back for you, if you want." Asher said with something slightly less than conviction.

Aly stopped and faced him. "Look!" she said, no trace of doubt in her voice. "I'll wait for you. You're going into G-d knows what, G-d knows where. What you do, what you see...Asher who knows what it will be like? Who knows what it might do to you? When you come back neither of us know what you might want. I love you. You're my best friend and I am definitely here for you. So whatever else happens, you remember that."

Asher told her not to wait, but just to be there. He would write.

And so it was. He had written and she did wait. Somewhere in the middle of it all they both got lost in the letters and fell to believe the relationship was real. But it wasn't. When Aly received the letter telling her that he was getting married in Europe she was shocked, then happy for her friend, then she felt betrayed. Finally, she felt freer and relieved of a great weight.

As she looked through the letters she remembered some of the emotions that had filled her during their earlier friendship and while he was away, but overall she was quite distant. She liked Rivka. She was elegant and friendly and approachable. Perhaps they might get along?

But that baby could not have been born only one year ago. She checked the letter. It was dated only 14 months ago! Unless she had been pregnant before they met or they had met in the middle of the war, something wasn't right with this. Aly hoped she was still a friend to Asher. That depended a lot upon Asher. But she was going to find out the truth.

If not for her own satisfaction, which may have even been a misguided revenge, then for the sake of truth itself. She would find out what had happened over there.

CHAPTER 22
Big Life

Although weddings were usually planned by the bride, Mrs. Teperman took charge of the wedding because Rivka was entirely unfamiliar with the American customs, conventions and currency. This was not an insult to Rivka. It was an acknowledgement of the real situation and Rivka was happy to be left out of the controversial responsibility. She was consulted on colour schemes, design of the invitations and the choice of wedding dress. The choice of dress was the part that pleased her the most.

Shopping for the dress was the most challenging and intimate activity that the two women had done together. It was more than the simple act of choosing a dress. It was an act of mutual diplomacy and tact requiring sensitivity and discretion. The choice of dress would reflect much more than taste. It would indicate a collaboration between mother and daughter-in-law strictly as individuals. It started when they met in the kitchen to go to the shop.

Rivka was ready first. She sat like a sentinel on a stool by the counter, wearing a simple dark blue blouse and grey pleated skirt. Leah was in the stroller beside her, quietly chewing on a soother. The wedding was not an entirely serious event for her. She and Asher had lived in Europe as husband and wife for a year before coming to Rochester and that had been a very meaningful time for her. It was the time when their relationship grew in both respect and love. She had come to know Asher as a seminal part of her life, and it was the time in which the loss of Miriam had become bearable. This second wedding was, to her, an act of theatre. She was performing a role to please her husband's family and their community and it was only ceremonial at best.

Rachel Teperman was a woman who seemed always to be surrounded by words. She came into a room like a radio, broadcasting information in a seemingly never ending stream. Yet she was not empty headed. She knew what she was saying all the time and it all had meaning. She knew when not to talk, when situations were awkward or tense she was very good at defusing them. Little known to others who knew her only through superficial encounters, she was an avid reader and was thoroughly well informed. Unlike many women of her generation she had gone to university and graduated with a sociology degree. She was also a Hebrew scholar. She was able to rival her husband in knowledge or the Torah, if not on interpretation then at least on content. Her presence in a group meant there would always be plenty of conversation.

When she came into the kitchen to meet Rivka, Rachel was in good form. She was pleased to be about to shop for something so special and personal as a wedding dress. She liked Rivka for what she seemed to be; a mature young woman who took her responsibilities seriously. But she was also a bit intimidated by her. Rivka seemed so sophisticated it made Rachel a bit unsure of herself. In fact, the two women didn't know each other very well. They were both relating to primarily superficial impressions of the other. There is very often some tension between a mother and daughter-in-law. Rachel and Rivka were not exceptions to the rule.

"Don't you look fine!", Rachel said broadly. "That blue blouse suits you beautifully."

Rivka presented a demure response. "Thank you. You gave it to me with some of the other clothes. I like it."

Rachel laughed. "Well, don't I have good taste! I'm sure it looks much better on you than it ever did on me."

At that moment Leah dropped the soother and began to whine and reach towards Rivka. Rachel responded first. "Let me hold her." She said. "Come to Bubbie, little darling. What do you think is wrong, little baby."

Leah had no biological relationship to Rachel, but she never showed that and never even thought it. The child was a war baby. Rachel saw her as the promise of a new generation and she was determined that Leah would receive every good thing possible in a new world.

"Let's go." She said abruptly. "This is going to be very difficult but a whole lot of fun!"

In the car during the first moments of awkward silence Rachel noticed Rivka gazing noticeably at the city as they drove by. She seemed to be in sort of dream. "Do you find it very different than what you are used to?" Rachel asked in Yiddish.

Rivka looked a bit startled as she turned her gaze to Rachel. She spoke in English. "Many things are similar, Mrs. Teperman." She said. "But there are also many things that are different."

Her mother-in-law looked at her seriously. "Let's clear something up. You don't have to be quite so respectful to me. Anyone who has been through the ordeal that you have deserves to be treated as an equal. From now on, you call me Rachel. That's my name and I want you to use it."

Rivka smiled and dropped her head demurely. "All right. That will be nice, Rachel."

Rachel smiled broadly. "All right. Now, what's different about Rochester?"

Rivka paused for a moment to put her words in order. "First of all, it's much faster. In Europe, people don't always rush and things don't always happen so quickly."

Rachel laughed good naturedly. "We're a young nation." She said with a wave of her hand. "We're in a hurry to grow up"

"Yes." Rivka replied. "You're a people that wish to get things done. Also, everything is bigger here. The houses, the streets, even the trees."

"This is a big country. Lots of space. Lots of space for everybody. We love people. All kinds of people."

Rivka went on. "And you live bigger. Your lives are more outgoing. Sometimes, I admit, they seem bigger than they should be. Everything is so important and busy. So much to do, only you to do it. Each person seems sometimes to be a movie star in their own little movie."

Rachel didn't know whether to be annoyed or amused. "It's just our way of copping with a massive burden. We believe we bring a most promising civilization to the world. We believe we have something new and fresh to offer.

"During the war Americans were very welcome. They always brought enormous relief."

"It's too bad we came to Europe too late to relieve it even more." Rachel glanced over to Rivka with a kind of sigh. She felt it was time for a sensitive question. "We didn't arrive in time to save your family."

Rivka hung her head. "That would have been impossible, Rachel. You came at the only time you could."

"I'm sure you miss them terribly." Rachel sounded her words in a low pitch. Rivka looked at her with some affection, although she didn't know her terribly well yet.

"You remind me of my sister. You remind me of Miriam."

Rachel was actually stunned by this statement. "Do I? In what way?"

"She had the same love of life, the same energy and strong will."

"Her name was Miriam?"

Rivka laughed. "Yes"

Rachel frowned. "How old was she when you lost her?"

Rivka grimaced slightly. "She was seventeen."

A shudder of anguish passed through Rachel's frame. "Oh my God. I'm so sorry, Rivka! I wish I could say something to wipe away that loss."

Rivka shook her head solemnly. "You have done so much. You have given me my husband. You have taken me in and you treat me as one of your family. We have Leah, and you have adopted her as your own grandchild. You have done more than I could imagine anyone could have ever done for me. My sister can rest more easily, I think. There is purpose here, and order." She smiled demurely at her mother-in-law. "Perhaps, even, there is love."

Rachel felt a warm rush rise from inside. "I don't suppose we could hope for anything more than that." She pointed to a store just ahead of them. "That's the bridal shop. Now, if only we can find a place to park!"

After several hours of looking at dresses and trying some on they found one that was just right. They were happy but tired when it was finally done. Two days later, while Rivka was at home giving Leah a bath her dreamy mood was broken by Rachel calling upstairs. "Rivka! There's a call for you!"

This was very unusual since Rivka had not made any real friends yet and the only person who ever called her was Asher. She was unwilling to leave Leah in the bath alone so she quickly dried her off in a soft towel and carried her with her to the phone in the Teperman's bedroom. It was Aly.

"Hi!" Aly said brightly. "I hope I'm not disturbing anything."

"No, no, not at all." Rivka replied. "I was bathing Leah but I'm done now."

"I thought perhaps we could meet for lunch."

Rivka was a bit surprised and a little confused. She hadn't expected an invitation but guessed it was not terribly unusual for a friend of Asher's to want to get together. "Yes, that would be fine. When?"

"How's today? Do you have any plans?" Aly's tone was pleasant, not pressing at all.

"Well, no, I have no plans."

"Why don't I pick you up at 12:30? There are several nice spots downtown. Are you willing?"

Rivka considered for just a moment. She was actually very happy to see someone. "Yes, I'm willing. You don't mind if I bring Leah? Mrs. Teperman is going out at one and I need to have Leah with me."

"The more the merrier!" Aly said buoyantly. "See you at 12:30."

The restaurant was cozy. Rivka, Aly, and the baby had a quiet booth near the back. Aly made chit chat last for the trip there and for the first few minutes while they looked over the menu. She helped Rivka order since she was not familiar with all the items and she asked the waiter to hold the order while she and her friend had daiquiris. When the drinks arrived Rivka looked a little abashed. Aly coaxed her. "Is it unusual in Hungary to have a drink with dinner?"

"No, no, it isn't. Usually wine or beer." She hesitated. "This looks so…special!"

"It looks special. American women like to have drinks that look special. It makes them feel more special, I suppose."

"Alright." Rivka agreed, and lifted her glass. "To being special!"

Aly concurred. "To being special. At least, to feeling that way." It wasn't her plan to get Rivka drunk but she felt a little encouragement might be appropriate. "How are the wedding plans coming along?"

"Good." Rivka was emphatic. "We have a dress!"

"We have a dress? Do Mrs. Teperman and you both intend to wear it?"

Rivka laughed nervously. "No, of course. It's just for me. It's my dress."

At this point Aly decided to pry. "It is your wedding, not hers, isn't it?"

Rivka was not the pushover Aly thought she might be. She pressed back. "I am already married. Asher and I had a Jewish wedding in Germany and have been living as husband and wife for quite a while."

Aly was quick to concur. "Yes. You have a one year old daughter."

Rivka seemed sure. "Yes. We do."

Aly could sense the firmness of Rivka's role. She could see that if she continued to make small talk they would get nowhere. Aly was sure that things were not as they seemed with Rivka, Asher and the baby. She wanted to know the truth, not because she was vindictive or wanted to hurt either of them, but because she was addicted to the truth. She had to know why Asher was not telling her everything. He was the person she cared most about.

"Did you know that Asher and I were very close before he left for the war?"

Rivka knew that Aly and Asher had been friends. "Yes, I knew you were close."

"I said I would wait for him. Did you know that?"

Rivka was surprised, but maintained her distance. "No. I didn't know that. I didn't know you were close in that way."

At that moment Leah began to whine. She was feeling very alone, so Rivka picked her up and bounced her on her knee.

Aly smiled. "I'll be clear, Rivka. We were friends. Really, that's all. But we loved each other, I think, in a way that was not entirely and certainly not always romantic. We knew each other over a very long period of years and were very close."

Leah was playing with Rivka's hair. "I think I see. Sometimes I'm not sure that isn't the way Asher and I feel about each other also."

Aly smiled and looked down into her drink. "He was the local boy going off the war. You can't send a hero off like that without giving him something to come back to. Someone special he can think about in the darkest times."

"Of course not." Rivka said quietly.

"I did wait, Rivka. I waited with fear and love in my heart for that special soldier to return. We wrote many letters. Eventually one that brought the news of you and him. That you were getting married in Germany."

Rivka was feeling sad for this. "I see. You were hurt by this. I didn't know."

Aly shook her head. "No, you don't understand." She looked directly at Rivka. "Well, at the very first I suppose I was hurt. But that didn't last long, it was quite superficial. I didn't really want to marry Asher. I only wanted to be here for him when he came back. But I would have married him, if he wanted to, when he came back. But Rivka, he found you and this was much better. I don't want to get married right now, to anyone. I love being a single woman. I guess I'm unusual in that way."

"Not so unusual." Rivka said. Leah was falling asleep in her arms.

"But there's something wrong. Even though I don't expect Asher to be as close to me as he was I still expect him to be honest with me."

Rivka wondered what was coming. "Of course."

"Asher never wrote to me that you were pregnant. Did you get pregnant before you were married?"

Rivka shook her head. "No."

"Then how can your baby be a year old?"

Rivka was shocked. She reacted defensively. "What do you want to say about our baby?"

Aly posed this sentence carefully. "I think she was born before you were married, Rivka"

Rivka was stunned, but her response was strong. "And if she was?"

Aly was clear in response. "There's absolutely nothing wrong with that."

Rivka assessed Aly critically. She saw a sophisticated woman who was not bound by the same conventions as most other people in this small American city. She didn't see someone to fear. "You are right. Leah was born before we were married."

"And you thought it was better if no one knew?"

"She was born to my sister, Miriam. She died just after Asher and I met."

There was relief in Aly's voice. "She's not your baby?"

Rivka was quick to answer. "No, she is my baby in every way. She's my sister's little girl and now she is my own. But why should she suffer?"

Aly was incredulous. "You don't want her to know who her mother is?"

"Someday she will know, but when she is old enough to understand. The Teperman's want no one to know she is adopted. Apparently, here in America, it is not a good thing for a child to know they are adopted, so we will do for her what other families do. Until she is old enough to accept who she is she will live like every other child."

"You're doing this for the Teperman's, or for you and Asher?"

"I'll be honest to you because you were so close to Asher. If it were up to me, Leah would know who her mother and father were. They are both dead. In Europe, this is no crime, but here it is not the same. There are not thousands of orphans. I am an immigrant, I hope to learn new ways. The Teperman's want everyone to think Leah is our child. If that is normal, then I agree. No one will know, until the time is right for them to know. I don't guess that you are going to betray our secret?"

Aly seemed confused for a brief moment. "I don't have any intention of betraying anybody's trust, let alone the trust of someone I love and respect. Rivka, you have every right to do what is best for your daughter. I want to be your friend, not your enemy. I just want to know the truth, because I expect, or at least hope for, that kind of trust from Asher and his wife. You may rest easy, Rivka. Your secret is safe with me. No one will ever know."

The waiter came back to take their order and as he did Leah awoke and began to cry. The two women gave their order and looked at each other with wan but hopeful smiles. Rivka finally said. "Thank you." She held Leah under the arms and held her out to Aly. "Would you hold her for a while? I have to leave the table."

Aly took the child into her hands and looked at her seriously. "Leah," she said. "You are going to be an international lady of mystery." She held the little girl to her shoulder and rocked gently.

The wedding was held a month latter at Rabbi Teperman's synagogue. It was modest by standards in that community but there was plenty of good food, there was dancing and there were speeches. The speakers praised Asher for integrity and courage. They complimented Rivka on her charm and intelligence. They addressed Rabbi and Mrs. Teperman for their dedication and courage. It was a very warm and personal affair. After the dinner had been finished and there was a lot of mingling going on, Asher found Aly at her table and asked her to dance a slow dance. When they reached the floor they were awkward.

"I believe I thought you'd be dancing at my wedding, but not as a guest."

Aly made light of it. "Oh, I'm much better at being the ex-girlfriend than being the bride. Am I the ex-girlfriend?"

Asher was quick to respond. "You're definitely not the ex, in this scenario. You are definitely the trusted friend. Rivka told me she likes you a great deal and thinks a lot of you."

"That's nice. I hope it's true." She replied almost politely.

"Aly, you don't know how greatly I am indebted to you."

"Oh, don't patronize me!" she said and slapped his arm playfully. "This is your wedding night! I couldn't be more satisfied with our relationship."

Asher leaned back and looked at her. He was glowing inside. "You're the greatest!" he said brightly.

They broke out of their two-step and began a waltz over the dance floor. The Teperman's looked out from the head table at the young couple and smiled at each other gracefully. Their son was home.

The next day Rivka and Asher faced the task of opening the presents. They had stayed overnight in a hotel and were prepared to leave later that day for a honeymoon in Canada. When they returned they would set up house in a home not far from Asher's parents. The gifts, though not unusual for an American wedding, overwhelmed Rivka. There was a toaster, an electric frying pan, a blender, an electric can opener, a waffle maker. There was a set of cutlery, plates, bowls, serving dishes, silver jugs, dishes. "We didn't have all this in Hungary!" she said. "We could open a small appliance shop!"

But secretly Rivka was both impressed and, at the same time, dismayed by all this apparent wealth. When she had been a young girl in Budapest, before the war, it was true that she sometimes dreamed of having material things. But in Hungary the quality of life had not been measured so clearly on possessions. As she opened gift after gift she felt a distance creep in. She became, for a moment, detached from all this. She missed her father. She missed Miram very much. In this moment of seeming joy there was an empty part inside of her and she slowed down briefly and sat on her heels. She was an immigrant for a moment, in a new and different world, not the blushing, happy bride that she was thought to be.

She picked up Leah in her arms and rocked back and forth gently. This little girl would grow up with everything going for her. Most of all, no war, no violence. Only plenty of things and unending love. Asher came across the floor from the pile of boxes. He smiled and held both his wife and daughter in an embrace. "Such a good start!" he said.

"Yes." Said Rivka quietly. "We must do our best to make good of what follows."

"Surely it will not be all laughter and no tears." Asher said. "But certainly there is hope. God willing, no mater what happens, we will always have hope."

CHAPTER 23
The King David Hotel

I had been hit in the shoulder by a British bullet. It had knocked me unconscious and my colleagues in the Irgun had dragged me into the escape vehicle and driven off to safety. I awoke in the car as is sped away, feeling enormous pain in my left shoulder. I didn't cry out. As I awoke, for a moment I was confused. I didn't know where I was. But one of the men put their finger to my lips, and I realized in an instant what had happened. I remembered shooting at the British, and the quick and brutal hit that followed.

We had our own surgeons. I was taken within a few hours to a modest house in a relatively poor neighbourhood. Our doctor was already there. He looked at my wound and smiled. "The bullet is lodged in the muscle. You're a strong boy! The bone doesn't seem to be broken."

There was no anaesthetic. One of my comrades gave me a large gulp of whiskey and the doctor dug the bullet out as efficiently as he could. The pain woke me from the semi-stupor I had been in. Pain is a strange thing. It can make you crazy or it can drive you to the clearest thoughts. While the doctor was working I imagined that I was floating on a cloud that was pouring rain on the other side. The pain was the rain; the side I was on was peace in Israel.

My wound was not too serious, but I would be out of action for a few weeks. It turned out that I was getting a reputation as a strong, reliable fighter. I took no account of that; I felt that I did what everyone else did and was in no way exceptional. Still, when I was sent back to the kibbutz to recover I was treated like a hero. I didn't especially enjoy the attention. Several people from off the kibbutz came to visit me. One was an Irgun administrator. I had created a reputation. This ersatz recognition seemed out of place. I was only a soldier doing what he had to do.

He was a tall, thin man with curly grey hair thinly covering a balding scalp. There was an air of order about him, as if he was obsessed by neatness, but his eyes were soft and full of thought. This seemed to be a contradiction. I was lying in my bunk, reading, when he appeared at my bedside.

"Avrum, I hope I'm not disturbing you! You seem engrossed. That must be a good book you're reading." His voice was strong and comforting.

"It's a biography." I said simply. "Of an Ashkenazi Jew who came to the Holy Land before the British mandate."

"Like me." he said. He smiled broadly. "I was also a kibbutzim when I was young."

"You must have seen a lot of changes here?"

"Many changes." He replied. "And you, please G-d, you will see changes too."

I am very poor at small talk. "May I ask, have we met before?"

He shook his head. "Actually, we haven't. My name is Eigherman. I wanted to meet you."

I was genuinely surprised. "Why?"

"To let you know people care about you."

I looked down at the ground. "I know that."

Eigherman's forehead furrowed. "Yes, you know that. What you don't know is that specific persons care about you. They want you to know that you are recognizable. They want you to know that you have made sacrifices they understand and that you are not alone."

"I've never thought I was alone. I live on a kibbutz."

"Yes, but everyone knows that you can be surrounded by people and yet feel alone. I can tell, even in these few moments of acquaintanceship, that you are independent. You saved the entire kibbutz almost by yourself. Now, you are hurt. Rest fully and recover well. I want you to know that your friends will not abandon you. I wanted to tell you that personally."

When Eigherman left I lay back down on my cot and put my hands behind my head. The wound was healing fast and I knew it would only be few weeks until I could be back to normal. I struggled with his words. Although it was good to be 'recognized' I knew also that it was absolutely necessary not to feel special in any way. This was not simply humility; it was essential to my survival. It was given that in the field you must be focussed and grounded. To think you were a hero was to put others in harms way. I regarded Eigherman's visit as sign of trust, not as a sign of any personal victory. I did my best to forget about it, or more specifically to consider it as a slight but meaningful part of my training.

Two days later I had another visitor. She came upon me as I was sitting on a stone beside the front gate of the kibbutz. I could see her coming up the road in the distance, a graceful silhouette against the backdrop of fields. There was something familiar about the way she moved, but I couldn't place it. As she came closer I felt my pulse quicken involuntarily, even before I recognized her. I stood as she approached to greet her and as soon as I did I knew who she was; Hannah, who I had trained with many weeks before.

I held out my hands in greeting, and she grasped them both in response. "Shalom, Avrum!" she said happily. "You look as good as I hoped you would!"

"Hannah! I can say the same for you."

"Is this your 'thinking spot'?" she asked playfully.

"I suppose so. The view is terrific."

I felt uncharacteristically demure. I was home here. She had come to visit me. I was flattered. She looked very healthy and fit.

"This is where you live?" It was more of a statement than a question. Her voice was low and husky, as I remembered it. There was an almost tense sureness to it, as if the very rocks would crack if she called them to.

"Yes, this is it." Despite myself I was feeling nearly proud of where I lived, as if I had somehow made it so beautiful. It was her face that made me feel that way. It was as handsome as the view. "Come. I'll show you around."

As we walked down the road toward the kibbutz, making small talk about the agriculture, I felt a low rumble in my stomach. Nerves, most likely. They were not caused by fear or discomfort. They were caused by a simple, physical craving. My experiences in training and the field had brought upon me a curious apperception of my body. It had become like a thing in itself; it seemed to wake to every impulse and I was like a creature with no mind, but instinct. Hannah affected me with an animal response. I've heard other people talk about this, but it was the first time I had felt it. This was the only woman I had ever known who could challenge me with her bare hands.

I expressed my feelings about kibbutz life. "Everyone has a function, and we work together to make the farm efficient and complete."

"Like clockwork" she asked.

I looked at her quizzically and shook my head. "You might think so, but no, it's not like clockwork. There are bells, it's true, and schedules as well. But it's not as mechanical as clockwork. It's more organic, like a living thing. We don't do our jobs because we 'have to', or even because we need to. We want to make the kibbutz work. We desire to help each other, to respect each other, and to support each other. There is always a sense that we are moving towards something, that we are making history. It's wonderful."

Hannah radiated appreciation at these words. "You sound happy and excited."

Perhaps I blushed. "I am. Is that bad?"

She laughed. "Not at all! I don't remember you ever expressing such emotion."

My embarrassment must have shown. "I don't think about it all the time. In fact, when you're working, you don't have time to be aware of all this. But while I've been resting, not involved in the day to day activity of the kibbutz, I've been able to see how it works. That's why I'm so impressed and excited."

She put her hand on my shoulder in a friendly gesture, one that expressed a touch of intimacy as well. "Avrum, you're an unusual man. A poet warrior."

"Ah, no!" I said. "I simply live in Israel. I'm not unusual at all."

We reached the first buildings. I told her what each place was for and little stories about each one to characterize them and the people who worked there. Because I was nervous I talked on and on, but Hannah never showed any sign of being tired or bored. We approached the dinning hall just at dinner time.

We sat with Dov. Our conversation was excited and broad. I introduced Hannah as someone I had met through a friend while taking classes in Tel Aviv. Everyone knew I was suffering from a gunshot wound, but the story was that I had been hurt in an accident. People didn't ask questions or press the issue. Anyone who pursued the issue would know the truth; it was certain that the underground pursued terrorist activities and news of the airfields had been broadcast in certain circles. I was sure that Dov knew I was a fighter. It explained a lot of incidents that surrounded me but were not fully explained, and he knew my feelings politically.

He didn't give any indication that he knew or suspected anything. He was gracious, funny and lively, a marked contrast to my own demeanour, which was more introverted. It wasn't that I was feeling moody. It was that I was enjoying watching Hannah and Dov relate to each other. They were enjoying themselves so much.

After the meal Hannah and I sat by the fireplace in the central square. A few people passed by but it was essentially quiet.

"I think a part of me yearns for this kind of life. It's so relevant. So valid." Hannah said. "I think this is what Israel is all about."

"If you think so," I said, "why don't you live on a kibbutz?"

She shrugged and smiled at me coyly. "Oh, I don't know." She looked me directly in the eye. "I have a wild nature."

This I knew to be true. I laughed loudly. "Yes." I replied. "But you have a pensive spirit."

I never expressed my actual feelings for Hannah, not to her, not to anyone else, not even really to myself. Of all the people I had met since I had arrived in Palestine, Hannah was the one who stirred excited emotions in me. She was the only person who made me feel something like the way I felt about Miriam. In fact, she reminded me of Miriam and at the same time she compelled me to feel that there might be someone else in the world that I could possibly love the way I loved her. In the back of my mind I knew that eventually someone would again be in my thoughts, but I encountered that possibility most when I was with Hannah. I don't know how Hannah felt, but when I waited with her when she caught the bus on the road in front of the kibbutz she kissed me goodbye with a kiss that was too deep for simple friendship. We were people who lived on the edge of life and death. I felt, as I waved at the departing bus with her on it, that something had happened in this unexpected visit. Our defences had dropped, and we were facing each other on potentially more intimate ground.

In late July, 1946, about 5 weeks after I had been wounded at the air field, I received a message to report to a location in Jerusalem for an assignment. I was, at that time, fully recovered and ready to participate in an action. When I reported to the place at 7 a.m. and gave the correct password to the guard I was sent to a large room where about 20 men and women were assembled. Some of them I knew and exchanged greetings with. None of us knew the target of this mission at that time. It was 26th of the month.

A few minutes after I arrived the senior command came to the front of the room and began to speak. He explained that the mission was complex, required precise timing and exact operation and that the target was an extremely important one. He revealed that we were going to blow up the King David Hotel.

The King David hotel had been a luxury hotel, built by Jewish financiers in 1931. The entire southern wing had been requisitioned by the British Mandatory Government in 1938 and was used as their central military command because it was easy to guard. It was an important objective, though a very tricky one. The plan was drawn up in two stages.

First, operatives dressed as Arabs arrived at the side entrance of the hotel by bus in order to assist the unloading of the van when it arrived. A group, also dressed as Arabs approached the King David in a van loaded with seven milk-churns packed heavily with explosives. When they arrived the 'porters', who were already in place, helped them unload the containers and, disguised as delivery personnel, they overcame the guards at the loading entrance of the 'La Regence' restaurant and hastened to the basement. They searched the adjacent rooms and collected the staff in the restaurant kitchen. Next, they brought the explosives into the hotel and placed them at strategic supporting pillars. When this was accomplished the fuse was set for 30 minutes and the staff instructed to leave the building 10 minutes after the fighters left. Thus, the bombs were set and secure and the explosives timed for half and hour

At this point the second stage of the operation began. I was positioned in a location outside the hotel as back up. As the agents, dressed as Arabs, left the building their activity was detected and they came under heavy fire from the hotel. One man fell from a bullet to the hip but was pulled into the van. Another was hit in the chest and was also taken aboard the van before it was able to pull out. When these men were clear I was able to carry out my specific function.

Two female operatives were dispatched to nearby telephone booths to call the telephone operator and also the editorial office of the Palestine Post. My function was to cover one of these women in case there might be any problem. Both of the female agents made their calls successfully and with no problems. At this point the bombs were positioned and set to explode, the press had been notified and instructed to contact the hotel immediately and the telephone system had been notified as well so that lines to the security forces in the hotel could be clear and the military presence alerted.

It was our turn to wait, now. Although we didn't know so at the time, the evacuation of the King David Hotel under this desperately real threat was detained. Word was received by both the staff of the government secretariat and the military command, that the Hotel was mined and that an explosion was imminent. Both decided not to take action or begin to evacuate the hotel. Apparently, they refused to take orders from the Jewish underground. I stood at a safe distance across from the Hotel as the minutes pressed on, waiting anxiously for signs of an evacuation. It never arrived.

Twenty-five minutes after the female agents had completed their phone calls a devastating explosion rocked the city. The entire southern wing of the King David Hotel blew with frightful fury. I watched in stunned silence as the seven story structure, with its people inside, collapsed completely. Windows in surrounding building, except those in the French consulate, were shattered. Apparently, they had taken the warning of the underground seriously and had opened all their windows. There was nothing more for me to do at this point, as rescue crews began to arrive. I left, with no feeling of having won even though our objective had been destroyed. I would have stayed to help pull survivors out of the wreckage, but couldn't risk it. It took ten days to clear the debris from the blast. On July 31 it was announced that 91 people had died in the explosion.

News of the attack spread very quickly over the entire world, and outraged was expressed from almost every quarter. In Israel the heads of the Jewish Agency were shaken. They denounced the operation in the strongest terms, fearing that the British backlash would be so severe it would undermine their political situation. They expressed "their feelings of horror at the base and unparalleled act perpetuated…by a gang of criminals". David Ben Gurion, the head of the Jewish Agency, declared that the Irgun was "the enemy of the Jewish People". This was said despite the fact the attack on the Kind David Hotel had been a part of the United Resistance activity. The attack had, ironically, pointed to two distinct issues. On the one hand, it showed the contempt the British had towards Jewish resistance. On the other hand, it illustrated that a clear and consistent line of resistance, though not real at the time, was necessary.

The loss of life at the King David Hotel caused me to pause over my commitment to armed struggle; it did not cause me to relinquish it. Conversely, it made me realize how important it was to maintain a military force of resistance in Israel. The British contempt for our struggle for independence was made clear in this unfortunate event. It was their stubborn refusal to even acknowledge the attack that caused the deaths. The Irgun was definite, in the leaflet accepting responsibility, that they had given 22 minutes to clear the building, and this was later proved in court. It was possible for me to arrive at this condition when I fell back upon my experience as a Jew in Europe. If the world wanted to express horror at the loss of life, it should recognize first the attempted genocide on the Jewish people. There was no doubt in my mind, now especially, that our actions were justified at the King David. Only by 'fire' could we fight 'fire'. The world would see that our cause was real when they understood that our intentions were just. And they would see this, I was sure.

A letter from a British commander shortly after the explosion and subsequently made public proved this point. Having issued a command ordering all Jewish places of entertainment, restaurants, shops and homes off limits to British personnel, he ended by saying: "The aim of these orders are to punish the Jews in a way the race dislikes as much as any, namely by striking in their pockets". The anti-Semitic content embarrassed the British government and diverted some public opinion from the King David Hotel bombing.

The final effect of this experience was actually to increase the validity and strength of the Irgun. The breakdown of the short lived 'united Jewish resistance' meant we were free from the Haganah to operate alone. Despite the disquiet caused by the loss of life at the King David Hotel, due to the success of the operation the number of recruits increased. Also, we were able acquire more guns and ammunition from British army depots. For my part, after a brief period of quiet, I had been brought back into action. I thought about my role every day. I was very hungry for the State of Israel.

Two weeks after the bombing of the King David Hotel it was clear that there would be a holding period within the Irgun before we would be called up again. Although we were all on standby, the leaders took advantage of a period of inactivity to reassess and restructure our activities. Now that we were no longer a part of a united resistance we needed to set goals and stage objectives.

I took the time to establish my working relations at the kibbutz after the period of recovery from my shoulder wound. I took up my role as security officer and began to work nights again. Fortunately, there were no incidents. During the afternoon I often helped with odd jobs around the kibbutz. There was plenty to do, and I enjoyed the activities because it kept my mind busy. I had learned that too much leisure could be a distracting, if not destructive, force. It was good to have some time to contemplate philosophical and emotional issues, but too much contemplation tended to hurt my objectivity. I had nothing against philosophy but preferred to find it relevant to a man of action. I was very slowly coming to see myself as a man of action although certainly not as a 'hero' as some others seemed to like to see me. I was still a *Yeshiva* Boy at heart, and my faith in God had not diminished. Indeed, my faith in God had become even stronger although my faith in religion had waned.

This last point had troubled me quite a bit until I was wounded. Up until that time I had tried to believe that I was fighting for the Jewish religion, not just the Jewish nation. I believed that God favoured the Jewish people, despite all that had happened in the camps. But my life did not confirm my beliefs. My life did not give me time to be observant or much chance to be observant. I thought of myself, even though I was a killer, as a moral person, and this was on account of Jewish principles. But the randomness of events, the frame of mind one needed to be a fighter, was in contrast to observance. There was no blessing to be said before you killed someone, no time to wash your hands before throwing a grenade. I had to shoot a gun on the Sabbath and eat *traif* when disguised as an Arab. The observance of the Jewish religion was not possible in the camps, and it's true I wondered what good observance was overall at that time. But even more so in the field a suspension of religion seemed essential to survive.

The laws of the Talmud were true enough but they were not what I was fighting for explicitly. The religion of the Jews made them a people, but it was mostly made up of customs and traditions. The laws had a place in the life of a Jew, but they could not be everything. One thing was absolutely clear. Although we might act according to these laws, God did not. His rule was invisible and seemingly arbitrary to the common man. I was respectful of religion because it informed people of what was right and wrong and enriched their lives with ceremony. It was essential to maintaining the Jewish people through the Diaspora. Now, it was time to physically fight for Israel. In Jewish tradition there are religious people and there are warriors and each is instructed to respect the other. I didn't know until I reached Israel that I was not a religious person. I had chosen to be a warrior and that had drawn me away from religion. The ironic element to this was that it had, perhaps, drawn me closer to God.

I received a message from Hannah several weeks into this period of transition. I contacted her by phone and we arranged to meet soon after in Tel Aviv. I looked forward to seeing her with anticipation and with trepidation as well. We would be alone together and, with the very strong exception of my time with Miriam, I was not actually used to spending much time alone with women I very much liked.

We met at a café. She was wearing a long taupe skirt and a simple white blouse. I was struck by her clothes, especially because she looked so good in them. She kissed me on the cheek when she arrived and squeezed my hand. I smiled brightly, but inside I was actually experiencing anxiety. I had a bus ticket in my pocket that was good for two days.

"How was your trip?" she asked. I was glad the first question was so simple.

"It was pleasant except for the woman beside me carrying a chicken."

We talked about things that had happened to us over the past few weeks. I told her stories from the kibbutz. She told me about her work in Tel Aviv. This was pleasing and it gave us a chance to be familiar without being intrusive. There was a break in the conversation.

"I thought we could go to the market. We'll pick up some things, take them back to my apartment, and I'll make dinner for you. Does that sound alright?"

I made my face seem very bright. "Yes, fine. Don't go to any trouble."

"No trouble." She replied almost coquettishly. "Vegetables. Maybe chicken? Something simple but delicious."

We began to stroll towards the market and she took my arm lightly but with purpose. I felt very flattered, despite myself. At the same time, I felt comfortable or, in the most positive sense, happy. It was unusual for me to feel happy. I normally didn't allow it, but this day was different.

Shopping in the market was rare. I had not ever done much of it, although I had often seen couples like us shopping together in Budapest when I was in the black market. I think at times I vaguely wondered if I would ever be in a similar situation, thinking at that time that it would be unlikely. Observant Jewish men and women don't touch. But this felt strangely right. Choosing the perfect pepper. Making sure the onion was fresh. Such everyday things seemed so special. They were special because I had met Miriam on the way to the camps and she was the first woman I had ever been close to. After the camps I had little chance to be intimate, except for a short while with Arly. I had never been in public with a woman like this before. It was special because I was a fighter in a war that was still going on. The realities of that life and the reality of this moment were distinct. And, most of all, it was special because of Hannah. She seemed so right to me, in the market, looking for the perfect things to cook.

When we were alone in her comfortable one room apartment and she was preparing dinner our conversation turned more serious and more intimate. We talked about the Irgun.

"Do you think it was a mistake to destroy the King David?" she asked cautiously.

"It was the military intelligence centre of our enemy. Is that wrong?"

"The war was won by the Allies. The world hates to hear about British soldiers being killed in Palestine. By the Jews."

"So you think it was a mistake?"

"No. It was the British who brought on their own tragedy. This is a land that is at war. I think the British have to realize the meaning of that"

There was a pause. I said, "The world must be aware of our situation. We have suffered an unaccountable tragedy by following without defence the actions of a people. We must obtain our land or disappear. There is no more Diaspora, there is only a homeland here. The world must give us that, and we must show them that we are serious in this matter. If the world doesn't respect the loss of millions of our people then we must risk upsetting the implacable world."

Hannah stopped cooking and looked at me with an expression of surprise. "You sound like a politician, not a soldier now."

I smiled. "Would you elect me?"

Hannah laughed. "Not until you've kissed a thousand babies."

Hannah was subdued during dinner. There was something going on with her that made her seem softer and more feminine than usual. I felt myself drawn in, as if to a net, that was as gentle and easy as floating in a pool. There was nowhere to sit together in her apartment except the bed. After dinner we sat on it, cross legged at first. I felt very relaxed. I felt very young. I felt a great deal of anxiety falling away. While we were discussing life in Europe, Hannah took my arm. It was under her initiative that I was slowly drawn toward her, closer until our noses touched. Then our lips.

We kissed for a long time. "You can stay the night." She said with a note of hope and expectancy. "Can I?" was all I said. In the morning, with the sheets loosely thrown about her, she looked more beautiful than any sight I ever imagined to see. I know that every man has a sight like this that is so wonderful. This was my time to be so blessed. Who can doubt the work of God when one sees such things and experiences such emotion.

CHAPTER 24
Acre

The period following the bombing of the King David Hotel was tense, but there was a break in offensive operations. Despite the appearance of indifference to world opinion in the ranks of our organization, it became important at this time to legitimize the work of the Irgun as a valid force fighting a just war in their own homeland. We had to show that we were not reckless renegades out on a rampage. We had to show that we were not bloodthirsty or random. The world had to see that the battle for Israel was a battle for a people and a civilization and in no way a war of attrition or an act of vengeance.

There were several very specific attacks in the year after the King David bombing that created interest in world opinion and helped establish legitimacy for our cause. I must say that it was not only the reasons behind our cause that created notoriety. It was also specifically the integrity and composure of our fighters that helped turn the tables. In this period, which lasted almost a year, the validity of creating a State of Israel for the Jewish people grew stronger.

An operation that took place before the King David Hotel bombing reached the public in January, 1947 with a military trial. Executing a daring plan to obtain weapons, a group of Irgun members approached a police station in a military vehicle, some dressed as Arabs and some dressed as British soldiers. Their apparent purpose was for the disguised soldiers to deliver the Arab prisoners who had purportedly been caught stealing at an army camp.

On a signal from the leader the disguised fighters pulled out revolvers and quickly occupied the station. When that was secured they approached the armoury and blew the door open with their weapons, but an armed guard who was posted on an upper level discovered the activity and opened fire with a machine gun. The fighters managed to get most of the target arms into the truck, however there were casualties. Two men were killed by gunfire and a third was wounded. The wounded man was Dov Gruner.

What caught the eye of the international community from this event was not only the fact that it was entirely directed at a military function or that it was both daring and well planned. It was, rather, the integrity and purposefulness of the accused when he came to trial in January, 1947. He refused to recognize the court, but issued a written statement. I have saved it, in part, here:

I do not recognize your authority to try me. This court has no legal function, since it was appointed by a regime without a legal foundation.

You came to Palestine because of the commitment you undertook at the behest of the nations of the world to rectify the greatest wrong caused to any nation in the history of mankind, namely the expulsion of Israel from their land, which transformed them into victims of persecution and incessant slaughter throughout the world. It was this commitment, and this commitment alone, which constituted the legal and moral basis for your presence in this country. But you betrayed it wilfully, brutally and with satanic cunning. You turned your commitment into a mere scrap of paper.

When the prevailing government of any country is not legal, when it becomes a regime of oppression and tyranny, it is the right of its citizens—more than that, it is their duty—to fight this regime and to topple it. This is what Jewish youth are doing and will continue to do until you quit this land and hand it over to its rightful owners, the Jewish people.

Gruner was sentenced to death. Appeals were made to commute his sentence both internally and abroad. He was urged to plead for clemency but insisted on being tried as a prisoner of war. He was hung in the Spring of 1947 with three other condemned Jewish fighters They issued a public statement before their execution in response to international appeals to them to ask for clemency:

Do you not understand that your requests for clemency are an affront to your honour and the honour of the entire people? It represents servility towards the authorities reminiscent of the Diaspora. We are war prisoners and we demand that they treat us as war prisoners.

At present we are in their hands. We cannot resist them, and they can treat us as they choose…But they cannot break our spirit. We know how to die with honour as befits Hebrews.

On the day he was hung I was on the kibbutz. At lunch time I could not eat, and I went to sit out near the gate of the farm. Dov came to join me shortly after I sat down.

"Is it a sad day or a good day?" he asked plainly.

I looked at his face. There was a helpful smile on his lips. Dov was a diplomat; he knew how to control other people's emotions. "It's both good and bad. It's good because what is happening may help our cause. But it's not good that a soldier has to die."

"It could have been you."

"In any way I can think of it, it was me. Gruner is a man first and foremost, but he is also a symbol of our cause. He is an articulate symbol. People understand, when they hear his words, that we are in a country that belongs to us and that we are willing to die for."

Dov sat beside me. "Do you think it is different in other countries?"

I didn't pause on my reply. "Look, there are patriots in every country, but there is no real parallel to the Jews in Israel. The war destroyed us, we were destroyed in the camps all over Europe. We are a displaced people with a just claim to our homeland. We have to show that, above all else, we are adamant and unerring in this purpose."

Dov wanted mostly to help ease my pain, but he had other motives as well. "Is there nothing else besides martyrdom and rhetoric that will lead to a consensus in world opinion?"

It was my turn to lead Dov. "You think I applaud martyrdom, Dov? Do you think I endorse violence for the sake of violence?"

Dov was defensive. "No, no I don't think that for a minute. I think you endorse the means to achieve peace."

My emotions had been engaged. I knew that I would not be purely rationale at this point. "Without actions that are violent no one will look at us, no one will see us and, inevitably no one will care about us either. How many times I looked into the faces of the nation that surrounded us in Europe and saw not a glimmer of hope or concern. They relished our plight, looted our houses, turned their backs on us and forgot us. They could smell our corpses burning in the camps. They endorsed it. Jews are cheap but Jews are rich off our backs. People believe what flatters them and they believe what others around them believe. There are millions of times more followers than leaders and the leaders only believe in one thing…power and the will to violence."

Dov was more hurt than shocked. He felt recriminated. "You're wrong!" he said with some emotion. "Most people do what they believe in if given a chance. Its not violence that changes the world. It's freedom. Freedom to lead a meaningful life in peace."

"But when you have no freedom, Dov, what then? You have the freedom to walk, crawl or be carried to the oven, to the battlefield, to the gallows."

"It's not my purpose to criticize the cause of Israel, Avrum, only to say that the goal of war is to create freedom and that there are many ways to fight for that."

"You don't understand oppression, Dov." I wanted to distinguish justice from random violence. "The oppressor doesn't want justice. Justice is, in fact, it's enemy. The British have to know that we are also here in Palestine and that we are not afraid to fight them. This is not their land, they are an occupying force and they have to experience pain and resistance or they will never leave. They will have no reason to leave. The Jews hold the seeds to civilization. We are a valuable people. We have to stand up for ourselves."

Dov backed down at this moment. "Every day, when I wake up and go to work on the kibbutz, I am stating my commitment to Israel, my commitment to a way of life and my commitment to justice. A good man was hung today. I am very sorry for it, and I acknowledge personally and politically that it was wrong. What is of grave concern to me is that it could have been you. It just as easily could have been me. My fight is not with the British themselves. It's with ignorance and hatefulness in every form. There are many ways to make strong statements that the world can hear. These statements can be heard from anywhere, not only, God help us, from the gallows."

BAR KOCHBA

Two weeks after Gruner and three others were hung in Acre prison, two other prisoners in death cells died also. Their names were Meir Feinstein and Moshe Barazani. On the day of their proposed execution fellow members of the Irgun and Lehi managed to smuggle to them two improvised grenades packed inside oranges. Before they could be taken to the gallows they exploded the grenades that were held embraced between them at the level of their hearts

Although I was previously aware of my own reasons for joining the Irgun, and although I had not be disappointed by our rationale or by the leaders, these executions and others that also occurred around this period were extremely meaningful to me. Certainly the death of comrades under any circumstances was tragic, but the executions were unusual because they gave a political face to the Irgun activity. The world could hear our voice, and we all knew that it was the opinion of the world, in our favour, that would finally turn the political fortunes towards us. The words of one of the fighters expressed the nature of this message very clearly:

You wonder how it came to pass that those Jews whom you thought to be cowards, who were the victims of massacre for generations, have risen up against your rule, are fighting your armies, and when they stand in the shadow of death, they scorn it... Their courage and spiritual force are drawn from two sources; the renewed contact of Hebrew youth with the land of their fathers, which has restored to them the tradition of courage of the heroes of the past, and the lesson of the Holocaust, which taught us that we are conducting a struggle not only for our liberty but also for our very survival.

On May 3, 1947 I was summoned to a diamond factory in the city of Netanya. There were about 30 of us assembled there to receive instructions for our mission. We were going to enact an escape from the walled prison of Acre, known around the world as being impenetrable.

Acre was an old city situated at a port which was considered the main gateway to Palestine. It had been conquered by the Ottomans at the beginning of the 16th century, at which time a strong fortress was established to protect the port. It was surrounded by thick walls and a dry moat. The fortunes of the city fluctuated for centuries, sometimes thriving for a time and alternately falling into disrepair. The fortress had been turned into a miserable prison which also had a varied history under Turkish rule. When the British mandate began the prison fortress was established as a central holding station for both Jewish and Arab prisoners. Many of the Jewish prisoners were Irgun fighters, some belonged to the Lehi and the Haganah. At the time of our briefing there were 163 Jewish political prisoners and approximately 400 Arabs. We could only free 41 of the Jewish fighters because it would not be possible to finding hiding places for more.

Prior to the briefing, several events had occurred to make our assault possible. One of the Irgun prisoners was informed by an Arab inmate that he had heard women's voices outside the wall by a kitchen storeroom for oil. The Jewish prisoners were in constant preparation for an escape. This particular inmate deduced that the south wall bordered on a street or alley of the old town. This news was crucial and an Irgun officer, disguised as an Arab, reconnoitred the site. It was subsequently discerned that a prison break was possible using the south wall as an escape route.

Careful plans were made which of necessity involved inmates of the prison. It was established that parents of prisoners were allowed to bring them food items such as jam and oil. It was clear that the inmates needed explosives to be used in the escape. Necessary materials were arranged to arrive in selected containers. A few of the parents undertook the dangerous task of delivering these materials to their sons at Acre. In several cases, gelatine was concealed in jars of jam. Although these jars were examined by the guards, the bearers explained that the specific batch had not set properly so that they seemed to contain hard lumps. The jam was passed on to the prescribed inmate. The detonators were placed in a false bottom of containers of oil. When the guard checked the containers with a stick he did not detect this false bottom. It was less than a centimetre thick. In this way, the Irgun fighters on the inside of the prison had the materials they needed to assist with the escape. It was decided by the most senior Irgun inmate which of the Irgun members would actually be freed. The members of Lehi decided who of their number should go.

Our briefing on May 3rd included this information as well as details we would need to know regarding the escape operation. Twenty of us were to be disguised as British soldiers. We were all given the official haircut of the British forces and we were instructed in how to act as British military personnel. Our mission was to enact the planned escape the next day.

Although it was not easy to act British, since my actual contact with the British military was not large, I attacked the role eagerly. It must be said that our leaders made this complex and difficult operation possible. Not only was the planning careful and precise, their utter confidence and complete sureness gave heart to the rest of us who followed their instructions. Never did I doubt that I could impersonate the British. Not a sliver of doubt was raised at any time that this effort could be undertaken with certainty. We understood from their behaviour and communication that everything we were about to do was legitimate and possible. I was both proud and excited to be involved with an operation to free others of my people. The danger was unquestionable, but the objective was so rewarding that it defied fear or doubt.

On May 4 we assembled at a strategic location and donned our uniforms. Twenty of us wore British uniforms and three others were dressed as Arabs. We formed a convoy including a 3-ton military truck, two military vans and two ordinary vans. We were headed by a Jeep carrying the commander of the exercise. I was with the military truck since my English was poor and I was less likely to be addressed in that group.

The operation of taking the wall and freeing the prisoners was meant to happen quickly and with clockwork efficiency. First the two civilian vans prepared to block routes leading to the prison wall. They laid mines at the roads entrance. At the same time our soldiers prepared the way at the wall itself where there were adjacent a Turkish bath and a market. Operatives took places on the roof or the Turkish bath posing as British personnel who had to repair phone lines. Meanwhile, the army truck was moved into position and in the necessary places along the wall were mined with explosives.

Inside the prison our inmates were ready. When their exercise period came up at 3:00 P.M. the designated escapees divided into 3 groups and each group gathered in a separate cell. Those who were not designated went to the prison yard with the intention of creating a diversion at the proper time.

We had a short wait before the major blast took place. At 4:22 P.M. it happened. There was a large explosion that rocked the entire area. When the smoke cleared a bit we were able to see the results: a large hole had been blasted in the wall of the prison. We could see the jail within.

At the moment of the explosion the designated inmates leapt out of their cells and hurried down the corridor towards the blast. There were a large number of Arab prisoners in the area running in confusion and making it difficult for our inmates to make their way. When they reached the first locked gate the explosives that had been smuggled into the jail were used to blow it open. At the same time, the Irgun fighters who were in the courtyard lit kerosene fires to create both a distraction and an obstruction to guards trying to follow the escape route of the other prisoners. Grenades were thrown at the roof to cause the guards to scatter. All of this created a great deal of confusion for the British and Arabs in the fortress. Under the cover of this confusion, 41 prisoners made their way to freedom. They were collected in the two vans and the army truck. My function was to guard the truck as it loaded prisoners and prepared to take off. At this particular moment there was no resistance. The British didn't know what had happened yet.

Just as we were loading one British soldier, who had been on the roof of the fortress prior to the explosion, realized what was happening. My commander was helping to load escapees onto the truck when this sniper opened fire. I was posted as a guard when I saw my leader struck in the leg. He fell wincing in pain. The smoke had not yet cleared so I could not see the shooter for a clear shot. I went to the assistance of the fallen leader, covering him as best I could. Another shot hit him in the shoulder. I knew I had to act quickly, not only to protect the man but also to be certain no one alive had seen our escape vehicle.

Everything suddenly became very still for me, in the midst of the smoke and confusion. First, I carried the wounded commander to the other side of the truck, out of the line of fire. Escapees were virtually pouring out of the devastated wall. My senses were very clear but my actions by contrast were almost dreamlike. The only way I could get a clear shot at the British soldier would be to stand on the hood of the truck. That would also give him a clear shot at me. I had to act very fast. In an instant I had jumped up on the hood of the truck. Without consciously taking aim I fired. I knew in my mind exactly where he was. A bullet whinged beside my arm and ricocheted off the truck's fender. Then the sniper fell from the roof and his body slammed into the ground. My senses returned to normal. I pushed my wounded captain away from the steering wheel in the truck, took control of the vehicle. The moment the last inmate was on board I took off speedily. No one alive had seen us load.

But everything did not go entirely well. Escapees in the first civilian van went the wrong way out of the city. They ran into a group of British soldiers who had been bathing in the sea but who recognized the van as an enemy vehicle. They were fired upon, and the van overturned. The two leaders were killed along with 5 of the 13 escapees. Six of the others were wounded. Also, both of the blocking units, the two military vans, failed to hear the signal to leave their stations. Both were engaged in battles and both were caught and suffered casualties.

Those of us who escaped were safely lodged throughout the country in various hiding places. I was able to return to the kibbutz within a few days, and my commanding officer was treated for his wounds. Before I left him with associates he took me by the arm. "I will make sure your courage is not forgotten." He said.

The results of our action at the prison of Acre were assessed soon after. Twenty-seven inmates succeeded in escaping (20 from the Irgun and 7 from Lehi). Nine fighters were killed, three from the operation and six from the prison. Eight inmates were caught and returned to prison (some of them injured) along with five attackers. Also escaping during the manoeuvre were 182 Arab prisoners.

It wasn't until I got back to the kibbutz two days later that I became aware of the political impact of the action at Acre. In contrast to the bombing of the King David Hotel almost a year earlier, the bombing at Acre had created headlines that were mostly in our favour. The precision of the attack, the earnestness of it and the daring nature helped make it clear that we were not acting randomly, but that we were a agency for political change and not simply an excuse for terror. The London Ha'aretz wrote, "The attack on Acre jail has been seen here as a serious blow to British prestige. Military circles described the attack as a strategic masterpiece."

The New York Herald Tribune said that the underground had carried out an 'ambitious mission, their most challenging so far, in perfect fashion." What is important here is that we are understood to be the 'underground', a reliable under-structure for a legitimate government in waiting. The world was beginning to see our actions as the struggle of a nation for both recognition and response. On example of this effect is that shortly after the action at Acre Andre Gromyko, the USSR representative to the United Nations stated that his country took a favourable view of the establishment of a Jewish state in Palestine.

The event of the prison break at Acre may have been part of a turning point in the British hold on Palestine, but it cannot be seen as an act in isolation. The free nations of the world had been inundated with horrible words and images of the Jewish people from the death camps, from Cypress and from Palestine. Many people understood that the Jews had been persecuted almost out of existence and many people were sympathetic to the Jews gaining their own independence in a State of Israel. It was also becoming incumbent on the world to recognize that the Jews had nowhere to go but Palestine. People wanted to see us with the strength and certainty of a homeland and they wanted to acknowledge that we had a place in their world in spite of the terrible images of persecution and genocide. The idea of Jews who are free setting other Jews free from yet another prison is powerful in a way that other images are not. The fact that it was well organized and expertly executed meant something as well. We knew who we were and what we were doing. Our actions were political in this sense and possibly even viable.

Also, the British had suffered another defeat. This is something they could not overlook. This is where the strategy and the detail are so important. We are an army, too. We are capable and effective and we will not stop until we win. The British would have a hard time deflecting world opinion, it's true. But perhaps even more true is how sure is their ability to maintain their presence in Palestine from a military point of view. That is where the line falls between control and defeat.

Shortly after returning from the action at Acre I had an opportunity to meet Hannah in Haifa. We met at a favourite café. I arrived early. I saw her arrive from the street dressed in shorts and plain blouse. It wasn't the clothes. When I caught site of her approaching I felt my temperature rise.

"Shalom!" she said. "Have you been waiting long?"

"No. I just got here a few minutes ago."

She placed her hand on top of mine and squeezed. "You look relaxed."

I didn't smile because I didn't want to express uncomfortable emotions. "I have some free time."

"I'm flattered that you contacted me. I want to spend some time with you."

"I have two days."

She looked at the ground, then looked up and smiled slightly. "You can't scare me, you know. I have some classes tomorrow. Maybe you can go with me?"

I maintained my distance. "That could be possible." I wasn't really non-committal about anything, I was simply frightened by my emotions. Hannah seemed so perfect to me, so self-assured. I felt awkward socially and awkward romantically. My personal life had not seen a great deal of relationships with women. I was afraid to miss and I was afraid to connect. Hannah could see that.

She looked at me closely. "What's going on, Avrum? What are you afraid of? Is there something I don't know that I should know?"

I shook my head and tried to appear casual. "No, no. Nothing like that. I'm just very glad to see you."

"Very glad? You're very glad to see me?" she asked inquiringly.

"I've never really had relationship like this. It's not terribly common for me to meet a woman in a café, despite appearances. There were no cafes in my village, only a kind of tavern where the Jews never went."

"I forget that you grew up in a shteitl. You seem very worldly, you know."

"When I sold food on the Black Market I saw a lot of things I hadn't seen before in Budapest. There were cafes. I used to see the couples drinking coffee and liqueurs and beer. I couldn't go. I had payas and a big hat. But I did learn something just by being there, by seeing it around me. It looked nice, I must admit. I think I felt a little resentful that I wasn't a part of it."

Hannah looked serious. "Do you feel more a part of it now? After all, this is Israel. You belong here more than anywhere. And I care about you."

I laughed a little at the irony of it. "Everybody seems to care about me, one way or the other it seems. In some ways I'd rather be a little anonymous."

"You have a low opinion of yourself, Avrum. You are many things perhaps, perhaps even you have many traits that are contradictory. But you are not anonymous. You have a very strong presence. You appear very strong."

"I've seen quite a bit of life, I guess, even though I am from a shteitl." I was thinking of Miriam although I couldn't show it. I could see how different Hannah was from her, but also how much they shared in common. They both had a feminine quality that I found rare and difficult to describe. It was a self control that seemed to hold their character together with a complete integrity. They knew who they were as women. They both seemed to understand emotions perfectly, whether their own or other people's. But whereas Miriam had been almost childlike in her softness, Hanna had a quality of hardness inside. She was more capable than Miriam of taking matters into her own hands.

"You have seen a lot of the world but you don't always see yourself as part of it."

I had heard enough about myself. "It's nice that you see this, Hannah, but I'm not able to participate in self-analysis. I need to know what I think more than I need to know how I feel."

The waiter arrived at that moment and took our order. Hannah laughed to ease the bit of tension between us. She leaned close to my face and whispered happily, "Would you like a beer? Just for a change?"

I laughed also to make things right. "Alright. Sure. I'd like a beer." The waiter left.

"You're not going to get me drunk, if that's your major plan." I said.

"I expect to drag you home by the hair." She said. The thing about Hannah that I so much liked and found remarkable was that she could make everything right with a word or a gesture. She had an uncanny talent for harmony.

"Did you read about the attack at Acre?" she asked.

"Yes. I did." This was public knowledge and therefore reasonable to discuss.

"I think it may be a turning point."

"Perhaps. The press seems a little more supportive of a Jewish homeland."

"They are taking our efforts at least seriously."

I replied, "It really depends on what happens at the U.N."

We chatted in a conventional way until the beer came, and then talked more about simple topics. It was amazing to me that Hannah could keep a conversation running through many twists and turns and make you feel fresh and interesting all the time. I wondered, as we were talking, if I was in love with her. It was hard for me to know because there were many emotions in my immediate experience and love was not one that I actually welcomed. I was thinking about my comrades who had been killed or captured only three days before. I wondered what I would be doing now if Hannah hadn't been there to help me. Quite probably I'd be ranging alone in the hills near the kibbutz, taking the whole thing very personally. I was thinking also about the Jewish heroes who had gone to their deaths, either on the gallows or in the field, with courage and dignity. Would I be as noble and example, if it happened to me.

Being with Hannah felt good, whether I was in love with her or not in a romantic sense. I loved her very much as a comrade. Late that night, after a full evening together, I experienced once again how much I desired her as a lover. I never doubted her independence. I never doubted for a moment that she was also a warrior, just like me.

CHAPTER 25
A Prelude to Independence

In the period immediately following the Acre operation our attacks on British installations flagged somewhat because there was a great deal of diplomatic activity at the U.N. we didn't want to alter. That time was tense, but also hopeful. We didn't have a lot of opportunity to relent in our general activity because there was an increase in activity by Arab factions. Much of it was seemingly random and we could only mount retaliatory strikes, but because the Arab activists were absorbed by the general community it was hard to know where to aim reprisals. Also, we didn't want to antagonize the U.N. situation by appearing random, so we often showed restraint here as well. From the middle of May, 1947 until the end of November that year I was involved personally in several missions dealing with Arabs, but these were essentially reconnaissance, not military.

The breakthrough at the United Nations came after months of manoeuvring and debate, not to mention the continued persecution of Jews who wanted to come to their homeland. The developed nations of the world felt something for what the Jews had suffered during the war. The acts or resistance on the part of the Irgun, the Haganah and the Lehi as well as the continuing political actions of the Jewish Agency paid off.

BAR KOCHBA

On November 29, 1947 the U.N. passed a resolution determining the partitioning of Palestine into Israeli and Arab sectors with Jerusalem as an international site. This resolution established that the existence of the State of Israel had finally been assured.

Although this resolution was certainly a turning point, we didn't have much opportunity to relax or vigilance within Israel. Arab hostilities dramatically increased, especially since the will of the British mandate was broken and they had the virtual freedom to mount attacks and operations without fear of interference. In the four months following the U.N. resolution approximately 850 Jews were killed throughout the country, the majority of them either in Jerusalem or the road to the city. The road to Jerusalem was blocked, settlements in the Galilee and Negev cut off and attacks were frequent. In early April an operation to clear the road to Jerusalem was initiated by the Irgun and the Lehi. It was called Operation Nachshon. When the Haganah learned of the plan to open up the town of Deir Yassin, they asked them to coordinate the plan with their own activity on another Arab town. Thus, a united effort to combine actions was undertaken. This was also an important step in the establishment of Jewish resources and a unified military force in what would soon be the State of Israel.

All of this I learned long after it happened. The increase in Arab attacks and the subsequent deaths were, of course, common knowledge but even members of the Irgun like myself knew little or nothing of their strategic plans or political activities. Following the U.N. resolution I was always prepared to be called away and the mood was tense overall. We were waiting, as a nation, on the brink of independence. I had a conversation with Dov and Hannah about our overall preparedness. Hannah visited us on the Kibbutz several times in that period.

The three of us were out for a walk on the roads outside of the kibbutz. It was late March. Beautiful spring. We were in an uncharacteristically light mood. Dov loved to be playful and he was teasing Hannah about her life in the city. "After the sun goes down you creep out of your dreary apartment into the nightlife of the city and soak up sophisticated life."

"Not true!" Hannah laughed. "My apartment isn't dreary. I don't creep out, like an insect, and I don't seek out sophistication. I merely enjoy urban pursuits like any natural person in most of the modern world. There's nothing wrong with that!"

"No," Dov chided. "except that you show our Arab friends a sign of Jewish culture that is not essentially from Israel. Its European."

"Its Israeli!" she cried. "Its as Israeli as khaki shorts."

"Are you criticizing my shorts?" Dov asked.

"I'm implying that they are natural, but no more than drinking espresso in a café. Goodness, we learned that from the Arabs."

"Soon to be our neighbours, not our hosts." I interjected. It wasn't my intention to dampen the conversation or to alter it. I wanted to be playful too. It was hard for me to be completely light hearted because I am by nature a more serious type. I am not always easy in casual situations. They have always seemed a bit strange and even mysterious to me. I am used to having a focus. I don't like this characteristic, particularly, but I have found it difficult to change. I would like to have the kind of easy wit that Hannah can display, but it always seemed strained for me. I envy Dov's kind and generous nature, but I am more pointed and clumsy. It doesn't show in my looks, which are somewhat graceful and natural. But I feel that touch of awkwardness sometimes. I suppose its more common a feeling than I am able to see in others. We are all, I suppose, self-conscious at times. My comment changed the tone of the conversation, though. Perhaps it was time to change anyway.

Hannah and Dov looked down at the ground. Dov said, "Our Arab hosts are not responding well to partition."

I replied, "Have they ever responded well to us?"

Hannah said, "They have no reason to kill us. We have offered to let them stay."

"Why should they 'be allowed to stay' in a land they have lived in for centuries" Dov said.

"We have a right to be here." I replied carefully. I wanted to express this to Dov specifically because I knew he had uneasy feelings about what was happening to the Arabs here. "Historically it's our home also. We were here for centuries, too."

"But in recent history?" Dov said this softly, like an apology.

Hannah replied. "This land has been occupied by one nation or another throughout almost every period. The Arabs know that."

"But it's still their home. You don't expect them to just get up quietly and humbly walk away!" Dov was expressing what I understood to be Jewish guilt.

I responded strongly but with concern, "I do expect them to be peaceful, whether they leave or not. But this is not really the question, Dov, because the world doesn't work that way. People have to fight for what they want in any situation. It's never handed to you on a platter."

Hannah broke in. "It's not a matter of the specific justice of what the Arabs want. We are in a situation. It's a difficult situation. No one can seem entirely right."

Dov expressed his dilemma. "Alright. So we have a right to our country which happens to be their country also. Should we kill them now?"

Hannah replied with some passion. "No one is killing them except as they kill us. Jews don't want to kill, but we know that we have to be strong in order to achieve what is, in fact, just. You want a State of Israel, you live for it. Do you think it comes without a cost?"

"I believe Jews want justice more than anything else in the world." Dov was also passionate. "But I believe that also means honouring others as ourselves."

"You don't understand, Dov." I had to clarify the truth of what we were saying. "We had to take this land from the Canaanites, and when we first failed to do that we were punished. G-d has His way. Now is no different. We have to fight to regain our land. That is a fact. The rest is merely rationalization."

Dov exclaimed, "How do we know who we kill! We have to be sure."

"Look!" I said to Dov. "I don't hate Arabs. I don't hate the British. This is war! Nobody wants it. Everybody hates it, but everybody is implicated in it just the same. Our right to survive is in jeopardy. We didn't start the war in Europe but we were victims of it. Now we are here, in Israel. We will not be victims here!"

Hannah turned to Dov and looked at his eyes. "Compassion is a human virtue. Even more, it is understood to be divine. But we are simple creatures. This land has two masters; that may be true. But it is not possible or right. The world has sanctioned Israel for the Jews. That's a fact, that's a reality that we must enforce. You don't need to hate the Arabs but you cannot ignore them. You can forgive them if they fight but you can't excuse it and go on like its not there. You have to deal with it. In this case, you have to fight. Maybe that's not great philosophy but its reality just the same."

It wasn't long after this that I was called back into duty. The British were no longer restraining us and were not operating against them. By April 6, 1948 the Arabs had successfully closed all routes into Jerusalem.

BAR KOCHBA

We were brought together outside the town of Deir Yassin to attempt to take the town and open a route to the city.

It was later called "The Massacre of Deir Yassin". This reputation was unwarranted. There was no massacre. There was a military assault, and I will show that great lengths were established to avoid bloodshed on the part of Arab civilians.

We assembled about 70 members of the Irgun at the Etz Hayim base at the entrance to Jerusalem. Since the British were no longer interfering, this was the largest number of Irgun soldiers ever assembled. We were about to test our resources in a military theatre for the first time. There was a political rationale for this operation, which would realize Jewish forces taking and holding an area. For the first time, the Irgun and combined forces would not be acting in retaliation for other actions. Also, we were fighting to establish, for both the inhabitants and for the world, that Jerusalem would not be given up by the Jews.

The Irgun fighters I was stationed with were moved into a levy outside the town of Deir Yassin. At about 4:45 a.m. an armoured car, which was rigged with a loudspeaker, was sent out towards the entrance of the town. Apparently, some guards in the town noticed movement and, due to a mistake in shouting the password, they became aware of our immanent attack and opened fire. Quickly the armoured car was forced to halt. I could see it from where I was, and it took an unprecedented step. It announced that our forces were going to attack and that any person who needed to leave could do so prior to the approach to the town of Ein Karem and that the road there would be open. We sustained some fire to give the townspeople a chance to leave, but within a short time I began to advance with my unit.

The fighting was very close; it was a fierce street battle from house to house. I had relevant experience in other operations as had most of my unit, but there were obviously going to be heavy casualties on both sides. This was complicated somewhat because we had been instructed not to attack Arab civilians, women or children. After entering the town, fighting was close, slow and deliberate. I could see the eyes of the foes I shot. It was impossible to see the source of gunfire in all cases and we were forced to use hand grenades at times. In some cases it was necessary to blow up houses.

Mid-way in the battle I arrived at a corner square. In order to get to the next street we had to cross a small road, but it was covered by fire from another low building. Two of our fighters lay behind the wall of one corner. Another was lying in the middle if the street. I came upon them from the rear with a comrade. Without thinking of the consequences I assessed the situation and, instinctively more than consciously, got into action.

"Cover me!" I cried to my comrade. I leapt into the intersection while he held down Arab fire and quickly dragged the wounded soldier from the street. Then, without stopping to make any further decision, I ran keeping low across the corner to a place below a blasted window. I took a grenade, pulled the pin, and threw it in the window. The blast was quick and loud. Before the smoke had cleared I rose up and, with my weapon ready, looked into the room. A shape moved to my left. I shot. Two more figures on the right, silhouetted in the smoke. I shot twice. There was no further movement. Carefully, I moved to the door. It was closed, but opened in. I kicked it hard. It swung back. A shot came my way from inside the building. I opened fire, then retreated behind the door again. No more shots, no more movement that I could hear.

A moment later my comrade was beside me. We flung back the door and looked inside. There were four Arabs lying dead on the floor. We had captured that corner, a key strategic point in the town.

BAR KOCHBA

Soon, at another part of Deir Yassin, a similar event occurred. The same comrade and I were approaching a large one story house. My companion was just ahead of me as we came around a corner we thought was safe. He was hit in the abdomen and fell to the ground. Without thinking I propped his body against the wall and assessed the situation. It was impossible to approach the house from this corner, but the enemy was firing from across it and they had to be stopped. There were no other of our fighters at that place.

Knowing that the Arabs could not see me at this angle, I crossed the street from behind them and entered the building from a rear window. The Arabs did not have it covered as luck would have it, but one of their number heard something and came through the inner door into the room. I shot first and he fell to the floor. Immediately two more came towards the door. Again I fired, as they did, but I was lucky and they missed whereas I didn't. One more of their group was in the other room. They were not as well trained as I. I stood by the open door and threw a babies toy into the corner to make a noise. The Arab fired, giving me a location. I quickly shot at where I now knew he was. An old trick, but it worked. There were no more enemy in that shelter. I went back for my comrade. Three of our men had arrived and he was being tended to. His wound was serious. We didn't know if he would live.

So it went through the whole town. It lasted most of the day. At the end we were able to destroy an important command centre and the fighting in Deir Yassin stopped. That house had been preventing civilians from leaving the city, but when it was captured hundreds of villagers retreated to Ein Karem as advised. Casualties on every side were very high. Villagers who remained behind were placed on busses and taken to East Jerusalem where they were handed back into Arab hands. I was exhausted. It was the longest sustained battle I had been in. The cleanup was also long, but we were given support by supplementary forces.

After the battle of Deir Yassin the press got word of atrocities committed by our side. The Arabs told of a 'massacre' of civilians, of rape and even of mutilation of pregnant women. 'Massacre' is defined as the mass killing of defenceless people. Certainly there was a battle, but it was a military manoeuvre and it was conducted by the rule of military conduct. There were certainly many deaths, and there were civilian deaths perhaps too. But you do not propagate a massacre by warning civilians be loudspeaker before attacking and leaving a route open for escape. The message the world press received and was perhaps eager to print was not true. Still, the effect lingers and the damage is done.

For my part, I did what my training and instincts required. My fallen comrade, who survived, was very kind to me. He reported to our officers what I had done in Deir Yassin and I was questioned on it. I told what I thought had happened. Word spread, again, that I had done well. Since this operation was not strictly an Irgun attack, word of my actions spread to leaders of the Haganah and the Lehi. I take no account of being a 'hero'; for one thing if I thought that were true it would impede my performance and for another thing I know it is not true. I know so because the blood of my companions tells me so in no uncertain terms. But this time, it helped me because we were in transition from a terrorist state into a politically independent State. That made my actions important in a different way. Soon, I hoped to be a citizen of Israel and acknowledged as a soldier in a legitimate army. It was my hope that I might gain from my actions then.

In late April, 1948 a large scale operation involving the Irgun as well as the Haganah and other independent forces was organized outside of

Jaffa, the largest Arab town in Palestine with a population of 90,000. It sat beside the Israeli city of Tel Aviv with a long, twisting border. Although the assault eventually came under the control of the Haganah it was first comprised of 600 Irgun fighters assembled at Dov Camp in Ramat Gan. It was the first time this large number of the Irgun ranks had gathered openly and, importantly, it was the first time the Irgun Commander, Menachem Begin, appeared publicly. He addressed us directly:

"We are going to conquer Jaffa. We are setting out on one of the decisive battles in the struggle for Israel's independence. Know who stands before you, remember who you have left behind. You face a cruel foe who wishes to destroy us. Behind you are our parents, our brethren, our children. Strike at the foe! Aim well! Spare ammunition! In this battle, show no mercy to the enemy, as he knows none towards our people. Spare women and children. Spare the life of anyone who raises his hands in surrender. He is your captive. Do not harm him."

This was a long battle by our standards up to this point. Like Deir Yassin, this was a military operation and not a reprisal, an again it was a battle to take and hold an area. But this battle was much heavier than the earlier one, involving more troops, more equipment and more integration of manpower and command. In the first day a key area of Manshiyeh was taken, and when it fell chaos erupted in the town. This may have helped our cause, but the British stepped in and deployed troops and equipment, taking full responsibility for the defence of Jaffa.

Despite this turn of events, and by the use of careful strategy and deployment of resources the Arabs surrendered on May 12. On May 13 the last of the British troops left Jaffa. In the meantime, negotiations between the Irgun and the other Jewish organizations in preparation for the impending independent Jewish State, were vigorous. This was, essentially, a formal agreement, and it was a bitter process. Although the Irgun had stated earlier that it would co-operate upon the formal establishment of the State of Israel and that its members would independently apply to the new national forces there were still differences between the factions that created some difficulties. In fact, it was not until later in the summer that the final events of the Irgun's existence came to an end.

After the taking of Jaffa the Irgun established the Jerusalem Battallion to protect the city until it was clearly established that it was to be a part of Israel. I was not a part of that unit. Although I returned to the kibbutz, I remained an Irgun operative, and although I was not summoned by them again until somewhat later I was aware of events.

There wasn't any time to be wistful over my period with the Irgun, which was now at an end. The State of Israel was soon to achieve Independence and would be immediately at war for its survival. I didn't have a chance to see Hannah soon after Jaffa but I did see Dov. He would also now be part of an army.

"Did you think this time would ever come?" I asked him at our evening meal.

He looked at me squarely. "I didn't 'think' it would come. I knew it would come. There was no doubt in my mind that it would come. I didn't know when."

"You have a university degree. You'll probably be an officer"

He laughed. "My degree is in literature! I don't know very much about being in the army."

I patted his shoulder with no hint of patronizing him. "You'll do well."

"I'm not as athletic as you."

"Sure you are."

Dov looked at my eyes with honesty in his. "I don't like to hurt people, Avrum. That's the thing."

I paused for a moment, then spoke as plainly as I could. "That's your strength, Dov, not a weakness. You don't like to hurt people but you need to fight for your beliefs. You have all the qualities of a good leader, you just don't know it."

"What qualities are those, I'd like to know?" He wasn't really asking, but I replied anyway.

"You act with caution but you're decisive. You assess situations very well. You're stronger than you think but you don't think about it. You care about people but you're not sentimental about them."

Dov looked up and around the dining room. "I'm fighting for this?" he joked.

"And for other things, maybe much more important things than even the kibbutz." I wasn't sure that I was making any sense. The conversation was awkward.

"You know, Avrum, I wouldn't go to war for any reason under almost any circumstance. I don't believe in war and I don't actually believe in violence."

"But now it is survival." I was stating what I thought was a fact.

"No!" he said forcefully. "As a matter of fact it isn't simply survival. In most any case I would rather withhold violence than perpetrate it. No doubt that sounds unusual, but its part of what I believe in."

I was not comprehending this. "You'd rather die than defend yourself?"

"That's not it. I'd rather not perpetrate violence. I am committed to peace."

I wanted to clarify this. "But as a Jew, you have a responsibility to defend yourself."

Dov slammed his fist down on the table. "Yes, you see, that's the whole point. As a Jew I have a responsibility to be a civilizing agent. I have a responsibility to defend that prerogative. I have a responsibility to defend it for the purpose of peace."

"So you have to defend your right to be a Jew?"

"Not exactly. I have the right to defend myself as a civilizing force, which means I have duty towards the purpose of being a Jew."

Despite some confusion I thought I was getting the point. "You have a duty to defend Israel because it is a civilizing force?"

Dov turned his whole body to face me. "What is my purpose in life?" he asked bluntly.

I couldn't answer that question. "You tell me."

He was emphatic. "G-d created me. Did he create me to have my own way?"

I had been a *Yeshiva* boy. "He created you to do his will."

The lines on Dov's forehead deepened. "Have I no will of my own?"

Again I didn't know how to answer. "He gave you free will. Isn't that an incentive to have your own way?

Dov leaned towards me with the passion of his argument. "I am nothing but a beast if not for free will. But unlike a beast I can do good in the world. And I can turn towards creation and not towards destruction. I can be an agent for progress. G-d made me a Jew. That in itself doesn't mean very much, I believe. But G-d also made me capable of civilization and progress and even, possibly, peace."

I tried to understand. "These are things you can fight for?"

He became even more passionate. "As a Jew, these are things I have to fight for. They are the rationale of my very creation."

I believed I understood. "You have to fight for civilization but you have to go to war to be a Jew?"

Once more Dov leaned forward. "I have a duty to fight a war that I believe in. But I am not the same as you, for better or worse. You can see cause and effect and you can act clearly on that basis. You have a political view, at least to some degree. For me, hurting people is deplorable, but for the survival of this Jewish mandate, the principle of eventual peace, I must also go to war and be a soldier. I must kill my neighbour because I have no doubt about my purpose. It is not out of anger or hatred that I go."

I spoke up here out of my own experience. "You say that now, Dov, but I will tell you something. When the time comes to act you only consider what needs to be done. Philosophy doesn't matter. Religion doesn't matter. That's how I know that you will be a good soldier; because your heart is sound and your mind is clear."

I had some time after dinner to look back over the events of the recent past and to speculate on what the future might bring. My activities as an Irgun fighter were essentially over. What had I learned?

I had released and developed parts of me that I didn't know existed. The part that could act effectively in a situation without thinking. The part that could react independently without breaking trust. The part that could keep a secret. The part that could go into battle and not fail. All of these parts had only emerged with the Irgun.

But also, I had learned about more philosophical things. I now understood why I believed ideas that were vague before. I learned that you must follow what you believe or serve the consequence of betraying your own trust. It is by the convictions of men and women who act upon them that the outcome of events are determined. I learned that personal integrity was essential to action and that my effectiveness in the world was rooted mostly in that. I learned that loyalty was a virtue and courage was only a matter doing what had to be done.

I didn't know, at that time, exactly what it would be like to be in a regular army. I would have a rank and military objectives and there would be a different kind of hierarchy and organization. It would be very different fighting behind the banner of a united Israel. Although it may sound strange, I was looking forward to it.

CHAPTER 26
Bar Kochba

Between the battle at Jaffa in mid-April and the Proclamation of Independence on May 15, 1945 there was a lot of pressure. The new independent nation had to create an army, since we knew that we would be immediately at war. The atmosphere was the opposite of panic. Everyone wanted to cooperate, everyone wanted to help and be a part of defending what they had fought so passionately to create. There was no doubt that this battle would be for our very survival. The overall approach could not have been more serious and determined, although conflict between the new government and Irgun was, in fact, inevitable.

In the few weeks before Independence we were busy training on our kibbutz. At this point it was no longer necessary to hide or ignore that I had military experience, and since I was a member of the kibbutz security command it was obvious that I would be at the forefront of this activity. The fact was that I was responsible for structuring and setting up much of the schedule. It wasn't known, at that time, who would be left to protect the kibbutz. Everyone took part in the training, even the children who were taught how to take cover.

On the first days of training members were instructed in the use of weapons. We didn't have much; there wasn't a gun for every person but they were trained to pick up a weapon if the carrier was shot. We had target practice, but because our munitions were limited we kept it to a minimum to save ammunition. At dinner after the second day of training I sat with my friend Orly and her husband Aaron.

"You're a good instructor!" Aaron said quite seriously. "You have a lot of patience."

"I'm pleased that you think so." I didn't really want to be the centre of this conversation.

"You know your weapons." Orly stated, with the hint of a question in her tone.

I wanted to evade this issue. "You know, they teach you in the security command."

"Of course." Orly went on. "But you seem to have learned more than the others."

My intention was to change the subject. "You know, I was a *Yeshiva* boy in Hungary. I was taught how to learn, so I pick things up quickly."

Orly and Aaron glanced at each other. Aaron inquired, "How are your wounds?"

I smiled briefly as if to pass by the issue quickly. "Healed!"

'Oh?" Aaron was pressing the point.

"They were superficial anyway." Again, I wanted to evade the topic altogether.

"Really? You arrived here quite badly injured at one time. Rumours say you were shot. Is that true? Were you shot?"

It was important to me to end this inquisition, but I had to do it diplomatically. "What does it matter, Aaron? Really, accidents happen. Its not important."

He backed off from the immediate point, but Orly picked up the questioning. "Do you remember that time the Arabs attacked the kibbutz? You were very effective and no one had to tell you what to do."

I replied more forcibly. "You know, security trained me and I did what I had been taught to do."

Orly frowned. "You just followed orders? That's all? Why so modest?"

"Well," I said, "Everyone plays a part here. I'm no exception."

Again Only and her husband exchanged glances. "Excuse us," Aaron said. "We don't think so. We think that you are an exception."

This made me nervous. "I'm definitely just like everyone else!" I said.

Orly took up the theme. "Do you know that people look up to you here?"

"No they don't." I said. "They have no reason to."

Aaron continued. "Most of us here are settlers, Avrum. We want to live on the land, we want to make it lush and vibrant and healthy. We don't just live on this earth. We cherish it. We want to devote ourselves to living as a community and doing so by Jewish means. We're farmers and we want nothing other than to live in our homeland in peace and with harmony."

It wasn't clear what he was getting at, but I was suspicious that it would be a reprimand. "Do you think I don't want peace and harmony too!" I said.

"Of course you do!" Aaron exclaimed. "As much as any one of us. But you're not like most of us on the kibbutz, Avrum. You seem to have a different kind of spirit. For one thing, you like to act alone."

I was about to become defensive. "You mean I'm not part of the community?"

Aaron was quick to answer. "No, no! You are an integral part of this community. But you're not truly a kibbutznik. You're training us now in warfare and its completely obvious that you not only know what you're doing but also that you love what you're doing."

Orly broke in. "You're a fighter, Avrum! At a precise moment when war has broken out! We're not really fighters, in your sense. We don't bear it like you do."

I was quite stunned. I didn't think of myself as a fighter, even at this point. I only thought of my objectives in helping to establish the State of Israel. "So you think I am a brutal person without the ability to fit into Kibbutz life?"

Both Orly and Aaron reached towards me with outstretched arms as if to comfort me. "No! No!" they cried. Aaron said. "We don't see you as brutal at all."

My anger was beginning to rise and it got the better of me. "Then how do you see me" I asked in a huff.

Aaron looked again at Orly. "Like a hero." He said.

I was stunned. The anger that had begun to rise turned to astonishment. "A hero? Why on earth…"

"We see you as a soldier, Avrum. But more than that we see you as a righteous soldier and, thank G-d, you are a Jewish soldier. We see Israel as a settler sees it. Fields and orchards and pasture. We want to protect it as that. But you see it as a soldier does; you want to protect it as a soldier does."

I wanted to dispel this idea. "If I'm a soldier it's because that is what I have to be to protect this nation. I believe I love peace as much as anyone."

Orly spoke up. "But that's the point. You are ready to do what you have to do. I think that's your nature, Avrum, and it's special. Right now, at this moment, war is here! And you are here to be a soldier. Most of us will fight and die for our country, but you are prepared for that alone."

I was shocked and not particularly happy about being singled out. "Is that really what I am prepared for?" I asked, mostly rhetorically. My head was turned down. Orly looked up into my face.

"We want to say thank you, Avrum. Thank you for training us. Thank you for being one of us."

I looked at the faces of Orly and Aaron and smiled. "No." I said. "I must thank you. For making everything worthwhile."

There was a very brief pause. Aaron said, "That Sten gun has one hell of a kick!" and the subject was officially changed.

As the days before Independence passed by and the training progressed on the kibbutz I became aware of two things. First of all, the community on the kibbutz became more and more secure, more and more like a well defined organism. There was a definite lack of the interpersonal friction that might have been expected. Instead there was clear evidence of competence and cooperation. Secondly, and this was less meaningful, people regarded me with appreciation, good humour and respect.

We set up security protocols and schedules for 24 hour surveillance. Everyone was drilled on what to do when attacked. Each member had a place to go, a weapon to use, a position to protect. We practiced defending the kibbutz to the last remaining soul. We also practiced all the manoeuvres for a retreat and flight.

As May 15th approached it was not anticipation that dominated our feelings. It was resolve. We were going to persevere, we were going to prevail, we were going to survive.

A few days before Independence would be declared Dov and I were free to walk the perimeter of the kibbutz just after dusk. We were both carrying guns. We knew that we would both be taken into the army very soon.

After a little small talk, Dov mentioned the training. "I now know who to shoot when we're attacked." He said.

"Once you know how to shoot, the next important step is to know who to shoot." I rejoined. We both laughed.

"It's not funny, really, is it? The tension must be making me a bit foolish. I've never shot anyone. I never want to." His face was looking down and his head was shaking gently from side to side.

"You are allowed to defend yourself."

"Yes. I know. It makes me just a little more easy with it." He replied.

"You are defending your home and your people. You have the right." I said.

Dov looked up. "That is the only reason."

"Look," I wanted to be positive. "No rational person wants to kill. At least not for the sake of it. You are not some lunatic with a gun bent on killing anyone. There is an enemy. You must know that this is so in your mind."

"Even if it is not so in your soul?"

"That is in G-d's hands, Dov, not yours. The enemy is what you have to know. You cannot see it otherwise. It's not philosophical; it's entirely realistic. He wants to kill you. You must do it to him first, or everything you have lived and worked for is in vain."

Dov looked into my eyes. "What I have lived and fought for is nothing if not peace. Now, as you say, I have to fight to survive, to prove, in a way, that I am worthy of that peace. I am not so naïve that I don't understand how desperate the circumstances are. I understand that if we don't defend the kibbutz, the whole country, we will be wiped out. I know we have become a nation of soldiers, but I don't enjoy it. I would much rather we be what G-d intended us to be...a nation of scholars."

BAR KOCHBA

I was touched by this idea, but my mindset was on the pragmatic. "You forget, G-d wanted us to be warriors too. When we failed Him at the land of Canaan the first time he punished us with forty years of wandering in the desert."

"This very desert!" Dov exclaimed.

"For this very reason: we would not fight for our nationhood!"

"So G-d is good and just. He promised us this land, we lost it, and now he has given us another chance?" Dov was asking this more than stating it.

My answer was plain. "Well, it seems to be a similar situation."

Dov rubbed his cheek. "You know something? That makes me feel a little bit better. To think that it is the will of G-d to defend ourselves."

This was the crux of my argument. "Which I believe to be so."

Dov was almost mocking his own reaction. "And by implication if I kill a man his soul is also in G-d's keeping, maybe even pre-ordained!"

I went along with this. "It is, like everything, in G-d's hands. Those who die and those who kill are all equal in G-d's eye."

We didn't take this too far, it was so out of place. But the idea seemed to make a difference to Dov because he became more sure of himself. It showed in his walk, which was stronger and more self-confident. "We're a nation of warriors again, are we not?" Dov said.

"Yes. I think so."

"We are fighting once again for our homeland."

"Yes. For our right to survive."

"Then I cannot possibly think otherwise." He smiled ruefully and took me by the arm. "Avrum! We have the honour and duty of being in this glorious generation."

I smiled back. "The same generation the Nazi's also tried to destroy."

Dov stopped walking and stood his ground. He took his rifle off his back and held it in the air. "For the survival of Israel I dedicate time!"

I did the same. "For the survival of Israel!"

Dov laughed ironically. "Right now thousands of Arabs are having exactly the same conversation about us."

"You're quite right." I replied. "It makes us strong to know that."

Just a few days later Hannah came to the Kibbutz for a short visit. She knew that after Independence we would probably not have a chance to see each other. She knew very well that we might never have the chance of seeing each other again. Normally, she would spend the night in a woman's dorm, but that night she stayed with me. Our love making was slow and deep. We knew all the time that we were both soldiers. Later, we sat by the centre square. There was no bonfire, but the moon was bright.

"Avrum, we have our soul's desire." She said.

"Yes. The nation of Israel."

"And this." She took my hand, squeezed it and held it in her lap.

I made no reply, but I did not withdraw my hand.

She asked a question she had not asked before. "Have you ever been in love with someone else."

I hesitated just a moment. "Yes."

"I don't know if love is possible at this time. Do you think so?"

I wanted to answer honestly. "I don't think there is a better time for love. It's an antidote to everything dark and therefore shines very brightly."

Hannah agreed. "It might even be necessary, don't you think?"

I laughed lightly. "I do think so."

Hannah couldn't say this directly to me. She looked quietly at the ground. "That's good. I want to say this to you now. I love you, Avrum, but not that more frivolous love that only knows itself. I love you as an equal and as a friend. And I love you for your character, which is the most beautiful character I have ever known. I want you to know this, in case I never have the opportunity of saying it again."

I responded not only to Hannah's words but also her sincerity. "I love you," I said, "in very much the same way. You are the only comrade in my personal history that I care to kiss."

She laughed. "I've never said 'I love you' to anyone except members of my family."

"Neither have I." I volunteered. "You are my first actual lover."

Hannah was curious. "But you said you were in love before?"

"In the concentration camps I had the memory of someone I met. I only knew her for a few days."

Hannah stroked my back. It was an affectionate gesture or recognition and condolence. "You've suffered many losses, haven't you?"

"I don't really think about it. We're Jews, we all lost a lot."

Hannah stopped stroking my back. "Now the war is over, and the new war is about to start."

I answered simply. "This will be different for us. We will be with regulars and we won't have to hide."

"Nevertheless." She said softly. "We won something."

I believed we both felt the same way. "Do you have a sense of victory, Hannah?"

She let some breath out slowly. "I feel we won a war of propaganda. We let the world know we would not become extinct or sit on our hands and be silent. I feel victory in that, but it is brief. It was a prelude to what is going to happen now...whatever that may be?"

"That was well put, and I agree with you." I said. "We fought a battle for recognition. Now the real war begins."

"I do feel ready to be a soldier, though. I'm ready for that, I feel."

I agreed again. "It's going to be different. But also, in many ways, it will probably be the same."

After Hannah left the next day I felt something I had not felt for a very long time. It was not exactly happiness. It was closer to a kind of certainty. I had realized, although mostly unconsciously, that one phase of my life was over. Importantly, it was over with a degree of success.

Of the events in my life up to this point, by far the most significant was not terribly far behind me. I had survived the camps. Although this was a decidedly personal experience, it was also a collective one. Being in the camps had brought me to an understanding of being a Jew. Surviving the camps had made me into a fighter. I had been transformed from a *Yeshiva* boy into a committed person with a desire to live. I had been, in essence, radicalized by the knowledge that the survival of the Jewish nation was only in the hands of the Jews themselves. But I had survived. That was miracle enough to justify the rest of what I had done.

I became a soldier in an underground army. I had some aptitude for it. I had fought and been ready to die for what I believed in. That was something. I took no pleasure in this knowledge, but it was knowledge at least. There was something external to me that was important enough to live for and to die for.

That was, I think, the real accomplishment of the first part of my life. I was 21 years old. There was something more important than myself to live and die for. It was not an abstract idea, but a very concrete one. This is what gave me strength and confidence at this point, the point at which Israel was about to be declared an independent state. To a large extent this factor alone proclaimed a victory of all that I believed in, but it was not explicitly my victory. It was the victory of a promise made, perhaps by G-d, 3000 years ago.

But the most essential element in all that I had lived with was not war or statehood. It was something entirely personal and subjective. I still remembered Miriam. I had experienced love. That emotion had carried me through all the days in the camps and all of the days that followed. Hannah and I had understood that love stands out the brightest when it is surrounded by darkness. The love I felt for Hannah, which was sincere and honest, was only possible because I had loved Miriam and had carried the reality of her through everything else. Now, at the moment in which everything was about to change, my love for Miriam was still constant and alive. Although love for Israel dominated my actions, love for a lost girl commanded my heart and set it to work. I had to fight for the sake of Miriam and myself in love. I knew this without consciously knowing it.

I had a bit of time to myself one night just before Independence was to be declared. I walked down the road and sat on that favourite rock near the front gate. I am not especially romantic about things; I lean more towards the pragmatic end of the scale. But I felt very acutely that a transformation of sorts had taken place for me. I did not like to think about myself and I did not indulge in it often. This night, though, I felt so very clear.

I was not the person I had been before coming to Israel. I was no longer a victim, nor was I a scholar. I had become a part of a cause. There was a part of me, still a very young man, that wanted to mark that change and there was a part of me, the part that looked ahead, that wanted to make the change real. I decided to change my name as I became a citizen of an Independent Israel. I knew that many people were doing the same.

I thought of names I could adopt. One stood out for me, above all the rest. There was a famous revolutionary Jewish fighter in history who I had always admired. His name was 'bar Kochba".

I decided that night to take that name. It was the choice of a young man, a choice that was naïve since it implied so much that I was not aware of at the time. I was reborn. I would become 'Avrum Bar Kochba' in the new State of Israel. I didn't know what kind of destiny that name would bring.

CHAPTER 27
The New Nation

On the evening of May 14, 1948, the British mandate in Palestine ended. The next day, on May 15, David Ben Gurion, now the Prime Minister, declared the creation of the State of Israel. Immediately, five countries declared war on the new land, with the stated intention of overrunning it and preventing its continuing existence. The countries were Egypt, Syria, Transjordan, Lebanon and Iraq. With no window to celebrate our birth, the single event of our military efforts up to that time, we were immersed in struggle.

The occurrence of Independence had been preceded by months of conflict with the Arab communities, especially after the UN had agreed upon partition earlier in the year. At the time of the declaration of the State of Israel our population was around 600,000. Our armed forces numbered approximately 30,000. Over the next few days, approximately 1,000 Lebanese, 5,000 Syrian, 5,000 Iraqi, 10,000 Egyptian and 4,000 Transjordanian troops invaded the newly-established state. They were aided by corps of volunteers from Saudi Arabia, Libya and Yemen.

Our kibbutz was slightly outside the main route of the Syrian army invading from the north, but we knew we would not escape an assault. Word reached me that I should stay with my people until notified otherwise, and this was very fine for me. I wanted to be there to help defend the community.

My boss Jacov and I were the only members who had any military experience. He was just short of middle age and had grown up on a kibbutz before joining the British army. He had been in the Jewish Battalion of the British army during the war and knew something of strategy. His dark hair formed a fringe around his bald head, but he kept it cut very close. Jacov was a romantic soul, always an interesting quality in a military man. I had a great deal of respect for him because he made what we did seem purposeful and heroic. I also had affection for him, since he loved the kibbutz and everyone in it so completely.

On May 15th we went on high alert. That meant that everyone had a defensive post, mostly around the perimeter of the compound. Everyone was placed in pairs and everyone had a weapon. There was an enormous amount of energy in the kibbutz, but it wasn't all as directed as it could have been. Some people were running to their tasks; a few were standing in some confusion not really knowing exactly what to do. The mood was serious and everyone wanted to be efficient and prepared. Jacov held a central position to coordinate our forces and I was appointed to rove the camp, making sure everything was in good shape and keeping the pairs informed.

We needed something to pull us together as a defensive force; this was clear to me and some others. The problem was not ignored by our appointed leader. Before everyone was dispersed Jacov sent out the word that we were to assemble in the central area. He addressed us as soon as we were all present.

"Today is the most beautiful of days. It is the very first day of a new beginning for us all, and for all Jews everywhere. Today, two thousand years of Diaspora are made one. Today, all of us realize an event we have only dreamed about. We are a nation! We have our own country! Today, we stand on our own soil. We will build, from today, a civilization among the community of civilizations. We are the first peoples to live in the Jewish State of Israel in many, many generations. We must thank G-d that it has happened in our time.

"But we are, as we are gathered here, a free nation that is at war. The enemy will soon be at our gates. Now is the time to make good upon our strengths. Now, we must fight together to protect our right to exist. We have trained for this day. In some sense, we must welcome it joyously and in the same instant we must be ready to defend ourselves. In any case, take heart! We are blessed in every way. Stand firm and we will give evidence to G-d that we are worthy of his blessings.

"Go now to your positions. Draw your courage from the knowledge that your cause is just. You are making history and you have nothing to fear."

Our people left the meeting area with high spirits and determination. The sense was good. I turned to Jacov and said, "Do you think we are ready?"

Jacov looked down into his rifle like he was about to sing to it. "You fail to ask the important question: Are the Arabs ready?"

"They have an army. They believe in their cause, too. " Although I had fought in several battles I knew very little about fighting a war. It was my hope that I would learn fast.

Jacov made a dismissive sound, like air escaping from a tire. "They are not well trained. That may prove bad for us."

"You think they are disorganized?" I was not sure I believed him.

Jacov looked up from his rifle and caught my gaze. "They harbour hate. They are motivated by a desire to kill. That is not good for an army. It compels them to make mistakes."

"They want the land back." I ventured.

Jacov put a hand on my shoulder as he often did when telling me something he wanted me to absorb especially. "That's almost always the case in war. It is a dispute over land. That's something you and I could discuss for a very long time. But they are driven by hate. We are not. We are driven by love. Love of our country, love of our people, even a love of peace."

I was curious about this issue. "You think we are better than them?"

Jacov gestured to stop. "Now is not the time to be philosophical. I am only speculating on the enemy. It is necessary now to have cool heads. You should begin to roam, now. Make sure everyone is in their place."

I began to make rounds, stopping at each station to give encouragement and support. I understood that a large part of my function was to make the parts feel connected to the whole. The kibbutzim at each post needed to be encouraged. None of them had ever seen a battle before. Half our numbers were in place, half were in the kibbutz ready to relieve the others every few hours. We tried to make each stand with a man and a woman but sometimes there were two woman since their numbers were greater.

The first day went by without incident. In the middle of the second day I relieved one of two women at a station so that she could go back for a moment to check on her infant. The other woman was Orly. "Do you think they will come?"

"Yes. I think so. Their main army is passing by not too far away. They won't pass by this close to a kibbutz without sending some kind of attack."

Orly grimaced. She was a pretty woman, even in this situation, and she exuded strength from beneath a gentle, feminine exterior. "I keep hoping they'll ignore us. Or not even know we're here."

I didn't want to frighten her, but I didn't want to mask the truth either. Especially in this tense, life and death, situation. "Orly, they know we're here. They know where all the kibbutz are because they have to deal with them. They may not mount an all out offensive. That could be true. But they will send scouts, anyway."

Orly expressed an easy good humour. "It's a beautiful day for a war, don't you think? It would be very depressing if it was raining."

I pulled the brim of her hat down. "It's fun in the rain!" I used the non-military term 'fun' because she was such a sunny woman.

Orly's partner returned and I went on, but not too far. About five minutes later a shot rang out from a spot further away along the perimeter. My feet could not move me fast enough and it was a long sprint to where it occurred. The two defenders were lying low behind a stone wall. They were Simon and Marlie. Simon said, "We saw a soldier creeping towards us. He's over there, behind that tree."

This was not good news. "Who fired the shot?" I asked.

Simon said he did. "Very good." I congratulated him. "You did the right thing."

Marlie spoke up. "After the shot I looked up over the wall and I thought I saw another one over there." She pointed to a short fence a few meters away.

By this time more members had arrived. This time the Arabs took the offensive. They fired as people approached our position but no one was hit. There were now five of us at the wall. Too many. I motioned them to go back, which they did.

"Look," I said with control. "They have good cover, but there must be more behind them so they're going to want to move up. You can't let that happen. Whenever you see movement, fire! Keep them pined down."

At that moment Jacov arrived. He assessed the situation in an instant. "This is a vulnerable spot. They're going to try to break through."

"So all we can do is hold the position?" I asked, although I knew the answer.

"Don't you think they're as vulnerable as we are?' Jacov asked.

"Who's holding who down?" I said.

Jacov winced. "One of us has to move first. We won't keep this station for long." He looked at me with a piercing glance. "What would you do?"

I thought I knew what had to be done. "We need to take that position and hold it. There's not enough cover at this wall."

There was resignation in Jacov's voice. "You think there's any way to break this tea party up?"

I looked at his face. "We could take it to them."

The older soldier looked in both directions. He pointed. "From that tree you can see one Arab. He won't be able to use it for cover."

I could see that. "The problem is to get there without being shot."

"We'll cover you completely and you will be masked by the orchard if you start further down the wall."

The risk was worth it. "Good. I'll go." Simon and Marlie looked very determined.

"When I tell you, raise yourselves up a bit and shoot at that soldier as you see him."

They agreed. I crept behind the wall for a few dozen metres until I was on the downside of the orchard. Then I leapt over the low barrier as quickly as I could and ran to the nearest tree. As I reached the trunk a bullet struck with a great thud. Shots were fired on all sides, so I had cover

I was armed with a handgun. There were five trees between me and the Arab soldier. To the first tree was easy; he couldn't see me clearly. The second tree was more difficult because the second Arab was drawing fire also. I was not thinking at this point. I was running on something like instinct. As I darted to the third tree I heard a scream. I didn't have time to consider it. I sprinted all out to the fourth tree. That was close enough. I could see the Arab soldier but I didn't have a clear shot. He was making a mistake; he was following the cries from where he had already shot. I darted quickly to the fifth tree. This was the mark.

The Arab looked to see me almost beside him. I saw the surprise on his face as he raised his rifle. Too late. I shot him in the side of the head before he could attempt a shot. From this point of view I could see the other soldier. He shot at me but the bullet was off the mark. I'm good with a handgun. I hit him once in the chest and again in the heart.

I quickly checked to make sure both men were dead, then I ran to the station of our people. Marlie was frantically trying to stop the bleeding from a gaping wound to Simon's chest, but I could see that he was past help. His head was in her lap. Marlie was sobbing without being aware of it. It was a reflex reaction. Jacov was sitting grimly beside her. None of us had time to let it all sink in because we heard screaming coming from down the line. It was the cry of real fear.

I left that station with a panther's speed towards the sound. It was coming from Orly's station. As I approached I could see one of the women on the ground. It was Orly's partner. Orly was standing beside her post, but her rifle was on the ground beside her. An Arab soldier was holding her around the neck, a knife poised to kill.

There had been no shots. The Arabs had somehow surprised the two women. As I sprinted towards the post the soldier began to use Orly and a shield. Just as I reached their post the purpose of the attack was revealed. The Arabs wanted to make this spot a gateway into the kibbutz, so they did not shoot. Only one soldier had tried to reach this gate so as to escape detection, at which he had been successful. He had killed Orly's partner but the two women had put up an enormous fight. He was struggling to kill Orly when I came into view. As I understood all this in an instant a second Arab leapt upon me from behind. As he struck the handgun was knocked from my hand. Although I was pushed back I was able to reach for my knife that was in my belt. The Arab was strong but I had been trained. As he reached his arm over his head he broke his guard. My left arm grabbed his shoulder and I pulled him towards me while my right hand, which held the knife, struck his midriff. Meanwhile, Orly was struggling with the first soldier, who couldn't overcome her completely. He saw that I was free to face him so he gathered his strength and plunged his knife deeply into Orly's stomach. She crumpled in shock and pain, leaving he and I facing each other.

Everything happened very fast, before other kibbutzim were able to arrive. I let the Arab move first. He thrust hard in the air but missed my chest. I wanted him to try again, because I thought it might throw him off balance just a little. I feigned back, he attacked, but his thrust missed again. He was off balance. I hit him hard in the face with my left hand. He fell back a step, and my right hand came up from below and struck up to his midriff. The knife cut deep into his ribs and cut his heart. He was dead before he fell.

Other Kibbutzim came quickly running up after that. Our doctor came straight to Orly who was conscious and being supported in the arms of friends. "Welcome to the State of Israel." She said quietly. They carried her back to the compound. Her wound was serious. I stood above my friends feeling helpless. I hadn't realized my feelings for Orly until I saw her lying on the ground bleeding from a knife wound. At that moment I knew something that I had been unaware of until now. I knew that this kibbutz was my home and that my attachment to it and the others who lived here was much deeper and stronger than I had known. It had been years since I had felt a sense of belonging to a place. I didn't have time to contemplate this understanding, but I knew that I would have to deal with it eventually.

Jacov, who was left with me as two more people took over the station. was stoic. "That was only a reconnaissance expedition. If there were any other forces they've probably gone back to report. Taking a modest sized kibbutz are probably not their biggest priority, and if we're lucky we'll give them enough to worry about in this battle to keep them going."

I wondered. "Do you think we convinced them that this would not make such an easy target?"

Jacov scowled. "Who knows? Maybe. We killed four of them." He looked at me squarely. "You killed them, Avrum. You did it yourself. Two of them with a knife."

I didn't see any glory in this. It hadn't struck me yet that I had killed four men. "Oh, well. I only did what I could."

Jacov laughed lightly and took me gently by the shoulder. "You're a good soldier." He said. "Luckily, we are going to have a suitable army."

As it turned out Jacov was right about the Arabs. The attack had been recognizance and the Arab armies were heading south, somewhat away from our location. That didn't mean we would be spared the fight, but in the few days following, as news of the war began to come in and the shape of it emerged we could see what might be coming. We prepared for a second and larger assault.

Orly survived out of sheer strength of will. Aaron stayed by her as much as he could. I waited for instructions from my commanders in the Irgun. I felt a great sense of loyalty to them although it was not entirely political. I fully accepted the government as completely legitimate and I agreed that there should be a united armed forces. The Irgun had been my place of origin as an Israeli and as a soldier and I was happy to have been given the opportunity of fighting for what was necessary in my eyes. I didn't want to make a move until I knew it would be the right one.

Two days after the first assault a second one struck. It was just before dawn when the alarm was sounded. This time they were advancing down the main road toward the gate. Some of us were still asleep, although at that time everyone slept in their clothes to be vigilant. I was in the security area checking our weapons. They included 50 grenades and two antitank launchers and 20 shells. Added to our arsenal over the past few days was a supply of Molatov cocktails. They had been Jacov's idea.

Making the cocktails had been an activity that served two functions. First, it made us feel more secure to have a simple weapon that people could use easily. Second, it reminded us of resistance in Europe during the war, when Jews had very little to fight with. The bottles filled with gasoline and stuffed with rags gave us a sense of courage and purpose that the sophisticated weapons did not. We were not exactly soldiers; we were settlers compelled to fight for our survival. Making the primitive bombs together in the kibbutz brought us together as a group far more strongly than the other military actions we undertook. We had the chance to laugh together, to band together and to feel close. That was well worth the time.

I reached the front gate seconds after the alarm went off. There were five of us there, including Aaron and three others. It was still quite dark and misty. Down the road it was hard to see anything through the mist.

Aaron passed me binoculars. "Look down there." He said. I looked down the road. Indeed, there was something there in the early morning light. It was a large shape, just a shadow at that moment. But it was clear enough be unmistakable. It was a tank.

Jacov came running up from behind. "What's going on?" he said in his commanding voice, but low like a whisper. I handed him the binoculars and he looked down the road. Then he turned to me.

"Why would they send a tank?" he asked briskly.

"I don't know." I replied without much expression. I actually did know but I wanted to hear his reasoning.

"It's not good strategy for a raid. It's too clumsy. It's not meant strictly as antipersonnel. Our location isn't strategic either. They could pass us by easily without bothering about it."

"So why send a tank?" I lay low on this. I didn't know much about strategic warfare, but that wasn't the main reason. I didn't want to interfere with Jacov's fine military reasoning.

Jacov spoke lowly, almost ponderously. "It's not a strategic attack. They want to blow something up. We don't know how many troops are deployed They don't have to be here."

"Alright." I said.

Jacov spoke to all of us. "This is a reprisal!" he said. "They're here to pay us back for the surveillance where they lost four men. They want to destroy the kibbutz and kill as many of us as possible. This is not going to be a military manoeuvre. They want a massacre. This is revenge."

This understanding could have daunted us. It actually had the opposite effect after the initial shock. Instead, it galvanized our sense of resistance and defiance. Jacov instructed me quickly to check the other posts and then return to the security area with a few people to bring weapons to the gate. As the word spread that this was an attack meant to destroy us an attitude of purpose spread as well. I heard people laughing together quickly, saying "If I die today it won't be for lack of trying." And "I'd rather die defending my home than ploughing it." There was anger, too. "If they want us dead they're going to have to pay for it!"

For my part, I had seen battle before; that was not new. But this almost celebratory attitude was unexpected. I hoped it wouldn't effect our ability as defenders, but I felt that it would not in the circumstances. My military instincts, though, had not left me. I kept a cool head, focused on the tasks at hand. I distributed grenades and Molotov Cocktails to the others, a number of them in carts to be hauled to the gate. When that was done I took the launcher myself and started back. There were a few kibbutzim remaining in the compound to guard it.

When I arrived there were about 10 of us manning the main gate. Everyone else was in position at the perimeter. Just after I arrived shots rang out to the north; there was a lot of sustained gunfire but it didn't last very long. After that it was sporadic but heavy at times.

Jacov said, "That gunfire may be a good sign. It's not sustained and it's sporadic. They don't have a great many troops there or there would be constant fire."

Aaron asked, "Why are they standing there in broad daylight?" It was quite bright morning now.

"They don't know what weapons we have, so they don't want to rush." Jacov said slowly. "But there's something else going on or they would have moved by now."

It wasn't long before we had an answer. From behind the tank, where it had been hidden from our view, there swiftly emerged another vehicle. It was an armoured car with a machine gun mounted on the front.

That was hard news, but there was something else. What was missing were troops. We could see soldiers on the ground, but not too many. Unless there were many more concealed off the road, this would be a rather small force.

Jacov broke our little silence. "Maybe we're right about this being reprisal." He said seriously. "They expect to kill as many of us as they can with the machine gun and blow up the kibbutz with their tank. They haven't committed many soldiers because they can't spare them and they don't want casualties. They expect a slaughter!"

"Let them!" One of our people said. "They won't find that it can be so easy." To tell the truth, it upset me when some of our kibbutzniks talked tough. It somehow didn't seem right that we sometimes talked that way. It was out of character. Although it was clear that we had to fight it didn't seem appropriate to act as if we liked it.

A few moments later shots rang out towards us at the gate. Even though there may not have been dozens of soldiers there were enough to pin us down. Those of us together on the gate opened fire. At the same time, firing began along the perimeter also. We needed a strategy on the spot. Jackov thought for a brief minute and then spoke:

"We have to take out the tank and the armoured car, and hope at the same time that the positions on the perimeter hold."

Just as he said that there was an loud bang and then a massive blast several meters in front of our gate. It was the tank, just slightly out of range. We had to think fast. Jacov gave instructions.

"That armoured car isn't going to wait and we can't wait either until it rolls right in. We've got to ruin it, and the tank.

"Avrum and Aaron, I want you to take the launcher and enough shells into the orchard. Slide in between our positions. Make sure the others cover you very well and take three fighters with you for cover as well. You must secure a position behind the wall surrounding the orchard close enough to strike at the tank and the armoured car. Go!"

Aaron and I took off for the position by the wall of the orchard. "I'm never going to think of this orchard in the same way again!" Aaron said.

"No." I replied. "I don't guess you will."

We gathered three fighters and tried to carry out Jacov's instructions. There was a lot of firing. One of the men stood up too quickly. He was struck by a bullet in the arm and fell beside the wall. Then one of the women bent over to help him, but she exposed herself to danger as she did it. She was shot in the hip.

We weren't experienced soldiers; that was so hurtfully clear. Immediately after she was struck I felt remorse for us. Then, immediately after that, I felt anger. For a moment I had lost the feeling of being a soldier, but it returned again with renewed strength. My objective was set once again. I became steady, focused and alert.

There were two others at that position. "Keep firing!" I commanded. "Shoot where you see gunfire."

I took Aaron by the shoulder. "Come on!" I urged him. "We have to make our way!"

But it was no use. Enemy fire was too strong. I managed to clear the wall and take cover behind a tree. Aaron followed quickly. We made it from tree to tree until we were close to the road but still to far from the tank to take a clear shot. Even so, the enemy had us in their sights. We couldn't get any further.

Aaron smiled at me from the tree beside mine. He was a brave soldier for someone who had never been in a war. He was trying to encourage me, to tell me that he was fine. I thought of Orly lying in the infirmary.

And then he was shot. The bullet passed through his back, through his heart and out his chest. His body fell forward heavily into the ground.

Just at that moment the armoured car began moving forward slowly down the road. It had come swiftly into my range. I moved quickly and with purpose, pushing my feelings for the loss of my friend out of my mind. I bent over his bloody body and took two shells, then as fast and as smooth as I could I loaded one of them into the launcher. I swung around, took aim and fired but not before it had done damage. The machine gun had raked the area of the gate with several rounds before my shell struck. It was not a direct hit; it was low. The wheels were disabled but the machine gun could function. Although the gunner was injured, another soldier quickly took his place and continued firing upon the gate. For some reason, it didn't turn on me and neither did the tank. I was able to load another shell and fire again. This time was better. The vehicle exploded loudly and it was entirely destroyed.

I took a grip on the launcher but left the remaining shells. I was coming under fire but I was able to quickly retreat back to that original position by the wall where the two kibbutznik had been hit. Now the enemy fire was more sporadic and I realized that they really didn't have many troops. They had supposed they could destroy our kibbutz without losing men and probably thought it wasn't important, considering they were intending to make progress elsewhere in more strategic territory.

Then the tank moved forward. It manoeuvred around the smoking armoured car and ran right on along the main road to the kibbutz. It fired. The gate exploded in flame and smoke. It fired again into the compound, since it was now in range. There was an explosion but I couldn't see what was hit. It continued to fire and it continued to move forward.

I was operating without instructions now. I was approaching the gate and could see bodies lying around. On the ground I could see shells, which is just what I wanted to see. I acted quickly and without thinking. That's a strange thing that soldiers and athletes sometimes do. I loaded the launcher, aimed at the tank, and fired. Again it was low, but it disabled its tread. Someone was behind me. It was Jacov. His one arm was broken, but with the other he loaded a shell into the launcher. I fired again, this time well. The turret was hit.

Suddenly there were people all around. Someone grabbed a Molotov cocktail and ran towards the tank. Then someone else did the same thing and followed him. Then everyone did. They threw the makeshift bombs at the tank and quietly watched it burn. The crew inside was taken prisoner. The other enemy soldiers left our site after the tank blew up.

Our resistance was successful, but at a price. Four of us were killed and seven wounded. Our meeting area had been destroyed as well as the mess hall, some barracks and two sheds. We all mourned the dead, but for me the loss of Aaron was most meaningful. Not only was he my friend, he was also Orly's husband. I told her the news, although Jacov offered to do so. There's no need to describe that part of this battle. I don't think there can be a more difficult thing to do than tell a young woman that her husband has been killed.

There was another less painful but unwarranted outcome for me personally from this unhappy fight. Once again others on the kibbutz regarded me as a kind of hero. I hate that. I only do what I have to do and I'm not special for it. If there has to be a hero in this battle, it should be Aaron. He put his life on the line. I only lived to tell about it.

CHAPTER 28
The Recruit

Ben Gurion quickly united the military factions into a new and unified Israeli Defence Forces, but the Irgun lingered for awhile and I resisted enlisting until I had word from my leaders that it was time. Even though it was the moment for the nation to unite as one people, there were still differences that had to be worked out. Menachin Begin wanted recognition for the part played by the Irgun in the battle for statehood and it was slow in coming. As a representative of the conservative Right, Begin had a certain pride to maintain. This conflict became manifest over the arrival of a ship commissioned by the Irgun off the waters of Israel. Although it arrived in June, during the first truce, it caused a certain crisis.

The actual end of the Irgun, the movement that had shaped this part of my life, did not occur until the arrival of the boat called the Altelena in a small port on the coast of Israel. This ship was chartered and its cargo carefully loaded by the Irgun. It was a dangerous operation because the ship was carrying weapons, munitions and about 1000 Jewish military volunteers. These fighters had been gathered together at great risk and had been commissioned by Menachim Begin to arrive in Israel on May 15. Due to a series of unfortunate circumstances it had been delayed with its significant cargo and, because the Irgun was no longer a fighting force and the IDF was now in control of the new state possession of the ship and its contents was in dispute. A divisive conflict arose between Ben Gurion and Begin. I had been called up to work with Begin's group who secured the ship. We boarded it at Kfar Vitkin. It was the first time I had been within speaking distance of the man who was my commander.

Begin was very much in control of his own people. It's hard to describe the charisma of such a man. He had done something remarkable; he had created an army where there had only been unorganized resistance. He had forged a credo where there had only been emotion. He had personally evaded capture while the British Army searched everywhere for him. Perhaps even more significant, he was a man who knew himself in the wake of serious questions. I felt almost aglow to be physically close to him. I felt a sense of purpose and pride. There was no doubt where his authority came from. It emanated from a strong heart and a razor sharp mind that were devoted to a single cause.

Although we were not immediately aware of it, Ben Gurion had empowered the army to use force to confiscate the ship and its cargo from our hands. It is likely that he misinterpreted Begin's intention. Some of the Irgun had been absorbed into the IDF as separate battalions and Ben Gurion might have balked at the possibility of an 'army within an army'. This was in no way Begin's intent and he did not expect the actions of the IDF. I know that there was never a suggestion in the Irgun that it would rebel in any way.

I was on the ship at the request of my group commander. It was meant to be an honour and a reward for my efforts in the Irgun. We learned about the details of a situation that was entirely unexpected when an ultimatum was delivered to us. It stated that we must surrender the ship and its contents to the government commander or face an attack. It granted us 10 minutes to respond. This was certainly meant to cripple and humiliate us. Begin was resolute. He refused to respond. After brief negotiations failed, a battle between the army and those of us aboard the ship ensued.

In the 10 minutes between the arrival of the ultimatum and the fight that ensued I had the opportunity to speak briefly with some of the recruits. They were mostly camp survivors like myself, some even spoke Hungarian and almost all of them spoke Yiddish. They were ecstatic to reach Israel at this time, determined to serve the country and the people. This introduction to the place of their dreams was a nightmare.

A man of about thirty took my arm and spoke to me in Polish. "Do you speak Yiddish?" I asked.

"I speak Yiddish." He cried out. "What is going on?"

"They want us to surrender you and the weapons to the IDF. They have given us an ultimatum. Either we give up or they fire. We have 10 minutes."

The fellow was aghast. "They would fire on us? But we are Jews. We are not enemies. We are their people!"

"It's some kind of misunderstanding." I was trying to calm him down but I was also speaking the truth.

"This is unacceptable!" He was shaking. "We have come to be in the Jewish army, not be shot at by it. We can work out details! Believe me, I have come home to be Jew in a Jewish country! Have I survived persecution at the hands of the fascists in Europe only to be killed by my own people in our own country. This is unacceptable!" he continued, and he leaned over the railing calling out at the top of his lungs "I am a Jew, you fascist idiot. Don't fire at me! I have come to be one of you!"

At that moment the IDF opened fire on our ship. When the shots rang out and the bullets flew I took a position in the bow. My heart was nearly sick, for I was firing upon my fellow Jews. There was no time to think, but unspoken in my brain was the question, 'Have we come so far only for this?'. Nevertheless, I did my part. Bullets whizzed past me and several of my comrades were hit. I knelt over one wounded fighter and continued to fire at our Jewish adversaries. I certainly did not feel like a hero.

A ceasefire was quickly established, but a lot of harm had already been done. Jew was killing Jew. Weapons that had earlier been sent ashore were left on the beach and transferred to the Israeli Defence Forces, while the *Altalena* left the port and headed toward Tel Aviv with Menachin Begin aboard. At this point the conflict was no longer military. It had become almost entirely political. The future of the individual fighters of the Irgun was at stake, as well as the integrity and importance of its mission prior to Independence. When we arrived at the Tel Aviv beach the army was waiting and they had big guns levelled at us. There was confusion on the ship as shells exploded around us. Eventually, we were struck. The ship caught fire and there was fear that ammunitions in the hold could explode. Begin ordered all the fighters to leave, but he stayed until the last of the wounded were taken away. Although he had his own guards, I stayed with him to the final minutes.

He actually spoke to me at one point, saying "You should go now!".

I replied, "Not until you are out of harm's way."

He looked at me with compassion in his eyes and said, "You have courage."

I will never forget that. It made me feel humble and strong.

Comrades were picking us up with rafts and when most everyone had left I also jumped ship. I am not a good swimmer, having never learned the skill, but once I was in the water, I just kept swimming away from the boat and away from the beach because I could see the IDF detaining our people as they landed. Where I finally arrived there were no soldiers. Eventually, 200 Irgun members were arrested, but I was not one of them. I learned later that 16 of our people were killed in the encounter as well as 3 IDF soldiers.

Perhaps it was inevitable that Jewish blood would be spilt by Jewish soldiers and that the Irgun would eventually be humiliated by the newly formed IDF. I understand that the new army, to be strong and unified, had to acquire a moral superiority over all the factions that had come before. The actions of the Irgun, directed and coordinated by Menachin Begin, were forceful, but they were necessarily so. I do not believe we were arbitrary and I do not believe we were not needed. Without our efforts, who is to say Independence would have arrived as soon as it did.

The Irgun went down, literally, in flames. Maybe that is more than a metaphor, maybe that was inevitable. But we were not renegades; we were not random assassins wreaking havoc wherever we went. We were an army of principle, a force of intent and we measured our actions with the armaments of purpose. There is neither pride nor shame in my period with the Irgun. I always felt that what I did was necessary and just. History may bear this out. I did what I believed was right.

I was soaking wet when I made my way through Tel Aviv to the only place I thought was safe: Hannah's apartment. The streets of the city were thronging with activity since the war was going on. At this time hostilities had been suspended in what became known as the first truce, but everyone knew it would be short and that fighting would resume within a short while. There were soldiers everywhere and activity of all kinds. Everyone had something to do. The café's were busy, full of people talking noisily and with great purpose. No one noticed a soaking wet young man, dressed in civilian clothes, walking purposefully through the streets. I kept to side roads to be as inconspicuous as possible.

Hannah wasn't home, as I suspected, but I found the extra key she kept hidden in case of emergencies. I hadn't eaten in a long while. I took off my wet clothes, hung then in the bathroom and wrapped myself in her own robe, which was fortunately quite plain and not frilly. It was characteristic of Hannah to avoid items that were especially feminine. When I was comfortable and dry I took a turn at her little galley kitchen and liberated some leftover salad and yoghurt. Then, without thinking about it, I crashed down on her carefully made bed and fell asleep.

I dreamed of Orly. In my dream she had died of her wounds but had come back to life, miraculously, and brought back a story of the underworld. She had seen Aaron in a restaurant in Gan Eden. He had told her that I was going to be a farmer despite my training. She told me, as we worked together in the orchard, that she knew my heart wasn't in the kibbutz. I woke up feeling a bit refreshed when Hannah returned from her business and called my name at the bedside. I sat up immediately and shook my head.

"This is a surprise!" Hannah sat beside me on the bed. "My robe makes an interesting fashion statement. If you like, I'll get one for you to use on the kibbutz."

I must have smiled. "I think there's a regulation against the colour powder blue."

Hannah was amused but a little distracted. "Does your unexpected company have something to do with my irresistible charm, or did you just want to raid my wardrobe and sleep on my bed?"

"There was an operation on the water off Tel Aviv." I didn't want to give her all the details at this time. "I had to escape in the sea. I was soaking wet and had nowhere to go, so I came here. You're not going to turn me in are you?"

She broke into a smile. "Yes, I am. I'm going to take you as you are to the police and tell them you went swimming without a permit. They do require permits to swim during the war, don't they?"

I played the game one more time. "Yes, I thinks so. I believe you also require a bathing suit."

There was a momentary pause while we just looked at each other with light smiles crossing our respective faces. "I had some leftovers." I confessed.

"That's alright. "she said. "They were old anyway."

"Do you mind if I stay until my clothes are dry?"

We were not trying to be funny any more, although we were still casual. "No, I don't mind. You can stay as long as you need to. I was going to make a bit of dinner. Do you want some?"

"That would be fine. I'm actually still hungry."

She went into the tiny kitchen. She looked very much at home. In about ten minutes she had a plate of humus and bread and salad. She also made tea and served some biscuits. As we ate at her small dining table we talked about the Irgun and the war.

"Now, what is going to happen to the Irgun?" Hannah asked after a few mouthfuls.

"It looks like Ben Gurion is determined both to destroy and discredit us. They were arresting fighters when I fled."

Hannah made a dismissive sound. "It doesn't seem necessary to persecute us. It seems entirely political and brutally unkind."

"Yes, I think so too." I wanted to talk about this with Hannah specifically because she was well informed and we both shared the emotional elements of having fought for the same cause. "The military factions that existed before Independence differed on methods, it's true, but we all contributed to making it possible."

Hannah seemed somewhat bitter, but it was mostly hidden behind a wall of objectivity. "Even though we shared a goal, Ben Gurion wants to distance the new government from so called radical approaches. Even though we were a necessary part of struggle for the state of Israel he's willing to discredit us and even throw us in jail. I don't think I'll ever trust politicians! They have no morals."

"I think you are right, but like anything some politicians are still better than others. This is more than simply politics, though. Ben Gurion wants Menachin Begin personally out of the picture because he holds too much influence. He wants the Irgun completely disbanded because he wants only one fighting force: The IDF. If remnants of the Irgun remained and if Begin had any military clout there could be trouble later on."

"We put our lives on the line for this country, just like everyone else. Now they're throwing us in jail."

"It doesn't seem right, but it doesn't seem irrational either. Although we fought hard, we fought by our own rules. We were illegal then and we are seeing the results of that now."

Hannah disagreed. "We're being persecuted because we were successful. That's the real crime. When we destroyed the King David Hotel the press was bad, but if we hadn't done that, or if we had tried and failed, this day of Independence may never have come. If the British hadn't felt a threat to their presence in Palestine they never would have left, and we created that threat, not Ben Gurion."

She looked at me seriously. "We were not terrorists randomly targeting civilians. We were a well organized army carrying out precise missions aimed exclusively at military installations and personnel.

She went on. "We should be rewarded for our stand by the government we helped make possible, not persecuted for it. Alright, we need a unified armed force, I agree with that. But they shouldn't be arresting us. They should be acknowledging us."

Hannah's features were clear and congruent. "You're right." I said. "We should be acknowledged. Its been a long road up to this point and the results are, I admit, complicated. But we knew what we were doing and we did it in spite of the fact that we were not popular. Now, Ben Gurion needs to make a point; we are a legitimate and sovereign country with a legitimate army. The new government does not want be associated in the view of the rest of the world as embracing random tactics. So they are distancing themselves from the Irgun even though morally they should be accepting the necessity of our role."

Hannah let go of some of the tension in her neck and her shoulders slumped. "I don't wand to feel ashamed in the State of Israel for the part I played in establishing it."

My feelings were touched by that confession. "We don't have to feel ashamed, Hannah. We will always know that we did what we believed was necessary and we have, thankfully, lived to see the results and our personal vindication. We knew what we were doing was not popular. Now, we have to accept that reality again."

Hannah frowned. She got up from the table and brought a letter from her desk in the corner. She threw it on the table in front of me. "I have received my conscription notice. I report to the office the day after tomorrow.

I looked at it. "You're going to tell them that you were a member of the Irgun?"

"I don't think that's wise, under the circumstances." She sat down lightly. Even when she was emotional she was graceful. "I'm going to be a regular soldier in a regular army."

"For a cause you believe in." I said.

"Yes." she replied. "With a uniform and a rank."

My clothes dried in a couple of hours. We were intimate like never before, perhaps because something was ending. We would be soldiers again soon, and it seemed as if the relationship, which could have gone romantic, would likely not go in that direction. I can't explain how we both knew that, but I knew that we did.

I returned to the Kibbutz that night by bus. The country was in a state of preparedness and anxiety. Everyone on the bus was talking about the war, but I kept pretty much to myself, short of being unpleasant and aloof. When I arrived it was too late to visit Orly. We had become quite close during the mourning period of Aaron's death, his shiva. There were no other attacks by Arab forces during that time, and I spent most of my hours that were free with her. When I got to my room there was a letter on my bed. It was my conscription notice. I opened it. I was to report to the military in 3 days.

The next morning I went to see Orly. She was in her quarters now, out of the infirmary, but her wound was still far from healed and she was restricted to her bed except for occasional accompanied walks outside. She was still grief struck. She was happy to see me on this morning. She sat up painfully in bed.

"Avrum, I was thinking about you!"

"That's nice." I was more happy to see her than I really wanted her to know.

"You're my favourite visitor. Did you know that?"

I smiled pleasantly. "I only dreamed that I was."

We made small talk for half and hour about events on the Kibbutz and about the war.

Finally I said, "I received my orders. I have to register in 3 days."

She looked concerned. "Was that unexpected, Avrum?"

I shook my head and made a sound like an owl. "No. Its part of the natural course of events."

"You'll be a good soldier, I believe. But don't take matters into your own hands! It was a blessing that you were here on the Kibbutz but no one wants you dead. You're not the only hero in the army, you know."

My visiting Orly was not only to try to help ease the pain of Aaron's death. I liked her personality and felt good being with her. I also felt, uncomfortably, nostalgia from or very early friendship, before she married Aaron. On the second day after my conscription notice arrived there was another piece of mail delivered by hand directly to me personally. It was addressed to the conscription officer and I was to take it with me when I was enlisting.

When I arrived at the conscription centre in Tel Aviv I was dressed in Khakis and a white shirt. The induction process was almost entirely impersonal. I waited in different lines several times. The recruits talked to each other rather freely and, of course, the women were separate from the men.

This was a committed induction line. Everyone wanted to help protect Israel. At this time the population of Israel was around 600,000. We were all soldiers, whether in the military or not. There were all kinds of men in the lines with me and of a wide range in ages. I looked around, I spoke a few words to a few, and I saw the future of Israel in their eyes. One conversation stands out. I was standing behind a short man who looked around 30 years old. He turned around to look at me.

"You look pretty fit!" he said.

I laughed. "I live on a kibbutz."

He smiled. "I'm a baker. I have my own company making bread and cakes."

"That must require hard work." I said.

"It's a living. I hope to live to see the day when I can pass the business on to my son!"

I enquired genially, "You have a son?"

"He's five years old. Probably too young to run a business."

I chuckled. "Most likely."

He turned a bit more serious. "My wife is coming here next week. It looks like we're both going to be in the army."

"Who will take care of your son?" I asked.

"The army will."

"That's good." I said simply.

He asked me quietly. "Are you married?"

"No." I replied. "I'm single."

"I'm happy, honoured even, to serve in this army. I feel the same way about my wife. But what if we're both hurt? I wonder about that."

I wasn't very talkative but I was interested in what this man had to say. "That would be hard."

"But I expect if me, my wife and people like us don't fight for what we believe in we'll all perish anyway." He paused and looked at me closely. "Are you from Europe?"

"Hungary." I said.

"My wife is from Poland. I'm from Austria. Can I ask? Were you in the camps?"

I didn't mind. "Yes."

He shook his balding head of dark hair. "That it should come to this!" he said. "That I should live through the concentration camps to possibly die defending Israel. I have no fear of death in this. I only have fear that we might fail, but I have even greater faith that we will not."

"I have faith that we will not." I answered.

"I didn't want to be soldier until this. Now, I want to with all my heart. I certainly didn't want my wife to be a soldier. But she's like me. She believes this is our cause, personally, and that we must sacrifice everything we have if necessary."

I looked at him squarely. His face was the face of a gentle man. "I want to be a soldier too."

When the line reached the registration desk I gave the letter I had received personally to the officer. When he opened it he read quickly. He looked at me squarely. "Are you Avrum Benjamin?." he asked with a mixture of contempt and curiosity.

"Yes." I replied, as straightforwardly as I could.

He motioned to a bench reside a wall. "Sit over there." He said gruffly. I did what I was told.

I sat there for more than an hour. The line had ended. I thought 'They know I am an Irgun and they are going to arrest me.' 'I won't get in the army.' Then an officer came out from the adjacent room with a letter in his hand and called me in. The office was small and contained a single desk. The officer motioned for me to sit in one of the chairs by his desk. He sat down.

"I want you to tell the truth." He said slowly. "Were you a member of the Irgun?"

I was scared. All the fighting I had done had not prepared me for this possibility. "Yes." I simply replied.

The officer was steady. "You are trained in weapons, explosives, combat."

"Yes."

"You took part in various military operations."

"Yes."

The officer sat back in his chair. "It's not often that I see a young recruit with this kind of experience. I don't favour the methods of the Irgun, but I respect the character of their fighters. I believe they are very valuable to our purpose. Do you believe that?"

I found myself swallowing hard. "Yes. I believe very strongly in the cause of Israel."

He paused. His tongue went to his cheek. "Alright. I'm going to give you a chance. You're to complete your induction and someone will speak to you again later. For now, let me assure you that you will benefit immeasurably by this training, despite what you might think."

I stood up as he did. "Thank you sir." I had to ask him a question though it might have been out of line. "Could I ask you sir?"

He was severe. "What?" he said.

"How did you know I was in the Irgun, Sir?"

He paused. "Well, I wouldn't have known and I guess you wouldn't have told me, except…"

I hesitated, but spoke anyway. "Except what, sir?"

He picked up the letter. "…except you are the only recruit I have seen with a signed recommendation from Menachim Begin."

CHAPTER 29
Latrun

The new State of Israel needed all the soldiers it could get in the war, so there was little time for training. Each recruit received a few days of readiness. It was mostly physical work and a few hours of weapons training. There were so few weapons available that we were instructed as a group and then placed in line to have a chance to practice briefly. There were no uniforms but we were all given shirts and slacks that had been sent from the U.S. Men and women trained together although it was known that women would not be deployed on the front lines. I agreed with this policy, not because women were any less effective as soldiers but because bonds between them and the men tended to form and it was a terrible thing to see someone you cared about in that way cut down on the battlefield.

I was, understandably, in better shape than most of my peers. I had already been through a period of training and this was not as rigorous. I excelled at most tasks and especially with weapons. This had an impact upon the others. No one was jealous or suspicious. After the first day they started to joke about it, pushing me to the head of a line saying "Avrum will do it and we will follow anyway." I can't say that it was 'fun', but it was good natured.

I liked being with these soldiers. It was different than the Irgun. There was a strong feeling of purpose and camaraderie. It wasn't only the idea that you were fighting for a new State that was at war; it was the sense that you were fighting for everything you believed in and that belief was shared both implicitly and explicitly. Our patriotism, our objectives, were not secret. They were very much shared and in the open. It wasn't exactly a sense of unity. It was more like a web of support.

At the end of the second day a man sat down beside me as I was taking some air outside. He looked to be in his early thirties and he was dark, most likely a Sabra. He set himself down beside me like we were old friends, put his arm around my shoulder and said, "You are a celebrity."

I laughed. I was a bit uncomfortable with his familiarity, but I understood it was appropriate in the situation. "It's not what I want."

"No." he replied. "You are not trying to get attention. That's clear. You're just good at everything. Is that the story of your life?"

Again I laughed and shook my head. "No, no. It's not. I most often blend in with the crowd."

He scoffed gently. "You're just being modest. You're a born soldier. Not like the rest of us. We do it because we love our country and we are awkward with it. You seem to be a natural."

I looked quickly in his eyes. They were smiling eyes. "I'm just in better shape. I live on a kibbutz and we have weapons there."

He scowled. "I have been on many Kibbutz and met many Kibbutzim. You are not like any of them. Your focus is naturally on the task you are performing. Kibbutzim are focussed but in a larger sense. You are different. You lack that sense of place, which is often true of soldiers."

I again glanced at his eyes. "So, is that a compliment or a criticism? I can tell you that I have as much a sense of place as anyone else. The place is here, Israel. This is my place. I am at home here."

"No." he said almost softly. "I'm not talking about politics or religion. Yes, you are at home here, I don't mean to infer that you are not as loyal or as bound to Israel as the rest of us. Perhaps you are even more but in a different way. What I can see, and the other's too if they could express it, is a restlessness that runs very deep beneath the surface, a state of readiness and an ability to lead. This is not bad, it's just rare."

I became defensive. I felt this man had gone too far but I didn't want to just get up and leave until I had dealt with his perceptions. "Is it rare to have an athletic skill? Is it rare to want to excel at tasks that may save the lives of others and yourself? Do you believe I want to be the centre of attention? Nothing could be more wrong. I want to be with my people, entirely one of them, not separate or different in any way. Do you think I will be a weight among my people? That I will go my own way and not follow orders, because you are wrong and I will prove you wrong!"

He waved his hand in the air. "You misinterpret me. We need people like you! You are an important asset in every way."

I calmed myself. I didn't want to be praised or patronized. "I will be an ordinary soldier in every way. I will do my duty and whatever else it may take to protect Israel."

He bowed his head in a gesture of acquiescence. "I apologize. I did not mean to imply that you had any fault. I only wanted to salute you as one man to another."

He changed his tone entirely and extended his hand. "I am Gershon. I am your friend."

I looked at his hand for a moment and then at his face. It was beaming and sincere. I could see that he was earnest and uncomplicated. I raised my own hand slightly in the air and brought it down with a slap to grasp his. "My name is Avrum." I said. "I am happy to meet you."

There was a short pause. "You are a Sabra?" I asked simply.

"Yes." He said, and nodded his head. "You are European." This was mostly a statement.

"I was born in Hungary."

Gershon reached into his breast pocket and pulled out a package of cigarettes. "You escaped the camps?" He asked this question almost tentatively, like a physician testing a healing wound.

"I failed to escape them. I was a prisoner."

He offered me a cigarette. Normally at this time I would have refused, but the moment was sensitive. "Thank you." I said and took one. Thus began a lifelong habit of smoking. He took one for himself and lit them both.

I inhaled the smoke and tried to suppress the cough that followed. Gershon laughed and I laughed with him.

"Good?" he asked.

"Yah!" I sputtered." We were silent for a moment.

"The Ashkenazim are brilliant at politics. They are very political. We Sabra's have been here since before King David. We believe in this place as this place."

I couldn't help coughing again as I took another puff. "I am not political."

He looked at me closely with a deep expression. "No. You are the first European I have met who actually seems at home."

"Thank you. I've been here a few years."

"I have heard that there are a large number of Ashkenazim coming right now to live here and help with the war."

"Yes, I have heard that too."

"They will be canon fodder."

"I hope not."

He smiled a sly smile. "I hope not too. I can tell you they are very welcome. I pray earnestly that we might emerge from this conflict victorious and build a strong nation."

I agreed. "I also pray we might survive."

Then Gershon smiled very broadly for the first time. "With soldiers like you and me, how can we fail!" he said.

We both laughed quietly and continued to smoke.

At the end of the brief period of training I was called into the office of the camp commander. This was no surprise since those of us who were to become non-commissioned officers were informed of our rank this way. The Captain was a tall man, very erect, who had been an officer in the British army during the war in Europe and who had been with the Palmach after that. He was an experienced soldier, although quite young. He had been a lawyer in civilian life, so his approach was very measured and seemingly analytical. Even so, he was more personable than I had expected.

When I entered his office he was sitting behind his desk intently reading some papers. He was dressed in a khaki uniform, unlike the rest of us who were finishing training. Although I was somewhat accustomed to dealing with superiors it was with the Irgun that I had gained experience. We didn't have formal ranks, we didn't salute, we didn't have uniforms. Even so, it was abundantly clear who had the authority and it was absolutely required that they be treated with impeccable respect.

In the newly formed Israeli Defence Forces we were expected to act as a traditional army. This was absolutely necessary because there was a definite and utterly necessary chain of command. We were a truly national army, the armed forces of a state. It was the Prime Minister who commanded us, and measures came out of his office. It was the high ranking military officials who created strategy and determined tactics. There were many troops in separate battles and missions that had to be coordinated. There was equipment that had to be deployed. The orders that we received on the field had to be be delivered through the various levels of communication without flaw, so the NCOs were a vital final link between the office of the Prime Minister and the actions of the ordinary soldier.

All of this was conveyed to me clearly and simply by the commander as he rose to stand before me. When he had finished his brief introduction, which happened to be information I was never actually considered, he uncharacteristically smiled at me in a way that implied I should relax.

"How was basic training?" he asked rather genially.

I was as plain and respectful as I could be. "Fine, Sir." I said simply. "It was comprehensive and challenging."

He pursed his lips slightly. "How did you get along with the other recruits?"

This question surprised me. "I believe we got along like soldiers, Sir. You would have to ask the others to really know." I felt very awkward, young and inexperienced with this man. I don't know why. He was my superior and an extremely experienced soldier. I guess I felt that.

"We don't have to ask the others." He said with quiet conviction. "We have eyes and ears and we can see even more clearly than them what is going on. The troops like you. More importantly, they respect you. You are strong in the field. You show steadfastness and determination in the things you do. You are personable but distant, independent but part of the team. You don't run over at the mouth. You speak wisely for your age. All these things are good."

I didn't feel flattered by these words. "Yes, Sir." I said. I treated them as if they were a medical report.

"So you are independent." He repeated. "This can be a double-edged sword. Do you understand that"

I wanted to be honest. I had an idea what he meant but I felt I should hear his point. "No, Sir. I don't believe I do."

"On the one hand," he said, "An independent soldier can think for himself. That may be an asset in combat. On the other hand, he may act without the consent or direction of others in command. This can be disastrous."

"Yes." I said.

He now had my file open in his hands. "You wee in the Irgun."

"Yes."

"I was with the Pal Macht." He frowned slightly as if to ask me, silently, if that was a bad thing. "Do you think the Irgun was an army?"

It was hard to form an answer to this question. "In a way, Sir."

"What made them different to the Pal Macht, or for that matter, the IDF?"

I spoke as clearly as I could since I felt I was on the carpet with this question. "The Irgun was an irregular force acting independently."

The Captain spoke quickly. "Yes, but of course we're all acting independently. There was no real country, only a promise of one. But the Irgun was unique. Why, do you think?"

I couldn't say what I suspected. "I don't now, Sir."

He dropped the file pointedly on his desk. "They were terrorists." He said simply but with some emotion. "They used every means available to them to persuade the enemy to leave." Then he looked at me directly for the first time in the interview. "What do you think about the bombing of the King David Hotel?"

Suddenly, for reasons I don't fully understand, I felt very calm and direct. "I believe it was a botched operation, Sir, but I believe it was effective. The British refused to evacuate the hotel."

"That may be so. The Captain replied. "It was botched, and whether it was effective or not is not a military matter. Even so, it caused some discredit to fall upon the Irgun and its methods. Do you still believe in their methods?"

"Sir, I believe that under the circumstances the Irgun did what it could to help establish a Jewish state."

He appeared almost angry. "They acted independently. They acted as renegades. If their purpose was to convince the British that there were radical Jews who would continually destabilize their mandate they partially succeeded, but at a great cost to the cause of Jewish sympathies in the rest of the world as well. This much I know about the Irgun. But there's something else..."

I knew that a reply was unnecessary and I felt that this lecture was misdirected. I replied simply "Yes, Sir."

"We have integrated the Irgun forces into the IDF. We have found something we suspected but had not experienced. They are dedicated and well trained soldiers who have a deep passion for justice and for Israel. And they can think for themselves while following orders. We are, I firmly believe, more comprehensive soldiers in the Pal Macht. We are better trained in conventional warfare. But I will tell you, reluctantly at best, that the Irgun fighters have a place with us if they can act conscientiously under the conditions of a structured command. Do you understand why I am saying this to you?"

I understood that he was addressing my own idea of an army. "I believe I do, Sir."

He was suddenly very calm. "You speak perfect Yiddish?" It was a statement, not a question.

"Yes, Sir."

"There are many immigrants coming into our jurisdiction at this time. They are being inducted directly into the IDF, but there is little time or resources for training. We desperately need this manpower on the field, but we are aware of how difficult this process of making soldiers out of camp survivors can be."

I understood that very well from my experience in basic training. "I can see that, Sir."

"You are going to be leading a group of immigrants. All of them are Yiddish speaking, none of them have proper military training."

"I understand, Sir."

"Even if you don't understand now, you will before long. You will be going into combat immediately. There is a shortage of arms, but you will have to do your best with what we have. In this context you will have to truly be a leader. I trust you in this, from the reports I have. Live up to your duty, and that will be sufficient."

There was nothing but strength and assurance in his voice. "Thank you, Sir."

His tone became a bit softer. "I understand that you requested a legal change of your surname.

"That's correct, Sir."

"To Bar Kochba."

"Yes, Sir."

"That's a name that will be hard to live up to. Your request has been granted and the paperwork is in your file for now. You have been elevated to the rank of Sergeant."

I refrained from showing emotion and, in fact, I felt that I was assuming a responsibility that was serious and grave. "Thank you, Sir."

The Captain almost smiled as he said. "Alright, Sergeant Bar Kochba. I wish you good luck. He shook my hand. "Dismissed.", he said.

By the end of the day I had been placed with my troops. Things happened very fast at this time. All my soldiers were men, there were 16 of them. All of them had just completed basic training. All of them were immigrants from Europe who had survived the camps.

They had courage and determination but they did not think like soldiers. In the first evening that we were a unit I engaged them in military way. I was strict and somewhat formal, but because we were to be a fighting unit I tried to be accessible to some degree. It must be said that Yiddish is not a language that lends itself well to military contexts. It tends to make people rather familiar. The men in my command had been bakers, shop owners, lawyers, small businessmen. Everyone had lost most if not all of their families and had been displaced from their homes. Some had spent time on Cypress waiting to come here. Their ages ranged from 18 to mid-forties.

It was a mixed group, but it all came together in that first evening. They gathered around me in the barracks as I told them our orders, which I had received before.

"One of the most essential operations for us at this time is to free the lines of transportation. Without free routes we can't move troops and supplies. The road from Tel Aviv to Jerusalem is blocked by a site called

Latrun. Jerusalem is not only an essential centre, it is the spiritual centre of Israel. Our forces have to take Latrun in order to free the road."

"This poses us a difficult battle. Latrun is on a hill, the only way is up, which gives our enemy the advantage. It is fortress and is well protected. We will need to fight hard."

We got some sleep and in the half light before dawn we were loaded into trucks and transported to the battlefield at Latrun. We arrived around noon. An offensive was underway, and without any time to organize the unit properly we were thrown into battle. The more experienced troops were already moving up the slope. It was clear that they were experiencing a lot of casualties. The Lieutenant in charge of my unit gave me orders; to follow the earlier troops up the hill, pick up the arms that were dropped and charge ahead. I informed my men, "We are going to charge up the hill behind the earlier troops, pick up their fallen weapons and attack the fortress. Bear down! This won't be easy, but it will work. Follow me. I will show you where the weapons are and you can pick them up."

We started up the hill. It was terribly difficult, the Jordanians were defending their position fiercely and they had to advantage. There were a lot of IDF troops working their way up the hill and a lot of them were falling. At the base of the hill there was some safety but as we ascended the slope the onslaught of bullets got worse. When my men reached a position half way to the top we had to stop behind a knoll. Before we reached that position I had seen my men falling one by one, hit by enemy fire. Three had been hit; they were lying behind me in the slope. I assessed the situation. My men were showing courage and composure given the circumstances, but they had never seen action before.

"Sergeant Bar Kochba!" one man said. "Are we supposed to die like dogs!"

I couldn't answer that question directly. "On my signal fan out so that you make a more difficult target." I pointed to another knoll about 30 meters ahead and to the right. "I want you to end up over there." There were dead and wounded men from the forward attack lying on the slope with weapons lying beside them. "Get those weapons as you go."

There were nods of assent. "Go!" I said, moving out ahead to lead the attack.

The enemy fire was heavy. I lay flat on the hill to allow my men to pass and pick up a rifle from a fallen soldier. As I did, I saw two of my men hit, one in the shoulder and another in the leg. They fell to the ground. I saw the rest of my unit make it to the knoll, but as I did something else occurred. I could see it from my position but my men could not.

The experienced troops, composed in part by former members of the Pall Macht, were clearly in trouble. They were pinned well below the fortress. I could see them try to move forward, but every time they raised their heads they were shot down. My men were in a better position. We would be able to move forward but not as far as the forward troops. I kept low and made my way to my troops.

"How many guns did we get?" I asked.

The strongest of my men answered, "Four. Now we have enough for all of us but two."

"Good." I said and I pointed. "We're going to make our way over there, to that position, to support the main army."

"What about the wounded?" another man asked.

"Don't worry. We'll pick them up on the way down."

"When will that be?" another asked.

I said clearly, "When the battle is over and we have taken Latrun. Let's go!"

BAR KOCHBA

We headed into fire, but the Jordanians were concentrating on the earlier troops and we got off a bit easy. Even so, I saw one of my men hit in the chest. It looked bad and despite some difficulty I made my way over to him. He was hurt badly, but conscious.

"Can you breathe?" I asked him.

"Yes, Sergeant. I'm alright!"

"Ok. I'll be back for you, just hold on."

I made my way to my unit. They were not frightened but they were concerned for the dead and wounded.

At that moment it looked bad as I surveyed the hill. Fallen soldiers were all over the hill, so many that I just knew this operation was a slaughterhouse. We were intended to take the hill, but the experienced troupes were decimated and the remainder were pinned down with inferior fire power just more than halfway up the slope. I looked at their position and I could see that they were in a nearly impossible position. They could hardly advance at all and the possibility of actually taking the fortress was limited. From the position of my unit we could offer some support by moving ahead to the next possible position, but because the Jordanians were firing from behind stone battlements it was hard to give them effective cover.

Even so, I felt we should try. I urged my men to go and we moved out towards a low ledge below and to the right of the first fighters. Then it happened. The soldiers ahead of us rose out of their position at once and attempted to move forward. It was a brave and daring attempt. There was fire all around. Many of our men fell. Those who remained made their way back to cover.

There was a break in the shooting for a moment. Then something very shocking happened. The forward troops began to retreat.

Effectively, that meant that the operation was at an end. As the soldiers retreated they were fired upon by the Jordanians, who were trying to kill as many as possible. I saw an opportunity to end this battle with some success. I ordered my men, "Take up their position and we'll cover their retreat." My soldiers did not hesitate. They made their way to the forward position and held the enemy fire. As they did so, two of them fell.

We held that position until the former front line was out of range. Then we started to take care of ourselves. I ordered most of my troops to work their way down the hill. I ordered them to pick up our wounded as they went. The rest of us covered them and they all made it back, carrying wounded with them. Then it was up to those of us who remained. I ordered the other men to retreat while I stood the ground and covered them. This was partly effective, but on the way down one of my men was hit in the back. It was now my turn to retreat.

It was pointless to try and fire, but one of my soldiers had remained lower on the hill to protect me. That worked to some degree. When I reached the wounded soldier he was barely breathing and he was unconscious. I hoisted him over my shoulder and worked my way down the hill. There were medics waiting on the site and I handed him over to them.

My men, those who remained, were collected below the battleground. They gathered around me. "We did our best, didn't we?" one man asked.

"We did our best!" I repeated. One of them gave me a cigarette. "You saved a life." he said. I felt very much a part of this group. I believe we all felt that.

We had failed to take Latrun on what was a third attempt. The experienced men ahead of us, who had retreated, were led by an officer named Ariel Sharon. He was a career soldier. Years later, after a long and interesting career, he said that the retreat at Latrun was one of the most significant tactical decisions he had ever made.

The Commander of the field came to see me the following day. He said we had done well, and that I was to commend my unit for bravery and steadfastness. I did that, and the men seemed pleased.

CHAPTER 30
The Protector

We were not relocated directly following the battle at Latrun. We were secured in a post away from the hill and beyond the reach of enemy fire. We had failed to achieve our objective, and this weighed upon the minds of my troops. We had lost 6 men; four wounded and two dead. This was a terrible blow to all of us. Now we numbered 11 including myself.

The night after losing the battle we sat in a circle outside one of the tents. The truth was that we barely knew each other. Even so, we felt very connected by our first military experience. We went over the names of the casualties. In both cases, someone who knew them said a few words.

"Issy was a family man, although his wife and children were lost." A soldier named Georgi said. "He had no pictures but he described his wife to me once. He said she was not an unusual beauty but she made everything around her glow. He said his three children were funny and well behaved. The oldest was 10. Issy had a lot of affection in his heart, more than bitterness and more than pain. He had an easy smile. I don't know his last name."

"Jacobson." I said. "His last name was Jacobson."

Another man, named Seymour, spoke about the other man who was killed. "He was quiet and strong" Semour said. "During training he hardly spoke to anyone. I was curious so once during a meal I sat with him. At first he was quiet, but when I started to talk about the future of Israel he opened up. He wanted to be a part of the process of bringing a new country to life. He was an architect in Germany before Hitler. He hoped to build here. He had two children, both in their teens. He couldn't find them after the war, but he still hoped somehow they had survived and were safe."

There was a moment of silence. I believed it was essential for my group to feel that they were a part of things, that they had bonds of trust between them, because their training was so superficial. As a fighting unit, in this case, the more we understood each other the better our chances would be on the field. I also knew that the most powerful bond would be action and I fully expected we would see more of that. We talked further about the events of the battle.

"It unnerved me to see a man hit very close to me. That was the first time. From now on, I will learn to live with it."

"I'm still not in the best of shape. Even though my adrenaline was pumping I found that I was winded half way up the hill. That will change."

"I had never held a rifle until training, and then I only used one a couple of times. It felt awkward to use one at first. By the time we were finished it felt good."

"Next time I will know where to fire. I couldn't always see the enemy. Now I know better where to look."

Every comment was a confession that ended with a positive statement. My men were committed to their soldiering. Among the 10 who remained there was consensus. They would improve as soldiers. They would accomplish their objectives.

My own feelings were positive. They were talking more like soldiers now, after seeing action, than they did before. I didn't see, at this time, the potential for internal conflict between men. This was a special unit. All its members had lived in various kinds of camps together with many other people. They had learned to get along with each other in order to survive, in order just to make things more tolerable. Also, these men had seen death and had suffered incredible loss. They were, each and every one, wholeheartedly committed to Israel's survival. In an almost ironic way, they were like the Irgun; they were not random soldiers. They were patriots.

After our meeting broke up Georgi stayed behind to talk with me. "You don't mind the men being honest?"

"No." I said. "I encourage it."

He was a man of about thirty. His hair was light, which was a bit unusual, and his skin was pale. He had escaped from Russia and wound up on Cypress for many months. He had an especially casual and engaging sense of humour which burst out of his conversation often. I had seen him in the field. He was unique in our bunch because he was a natural soldier. No one else had yet shown such instinct.

"You know, if we get too lovey-dovey we'll forget to hate. We'll converge upon the enemy and ask them for a cigarette."

"It's good for them to feel comfortable with each other."

Georgi pulled out a package of cigarettes. "Do you smoke?" He offered me one. I took it.

"Thanks." I said. He lit it for me.

"We lost today." He said.

"Well, it does happen. We will certainly find a way to win in spite of that."

Georgi smiled. "That's true. I know that. We all know that." He looked at my face from the corner of his eye as he pretended to look at the night sky. "Do you know what's next?"

I said flatly, "No."

"We won't be here for long."

I looked him in the eye. "You ask a lot of questions. When we receive orders, I'll give them to you. Can I give you some advice?" I asked.

"Sure." He said.

I spoke evenly. "Clean your gun. Think about things that concern you specifically as a soldier. Be even handed with the other members of your troop."

"O.k." he said.

"The more you worry about things that don't concern you the closer you get to being sloppy in the field."

"I see." He said plainly. Then I focussed in on his performance.

"I saw you in the field." I said. "You have the right instincts. Rather than getting close to me, turn your attention to the other men and what you can give to them. They will look up to you if you let them. I'm your sergeant, not your best friend. I have to stay distant from you to be able to protect you. It's not personal, it's practical."

Without a hint of sarcasm Georgi saluted me and said "Yes, Sir!"

"Look to me to save your life, not dally in conversation, because that's what I'm partly here to do."

Again he said "Yes, Sir."

I lowered my stance. "You can call me Sergeant Bar Kochba."

"O.k."

"Or just 'Sarge'"

"Yes, Sarge." It was clear that I was establishing military protocols. The truth was that I liked Georgi and could possibly have been friends with him. But I knew that if I let that happen the necessary order within the company would erode. It was essential that I keep my command separate from personal relationships even though I was looking at them among my men. I didn't actually know if that was right either. I felt they had to fight together so as not to die apart.

"Alright, Georgi. Dismissed."

He saluted and left. We both knew that this was all formality, but I could see that we both agreed, in some way, that it was essential. I couldn't risk loosing respect among my men, respect I thought I had won that day.

Over the next few days there was a great deal of activity. Shortly after failing to take Latrun an unforeseen stroke of luck struck for our cause, specifically for relieving the siege on Jerusalem and bringing in supplies.

Somehow, the Command got word of a small path leading to Jerusalem from somewhere in our territory behind the fortress at Latrun directly to Jerusalem. They quickly checked it out and determined that a road might be secretly constructed large enough to transport a line of vehicles into the besieged city. This was a bold plan, since the road would have to be constructed secretly, at night, and very quickly. This route became known as 'the Burma Road".

My troop was ordered to help with the construction. This suited my men quite well. They worked hard and they worked together and they caught the attention of some of the other officers. After the third night I received orders from the Command. We were dispatched along the yet to be constructed part of the path to go into Jerusalem. Our task was to assist with the operations there by both civilians and Pal Mach troops who were defending the city.

We traversed the path into Jerusalem at night. My men were steady but there was a ripple of excitement in their ranks as well. They knew they had been chosen for this assignment and their confidence had been raised. We reached the newer part of the city in the south just before dawn. I had briefed them on their mission. They were to assist and refresh the troops that had been in the city for a long while.

We were greeted by artillery fire from the Egyptians in the south. There was a combination of street fighting and conventional warfare going on. A line had been established in the city which held back enemy forces, but there was also street fighting to maintain a hold on the perimeter. My men and I were unaware of the ultimate situation when we arrived. I immediately reported to the head of the operation, which wasn't an easy job. When I finally succeeded in locating him he had his hands full with keeping up with the overall situation.

"What do you want?" he virtually barked to me.

"I need orders, Sir. 'D' company reporting for duty."

"How many are you?"

"Ten, Sir."

He clicked his tongue. "Ten. Get into the city and support those troupes on the street. Make sure no artillery gets past you."

"Yes, Sir!" I said quickly and left at once.

When I got to my men I told them we were going to fight house to house. We had been armed lightly with our rifles and some grenades. No one was thinking very deeply about this. We accepted our assignment gladly, without question. I think every man among us believed they would soon be dead.

As we approached the active part of Jerusalem we slowly began to take fire. No one was hurt. In a short time we came across a unit that was holding an intersection of the new city. We left them and went on further. Two blocks down the line we found ourselves in a fire fight with Egyptian forces. They were barely being held by a group of IDF troops. We fought hard to reach our force. My men showed professionalism in the face of grave fire. We reached the corner where our troops were positioned. There were only five of them left, the other five having been killed. We fell into that position, giving their men some cover and some rest.

We held that position all day and made some progress to an adjacent corner. The enemy couldn't move, which was the whole idea. One of my men was hit as he crossed the road but it was only in the hip. My soldiers were solid. They followed my orders clearly at all times, used their weapons professionally, acted independently when required and some times creatively as well. At one point, on their own initiative, two men covered three others as they took the enemy out of a doorway that was a strategic barrier. But mostly, they showed unity. They worked well together and this was evident to any experienced soldier.

In the course of the next few days our troop fought at several positions. We showed some pluck and we showed that we were effective. This was especially meaningful because of the meaningfulness of the location. It was conceived by most Jews that it was essential to hold Jerusalem, not only for strategic reasons but because it symbolized the very essence of what was Jewish and the core of faith. Even so, Jerusalem was very hard to hold although fierce fighting by both the military and civilian forces was focussed there. In the old city especially difficult urban warfare was engaged. In the end, when the Egyptians finally retreated from Jerusalem to shore up their positions in the South, Old Jerusalem was lost but the new city remained in our hands.

My men were in the battle until it ended a few weeks after we arrived in Jerusalem. We were rewarded with a few days rest within the city. On the first day after the Egyptian retreat, while I was sanding by a corner looking at the street, Georgi came up beside me with a box of juice in his hand.

"You want some?" he asked. "It's allowed."

I waved him down. "No, thanks. I'll go get one later."

He smiled wanly. "Nice to see a city street with no bodies on it."

"It's a relief."

"Well?" he asked. "Did we do alright."

I knew he wanted something specific. He wanted approval and encouragement for the platoon and I wasn't about to deny him of it. "You proved yourselves well. It wasn't an easy assignment."

Georgi looked into the sun. "And we didn't loose a single man!" he said. "That's your reward and your accomplishment."

I shook my head. "It's not my accomplishment."

Georgi looked away as if in abstraction although he was being very specific. "Oh, yes. There wasn't time to teach us how to fight, so you taught us to be a unit instead. You let us learn to use our weapons and to know what action to take. You directed us like teenagers, and it worked."

I smiled at him briefly. "I accept that as a statement of confidence. Thanks."

"You're welcome." He said and gestured broadly with his arm.

"It's not over yet." I said. "The war's not over yet."

"Alright." He said. "We're ready." I knew he was speaking for the group.

Indeed, we saw further action. My platoon was involved in several other operations having received some new recruits, to increase our number, but the last one was the most treacherous. We were sent to the Negev to attempt to regain ground held by Egypt and free several roads as well as the capital of the region, Beersheba. It was an operation that took, in all, seven days of fighting. On the third day our unit, along with several units of more experienced soldiers, were ordered to take two important hills that were strategic necessities. These hills were strongly held by the enemy.

Just before dawn we started our ascent. Tanks battered enemy positions as we fought our way up the hill we had to take. The stronger troops went first while we provided cover from behind. One of my men was hit during the initial assault but it looked like a wound he could survive. The enemy was entrenched at the top of the hill and it became clear that they would not be easily taken. No one had to say so, but we all knew that this battle would end in hand-to-hand combat.

At this point my men were experienced in battle, but they were not well prepared to meet the enemy head on. The Egyptians were much more thoroughly trained for this than we were. Still, when the moment came for a hand-to-hand fight, my men leapt in. Those who had no experience in close fighting held back a bit and covered their comrades with weapons fire. This was most helpful. Several of my men fought in pairs, which proved effective.

Hand-to hand combat is a final outcome of an attack. It's unpredictable and to be successful it requires an enormous amount of will and skill on the part of the soldiers. It is very hard to kill a man you are struggling with. It's not a natural thing for most people. The fight becomes crazed and each man begins to see only what they are doing in the bubble of awareness that surrounds them. Despite what some would have us believe there is little joy in defeating a soldier and cutting his guts with a knife. You hear his cry, you see his face contorted with pain and death. Victory may be real; there is some question about how sweet it is at that time. Although you are happy to survive the outcome doesn't necessarily create pride.

Blood flowed on all sides and courage illuminated a horrendous spectacle. This was not so new for me; I had fought soldier to soldier for the Irgun and I had been trained in it. My effort was spent in defending my men. The truth was that we shouldn't have been involved in this close a battle at all. We couldn't easily have avoided it, however.

Two incidents stood out. Two of the more experienced troops were in trouble near the top of the hill. Several Egyptian soldiers had the best of them and it was clear they were failing. Without warning two of my men attacked the Egyptians, wedging themselves between them and the falling Israelis and killing both of them. This was a brave act. They were put upon themselves by other enemy troops and badly wounded.

My own part in this battle was more defensive and strategic. I covered my own men as best I could. This involved struggle with a number of Egyptians in various manoeuvres. I had an obvious advantage over my men since I was trained and experienced. It is no exaggeration to say I saved many lives that day. My ability and my technique were clear. My men did not know I could fight like that. Neither did the other Israeli troops who saw me in action and often benefited directly by my abilities. To some, I seemed to defeat my enemies almost effortlessly. This was not at all true, but a factor of the issue that I knew how to fight effectively.

Our platoon actually lasted only 30 minutes in actual hand-to-hand combat. In that time all of them were wounded, two mortally. When we fell back, we continued to add cover to the other units. In the end our assault was successful; both hills were taken by our soldiers, with heavy casualties inflicted on both sides. As the sun reached its apex it became clear that this operation was over.

My men regrouped by the crest of the hill. We were able to count our losses and tend to our wounds. Several were quite serious; one of my men was cut in the stomach, another in the lungs and another had a deep head wound. Three men had been shot in or near vital organs and the rest had various wounds that were not life threatening. Those who could helped the others. There was a lack of sound around our position except for the men giving encouragement to each other. There was a kind of buzz in the air. It was the sound you can almost hear in the midst of pain. Medics arrived fairly soon and we carried those of us who couldn't move down the hill. From there the worst were transported to a field hospital set up several miles away.

This was the end of our platoon as an immediate fighting unit. It coincided with the end of the war within a few days. A "sincere ceasefire" was established on October 27th, soon after the last operation. I went to visit some of my men shortly after the battle. I had received some wounds myself but they were not too serious. Georgi was in the field hospital with an injury to his lungs and abdomen. I had seen him in the battle fighting with an Egyptian who out classed him visibly as an aggressor. He fought hard but was wounded before I could get to him and take his enemy down. Now he was smiling up at me from his cot.

"I want to thank you, Sergeant, for saving my life."

I didn't want any thanks. "How's the lung?" I asked.

He rubbed his chest lightly and coughed. "Good!" he laughed. "The nurse says I shouldn't smoke! Can you believe it! I joined the army and all that I get out of it is to stop smoking."

"It's part of the Israeli health package." I joked. "A 'join the army and quit smoking' policy."

"Is it true what I hear, that the war will be over soon?" Georgi was not attempting irony or humour. It was a sincere question.

"That's what they say. The U.N. is going to bring in a ceasefire, probably in the next few days."

"Will that be before or after we won?" he said.

I laughed. "Do you think we have won?"

Geogi smiled. "Yes!" he said emphatically. "Yes, we have won! We have not been pushed into the sea! We did not surrender! We are not all dead! Can we count that as victory?"

"As far as I know we protected the areas given to us by the U.N. resolution. The strategic position here in the Negev has been mostly won. You can tell your children to be proud of you."

"Ah, believe me, Sergeant, at this time the last thing I am thinking of is children. We have won for now, perhaps that's so, but I have seen war for what it is, if you don't mind an amateur saying so. Let my wounds heal for now. I'll think about the rest later."

The rest was soon to happen. Our platoon was cited for bravery and several of my men received awards of distinction. The regular troops who fought on the hill noticed our effort and recommended us. I never saw that group again as a unit but I made a point of visiting each one individually. For my part, I was awarded a medal as well and cited on my record for my leadership. A gang of European immigrants had distinguished itself in battle, which was unexpected by the military. My men were certainly noteworthy.

What cannot be forgotten regarding that platoon is that they were soldiers in their own way, having somehow survived the camps and made it to Israel. It would be crude to say they were men who had nothing to lose; they had new horizons to look forward to and new lives to live. They wanted to fight for Israel, having been victimized so viciously in Europe. Their purpose was forward looking and positive. They perceived a dream that could come true and they knew that they, personally, must show responsibility for it.

After the ceasefire things slowly began to fall into some kind of normalcy. The army, which included almost every Israeli citizen, was divided into two groups: a standing army and the reserves, which include everyone over 18 and under 40. By the end of November I was back on the kibbutz, but I had time to visit Hannah before going home. Her experience had deepened her rather than hardened her. We met at our usual café.

"So, Bar Kochba, now a peaceful retreat to the country?"

I laughed gently. "For now. I don't know yet what I'm going to do. I may stay on in the army as a regular. What do you think of that?"

She took my hand, which was rare for her. "Avrum, you don't know this…you're the last to know. Whether its fate or nature or choice. You are a soldier. Everyone knows that about you; you glow with it."

I felt defensive. "I'm not a killer. I don't want to kill, I want to protect."

"That's what makes you glow!" Hannah said strongly. "You are not a violent man, but you are a very good soldier. You are the kind of soldier that believes in what he is fighting for. That's best!"

The truth about Hannah and me as lovers was mundane. It really wasn't me that wanted to be friends. It was Hannah. I wanted to settle into a relationship. Hannah wasn't ready. It made us both a bit uneasy, but the innate affection between us was so real we couldn't avoid friendship. Hannah was an inspiration to me and an anchor. She always seemed to know what she was doing for herself, whereas I was mostly a mess when it came to self knowledge.

When I arrived back at the kibbutz at the end of November there was a strong sense of focus. About half of the kibbutzim had been in the army. I was among the last to return because I was an officer. I received a very warm welcome when I stepped into the dining hall that evening. Everyone stood up and applauded. I sat down with Dov and Orly, both of whom I was extremely pleased to see.

I don't know why people treat me with so much respect. I don't deserve it. I'm just a soldier, I only do my job. The fact that I kill other soldiers cannot be applauded, and certainly it is not something I'm proud of.

After dinner I went for a walk around the perimeter of the kibbutz with Dov. I had to ask him, although I was embarrassed, why people treated me with such respect. "It can't be simply because I'm a soldier?" I said.

Dov looked at my face. "You really don't know, do you?"

"No. Of course not. I know I don't deserve it."

"What do soldiers do?" Dov asked.

I let out a guffaw. "They kill each other." I said.

As we talked I began to understand something about myself that had been hidden. I understood that I had not escaped unhurt from the war. I had, like every soldier, been traumatized by the violence and death. It had taken the place of any kind of objectivity. All I could think was that I had killed others and I tried to justify that with guilt.

Dov sensed my concern. "Look at it from our point of view, Avrum, on the kibbutz. We know soldiers kill but we also know that they do this to protect us. That is the function of a soldier even if they don't see it. To protect. To protect Israel."

"I'm as much the *yeshiva* boy' as I am the warrior, Dov. I do what I do with the belief that I must in order to fulfill G-d's will. But every soldier does this and they don't all get applause for it in the mess hall!"

"Yes, because your purpose it more clear. You are not just a natural fighter, you are someone very rare and very valuable. You are a protector. You instil confidence and trust in your abilities and faith that you will do everything in your power to actually maintain the peace. That's why people respect you. You have integrity, and it spills out all around you."

I didn't accept Dov's words at face value. I was adamantly determined not to be special for what I did. I changed the subject.

"Orly seems better." I said.

"She's better. She's still getting over losing Aaron, I think. She's smiling again, that's a good sign."

"Such a beautiful smile." I said wistfully.

Dov stopped walking and we stood facing each other. "Do you think she has a beautiful smile?" he asked pointedly.

"Yes. Radiant."

"She's missed you." Dov said this as if I should already have known it.

"Oh, really! How do you know that?"

Dov seemed almost angry. "Avrum, you are a hero but you have the intelligence of a carrot. I know she thinks about you because we talk about you from time to time. Sometimes on walks just like this one…maybe even in this very spot!"

I was surprised. "Well, what do you talk about?"

"You. Briefly. What a fine person you are. How she misses you and hopes you're alright."

That was news to me. At dinner Orly was beautiful but uncharacteristically quiet. "Should I visit her?"

"Why not! You're going to be around for a while, aren't you."

Dov had touched a delicate point with me. I hadn't yet decided what to do with my future. I knew the life of a career soldier was hard, but I didn't know what else I could do. The fact was I felt like a soldier. I liked being one, despite my protests. I didn't feel that the kibbutz, much as I liked it, was where I wanted to spend my life. I did not see myself settling into so pastoral a setting.

"I'm considering joining the regulars." I replied.

We started walking again. "I see." Dov was stroking his chin. "Interesting choice for you. Certainly one thing Israel needs is a standing army."

Our conversation wound along, and as we talked I felt more sure about certain things. It was the first completely civilian conversation I had had in a long time, especially with someone I knew very well from the kibbutz. I drew out the facts. I suspected that I wanted to be in the regular army, despite my attachment to the kibbutz. The War of Independence was over but my future in the military probably was not. And I determined to visit Orly the next day. That was a priority.

In the early winter air my senses seemed more fresh and uncomplicated than they had in a long time. I was a protector? That sounded better than killer, but was it really any different? I would have to learn to make that distinction. Right at that moment, I could sense something close to peace in the air. It was extremely bracing. I wanted to see what kind of soldier I really was; a simple murderer or a man of God.

CHAPTER 31
Suburban Girl

Leah Teperman squirmed slightly in her seat. It was 20 minutes into her grade 7 science class and the light haired young teacher at the front of the room was writing the definition of 'mammal' on the board. His face turned every few seconds towards the group to speak as he wrote. His oval face, narrow at the forehead and at the chin, was alight with both eagerness and purpose. Most of the teachers at this Hebrew Day School were more laid back, but Mr. Brandeis was bright and shiny new at teaching and he took it very seriously. All the kids liked him even though most of them didn't like science. He kept the period lively and he made them laugh often by making funny comments and embarrassing individual students lightly by centring them out and asking questions.

Leah was restless as usual. Science was the last class of the day and she wanted it to end. She had to go to her piano lesson after school, but it was her best friend's birthday and there was a party after at her house. She had her gift in her satchel. It was a charm for her friends charm bracelet, a gold angel because she was volunteering at a local nursing home and Leah thought it was so appropriate. She had hunted for the right gift. Her friend was 12 and was going to have a bat Mitzvah later in the month. This afternoon's party was only for a few close friends.

Leah was busy most of the time. School ran from 8:30 to 4:00. There were lessons of one kind or another four days a week including Hebrew, ballet, swimming and piano. She was a good swimmer, an elegant and athletic dancer and a promising musician. She was good at whatever she did, but she didn't know it. She thought she was ugly. She thought her face was not pretty most of the time and her hair was messy. But she never dwelt on these misgivings, except in private sometimes and sometimes with her mother when she would whine about them and get a little comfort. She didn't know that she was special in any way, that she was the focus of a great deal of attention even though she did feel loved by her parents and grandparents. She didn't know that girls in her group always wanted something, that they were in a constant state of anxiety over their appearance, their possessions, their activities. It was partly hormones and it was partly training. Suburban girls had to protect their status at all times. It was not only their birthright, it was also the cornerstone of their usefulness and identity.

The final forty minutes of the science class dragged on for Leah because she was so anxious to go. When the bell finally rang, to make matters worse Mr. Brandeis asked her to stay after class. She didn't know what she had done, but it probably wasn't good. She wondered. He had collected their notebooks earlier last week. Maybe hers was the worst! They had a test three days ago. Maybe she had failed!

Mr. Brandeis had a pile of student's notebooks on his desk. She approached sullenly, certain there was a problem. Mr. Brandeis was frowning. Her test was also on his desk. It had a large red A+ on the top. What did he want? He looked at her and smiled.

"Leah," he said in a serious tone. "This test is perfect. I want you to know that. You made no mistakes. Every definition is correct. Every multiple choice, fill in the blank, short answer is correct. Your short answers are clear and correct. What do you think of that."

Leah didn't know what to say. She was, perhaps, ashamed? "I'm sorry, sir." She said.

"And this notebook." He took her notebook off the top of his pile. "Look at it. Every word is written in a very nice script. The sentences are all complete. The information is correct, the spelling is good, the choice of material is thoughtful and well chosen."

She blanched. "Oh." She said.

"And the diagrams. They are simple, accurate and most of them are coloured."

Leah had a lump in her throat. "Yes. I tried to stay in the lines. Is that good?"

Mr. Brandeis laughed. "Yes, Leah, its good! It's all good. In fact, it's almost exceptional. You have almost perfect marks in this course. Are your other courses this strong?"

There was no lying about this. "Oh no! Not really. I mean, I'm not failing or anything. But I'm only getting 'A's in most classes. I'm not getting many 'A pluses'."

Mr. Brandeis leafed through Leah's notebook. "It's not only that it's neat, Leah. Other pupils are as neat. You have a grasp of the material that is strong, stronger than the other students. I think you have an aptitude for science, that's what I wanted to talk to you about. It's not so common to have a girl who is so gifted at science. Do you like science especially? Is it particularly interesting to you?"

This was a tough question for Leah, but she answered without hesitation. "Yes! Well, I really like the biology part, especially when we learn about the organs. And I really like learning about other animals! And insects!" She started to gush. "I mean I don't like real insects. They're a nuisance. But I like learning about them in books. Oh! And plants! I liked learning about the pollen, and the stamens and the pollenization."

"That's very good!"

"And genes! I liked learning about genes!" She had forgotten that she was nervous.

"So you find this class interesting?" Mr. Brandeis interjected.

Leah caught her words. She instinctively knew this was a leading question so she hesitated a little before answering. "Science is interesting. Everything is so simple." She stopped short as she saw Mr. Brandeis' smile turn upside down. "I mean, it's not simple like easy simple. It's simple like it makes sense. It's all about real life, isn't it? Flowers and animals and the human body. It's not like English! English is ok, but its not about anything. I mean, I liked "The Red Pony' because it was about a pony and I liked "Black Beauty" because it was about a girl and a horse. But I don't have a horse, so it's not that real."

Mr. Brandeis looked serious. His brush cut made him look like a newspaper reporter, not a teacher. "So you like science better than English?"

Leah looked down at the floor. "I guess so." She didn't know what she had done wrong.

"Leah, I think you have an aptitude for science and I want to encourage you."

Leah was surprised. "You think I'm good at science?"

The teacher smiled. "Yes, I do. And I want to encourage you."

She looked directly at Mr. Brandeis for the first time. "You want to encourage me?"

"Yes." He licked his lips gingerly. "America needs scientists, Leah! We need them very badly. The Russians are strong in science and we have to be stronger! That means we have to encourage students to excel at science, especially those who have a talent for it. That means you!"

Leah was stunned. "You think I should be a scientist?" she whined.

"If you want."

Leah let out a kind of moan. "But Mr. Brandeis! I'm a girl!"

Her teacher laughed. "All the more reason!" he said. "We want women in the sciences too! That's also very important! What makes you think all scientists are men?"

"You never see girl scientists in movies. Or on TV. They're usually men dressed in long white coats with a pen in their breast pocket, or something like that."

"That's only movies. In real life there are lots of female scientists, especially in medicine."

"Oh." Said Leah knowingly. "Women doctors! I know there are women doctors. My mother has a woman doctor. Her name is Dr. Segleman. She was my mother's doctor when she had my little brother."

There was a slight pause during which Leah looked at the floor and her teacher looked at her. He saw a small, well groomed, polite and obedient little girl who he knew was bright and worked very hard. "Leah, you're not in any trouble, believe me. I think you are good at science and I want you to think about that a little bit. It's very good that you enjoy learning about animals and plants and people. And you're good at it! I only want to encourage you to follow your interests and to do what you're good at. Is that alright with you?"

Leah caught his eyes for only a moment. She saw that he was happy, not angry. "So you think I should be a scientist?"

He wanted to be careful not to scare Leah. "I want you to do what makes you happy. That's the most important thing and you have plenty of time to figure out what that is. But I think you have a talent for science and I want you to know that, Leah. That's all."

Leah was a bit confused. "Is that what you kept me after class for?" she asked tentatively.

"Yes, that's right. I just wanted to let you know that I see a talent for science in you."

Although she didn't exactly understand this because she had never thought a girl could have a 'talent' for science, Leah realized that she was not actually in trouble. This was enough to cause her both relief and excitement.

"Ok." Mr. Brandeis said brightly. "You can go now, Leah."

She literally skipped on the spot. "Thanks, Mr. Brandies. I'll remember what you said. Oh! Can I tell my Mom?"

Mr. Brandeis was already stacking notebooks. "Sure." He said. "You can even have her call me if she wants."

There were two children in the Teperman home; Leah and her younger brother Abe, who was 9. There was a third child on the way, due in four months. There had been a miscarriage three years after Abe was born and Rivka had been reluctant to get pregnant again for a while after that. Now, she was being careful. She was still young at 32 years of age and she wanted a larger family. She loved raising Leah and Abe. Although she was a strict mother she was also given to luxurious and spontaneous affection. She cuddled and hugged her children often and they were both very open to it. Abe especially liked to hug his mother around the neck and kiss her on the cheek, while Leah was a bit more reserved.

Asher was a gentle, caring father who spent as much time with his children as he could. From the time they were babies he plied them with insightful anecdotes, stories, parables and humour. Religion was the heartbeat of this family. It set the pace for every interaction and informed every hour. Although his congregation was Conservative and mostly didn't observe the Sabbath, Asher's family did observe it faithfully although not to the same degree as a strictly Orthodox family would. Asher was busy in his congregation. There were many weddings, bar mitzvahs and bat mitzvahs, holiday services. There were also funerals. Life was very full and they were mostly a happy family, firmly rooted in their community and their own business. They were also happy with their country. Being American was natural for Asher and the children. It was not always so easy for Rivka. She saw the United States through a more remote lens. She didn't experience the patriotism that was strong all around her.

She didn't like TV. That was unusual within her community. She had heard the unending propaganda in Europe during the war and she knew what it could do to a people. When she watched television, she didn't see cute characters living a perfect life in wealth and comfort. She saw characteristics cut out of American culture and pasted on two-dimensional figures to portray a kind of folk art for the 1950's. She had seen patriots as rosy and robust as the people of the U.S., but in her experience that had led to fascism and hatred. For this reason, she was highly aware of the discrimination of the black people in America. It was so much a part of the culture that it rarely dawned on people that they were persecuting anyone. More than most, Rivka could see the flaws and gaps, the dangers and potentials of the American political and cultural map. She knew how good it could be and was both grateful and thankful that America provided the means for a very good life for her and her family. Far from being anti-American, she supported the country in every way and was, in a muted sense, very proud that she had been adopted by this culture. She didn't think it was perfect, which, it appeared, a lot of people did.

On this November day Rivka had a luncheon date with Aly, a friend she saw only rarely since she lived in New York and returned to Rochester just once every few months. Their friendship was based on a simple pleasure. They shared a love of the arts and Aly was a sculptor in the big city. Aly also perceived culture differently than the other women Rivka knew and even liked. She had been to Europe, had studied there for a year, and she could see that American art, at this stage, was not yet original. She knew that her own art, influenced as it was by a more established set of traditions, was not unique. She was constantly frustrated by her inability to reach a level of concept and skill that would make for truly excellent art. She had good technique, but not as good as she would like and she knew it. Sometimes, she would create a mental image of the painting she wanted to do, but when it came to putting it on the canvas or sculpting it in her studio the product did not meet the quality of the idea.

Of course, her patrons didn't know this. They had no idea that the artist was frustrated and did not feel she could fulfill her personal expectations. The critics liked Aly's work, saw it as spontaneous and, ironically, accomplished and original. Although she was not among the top ten ranked artists in the country she was noticed and respected. But she had not fallen into the trap of churning out her work without continuing to learn from it. She had a notion about the artist, if not every other kind of worker also. She saw herself on a journey, travelling upon a road to perfection and accomplishment. Along the roaming bends and twists along the road were stations where she could stop. She could rest at these stations and then move on to the next if she could, if she wished, stay there, settle in, even decide to go no farther move in. Aly, in her own mind, had not yet settled in. She was still travelling towards more knowledge, more competence. That's what made her work so interesting. It was still dynamic. It still showed progress, although she was reasonably well established. Her last show, almost a year ago, was very successful. She had made enough money to work for a few years until she had more paintings and sculptures for a new show.

She was restless but satisfied. The first few years in New York had been difficult and she had worked teaching art in a high school at night for awhile. Now she was recognized. She didn't know how long her vision and skill could take her. She was pragmatic more than romantic. That had actually always been true.

She arrived a few minutes early for her meeting with Rivka. She liked Rivka because, like her, she was a pragmatist. Also, she liked Rivka's point of view on things. Rivka could see through the smokescreen thrown up by conventional wisdom to the deeper meaning of a situation. Aly found this extremely useful and refreshing in contrast to the hazy logic of her friends in New York. They were brilliant at following the vagaries of art, but they were less astute about the more mundane aspects of life.

Aly was gazing abstractly out the window beside her table when Rivka came in. She didn't see Rivka until she was lightly perched beside her at the table. Aly looked up and there she was, long hair tied up neatly in a close bun, warm and careful smile across her lips. "You are thinking about painting a portrait of Rochester at noon?" she asked.

Aly laughed. "It's not a bad idea, but they wouldn't buy it in New York. Rochester is not considered to be 'avant-garde', even at noon. I know! We could call it 'America at Lunch'!"

Rivka smiled. "How is the famous artist?"

"Very well. It's actually good to be here. It kind of recharges my engines."

"How are your parents?"

"Tolerant. Patronizing. Entirely wonderful."

Rivka sat down opposite Aly. "How long do you plan on staying?"

A wan mist passed over Aly's face. "Just a few days. My cousin is getting married on the weekend. I came in for the wedding. We were close when we were children."

Rivka looked concerned. "That's nice. You have no escort?"

Aly gestured broadly. "O, Rivka! I don't need an escort! I'm the single career woman in the family. It would ruin my appeal."

Rivka frowned lightly. "Perhaps, but it might make you happy."

Aly ran her fingers through her hair. "What would make you think I'm not happy, Rivka? Because I'm single?"

"No, of course not. I'm not so conservative. I don't think a woman has to be married to be fulfilled these days. You must have plenty of men in your life."

Aly sat back in her padded chair. "The kind of men that I meet in New York would mostly not feel comfortable at a wedding in Rochester. They often don't acknowledge that life exits outside of the city, or at least not culture. Ironically, that makes them more shallow and boring. I've met a few who are truly cosmopolitan. But they are usually married. I tried it like that once, but I got hurt quite badly. What do you think, Rivka, that I'm such a prize?"

Rivka shook her head slowly. "Yes, I think you are a prize, Aly! You know it!"

Aly sat forward. "I'm independent and I'm self sufficient and successful at my work. I expect the same from any man I might get involved with. Oh, Rivka, let's drop this right now. I do think of finding a partner to share life with, but not necessarily the way you have in mind. Not necessarily marriage as you see it, as you have it."

Rivka took hold of the pink cloth napkin under the cutlery on the table and put it on her lap. She looked at Aly with her head cocked slightly to one side. "Asher is beautiful and I have two healthy and gifted children."

"And a third on the way!" Aly pointed out.

"Please God." Rivka said quickly. "Do you think I am not content?"

"I think you are blissfully content, and I envy you."

"You can't envy me because I am only a mother and housewife with conventional dreams and no ambition to speak of. I envy you because you are your own person. You are free."

"At a price." Aly added.

"Yes, undoubtedly at a price. Every choice leaves another choice, equally promising, in its wake. We envy each other, it's true, but not terribly much I think. You know who you are. I know who I am. Neither of us should harbour regrets. It's not worth it."

Aly put her hands in her lap to keep them out of the way. "Asher's fine?"

"He's glowing these days. I've never known anyone who loved their work so much. With the baby on the way things are unbelievably happy at home."

"That's wonderful." Aly said.

"It can't last, Aly. Things are just too good. They're bound to slip. God doesn't mean us to be this happy all the time. I know that from the war. I'm in a condition of suspense waiting for this bubble to burst. I only hope that when it does things will return to normal, a case where both good and bad exist in balance."

"You are the most sensible person I know!" Aly responded. The waiter arrived at the table. Aly ordered a glass of wine and Rivka asked for tea. The waiter filled their water glasses. Aly raised hers to mid air. "To maintaining the normal!" she said.

Rivka raised her glass. "To the normal." They each took a sip.

That night, when the children were asleep and they were preparing for bed, Asher approached his wife while she was brushing her hair at the mirror. He looked passed her at the reflection and placed his hands gently on her shoulders.

"You look great!" he said brightly.

Rivka smiled. "I'm so happy when I'm pregnant." She said. "Don't get me wrong. I'm not giddy, like some women. And I have concerns because of the last time. But I'm happy."

"So am I." Asher said quietly.

"Do you think I am the kind of woman who only finds her self in her children?"

Asher squeezed her shoulders. "I think you're the kind of woman who brings fulfillment to her children in any way she can."

"Leah's science teacher called today. He wanted to tell us that Leah has a talent for science. Do you believe that, Asher! She has a talent for science."

"She also has a talent for piano."

"She's not a genius, Asher. She's just a normal child in every way. God knows that's all I want for her. To be normal."

Asher moved away from the vanity and began to change into pyjamas. "Was her father bright?" he asked.

Rivka frowned slightly as she finished getting ready for bed. "Who can know? I only saw him for a short time. We were human chattel in a closed cattle car. I didn't really know him, but in the few minutes we did actually communicate he seemed strong and polite. He was a *yeshiva* boy and he had run a bit on the black market. To be truthful, even though I didn't know him well I think I see some of him in Leah. The dark parts, like when she gets moody, you know, from time to time. I see what might be him in that part of her."

"She's more gifted than her friends" Asher said.

"She works harder, Asher, because of you. You're a strong influence upon her."

"And you." Asher cut in. "You motivate her and keep her on track."

"You know, I think of Miriam every day because of Leah. Isn't it amazing how great the parent is part of the child."

They met either side of the bed and each got in under the covers. They faced each other before turning out the lights.

Rivka spoke. "In the summer, do you think we should send her to stay in Israel with Wanda?"

"Have you been in touch with her?"

"I have. I sent her a letter last week and she wrote to me a few weeks before that. She said they welcome young people to her kibbutz and that it would be possible to arrange for Leah to stay there for a few months. It has to be arranged in advance."

"Why don't you go with her for a few weeks. Take Abe with you, and the baby, please God."

"Oh, I don't know if I could travel easily with the baby."

"Let's wait and see. It is a long trip." He stroked Rivka's cheek. "Did you have a good lunch with Aly?"

Rivka touched Asher's hand. "Very nice. She says she's very happy but I see the truth."

Asher laughed. "You are incorrigible! You think you are a true judge of human nature and, in fact, you are almost always right!"

Rivka made a sour face. "If you see something, Asher, you just see it. I don't try to see things that aren't there, I just see what is there but what other's don't always see."

"You mean you interpret things."

Rivka playfully slapped Asher's hand away. "Don't make me seem like some crazy magician."

Asher teased her further. "Don't be surprised at Hanukah when instead of receiving a bowling ball, like I know you want, you receive a crystal ball instead."

Rivka brushed that comment aside. "Aly is very happy. She says so and it's true. She doesn't think she's lonely because she is married to her work. That's fine. She has a good heart, but it's been broken more than once and is, actually, very prone to breaking again."

Asher was concerned at this. He had an even greater emotional attachment to Aly than Rivka did, more than she even knew. "Is she involved with someone?"

"She didn't say that, but I thought she might be anyway. The thing is, work cannot be a substitute for another human being. She doesn't see the problem, but I see it. Has she ever been in love, Asher? She hasn't said that she's in love since I've known her and that's ten years."

Asher felt a blush of emotion rise to his cheeks. He still had feelings for Aly that he couldn't acknowledge even to himself. "She's very capable of love, but she doesn't give it easily or in the spur of the moment. You say she's been hurt and I believe it. She's more vulnerable than she imagines and that could be the result."

Rivka pulled the covers closer around her shoulders. "If the right person comes along, she could make it work. She's at a point in her career where she could perhaps accept attention. I hope it's the right person who she meets."

Asher turned towards his side of the bed with a crush of covers. "Yes." He said. "She should meet the right person." Then he rolled back to Rivka. "Do you think that Leah may be something like Aly? She does work so hard."

Rivka answered thoughtfully while looking for the first time that hour directly in her husband's eyes. "No, I don't think so. Leah is strong but she has small insecurities. She may want a career and certainly both of us are encouraging that in her. But when the time comes, I think she will fall in love. Hopefully, with the right man. Aly is unconventional, but Leah is not. She likes to move with a small crowd although she is not the leader. Like Miriam, she is vulnerable and romantic as well as focused.

"How can we know anything except that she is a clever, sweet, hard working little girl? We do the best we can. We hope and pray we can give her what she needs to be happy."

CHAPTER 32
Parallel Universe

With the war over in Europe and Rivka, Asher and Leah gone to America, Wanda was left alone as a refugee in Germany. Although she met people like herself at the camp it was not easy for her to create bonds of friendship with anyone else. Everybody was in pain. Everybody had lost most of what was important to them. Perhaps it would seem that each of them had a future, but almost all of the refugees felt such a devastating sense of loss they were unable to look ahead. Those who had been left behind in the camp with Wanda were the ones who felt that they had nothing. Their faith in everything meaningful had been broken. They remained in the camp because they didn't know where to go or what to do.

For the first time since she had arrived in the Warsaw Ghetto 3 years before, Wanda was unable to repress the memories of the war, and very strong, very dark and very emotional feelings began to surface. The most persistent of these feelings was grief. In her soul there was an emotional crater where the love for her husband and children had been. In the weeks after Rivka and her family had left that crater had filled with poisons and she felt a constant ache. Sometimes she would imagine what it felt like to love those she had lost, and this would be a soothing balm. But it never lasted more than a brief time and she would sink soon sink again into pain.

The worst feature of her empty soul was the loss of faith. Wanda had never been religious. Before the war she had been a secular Jew, but she did believe in the manifest goodness of a G-d, even if that belief was seldom acknowledged or considered. Early on, in the battles in the ghetto the situation had been violent and she hadn't felt like a victim. It was war, she was a fighter, who ever thought of justice?

The camps destroyed her sense of purpose, as well as her belief in natural law. Whereas before the camps Wanda had believed, at least unconsciously, that there was order and meaning in the world her experience now told her that this was not so. Human beings, it had been proven, knew no law and were capable of complete and uncompromised brutality on a scale that condemned not only the individual but the entire species. There wasn't, as far as Wanda could see, a shred of evidence that G-d cared or even existed in the world. Although Leah had been born, Miriam had died. Where was the justice in this? Where was the active intervention of a deity in anything that had happened? When Wanda began to finally grieve, after her only friends had gone away, she couldn't avoid the question of where G-d played a role in her life. She didn't see G-d when she looked around her at the aftermath of the war. She didn't see G-d when she looked inside herself. After a while her grief, which had been so consummate, turned to anger. It was both inside her like a constant heart beat and it also cloaked her like a garment. It became so aggressive that she couldn't deal with it, and as a measure to eliminate this impossible state she eliminated the possibility that there could be a G-d who was responsible for all this. There was no G-d, she concluded. The war, the camps, the destruction was simply man made.

She could deal with that. Human beings in and of themselves had done this. Therefore, they could change it also. There was no force in the universe dealing out destinies. There was only human will, human intelligence, human understanding. This is what she turned to for hope.

There was a man Wanda became friendly with before she left the base. He would often sit outside the dining hall and smoke in the twilight after the evening meal. Their needs were met now by the Americans. They had plenty of food, they had shelter and there were activities they could join in. Agencies had been set up to help the refugees and the base was emptying out as people dispersed to different places. Wanda hadn't decided where to go. She didn't want to go to a kibbutz. She didn't want to spend any more time in a structured, community environment where there were only refugees. Although she believed in Israel she didn't feel ready for it. She wanted a taste of independence and what she thought might be a sense of freedom.

The man's name was Gil. He was about 10 years older than Wanda, slight and short with a ready smile. His close cropped scalp revealed a long scar along the top. Wanda had reached the end of her personal deliberation about what she would do and where she would go. She had finally made some plans on a peaceful evening in April when she went out of the dining hall this time and sat with him.

"You look different tonight." He said. There was a suggestion of humour in his voice, but not of any irony.

"Oh.", Wanda dismissed it. "I washed my hair."

Gil smiled at her easily. "That must be it! It's very long. It looks good on you."

"Thanks. There's nothing like washing your hair to make you feel good." Wanda normally didn't like small talk, but with Gil it was so good natured she enjoyed it. He created the impression that washing your hair was beautiful and important.

"Would you like a cigarette?" he asked, holding his pack out to her.

Wanda didn't often smoke, but at this time she thought she would have one. "Thanks." She said with a polite gesture of her hand towards the pack. "I'd like one." She was ever so slightly formal with Gil. His pleasing, comfortable manner always made her feel more intimate than she felt with any of the others.

She took a cigarette and placed it between her lips. Gil lit it with an American lighter. "Have you decided where to go from here?" Wanda asked.

"Yes. I'm going back to my home town in Poland soon. I don't plan on staying there. I'm only going back to see if I can find any of my family."

"Apparently Jews are not welcome there." Wanda said cautiously.

Gil grimaced. "I'm a citizen. I don't care if they don't welcome me. I'm not looking for affection. I want to know who in my family survived. I'm alive, maybe others as well."

"I wouldn't go back. I know my husband and children are dead. As for the rest, I can wait to find them if anyone is alive. I can't think of going back to Poland now, even for that. I want to forget."

Gil looked towards the ground. "That's funny, you know. I want to remember."

Wanda was surprised. "You want to remember? The hatred, the violence, the killing?"

"No, no. I can't forget that, it's so strong in my memory. I'm not going back for that. But before the war, I had a life that was mostly good. I had a wonderful marriage with two children. We weren't rich but I was a craftsman with a reasonable business and we had everything we needed. I want to remember that, so that I can reclaim it again now. I want to remember our old study hall, the little synagogue with the ark and the beautiful light above it."

BAR KOCHBA

Wanda was querulous. "Yes, you had those things before, but do you think you can recreate them now, in Europe?"

"Perhaps not the identical things. That's not what I'm after. I want to rekindle the knowledge that this goodness can exist. I worshiped every day. I put on *tzphilim* every morning in the synagogue and I loved G-d for giving me what I had. Now, it's a different story. I want to know that G-d still exists in this world. I think he does, but I want to jog my memory."

Wanda puffed absently on her cigarette. "If you find G-d there please tell him to do a better job in the future."

Gil laughed. Wanda was surprised and laughed also. "You think it's funny?" she complained.

"I think you're funny." He said with a hint of good nature. "You seem so strong and yet you are really so tender."

Wanda was serious. "G-d let me down. That's all. He failed me, all of us."

"All through history this has happened to us. We are persecuted, we are afflicted, we are tortured and tested. G-d is always there, I think, but we lose sight of him. He doesn't come to you, you know. You have to look for Him."

"That's alright. If he did all this, I don't want Him, and if he simply let all this happen I don't want him either. The last thing I want to do is find G-d!"

Gil made a large gesture and patted Wanda gently on the back. "You see, you are both tough and tender."

"And you are going to be extremely disappointed."

"Perhaps so." They sat for a moment in calm and silence, finishing their cigarettes. "What will you do now?" Gil asked.

Wanda threw her cigarette to the ground and stomped on it. "I'm not sure. I want to get a job somewhere and an apartment. Maybe in Holland."

Gil seemed surprised. "You're not going to a kibbutz? I thought you would go to a kibbutz."

"You know something?" Wanda said persuasively. "I've had enough of 'Jewish' for now. I've had enough of G-d and ritual and religion. I want to have a normal life, a secular life where being a Jew isn't the only thing to think about or talk about or act on."

"You can't deny what you are?"

"No?" Wanda's voice rose only a little. "Listen. I'm a human being. I deserve all the rewards and benefits a human being is entitled to. So I'm a Jew. Everyone is something they are born with, I was born a Jew." The pitch in her voice increased. "So what! So they wanted to kill me for it. They killed my family, my friends, even my children for it. I've had enough. I don't deny I'm a Jew but I affirm that I am a human being first. I have to investigate this phenomena, not as a Jew but as a person."

Gil struggled to respond. "I hope in that way you can find truth. I hope you can find G-d."

"There is no G-d." Wanda was emphatic. "There is only a pathetic desire for meaning and justice."

Gil was gentle in his reply. "No matter which way you go," he said quietly, "and you have chosen a very true way, you will find what you are looking for."

Wanda's look was calm but confused. "I am looking for reason at the end of insanity." She looked into Gil's face. "I must confess, reluctantly, that I do perceive it now from time to time."

Shortly after this conversation Wanda traveled out of Germany to Holland. It was a bit complicated to cross the border but she was both persistent and patient and passed through in good time. She arrived in Amsterdam in the Spring on a mild, sunny day with something like hope in her heart. The city had recovered most of its cosmopolitan charm by the time she arrived there. It had an exuberant energy and there was money changing hands in trade and commerce easily. Wanda felt a sense of recovery there. Everyone knew that the Dutch did not give up their Jews as easily as other occupied counties and knowing this made her feel more sure and confident. She could not remember being in a place where hatred and suspicion were not constant.

At first she was tentative about what she would do. For the first week she was sheltered by a refugee organization, but after a few days of wandering through the city and several afternoons drinking coffee in an outdoor café she felt more bold. She was able to watch the people as they passed by, at first with pain that later subsided, then with envy which quickly passed and then with growing confidence. No one bothered her with cold stares or mean looks. She saw things she hadn't known even existed anymore. Lots of smiles. Children running easily in the streets. Couples giggling, playing with each other, holding hands and kissing.

It didn't really dawn on her that she could have a new life, but the evidence of a natural recovery from the war had a deep affect. Without making a conscious decision to leave the past behind her she decided to look for work. Most of the refugees in Amsterdam were not working yet. Almost all had support from some relief organization or other and most were making plans to go to America or Israel. Wanda didn't know where she wanted to go. She thought Amsterdam was a good place to be, and she wanted to blend in. She did what she thought was right, although it was uncharacteristic for a refugee. She went from café to café, from bistro to bistro looking for a job. Her German was passable but she didn't speak

Dutch, so finding a place as a waitress was not likely. She went to find a job in the kitchen.

People were very kind to her. The third café she approached didn't have a job for her, but the owner took her outside to a table and ordered espresso for them both. He was a very thin, somewhat tall man with a neat moustache.

"Do you need money?" he asked politely.

Wanda shook her head and smiled slightly. "No. That's not really the thing. I mean, yes, I need money, but not desperately. I'm being taken care of."

He frowned. "But you need to work?"

"I need to do something. I can't just linger."

"Why not? Everyone else seen comfortable with that right now. Why are you different?"

Wanda was unsure, but offered an answer. "I like Holland." She said.

The owner let out a small laugh. "Yes, that's wonderful. I love it too. But why do you want to work?"

"I want to feel more useful." She was stammering just a little. "I want to fit in more." Further stammering. "I want to be a part of something that is not completely broken."

"Oh!" he said lightly. "Where are you from?" he asked.

"Poland."

The kind man paused for a moment. "Your family?"

Wanda looked down. "They are all gone."

"What did you do in Poland?"

"I was the mother of two children."

The man gazed into her open face. "I see." He said gently, then he said, "Excuse me." He got up and went back into the café.

Wanda was left alone. She had answered his questions directly because he seemed honest. She glanced at other tables where people chatted amiably, some with large friendly gestures, some with big smiles, some almost whispering to each other. It was very emotional for her. She wanted some of that too, not just to be a remote and removed observer.

The owner of the café came back in a few moments. He sat down again facing her. "Look. I called a friend of mine who owns a restaurant not far from here. He's nice but very demanding. If he likes you he'll hire you to work in the kitchen. He won't pay much at first, but he's fair. It's a few streets away. You should go there now."

The owner of the restaurant, whose name was Fredrick, liked her and put her to work the next day. It was an enormous step for Wanda, not because the work was so hard but because it represented something she would not permit herself to acknowledge yet; the promise of a new life. After two weeks at work the agency helped her find a room of her own in a small building. Each day she went to work. Each day she grew a bit more confident. By the middle of the summer she no longer felt completely like a refugee. Although she was quite like the Dutch, she was not totally apart from them either. Her room had a metal bed, a chair and a wardrobe. Even though it was meagre, it felt warm and homey to her. She liked it. She liked sitting in it at night and sometimes reading. With the warm weather, she walked through the city at night. The past still haunted her. She could not forget the brutality of human beings. But she slowly realized something she had not been able to conceive of only months before. She was happy. She felt safe.

In June of 1947 there was a meeting at the agency that had helped her settle. It was an informational meeting about Israel. Wanda had been thinking about Palestine. Although she was happy she thought of

Holland as a transition. Israel seemed to be her hope, not because she was very hard on being Jewish but because she did believe that her people needed a homeland and she wanted to be part of that. She went to the meeting out of pure and simple curiosity, hoping to pick up information.

The room was a modest size and held about 50 chairs in rows. Wanda sat near the rear. Before she sat down she picked up several information sheets, and while she was reading them over a man sat beside her. She looked at him innocently from the corner of her eye. The room was not overcrowded, but he could have chosen that seat because it was near the back, not because it was next to her. He was dark in overall appearance. His brown hair fell over his forehead in a short wave. His eyes were green. He was muscular without being square.

He smiled at her. Wanda couldn't help but smile back. He spoke in Yiddish. "This meeting promises to be informative." He said. "I've been to two before this one but there's always more information."

"Oh, I'm just here for an introduction" Wanda said.

"Yes. I can see that. I haven't seen you here before."

"No. I haven't been here."

The dark fellow pressed her a bit. "Are you staying with the agency?"

"No. I live in the city."

He was surprised. "Really! That must be interesting. My name is Simcha." He extended his hand.

Wanda took it lightly. "Wanda." She said with a small smile.

"Wanda." He repeated. "Who lives in the city and wants to learn about Israel."

"Correct." Wanda said, wanting to play the game. "Are you with the agency?"

Simcha shook his head. "Me? No. They helped me when I arrived and for that I am very thankful. I share an apartment with two other fellows.

It's good. We like each other. Except when Anton doesn't wash his socks. Then we throw cold water on him and make him sit on the fire escape."

Wanda laughed. That surprised her. She laughed, like a schoolgirl. Something was happening to her. They were flirting. Something inside of her was natural enough for her to giggle at a silly joke. It stuck in her mind and for reasons unknown to her the fact that she giggled made her giggle some more. It seemed that she actually blushed a light pink.

Simcha looked at her and smiled ruefully. "You have a very nice laugh." He said quite boldly. "But you haven't yet smelled Anton's socks."

Wanda recovered. "And I hope I never will!"

This conversation was the kind of silly, personal moment that a couple remembers all of their lives. It was a conversation about dirty socks. Not original, not brilliant, not memorable in any normal way. But it was the moment that they met and it provoked laughter and happiness. That was worth remembering.

As it turned out, Wanda did actually have a chance to smell Anton's socks. She saw Simcha at first every week after that meeting, then every few days, then every day. He was always funny, always sincere. He never pushed himself on her, he never asked anything of her. He had survived Dachau with a view of life that was tinged with humour. It was how he had survived.

In late September they slept together for the first time in Wanda's room. Sex had not been a possibility for her for what seemed like forever. Earlier on, it had started with a kiss goodbye on the cheek. That made Wanda wonder if they liked each other in that peculiar way. It's funny how lovers most often don't know each other's feelings. 'Do they like me?', 'Am I attractive to him?', 'He kissed me on the cheek. Is that a good sign or a bad one?'. The night when Simcha awkwardly turned her face to his and tentatively kissed her lips like they would be angry about it was a night in which everything stopped and began again. It was a second chance for both of them. They felt like they were living in a magic place.

Making love was slow and awkward at first. They stood apart on opposite sides of Wanda's narrow bed and took off their clothes, not looking at each other directly but lowering their heads as if they were embarrassed. When they turned to each on the worn sheets. Simcha smiled a broad toothy grin. "I wouldn't do this if I didn't love you." He said.

"If I thought you didn't love me you definitely wouldn't be here." She was nervous but she desired this. Who knew what the future might hold?

Two months later, in late March, they met as usual at their normal café in the late afternoon. Wanda arrived early. She was sitting down drinking a cold, sweet drink when Simcha joined her. "Did you ever think you would be sitting in a place like this again when the war was going on?" She asked.

"You know, it's what kept me going. I thought of this café and you sitting here and I knew it could happen."

"You knew this would happen?"

"I knew that it could."

"Of course, you didn't have children."

Simcha smiled ironically. "No, I didn't. We wanted, but it never happened." He was two years younger than Wanda and although he lost his wife they had never had children.

"Did you think that was because of you or because of her?"

Simcha gestured in the air. "We never got that far. We were only married a year and a half before the war broke out. We didn't try after that."

Wanda sighed. "Well that's a good thing. Before that, it wasn't you anyway."

The meaning of this didn't strike him right away. He looked disbelieving. "Now, how can you know that?" he asked.

"How do you think?" she asked with an exasperated smirk oozing off her lips.

Simcha looked blank as he processed the information. Slowly, his face recomposed into an uncomprehending pout. "No!" he said with the escape of a great deal of air from his lungs.

"Yes!" Wanda said with emphasis. Her face was full of wonder, pride and fear. "I'm pregnant."

Simcha forgot where he was. He fell to one knee beside Wanda's chair and held her hand in his own. "I think that's wonderful news." He said. "I can't believe it's happening."

Neither of them believed in marriage, although they were quite romantic about having a baby. It wasn't new for Wanda, but it seemed new since Simcha was so excited. They moved together to a larger studio apartment and in late November of 1947. Their daughter Naomi Ruebens was born in central Amsterdam. The parents were proud and happy. Still, Simcha was serious about going to Israel. It had not been possible due the situation with the British, but there was hope for the establishing of an independent state looming in the near future. Wanda was not so anxious to emigrate as her partner, who retained more of the colour of his Jewishness than she had. She felt more affinity with the Dutch than Simcha, had suffered more loss in the camps if such a thing can be measured and, importantly, had an infant girl to nurse and care for.

When the news of Israeli statehood was finally certain, Simcha wanted to go immediately. Wanda agreed but with some remorse. Everyone was aware that they would be sailing into a vicious war. Wanda settled into a state of resigned determination. As they attended meetings and community occasions to prepare for the trip she began to see an energy she had not expected. Everyone was excited, purposeful, optimistic. These were not the same people who were broken and ruined. They were hopeful, strong and directed. In a short while, Wanda felt a direction and a reason she had never felt before. It was not as brilliant as it was in most of the others, but it was more than superficial. She was reluctant to give up her life in Amsterdam, but she realized it would not be an answer to her destiny if she knew she had not done everything she could to help to establish the country of her people.

They set out for Israel in June of 1948. Naomi was the youngest passenger on the ship, still nursing at her mother's breast. When they arrived at Haifa there was nearly chaos, but before long she and Simcha were separated into different groups. They had a little time to say goodbye. "I'll be back." Simcha said. "I know you will." Wanda told him. He was taken to join others at a training camp. She was taken to train in communications on a kibbutz.

He didn't come back.

He was killed in action in the south.

He and Wanda had known each other for less than two years. She had already lost another husband and two children, but the loss of Simcha was unbearable because of the tragic happiness they had. Unlike the earlier grief, Wanda took this personally. It seemed a total affront of G-d, an insult or a rebuke that was impossible to ignore. But her mourning was as deep as if it had been a lifetime. Every day she missed him. Every day the thought of his baleful smile and his gentle humour. Although she was in a new land, it was a land of fresh starts and past difficulties and she felt at home. When the war ended she settled into a small kibbutz, worked in various positions but found the farming most enriching. Even so, she was given the role of teacher to the children, a task she had never thought of doing before. She grew to like it and she was, overall, satisfied. Her daughter was good natured like Simcha. She was raised communally like the other children on the Kibbutz and she was laughing all the time with childish comforts and joys.

Wanda didn't think of divine justice or the absence of it after Simcha's death. On the kibbutz, people didn't give philosophy much thought. She didn't turn to G-d with anger and she didn't turn away from G-d with remorse. There was no reason to consider G-d's nature. Everyone had suffered loss and now there was also gain. And so much to do. She had Naomi. In some way, that answered every blow.

In the summer of 1955 Wanda and Naomi, who was eight years old and tall for her age, received a visit from an old friend. Rivka, her son Ari and her eleven year old daughter Leah. They came from the U.S. to stay with them for a month. The women were in a near ecstasy in each other's presence. Ten years after the war ended there was some personal peace to be enjoyed. They compared notes on each other's state, the remarkable aspects of America and the equally remarkable elements of the Israeli nation. But most of all, for the two mothers, was the way their daughters played together. Of course, Wanda had known Leah when she was born and had known her birth mother, so this was all very natural and right to her and Rivka. The significance of Wanda having known Miriam was so real to Rivka; it was a link to a past that did not exist in Rochester, N.Y.

Leah seemed to take to Naomi in a nearly supernatural manner. The way they played, the games they chose, the funny things they said stayed with Wanda and Rivka for years after. In 1956 war came again to Israel.

Wanda was as ready as she could be for such a thing; everyone knew it was coming. They didn't know how immediate the danger would be to them on the kibbutz. Wanda took care of the children. Now it seemed like she had been four different women in her life. First, the wife and mother of two. In Warsaw she had been a fighter and after that, the persecuted and broken refugee. Now she had become the strong and steady protector of babes. She was a fierce protector. Circumstance has made her that complete a human being.

CHAPTER 33
Salvation

There is a good story about Wanda. When she received the news that Simcha had been killed in action it was more than a blow and her reaction was deeper than grief. Through the war in Europe her experience had been cushioned by the reality that everyone was suffering. In the Warsaw ghetto she knew the consequences of her resistance, knew the desperate odds, and somehow that had made her losses collective. Also, in Europe, she had been distracted by circumstances that required her full attention. She had been a warrior, a prisoner, a friend.

Now, in Israel, it was different. The war was real and very immediate, but she had felt immune. She was a stranger mostly among strangers in a battle that had been made more personal because of its nature. Since she was on the kibbutz she felt a safety that was not, in the end, real. She hadn't seriously considered the possibility that Simcha might not come back since he was so close to her in spirit and yet so far in fact.

It was as if a wall holding back the remorse of all those years gave way when she learned of Simcha's death. The psychological structures that had held up her sense of reality broke and she was shaken to the very foundation of her nature.

The day she received the news she was working on communications in the cluttered office on the kibbutz. It had become a world for her, and her concentration was focused. She didn't see the envoy come into the room, didn't notice her supervisor point to her at the desk, didn't recognize the expression of sorrow and concern cross her face.

Wanda was tapped on the shoulder by her supervisor, who told her gently that she had to go to the kibbutz administrator's office. She didn't even think of what might be the reason, she was still thinking about her work. The administrator was a short woman dressed in army khakis who had a natural and normally easy manner. Her light brown hair was pulled back into a loose bun.

"Hello Wanda," she said, more carefully than would have been usual. She gestured. "Please sit down"

At that moment Wanda realized something must be wrong. She realized that something had happened to her husband. A rush of panic rose from the centre of her stomach. She almost fell, but grabbed the back of the chair in the small office and eased herself clumsily into the seat. Without meaning to a single word unwillingly escaped from her throat."

"Simcah?"

The administrator didn't try to draw out the pain. "I'm sorry, so sorry Wanda. He was killed in action two days ago."

Wanda felt, at that moment, something she had not felt through all the hardship she had so far endured. It didn't strike her immediately. At first she just felt numb and unable to speak. She didn't know what else the administrator might have said. Without being consciously aware of what she was doing, before the administrator had actually finished, she rose out of the straight backed chair and worked her way to the door. She stepped outside into the direct sunlight. It was as if her consciousness had turned to stone, as if her blood had turned to lava. She moved three steps from the building and her legs gave out. Without feeling anything but unchallenged pain and deadly blindness she collapsed into unconsciousness on the dusty ground. It was 48 hours before she woke up.

She was in shock. Her body had shut down in the wake of emotions that were simply too strong for her to handle. When her eyes opened as dawn rose on the second day, she screamed one sharp note. She hadn't had time to make any close friends on the kibbutz, but she had begun a new but promising relationship with a woman named Rochelle, who was watching over her in her room Wanda's scream was piercing but brief. It was a result of bad dreams and an unacceptable reality. Rochelle came to her side immediately, put her hand on her forehead, clasped her hand in her own. Wanda turned to her, looked in her eyes with a penetrating glare.

"What is the reason?" she asked in a desperate voice. "I demand an answer. What is the reason?"

"We have won peace." Rochelle said in reply.

"No, no." Wanda said. "There is supposed to be G-d. Where is G-d? There is no order in this life, no reason. G-d is reason. Where is He?"

Wanda recovered her ability to eat and sit and slowly walk. She didn't speak. The following morning she went outside and walked in the air. No demands were placed upon her. For a few days her pattern was stable. She sat or lay down in her room, walking in the perimeter around the kibbutz for a while during the day. On the fourth day, Rochelle found her slumped in her chair in a pool of blood. She had slit her wrist with a sharp scissor. It had been a real but botched attempt at suicide.

Ephram Greenberg was a member of the kibbutz who worked in agriculture, but he was also a rabbi. There were no counselors as such on the kibbutz since it was quite small and emotional troubles were not too frequent. Ephram was asked to talk with Wanda and try to help her out of her state. No one figured the problem was a long term one. Virtually everyone believed that it was an immediate reaction and not a life altering one. Ephram didn't assume that was actually the case. He knew suicide attempts were desperate actions at any time, and that it would be irresponsible to think they were not indications of a serious concern. He was young, in his early thirties, but he had come from Europe like Wanda, although before the war, and had wrestled with some issues.

When he approached Wanda in her room she was sitting in her chair looking out the open window. It was warm in the room and Ephram's collar was damp with sweat.

"Wanda?" he said softly. She didn't look at him at first. "My name is Ephram. How are you?"

Wanda turned her face to him. "Hello, Ephram. I'm alright."

That was a good start. "Can I get you anything?"

Wanda looked sullen. "No." She said. "Thank you."

Ephram wasn't sure where to start. "You know you have friends here who care about you?"

Wanda's expression didn't change. "Is that so?"

"Yes. You are a member of this community and you are a citizen of the State of Israel."

A wisp of a smile crossed Wanda's lips. "Is that so? What does that mean? What is the reason for it?"

Ephram responded. He had encountered this kind of question himself, even dealt with it himself in is own struggle. "We fight a sometimes uphill battle to bring peace and hope both collectively and personally."

"And is that possible?" Wanda asked.

"Yes. Definitely. We have had it, mostly we have it, but not all the time. The world has been at war, we in Israel have been at war, for a very long time. But to think it will not end is impossible."

Wanda let her smile pass. "Who makes wars?", she asked.

Ephram hesitated. "Evil people who want to control others and inflict pain."

"Who makes them that way?"

"It is their choice."

"They have choice?"

Ephram's face moved closer to Wanda's. "Yes, they have choice."

"And G-d does not protect all the other's, who do not choose to be evil?"

Ephram had studied this problem. "We do not know who G-d protects and why."

"Why not?" Wanda slammed her hand loudly on the arm of the chair and spoke loudly. "Why can't we know what G-d wants?"

There was patience in Ephram's response. "We would not be human if we knew G-d's mind. We would be angels. We are not angels but we must struggle to understand what we can so that we can be always and ever better."

"You mean there is a reason my first and second husbands, my two children died? But that I cannot know that reason?"

"You can know, but not right away. You have to search for the answer, pray for it, and it will come to you."

"And when it does? Does that make it all better?"

Ephram seemed surprised. "That is the value of searching for the answer. It will make it better."

Wanda was matter-of-fact about her response. "If there is a G-d, and he can make it better, he can also make it worse. How can we know? For me, to make it better, is no answer because G-d is all powerful and can do as he likes. If there is a G-d, who does what He likes, there is no way for reason. And if there is no G-d, there is no reason either. Any way you look at it, there is no reason."

Ephram could see how hurt this woman was. "That is what faith is, Wanda, a knowledge that G-d is not only reasonable but good and that, in the end, that goodness is real and strong."

"There is no G-d.", Wanda said lowly and steadily. "There is only the fleeting chaos of human will."

Ephram impulsively took hold of Wanda's arm. "The fact that I am here, the reality that on this facility there are people who know and love you, the existence of your daughter Naomi who needs you so desperately…these are signs of G-d's goodness and his existence. Always, these signs will be stronger than the chaos of disorder, evil and destruction. Here, in Israel, we are building for a future. You must have faith that this is possible because we know that reason and faith both demand it. The demand itself is an ultimate proof of order and goodness and that is proof of G-d. A small bit of faith can take you a very long way."

Wanda stared unrelentingly at Ephram. "My daughter is a cause for faith, I confess. You are a reason for having faith even for my daughter. But for me, there is not a G-d right now. I choose to look away from Him. I have no intention of harming myself again. But if you want to talk to me again, I will be available. At this moment, I do not really want answers. At this moment, I am concerned with coming up with the right questions."

After Ephram left Miriam, despite herself, felt better. The reality of her daughter's presence in the kibbutz and the knowledge that she had her whole life ahead of her was a healing ointment for Wanda's grief. But she didn't want to feel better. She wanted to feel all the bitterness and pain of her life so that it would make her feel stronger. Although she was clinging to the idea that there was no G-d, no order, she also wanted, at the same time, for this conviction to break and actually lead her to knowledge. She wanted the pain to guide her to its opposite.

She got out of her seat and went to the children's centre. Naomi was playing loudly with several other children, laughing and crying out with exuberant joy. When the little girl caught sight of her mother she reached out her arms and laughed. Wanda picked her up and held her solidly in her arms.

"Are you having fun?" she asked with kindness.

Naomi leapt joyously in her grasp. "We're building a house, with a garden and a ocean."

"Isn't that nice!" Wanda said. "Will there be boats on the ocean?"

"Yes!" Naomi cried. "And big whales too."

Wanda laughed quietly. She experienced an emotion that is somewhat rare, the feeling of great sorrow and great joy all at the same time, so that she was both laughing and crying at once. She also felt something odd; she was thankful. She was almost breathlessly thankful for this moment, as if its paradoxical significance was ultimately special.

When she returned to her quarters half and hour later she did something uncharacteristic. She lay down face upward on her bed and looked up. She crossed her hands over her chest and took a deep breath. Then she spoke to G-d.

"The sorrow and the joy I am feeling at this time are not compatible, and yet they exist at the same moment. Day follows night and eventually the storms subside. I don't believe in you because I do not see a purpose for it all. That is the very worst of what I see, the rest is only circumstance and perhaps I simply have to live with that.

"And yet, amid all the chaos, there is beauty. The beauty of a child's hopefulness, and a mother's desire to see it fulfilled. This wonder, even though seemingly small amidst the horror and pain, shines through all the rest. I want to give my daughter hope. I don't want to dirty her simple childhood with despair.

"But I don't see you. I don't experience your power except how it destroys, condemns or ignores. I think at this time, because beauty exists, that you must exist also. But I don't believe in you. I can't worship you. Not until you show me reason. Not until you show me that you have care for me and my little girl. Not until you show yourself to me."

As Wanda lay on her bed something unusual happened. A pale yellow light, an almost imperceptible glow, appeared in the room.

Wanda had suffered a lot. She was beyond betrayal. She saw the miracle of the light, but it didn't move her.

"It's not miracles that will convince me. I am not a dog who can be satisfied by a bone thrown to her by her master. It may be clear that you exist, but what you mean is a different issue. If you are a G-d of mercy, I will know that. I am going to search for it. If I find you, I swear that I will serve you in whatever way I can. That is my prayer, now. Let me find you and then let me serve you. From this moment on, I will constantly search for you."

A few days later Ephram paid a visit to Wanda. "We want you to work with the children. That way, you can be close to Naomi help teach the little ones."

Wanda actually didn't know if she was particularly good with children. At first she didn't know how to act, but quickly she learned to be natural, kind and strong. In a few days, she began to glow. She began to look forward to being with them. She felt a renewed happiness. In her heart, she began to thank G-d for it, but her resolve to disbelieve was still earnest.

A week after she began to work with the children a letter arrived from the military office. She received it but had no idea what it might contain. When she opened it, she read that Simcha was receiving a citation for courage under fire. As she read it she stood with her mouth opened in stunned silence.

It meant so much to her. She didn't know why. Somehow, this was a vindication of her pain at her loss. Naomi would have something, at least, to remember. Somehow, somewhere, someone cared.

When she went to bed that night she did something that was to become a regular event. She lay on her back and she talked to G-d. "I don't see angels and cherubim." She slowly said. "I don't know yet what the nature of G-d is. But I take this as a sign. And I must do something that I have not done before. I must thank you."

Over the following three months Wanda looked for signs from G-d. At first, she saw little things: a helpful smile from a fellow kibbutznik she didn't know very well, an unexpected hug from her daughter, an amusing story told to her by a friend. Still, she was not convinced. The pain of the war and the loss of Simcha were too great.

In the fourth month, she walked out of the kibbutz in the evening to a nearby hill. She sat down and spoke to G-d with tears in her eyes. "I know you exist. I have no question about it. But I am still suffering and that suffering does not seem to go away.

"Those who serve you, the rabbis and the others…you must have done something for them personally to have created in them faith. Abraham, Sarah, all the patriarchs and matriarchs. You gave them reason to believe in you, and they were faithful on account of it.

"I am no matriarch and I am no rabbi. I have killed men in war and I am a cold person in some ways. But I want to serve you, even in my own small way. I pray to you, give me reason to believe before I die of exhaustion."

A few days after that prayer Wanda received acceptance into the education program at the university through a correspondence course. As she studied and worked with the children, and as life on the kibbutz became more rich and varied, something happened. She began to fill with joy. Ever pragmatic and sometimes contrite, she experienced a balance between cynicism and realism. The people around her found her humour delightful and her down-to-earth approach to every problem rewarding. Wanda herself began to experience rewards for her actions from the people with whom she shared the kibbutz. For the first time in more than a decade she wasn't always anxious, always wary, always in pain.

Three years later, in 1952, she graduated with her degree in education and began to study Jewish theology. Her teachers found her writing sharp and perceptive. In her life, she had found purpose and in her studies she had found reason.

In the summer of 1955 a marvelous thing happened. Rifka and Leah, now 11 years old, came to visit Wanda for a month in Israel. The meeting was exciting and eventful, but the best of it was the way in which Leah and Naomi simply clicked. It was as if nature had created two friends out of one cloth. They ran together over the hills, they played constantly as if meant to, they talked together as though they were characters in a divine play.

For Wanda and Rivka there was also enormous laughter and joy. Rivka was especially overcome by the kibbutz. In contrast to her life in suburban New York, life on the kibbutz seemed vivid and authentic. She participated in everything she could, from the noisy group sharing of the meals to working in the orchards. Most gripping to her was the communal care of the children and the operation of the school. There was a lesson in this for everyone.

Over the course of the few weeks they were together each of them noted changes in the other. Several days before Rivka and Leah were scheduled to go, the two women expressed themselves to each other on this account. Wanda had made a simple joke about her hair and they both laughed.

"You know, you have changed in other ways too, Wanda." Rivka said lightly.

"And you too!" Wanda replied.

"Oh, I'm the same old lady I always was." Rivka said laughing.

"No. You are even better. You know yourself even better."

Rivka was disparaging. "Oh, everyone knows themselves better when they grow up."

"But not everyone gets better. You have."

Rivka looked briefly at the ground. "I'm very lucky, Wanda. I have a wonderful family. A very kind, bright husband."

This might have been in contrast to Wanda, had it not been for her life on the kibbutz. "I know." She said. "But you deserve credit for making it so."

There was a pause. The women flashed warm smiles at each other. Rivka spoke first. "I envy your life. You don't seem lonely."

"I'm not." Wanda said plainly. "G-d has been good to me."

Rivka's mouth dropped in mock amazement. "Wanda! Did you just say 'G-d has been good to me?'"

Wanda smiled. "Is that a crime? What? You, the wife of a Rabbi, has never heard the expression before?"

Wanda chided her. "Not from those lips, I think. Oh, wait a minute, only about 10 times since I saw you. I let it pass before but now I must say. The Wanda I knew in Europe was an atheist. When you first mentioned G-d, I thought it was a feature of speech in the Kibbutz, but I know now that is not true."

"I was an atheist." Wanda confessed. "The Warsaw ghetto, the camps, the loss of my children and then the loss of Simcha made sure of that."

The conversation was serious now, though still intimate. "It challenged ones faith."

"I thought I would go mad when I lost Simcha. I actually think I did go mad. I had nowhere to turn but to G-d and when I did I was livid. I didn't want to believe in Him. I wanted to hate him instead."

Rivka understood. "When Miriam died I felt that way too. But time heals."

"Yes. When I turned to G-d, without my knowing it, He was there for me. He absorbed my hate, he didn't erase it. Slowly, things got better and slowly I began to realize. He was answering my prayers."

"I've found that too." Rivka said softly.

Wanda shook her head. "I still can't believe it. He didn't make the past go away. He didn't correct it or discredit it. He didn't take away the emotions or cause them to be rationalized."

"I know. That's right."

"But, somehow, its better. I suppose that's the miracle. Life is better with G-d in it."

"It's a sign of His meaning."

"We all know there's another war coming up. Everyone is getting ready. This time, I feel purpose. Not the murder, the bloodshed, the hate. I still can't deal with that."

"It's an awful knowledge."

Wanda's breath was sucked in as she spoke in a sound like wind. "It's the inevitability of it that seems almost tangible. Why do people hate the Jews so much? Why to they want to wipe us out, even as we sit in our own land?"

"Is there a reason?" Rivka wondered.

"In heaven, maybe? Maybe G-d wants to show that we are bound to survive in any case." Wanda said. "In the past years, I've learned not to blame G-d but rather to turn to Him, Not as the Father but as a kind of supernatural force. People have free will, that's a gift that is never taken away no matter who you are or what you want to do with it. Wars are unnatural, but real. We're only human beings and we have to face that."

Rivka smiled at her friend. "So philosophical, Wanda! You have seen the burning bush."

'No." Wanda ventured. "I have only had to deal with pain."

When Rivka and Leah left a few days later and Wanda and Naomi waved them goodbye from the airport lounge there were ghosts among them. Miriam rode with Rivka while Simcha and her earlier family stood and waved with Wanda. War was coming to the Middle East once more and heaven and earth would be again in turmoil. This time, Wanda was not frightened. But neither was she prepared. The warrior inside her was peaceful and to some degree in a state of awe. It was sure to arise when shaken once again by mortal cries. Until then, it would remain in its place.

Rivka ran her hand along Leah's brow. Her daughters hair was thick an damp from the hot sun. The cool breeze of the air conditioning on the plane was drying it fast. Such a nice looking little girl, so well composed and bright.

"What an exciting trip!" she said to her. "You're going to remember it for a long time!"

Her daughter's calming, childish voice rang in her ears. "Yes and I made a new friend. Can we come back next year to see Naomi and Aunt Wanda?"

"We'll see." Rivka said quietly.

Somehow, as she looked carefully at Leah's face looking calmly out the window, she saw something she rarely noticed. Often she could see Miriam's features. They were as clear to her as rain. But rarely, such as at this moment, she could see something else. It was Avrum, relected in his child's face. She thought of him, a boy she really never knew, and wondered in passing what had become of him. All she could assume was that he was dead; there were so few survivors. Even so, some did survive. He could be anywhere if that were so, even in Israel.

Eventually, when she was old enough, Rivka expected to tell Leah who her birth parents were. But not for a long time. Not until she would be able to handle the truth.

CHAPTER 34
Love and Study

I spent a lot of time after the formal end of the War of Independence contemplating to what degree I was a simple murderer or a soldier doing what was necessary and right. It was difficult to think of myself as a vicious killer, because my nature was not vicious or malicious. To be honest, I still thought of myself as a *yeshiva* boy who only wanted to study. This was in stark contrast to the reality of the past few years in which I had been a member of the Irgun and a IDF soldier.

Without doubt I had committed myself to violence from the start. This is due directly to being in the camps. I understood with painful clarity that if we didn't take a stand, a forceful stand, the Jewish people would be wiped out by brutal and well organized forces. I could have sat by and allowed that to happen without doing my part, but the results would then have been as much my fault as the fault of the aggressor. I had decided that I had a responsibility to oppose oppression, whether I was Jewish or not. I actually did not believe G-d was on the enemies' side. I believed G-d wanted us to forge a civilization tested by opposition.

Even so, I felt a great deal of personal guilt. I avoided looking back on men I had killed in hand-to-hand combat because that was most painful. The more I contemplated the war, and the more threatening political circumstances became in the months that followed, the more I vindicated myself as a soldier. I was living on the kibbutz. The natural beauty was an unavoidable presence. I began to see that this was at the very centre of what we were fighting for, and I believed entirely that this was our right. It may seem parochial and narrow minded, but increasingly we had no choice but to go on. The idea that Israel had a right to exist was beyond philosophical. It was an edifice of reason, reality and purpose.

This direct contemplation took place over only a few days. I had only just arrived home from active duty and it was my purpose to decide if I would enlist in the standing army as a full time member. This would mean living part of the time at the army base and part of the time on the kibbutz. After talking with Dov that first night back I had said I would see Orly the next day. I didn't. I was too disturbed by violent images and ideas and I felt too awkward to see her. Every soldier thinks of someone waiting for them when the battle ends. Somehow it is necessary to believe someone cares for you, and I believe quite simply that in the midst of the most primitive and brutal environment that war represents a soldier has to believe that there is love and that it is this that actually, and ironically, makes it not only worthwhile but also absolutely necessary.

It was my secret. I had thought about Orly in that time. It might have seemed that Hannah would have played this philosophical muse, but Hannah was also a soldier and I was not romantic about her. She was a comrade and more like a sister to me. I knew, in the end, that she felt likewise about me.

Orly was, by contrast, a more simple person. It would be unfair to say she was more feminine if that were to imply that she was more fragile. Orly was independent and strong in her own right. She was not overtly political and she was devoted to the life of the kibbutz. But the most crucial thing for me, perhaps from a psychological point of view, was that

BAR KOCHBA

Orly had been hurt. She had been wounded physically and she had suffered at the same time the loss of her young husband. She was vulnerable, and this brought out that protective, chauvinistic and masculine side of me, I am almost ashamed to admit. It made me dominant in a way, and I likely responded to that.

On the battlefield, where the smoke and blood are the terrible scenery, in those moments of blessed rest, thoughts come to you like a salve. You think of the opposite and why you are protecting it. In those moments pictures of Orly often came to me mind. I imagined her with blood still on her khakis cradling Aaron's head in her lap. And I was there, beside her, waiting and protecting.

I'm not proud of these fantasies. They worry me. But at the time, before I returned home, they occurred to me and I relate them reluctantly because they have significance.

During the first few days after I arrived back at the kibbutz I was kept busy with simple tasks and talking lightly to a number of individuals who tried to help me make the transition from both the events before the war and during it. Everyone was very kind. I saw Orly from a distance several times and she would wave at me and smile. Once or twice we actually said a few words, but I was embarrassed and not ready to carry on an extended conversation.

Then one day, as I was working on a fence at the periphery of the land, she came out to join me.

"I've been appointed your co-worker here, Avrum. They thought you might need some help." She looked at me appraisingly for a moment. "Maybe even some company?"

I've been through a lot. Orly had been a friend for a long time. Even so, I felt a slight rush of blood run up my spine. I'd been thinking of her for a while, almost a voyeur on her spirit. I was embarrassed, but it probably didn't show and it passed almost instantly.

I grinned brightly. "Help? Sure, you're welcome." I gestured to the ground beside me. "Pull up some grass and make yourself comfortable."

She knelt down beside me. "I brought some sandwiches and a vacuum of tea."

I avoided looking her directly in the eye, busying myself with the details of the fence. "This is tedious but not difficult. And you know what? It's time for a break anyway!"

She broke out some sandwiches from a knapsack she was carrying and without much chat we began to eat and drink sweet tea from metal cups. "You feeling better now?" I asked simply.

She nodded empathically. "Yes. Much. I have to avoid strenuous work for now, so I'm not doing much farming. But it's ok."

"You have time to relax?" I asked.

She shook her head. "That's the last thing I want, I mean at least not in massive doses. I'm a simple girl and I like to keep busy. You know, too much time to think is not good either. I work in the office, I do sewing and mending. You know what? I read a lot, mostly Hebrew but I'm also learning English. There's a wonderful American writer, his name is John Steinbeck."

"I know English, but I've never read an American writer."

Orly clearly enjoyed talking about it. "There's this fabulous book called "The Grapes of Wrath", about migrant farmers in California. So relevant to us, Avrum. We're like the migrant workers. Perhaps the Arabs are like the owners in a way. America is a new country too, like Israel."

It was very pleasant to listen to Orly. Inside, I was admiring her plain physical and inner beauty despite remaining distant. "I can't think about the Arabs with any sense of fairness. They are the enemy, and I can't think of them."

"It's the same for me. They want to destroy us. We can only resist. There's no fairness in it."

We both spontaneously stopped eating. "Are you here to stay?" Orly asked, one eyebrow lifting slightly to indicate a keen question.

I was wearing a peaked cap. I lifted it to wipe my forehead. "I'm going to join the standing forces." I said simply, but for the first time I made direct eye contact with her. A fine mist seemed to cross her face and she looked down.

"I wondered about that." She said.

"Of course, our war is not over." I went on.

Orly shook her head with vivid strokes. "No, no, of course not. I know you're not really a farmer at heart."

We were on the verge of an uncomfortable silence, but I continued instead. "It wouldn't seem right to give up now."

Orly reacted with some emotion. It was hard to tell just what emotion it was. "Well yes." She said strongly. "It would not be right to sit out the war for our existence. Israel needs a standing army and people have to enlist." She paused for a moment and her radiant face shone up at me. "It would be irrelevant to say 'but why you?' You need to be a soldier, that's what I think. But, you know, we are waging a battle right here on the kibbutz."

"I know." I said.

"I'm not so sure you do, Avrum Bar Kochba. It's a battle for civilization and order and plain old fashioned sanity and it's just as important and meaningful and just as the battle the army wages."

I knew she was right but the emotions seemed out of place. "I know,

Orly." I said with sincerity on my mind and in my voice. "I can't help myself."

"That's right!" she shot back. "You lost everything that ever meant anything to you in Europe. Being a fighter is the only cause you have left. Home, family, religion, community, maybe you believe in these things as much as anyone but they don't stick to you. You have to be a fighter." She said and then, almost under her breath she said, "You have to be a hero." She was looking down as she said this.

I was a momentary loss for words. I had to struggle with the meaning of what to say before I could reply. "Orly, maybe you're right. But I'm not sure. I'm drawn to be a soldier, it's true. It's true that I have chosen that in the past and that I am continuing in the present. But I want those other things also. I want to have them much, much more than ever wanted to be a hero. I never wanted that. I never think of myself as that."

Then Orly did something that has been a stone pillar in the wreck and nuisance of what has been my life ever since. From her position below my eyes, like a sleek, silent and purposeful swan she brought her face in a smooth arc up to mine and kissed me fully and deeply on the lips.

At first I was merely stunned, but my reflexes quickly gave way to the truth of my feelings. I took her face gently in my cupped hands and held her lips on mine for what seemed like a long time.

When we let go of that kiss, Orly let herself down and curled up in my arms. She said, almost angrily, "I thought about you all the time during the war. I prayed for you all the time."

"I'll tell you the absolute truth, Orly. I thought about you also. More than I care to say."

"When you join the army will you still be living on the Kibbutz?"

"I believe so."

She sat up and faced me. "Do you want this, Avrum? Do you want a relationship with me."

I'm not the best conversationalist. "Orly, I want it more than anything on earth. I never thought it could be possible."

Her face went quizzical. "I've never met anyone who knew themselves less than you, Avrum. You do the most amazing things and they just roll off your back. You think you have no presence but you are so wrong."

I felt a bit weak for the first time in a long while. "I know myself well enough to know that this is definitely what I want." I paused, but said clearly. "I love you, Orly. It may not show, but that's the truth. I think I've loved you all along."

Orly smiled a wan but true smile. "Alright, Avrum. It's a start. I love you, too. And I, also, think perhaps I have right from the start." We were both thinking of Aaron and of the relationship we had before they got married.

It was several weeks after we began our relationship that I was called up as a regular by the army. I was stationed in a camp just outside of Haifa and I was able to visit the kibbutz on my time off. Orly and I were in a somewhat blissful state at that time, enjoying a love that was based on very deep friendship tinged, for me, with a ring of wonder. Although I had an earlier love affair with Hannah, this relationship brought out emotions that I didn't know I had. There was a domestic side that was rich and happy, even though it was intermittent. After a few months I felt closer to her than I had ever felt to any other woman except Miriam. And at first, Miriam was on my mind a great deal. I imagined she would have been approving of this. It was a sincere arrangement, legitimate and gratifying.

In the army I was involved at first in training reserves. It was honest work and gratifying, especially because we were not involved in any combat at the time. I was only 21 year old but I had seen a lot of action. My education, however, had been left behind many years before and the army had a policy of bringing permanent recruits up to a post-secondary level of education whenever possible. I was selected as a candidate for further learning.

Our neophyte nation had no university yet, so classes in various subjects were set up near the camp and we studied at night. I took courses in history, social science and literature. It was an enormous pleasure for me to study and a wonderful contrast to the task of training soldiers.

Eight months after I enlisted I received news that surprised and excited me. The army was sending me to a university in Toronto, Canada on an exchange program for eight months. I would be there through the winter of 1952 through 1953. It would be an accelerated program and on completion I would receive a degree. They gave me a calendar from the university to look over. I had never seen such a document. It was like a mansion full of dozens of open doors, each one shining with a brilliant light. I decided to focus on history and social science.

This was, for me, an honour and a special reward for all my experience. When I learned about it I was trembling with a happy excitement that didn't let up right up until I left. It must have showed a bit; the veil that normally hid my deeper dark feelings was less visible for a while.

Orly was appreciative. We were both naturally concerned about how we would deal with eight months apart after only a relatively short time together. The truth was that because our time together was both limited and intermittent we were strained already. Although we were clearly in love our actual relationship was still tentative. It became emotionally charged when we knew I was going away. Everything seemed heightened.

As the time for departure approached we were very close but also very tense. In the autumn air we walked together one day off the kibbutz down a pretty path. We didn't hold on to each other like we sometimes did and we barely engaged in the excited conversation that had been our custom.

"Avrum, we have to talk about this."

Knowing this conversation was essential I was happy to begin in this way. "Yes. I know we do."

"You need something from me when you go."

I wasn't certain what she meant. "Alright. What is it?"

"This isn't like going to war. You're going to do something you should enjoy and get the most out of."

"And that means..." I asked quizzically.

"You don't necessarily need a girl back home."

I grimaced slightly, stopped walking and looked at her directly. "Is that what you think you are to me? A girl back home?"

Orly's features tightened with resolve. "Eight months can be a long time. You're going to meet people and want have friends. Some of them will be women. One of them might like you."

"You think I'm a flirt?" I asked honestly.

"No. I think you are a young, single attractive man. You are going to be popular."

"Orly, you underestimate my feelings for you." I felt strongly that I had to assure her that I intended to be faithful.

"But that's just it. You should be free to have intimate friendships. I don't want you to go to Canada in chains."

"To me you are not chains. It's the opposite, Orly. You are freedom."

"Whatever, Avrum. You don't understand. I'll be here when you come back, but you must go a free man."

I hurriedly assessed the circumstances of Orly's feelings and quickly decided that her sincerity was worth more than any argument I could make. I didn't want to be a free man. I wanted to be someone who had something valuable to return to. "I'll write often."

"Very good. I hear the winters are very cold but very beautiful. Send me postcards."

In late August I made the long trip to Canada. All the while something slowly happened to me. For the first time in many years I began to let the idea that I was a fighter slip. There would be no war in Toronto, although there would be many veterans. I knew there was a strong Jewish community there and had, in fact, been put in touch with local organizations who had arranged a place for me to stay with a Jewish family. I thought about that on the voyage there. Wondering what living with a family would be like. When I arrived at Union Station there were five people there to meet me. Each of them smiled broadly and shook my hand. "Avrum bar Kochba," one of the men said. "You are welcome to Toronto." They were unaffected, generous and open. I gazed at their faces fleetingly and saw something I not seen in a very long time. In fact, I don't think I had ever seen it before. It was safety. It was the absence of the tensions of abiding fear. It was 'shalom', peace, in as simple a way as I had ever seen.

In point of fact, my winter and spring in Canada happened in a kind of muted daze. I had never been so simply comfortable and almost dizzyingly happy. The family I stayed with had three children under fourteen. They lived in a large three story house near Spadina and College streets, in the heart of a thriving Jewish district and within walking distance of the university. The father and mother were always hospitable and I became quite close to Sol, the father. But it was the children that made my stay very wonderful. They were always funny and mischievous, always friendly and affectionate.

I met many people my age, at the university and in the community. Orly had been right, I was popular. I thought of Orly a lot and I didn't get involved with any other woman. But surprisingly, perhaps, I thought of Miriam mostly. I don't know why; perhaps because it was with Miriam that I had first experienced this kind of happiness, and it was my bond to Miriam that kept me from getting involved with another even more than my bond with Orly.

One day in December I had a conversation with Sol that remains an emblem for that time in Canada. We were having cigarettes on the front porch of his house. It was dusk, getting cold, and there was some snow on the ground though not yet deep.

"I wonder if this reminds you of home?" he asked.

I didn't quite know what he meant. "Home? I said. "You mean Israel?" I was puzzled because there is no snow in Israel.

"No." he said clearly. "Home in Europe. That's where you're originally from, isn't it."

I laughed gently. "Yes." I said. "Hungary. This is quite different, although it does remind me of Budapest, now that you say so."

"This is something like Poland. I was born in Poland. I came here when I was 13."

"Yes. I imagine it was something like this." I didn't mention that I had been in a concentration camp in Poland.

Sol looked at me and smiled. "But this is the 'new world', Avrum! The land of opportunity."

I'm so dreadful at conversation. "Yes," I said, smiling back. "I see it that way, too. Busy. Young."

There was a very brief pause. "Of course, Israel is new too, isn't it."

I laughed genially. "Oh yes. Israel is young."

"I admire that you live there, Avrum. I don't expect it's an easy place to live."

This could have had any number of responses. I decided not to beg the question because I liked Sol and respected his insights. "It's very beautiful in a way that is almost the opposite of here."

Sol laughed. "The opposite! I like that! The climate is almost opposite, isn't it."

"You can live in peace here. That's what is, to me, so different."

"Ah, peace. Yes, we have peace. And you know what? We probably take that for granted. You have to work hard here to get ahead. Business, that's tough here." Sol was a tailor who was building up a small clothing factory."

"Here it's all about business, isn't it?" I asked.

Sol looked like someone had struck him with a wet sock. "Business. Work. It's all about money. You want to give your kids what they need and it takes money."

"And yet people here are friendly."

"Friendly, yes, to a degree. Don't you think people are the same everywhere? You've been around."

"Yes, in a way they are the same. But in a way, you know, I see it differently too. There are people who want peace and there are people consumed with hate. There are people who hate us, the Jews, so much so that they just want us dead."

A dark look came over Sol's face. "There are certainly people like that. Here as well. But Avrum? Do you hate them back?" He wanted to know how I might feel.

I looked at him with a curious expression at first, then I made brief eye contact. "No." I said. "I don't think they know what they are doing. I don't hate them for it. I feel very sorry, but I don't actually feel hate."

BAR KOCHBA

He slapped me on the back. "Good for you!" he said. "No matter what, we must learn never to hate. It makes us rash and irresponsible. Jews aren't perfect but we have to try to live by our own example. You see, people are always no more or less than human beings. We must copy G-d's image as well as we can. Here there is anti-Semitism but they haven't built the ovens yet. Please G-d, it will never come to that."

I decided to comment about the country to Sol. "Can I tell you something, Sol? I love Israel in every way, for it's natural beauty, it's history, its spirit and it's soul. But here, to be truthful, I feel light and real. I feel very natural and almost untroubled. I didn't expect it and I hadn't thought about it before I came. I think I could live here very well. It is a very amazing place. It's a closely guarded secret only a few expatriate Europeans actually know."

Sol stared at me in some wonderment for just a moment. "Well, you have put into words what I have often felt. I was a young man during the Depression and life was hard. But we shared with each other, we helped each other and we got through it somehow. The U.S. is a great country in every way, but we also have some greatness, little known as it may be."

The winter went by quickly. I trudged through the new fallen snow often to the campus, sat for hours in the wooded library, read and read and read. There were campfires, snowball fights, restaurants and coffee houses at night. There were people, it seemed like so many sometimes, always laughing and chattering and seemingly in a perpetual state of celebration. In April I wrote examinations in all my courses and did quite well. What had I learned?

Mostly the order of things. How the events of the world make up history and how history is also made up of slants and bias. How political systems evolve to serve the needs of both society and the ruling class, how they can be just and how they can abuse. I learned about human nature, about the natural structures of society and cultures. I learned a lot about war, especially strategy. When I finished, I wasn't even aware of what I now knew that I didn't know before. When I waved goodbye to Sol, his family and my friends at the train station I said farewell to a rich and beautiful moment in my life. A moment of learning and reflection, of friendship and happiness. A moment when I was not, for a brief time, a soldier and a fighter. It was a moment of peace made even more precious because it couldn't last.

When I reached Israel it was hot. Orly was waiting for me at the airport with a car borrowed from the kibbutz. I was very happy to see her angelic smile and soft features. She didn't run to my arms. She stood her ground in the waiting area until I approached her. As I came closer, she began to smile. I couldn't resist. I dropped my bags, hurried the last few steps and swept her joyfully up in the air. I was surprised. After eight months away and in a pleasing environment as well, with it's danger and it's pain and it's wonderful endurance this felt like home. I was happier than I ever thought I would be to set foot again in my homeland.

A short time later I reported for duty. To my surprise I was told that I had an appointment the following day with the officer in charge of my camp. It made me nervous but I managed to sleep soundly despite disturbing ideas. I wasn't kept waiting long at his office. Quite promptly I was let in to see him.

He greeted me with military formality. Then he said, "You have been overseas, Sergeant Bar Kochba. Did you have a good time."

I replied formally. "Yes, Sir."

He grimaced. "Glad to be back?"

"Yes, sir. Very glad to be back." I didn't want him to have any doubt about that.

Something like a smile passed across his face, tinged honestly with a sign of relief. "At ease." He said. I relaxed slightly.

"You have a remarkable record. You know that?"

Such a direct question. "Sir, I do what I can, Sir."

"No, No." He said. "I beg to differ. You have done more than your share."

I simply acquiesced. "Yes, Sir."

He placed my file, which he had been holding in his hands, easily on the desk. "Avrum, I'll get right the point because you know your record and I think you even know the limits of your abilities. Do you think you are ready to take a combat role at this time."

I thought about it for a moment but couldn't imagine what that role might be. Still he was right, I knew my limits. "Yes, Sir. I would like a little time to get back into physical readiness. But I'm very able to take up a combat role."

He looked through me at that moment as if to analyze my soul. "You'll get back in shape." He said. Then he paused, looked down and looked quickly back up at me.

"We're starting a new elite commando unit with a select group of soldiers. Very dangerous. Potentially very bloody. We want you to be in it, if you make training. We've been scrupulous in who we select for this task. Are you interested?"

I know I swallowed hard, but I also knew that all my instincts were in line with this. "I'm most interested, Sir. Thank you, Sir."

He smiled and held out his hand. "Alright, Sergeant. You'll be briefed in the next few days. You're not to go back to your former duties at this time. Stick around, relax a little, and we'll see if we can get you going on this."

I took his hand firmly. "Thank you, Sir."

I turned around briskly and left the office.

As I walked to my barracks my mind was racing. During the war I would not have reacted with so much anxiety but I had just spent eight months away from duty. A commando unit? I knew what that meant. I can't say I welcomed it. I can say, at least, that I met it head on.

CHAPTER 35
The Most Painful Things

Within a week I began training with the commando unit, called 'Special Forces Group Zero". We were moved to an isolated camp located somewhere in the Negev desert. There were 12 of us, each one a combat tested and highly trained man. We were transported there in the closed back of an army truck. We were encouraged to talk to each other during the two hour trip. The Commander wanted us to trust each other.

At the beginning of the trip we only nodded at each other in acknowledgement. Then one man turned to his neighbor, said "Shalom" and then his name. They started to talk, about immediate things like their weapons, equipment, what to expect in training. Soon everyone was speaking with their neighbor in low tones. Before long the general silence was broken by a pleasing hum of discussion, punctuated by the odd quiet laugh or exclamation. We were nervous, but we were also excited. This assignment was special and we all anticipated that it would be challenging and worthwhile.

My neighbour turned to me and offered a cigarette, which I quietly accepted. Although we were all career soldiers, we were not a coarse bunch. All of us were young, most had seen action in the Pal mach, Hezbollah, Irgun or other resistance before the war of independence, most of us had emmigrated from Europe but there were several Sabra. The comrade nest to me extended his hand. He was muscular, average in height and bore a friendly smile. I could see a wide scar running up his neck.

"I'm Zal." He said with comfortable assurance. "I was a sergeant until now. Do you know if we keep our rank?"

I took his hand. "Avrum. I don't know. I'm a sergeant also. Do you think we can all be sergeants?"

He laughed. "Sure. We'll all be officers. That's the Jewish way, everybody is in charge."

I shook my head. "They'll give us n new rank most likely. It won't be Private."

"No." Zal said. "What did they tell you about this mission?"

I raised my hands to indicate that I didn't know much. "Special forces. Commando unit."

"Elite group." Zal added. "Do you feel elite?"

I laughed. "After the war? No. I feel commitment. That's really what I feel."

"If any of us had any doubts we wouldn't be here." Zal smiled.

We rolled along for few moments. The rocking of the truck seemed to affirm our statements. My skills in conversation are not the best, but I didn't want to seem indifferent. Zev's accent was Israeli. "You were born here?" I asked.

"Indeed. My family were settlers from Europe. I grew up on a collective farm. Now it's a kibbutz. It's not too far from Tel Aviv."

"I also live on a kibbutz. In the North."

He nodded. "But you are from Europe, right?"

"Yes. Hungary. I came in '45."

"I see. Very good. How did you get in?" he inquired.

I laughed. "I was a very special case. They allowed me in as a unique exception."

Zal chuckled lightly. "Part of an elite force." He said. We both laughed at the irony. "I was in the Pal mach. By the time Independence arrived I had seen some action."

"Very good." I said simply. I didn't want to discuss my experience and Zal didn't ask. There was a moment of silence between us. Then Zal said, "I anticipate our training will be severe and thorough."

I let out a low whistle. "It will be thorough."

"You know what? I'm looking forward to jumping. I've never done it, but I've watched it and I look forward to it. The idea of leaping from a plane, falling through the sky, floating with a parachute? It pleases me."

"You know what?" I said. "You're right. I expect it to be a worthwhile challenge."

We didn't talk much further. At this time neither of us wanted to probe the other's background or experience; that would come more slowly over time. The truck rolled on and the rhythm of it's travel helped me think. I looked secretly at the faces of the men around me as they spoke to each other or looked at the floor or out the back of the truck. They were not especially brutal faces, although several of us were hardened. Like soldiers anywhere we were aware of our duty, cognizant of our commitment. The fact that we were Israeli didn't make much difference, I thought. Like any other soldiers we were anticipating battle. That element is the same, I think, wherever it occurs.

In the first few days we were pushed very hard, almost to the limit. Not one soldier complained. We were constantly kept on the move with calisthenics, miles of running with heavy packs on our backs, infantry maneuvers, combat exercises. At night we studied strategy, anatomy, languages and communications applications. We were in basic training for six weeks. By the end of the second week were in good physical shape, but there was nothing unusual in it except the degree. Around the third week we began more specialized training; parachute, stealth operations, combat techniques. My first jumps were remarkable. Initially, I confess I felt some fear, but soon it became so familiar I forgot the actual act of jumping and began to focus on the objective of the fall. Combat was different. Combat, as I had known it, was virtually forgotten, like a language that you never use any more.

We learned techniques of murder in all its forms. We learned to kill a man with one blow. We learned where to stab, where to shoot, where to strike on the human body. We learned how to fight hand-to-hand to the final breath, how to use any object as either defense or as a weapon. We learned how to draw upon every resource of our bodies and our psychology to maintain and achieve a purpose. We learned how to block out pain as well as how to inflict it. We became precision soldiers capable of achieving almost any objective.

We learned teamwork. We leaned complete trust in our partners and we learned how to deliver exactly what was demanded. We learned both to depend and how to act independently.

It would be inaccurate to say that I became friends with any of my teammates. Friendship would have been thoroughly inappropriate in the circumstances in which we existed. It would not be completely wrong to say we loved each other, although this would not be in the conventional way. Personalities were the thing that could cause failure or death, and we did not judge each other on the basis of personality or depend on each other on that basis. We were entirely focused on immediate objectives and our ability as individuals and a team to achieve them. To be friends with a particular individual would counter to or existence, since that would be as likely to tear us apart as it would be to bring us together.

Still, all of us were united by a bond, and it was a bond that transcended personality and the explicit task of our group. We wanted to defend Israel. It was not love of murder or the military or being a soldier that motivated any of us. Not a single man was a natural killer. Among us there was, in place of friendship, a deep camaraderie so pervasive that it might qualify as a kind of love. There were, of course, some individuals that were more approachable than others for various reasons, but we were trained to overlook those differences.

At the end of this first period of training I had occasion to talk with Zal again individually. We had worked closely but had not interacted a great deal on a personal level. Nevertheless, he had impressed me as a strong character very capable of immense damage even though his manner off the field was easy, almost casual.

We were allowed to stay up for 15 minutes after training to reflect in the night air. Just before we were to break up for a three week furlough I met Zal coincidentally just outside the mess tent. I was having a short stroll. He called me over: "Avrum!" he called softly. "Come here!"

I approached him curiously. "Here," he said. "have a cigarette?" He offered his open pack. I took one.

"Thanks." I said.

"I really should quit." He joked. "I only have one on special occasions, but you know what? That's too many."

I laughed quietly. "It's good for me." I said. He lit my cigarette.

"It's a beautiful night, don't you think?" I could see his teeth smiling in the moonlight.

It was clear and warm and the sky was lit with many stars. "Incredible." I said.

Zal seemed reflective. "It's been a rather incredible period. Do you agree?"

I looked at him. He was still smiling. "Yes. What's next?" I asked.

"Don't you know? We have exercises."

I looked down. "I know. I mean, it will be incredible, whatever's next."

Zal gazed directly at me. "Do you feel good, Avrum?"

I wondered what he might be moving towards. "Sure." I said. "I feel fine."

Zal gestured in a grand arc. "I feel good." He said. "I feel very good. You know what I feel, Avrum"

I did want to know. "What?"

"I feel safe. Isn't that strange? After a lifetime of fear and worry, I now feel safe. Why is that, do you suppose?"

"I don't know."

He waved his cigarette in the air for emphasis. "It's not because I've learned to run and jump, fall from a plane, kill a man in any one of many ways. That matters, but for all that I don't feel dangerous. It's not really anything about myself that makes me feel safe." He looked to my eyes."

"It's you, Avrum. It's you and all the others. It has given me confidence."

I thought this was appropriate. "That's what should be." I said.

"But no." Zal exclaimed. "I'm not being clear about this, I don't think. I didn't think about it much before this because there was so much politics involved. I think G-d wants us to be brave. I think He wants us to be strong and capable. I think He means for us to survive. Like when we first came to the land of Canaan and refused to fight for it. I feel good about it."

None of us had talked bout this for a long time. "I think we have no choice."

"I'm not a zealot." Zal continued. "I'm not a natural killer, I don't believe. I fight for survival. Maybe that's the most dangerous kind? Do you think?"

"I don't think there's any such thing as a natural killer, Zal. I think most killers are forced into it or they have unnatural motives."

"Yes!" Zal said simply. " I confess, I had some doubts coming into this unit. Self doubts, most likely. But not now. I'm satisfied and I feel happy about it. This is right. This feels right."

Zal was expressing my own feelings as well. The idea of safety was manifested in competency and preparedness, but even more than that I felt something about what had come out of my training. It was a commitment that ran far further than just my training. It ran through the whole country and I knew that it was expressed in our blood. Even though I had not been in touch with any other community in six weeks I understood that this experience was common.

We would fight to the death to keep the independence we had won. We would prepare, we would train, we would persist because, in some recess of our understanding this was required by more than just the situation. It was not a holy mission; it was, rather, an understanding. Israel was no longer a distant purpose, it was an immediate responsibility. I felt that Zal had expressed this quite correctly.

When we arrived in Tel Aviv a few days later I had only one thought in mind: to contact Orly. We had written a few letters while I was training and in hers were expressed very hopeful thoughts for my return. She met me at the base in a vehicle loaned from the kibbutz. I was standing outside the dispensary when she pulled up. I saw her coming in the distance and watched as her jeep approached. At first she was just a silhouette against the horizon. I felt an excitement grow deep in the core of my spirit. As she approached and her form became more clear that energy turned into a muted joy. Soon, I could see her face, her deep red hair blowing back in the wind, her warm smile spread happily across her face. We really hadn't been intimate for more than a few days before I had to leave for training, so our romance was still young. And it had been six weeks since we had seen each other. Neither of us knew exactly how to act. We were both nervous.

Orly stopped the jeep in front of me. Her teeth looked shining white in her wide smile. "Shalom, Avrum!" she said from her seat. "Did you wait long?"

"Not long." I said. "About a month and a half."

She tossed her head back and laughed. It wasn't terribly funny, but it broke the ice. She got out of the jeep and came around to where I stood. She was a few inches shorter than I and it made her seem adorable, with her petite frame and wide, clear green eyes. She banged gingerly on the hood of the car. "This old horse rides like a disaster. You could swear the frame was going to absolutely collapse at every pothole. And believe me, the road has as many potholes as solid land. It's like driving over Swiss cheese."

She looked up at me and I struggled for a witty reply. "Israel is a poor country. I hear they're waiting to fix that road until the Messiah comes. Our works department is run by a rabbi, I hear."

Orly laughed loudly, much more to be pleasing than because it was really funny. It was odd to me; she looked even better than I had remembered, shinning with an almost supernatural glow. As if reading my thoughts she said, "You look well. Fit. I think you've grown an inch or two."

"They had me on a rack."

"Well, it worked! I think you're thinner too."

We paused on our words and just looked at each other quietly, unconscious of the few seconds that passed silently. Orly broke the moment self-consciously. "Can I help you put your bags in the jeep?"

I only had two bags. "Do you want to drive?" she said without pressing.

"No." I said. "You can drive. I'll sleep in the passenger's seat."

Although these first exchanges were awkward they were innocent. We were very happy to see each other, that is what we were clumsily trying to communicate to each other and that is what I felt. As I climbed into the jeep beside her. "Hang on!" she said, as we turned around and drove out of the compound. It felt very good to be going home.

It was home, where we were going. That is what struck me hard as we headed toward the kibbutz. Sometimes it's been hard for me to know where my home is, but at this moment, beside Orly, I did truly feel like I was going home. For the first time in my life, I was with a woman who was not going somewhere else. I liked her so much and we were together. That was a very wonderful feeling as we made our way along the poorly paved road towards the kibbutz.

On the way, Orly steered clear of asking about the training. She told me news of the kibbutz at first. One woman was newly pregnant and another was about to give birth at any time. The early citrus crop was good. There had been an Arab raid at a nearby farm and one person was killed; otherwise there had been no attacks.

When the list of details was empty, Orly made the first personal gesture. She took my hand and squeezed it. "Everyone is going to be very pleased to see you." She said. "We missed you." I made a face. "Really!" she said with emphasis. "You're popular."

I looked at her profile as she turned back to watch the road. I was glad she had said that because it made me feel both relaxed and confident. "I'm happy to be back." And then I said what I really wanted to say but had not until the right time. "I'm very happy to see you. I thought about you often."

She looked at me smilingly. "I thought about you. And I wondered, are we 'a thing', or is it only a mindless fling for him?"

I liked her straightforward approach. "Oh, that's exactly the same question I asked myself."

A light, pretty laugh escaped from between her lips. "For my part, I waited for you, Avrum. I didn't look at anyone else because I didn't want to be with anyone else."

"I don't want to be with anyone else." I repeated her words. "I can't even think of anyone else." I picked up her hand and kissed it lightly. "I'm only back for three weeks."

Orly looked at me and grinned. "Let's make them count."

The following twenty days on the kibbutz did count. They were made most meaningful because they were so fleeting. I had never felt so much a part of anything. Working on the farm, being with so many people sharing a single wish, loving someone who was so much a part of it.

At the end of the second week Orly and I were walking in one of the orchards. The aroma was so beautiful and the colours were romantic. We were laughing about some of the equipment that was broken down and Orly took my arm. Something about the way she touched me gave me the courage to do what I wanted. We stoped walking and I turned to her. I took both of her hands. "Orly, I'm only a soldier. In a keen way, my life is not entirely my own."

"Avrum, that's your calling I believe. You don't have to apologize for it."

"I can't tell you how much you mean to me."

"That much?"

"More than my poor vocabulary can create."

She appeared serious but restrained. "Don't tell me then. Show me."

I grasped her back and drew her to me. I kissed her with every good intent. She lay her head lightly upon my chest. We held that embrace for a few moments. Then she shifted away. I didn't know how to say the words but I knew that I very much wanted to. "Orly, Let's not bring this to any end. I love you so very much, like I've just invented it. A soldier's life is not the best, I know. I'll understand if you say no. We'll live on the kibbutz I promise you, but you would make it all worthwhile by saying yes."

Orly laughed. Her eyes shone radiantly in the starlight. "Well say it!"

I was nervous. I said, simply, "Will you marry me?"

Orly's face was almost at rest. There was no visible tension or anxiety. "Avrum. You are the wonder of men to me in so many ways. I want to marry you. I will marry you, yes."

We fell to the earth in that orchard on our knees and held each other in a tight embrace. I was more than happy. I was filled with both pleasure and relief. I confess that I thought of Miriam in that moment, of the love I had felt for the first time in the grim train heading towards the death camp at Auschwitz. I felt almost the same, now, about Orly. But the circumstance was so different. Here was life. There was death.

We broke the news the next morning. All day long men and women came to me with happy words and kind greetings. Dov brought some bottles of beer and by supper time I was quite drunk. From that time until the time I left a week later it was as if I didn't have a care in the world. Uncharacteristic for me. My time with Orly was deep and sensual and warm. I didn't think about training until the last two days. I began to mentally prepare for the weeks ahead. The wedding was set for shortly after I was scheduled to return.

When the moment finally came for my return to duty Orly once again drove me to the base in the old jeep. We didn't talk very much on the trip. Orly kept the emotional space clear by talking about detail of the wedding, which she knew I wasn't too concerned about. She hadn't mentioned Aaron more than a few times in all the while we were together, but I understood that he was in her thoughts to some degree. The mood she created, wisely so, was more like we were going shopping than to see me off for at least a month.

At the base she didn't get out of the jeep. I removed my bags from the back and came around to the side to face her.

"Well, take care of yourself." She said almost casually, although there was concealed emotion in her voice. "When you're out there, doing your exercises, jumping from the plane, remember. I love you. You're my man."

"I'll see you in a month. Believe me, Orly, I remember you all the time."

We kissed with loving kindness in it and she put the jeep in gear, waved brightly, and drove off. I went towards the barracks with the memory of the orchard playing in my mind. I never saw Orly's wonderful face again.

BAR KOCHBA

Exercises were hard and stressful. They were designed to test every element of our performance. Many jumps into difficult terrain. Many situations to test our weapons use. We had to work together as a team in extreme conditions and fight hand-to-hand in simulated settings. It was exhausting and unrelenting. We had no contact with the outside world.

At the end of three weeks the C.O surprisingly pulled me out of an operation. I was taken to the field headquarters where I met an army Captain from our unit. I was brought into the field tent. I was greeted and asked to sit down.

The Captain said. "Under different circumstances we wouldn't do this. Certainly, under real combat conditions, it couldn't be done. We had to weight the effect of waiting a week until your operations were over or pulling you out early. It's your record that decided us. We decided waiting would impair your overall, long term performance more than letting you go. The Israeli Defense Forces believes in it's personnel. We do have what some might call, compassion."

I had no idea why I was being told all this.

"Your fiancé is very ill. She had an accident with farm machinery. You have been given relief to go to Tel Aviv. She's in the hospital there."

At first, when I heard this, my grief was so great I didn't know what to do. I didn't stand up right away. I simply sat immobile for a moment. The first thing I heard consciously was gunfire. It shocked me, because I had momentarily forgotten where I was. Then I remembered. I am a soldier. I have to handle myself competently.

I stood up shakily and saluted rather weakly. In a state of distraction I was shown to a jeep and driven the hour and a half to the reconnaissance point, then flown by helicopter to the base in Tel Aviv. During this time I was not thinking exclusively of Orly. Rather wonderingly, I kept thinking of Miriam and, in some way, confusing the two. It was like there was a dark smoke where my feelings should be. By the time I reached the hospital I was more clear. Although my faculties were numb, I was able to function and perform. It was like I had been hit with a grenade.

Dov was in the waiting room. "She's in that room." He said simply. "It's her old knife wound. She was helping to push a broken down tractor and an internal lesion broke. She was bleeding inside for a long time before telling anybody. They can't do very much, Avrum. She's in a coma."

I went into her hospital room and saw her on the bed with tubes running into her nose and arms. Her face was pale, her eyes were closed but she looked very beautiful to me. I've seen an enormous amount of death, from the camps to the army, but loosing the person you have been most intimate and caring with is different. I wasn't prepared for the way I felt.

I sat down beside Orly and took her hand. I didn't know what to say and I decided to pray. "Lord, this is Orly, a good person and the woman I love. I know we cannot know your work or guess your will. There's a lot of death in the world and I've been the cause of some of it. We need love more than ever. I beg Thee, give life to Orly. I will do anything you wish."

For the first time I could remember tears flooded my eyes.

"I will do whatever you wish, suffer whatever you wish. Only let Orly live. I beg of you."

I stayed all night. Sometime before dawn she slipped away. I saw it happen, that last breath, that horrible shudder and then that glorious peace. By that time my emotions were hardening. I was thinking of army death, not this. Yet, as I was increasingly aware as the night passed, this was not simply an agricultural accident.

Orly was a casualty of war, she was dying a soldier's death. She had been a fighter and had died of wounds received in battle.

By the time the nurses were telling me I needed to give them a chance to take care of Orly I was starting to feel the beginning of something different. In the pit of my stomach, in the same place Orly was stabbed, something was beginning to grow. It was anger. As it grew, paradoxically, I felt better. I felt as if molten steel was slowly creeping up my veins, hardening my resolve, even my muscles.

The funeral was nearly unbearable for me, even so. I shook with grief, but managed to stay erect and go through the social functions. The kibbutzim were very kind and gave me an enormous amount of support. After the funeral, which was on the kibbutz, I walked out of the camp into the roads surrounding it. Not into the orchard; I wasn't ready to go there. With the open space and the cool evening breeze I felt better. I felt the dull ache of loss, but not the acute pain of trauma. I wasn't thinking only of Orly. I was thinking also about myself.

I had lost the two women I had passionately wanted to love in my life. I wondered if G-d was telling me something. Perhaps love wasn't for me. Perhaps it was bad luck, perhaps it was the world that was bad. Millions had died in the past 10 years. I was only 21 years old. How would it go now? I was a trained assassin with no ties any longer to the civilian world. Perhaps I had no ties to the civilized world? Perhaps it was intended that I be a soldier and little else. Perhaps it was meant that I should be strong and feel anger not as an emotion but as steel in my veins. Perhaps that is what it all meant?

When I returned to duty several weeks later I was again called to headquarters. This time I was composed.

"Avrum," the Captain said evenly. "You did well during training and you have done well on the other pen and paper tests we administered."

"Yes, Sir."

"Your English is quite good?" he asked plainly.

"Fair, Sir." I responded honestly.

He looked at me seriously, then smiled. "You see yourself as a career soldier, don't you?"

I wondered where this was leading. I hoped I wasn't being given a discharge. "Yes, Sir."

"But you're only Twenty-three. That's early to decide on a military career, isn't it."

It seemed advisable to be honest. "I've been in a war, Sir, one way or another, since I was 10. It seems natural to me, Sir."

The Captain looked directly at me but I, of course, did not look directly at him. "An opportunity has come up, Sergeant Bar Kochba, and I've decided that a good person to fill it would be you. There accepting several cadets at West Point, in the U.S.A. Have you heard of West Point?"

"Yes, Sir. It's a military academy."

"Just so. You're going there in a few weeks if you pass their entrance exam. Everything will be taken care of, you don't have to be concerned about larger details. We want you to get thorough officer training. It's an honour, Bar Kochba. You'll be representing Israel."

"Thank you, Sir. I consider it an expression of hopeful confidence."

"Very good. You'll receive more instruction as needed." He smiled more broadly than was characteristic. "You make us proud, Avrum. You be a good man."

I can't say I was exactly feeling good about myself at this point. I was feeling instead a kind of muted strength of will. Until Orly's funeral I had thought I was a good person doing a necessary job. That wasn't sure any more. I didn't know if I was a good person doing bad things or just a bad person. Moral absolutes, in the vacancy of personal terror and erratic outcomes, didn't seem so sure any longer. I was going to West Point, which was known as a hotbed of moral absolutes. I understood very well that something had to give.

CHAPTER 36
West Point

I boarded the liner to America in a kind of daze. Orly's death had left me shaken, more than all of the killing that had surrounded me before. I had thought to settle with Orly, something I had wanted much more than I even knew. I had thought I was a soldier first and foremost, but that turned out not to be true. Actually, with her death the centre had fallen out of my life; that, and the end of the War of Independence. I no longer knew what I wanted for myself and it had left me empty.

Most of all, the crisis of faith that was begun by Orly's death had grown both deep and furious by the time I boarded the ship. Perhaps I expected some reward from G-d for having devoted my life to establishing the state of Israel. Instead, the very thing I wanted most had been taken away. This seemed utterly cruel and unjust. If there was a G-d who both gave and withheld favour, why had He punished me instead of giving me some measure of reward and incentive? How could I go on without faith?

The answer that was forming in the haze of disappointment and pain was that it was not possible to trust G-d in my personal affairs. Clearly it was meant, if such an assumption can be made, to be a soldier. Not only had I survived a number of battles, but I was even now on my way to be trained even further. G-d wanted me to be a fighter, perhaps so much so that he took away every other means for my happiness, first with Miriam and now with Orly. In response to this conviction, I felt a loss of moral purpose. My life, any way you looked at it, was not in my hands. As far as love went, it appeared to be both dangerous and meaningless. The two women I had loved had both died. I was certain not to be in love again.

From the moment I set foot upon the boat that would carry me to America, everything seemed to change. It was a medium size luxury liner, equipped with many comforts. When I boarded I was greeted by friendly faces who were both pleasant and efficient. I was dressed in uniform although I had some civilian clothes in my bag. I was traveling very light and I did not expect such an elaborate crossing. My cabin was small but comfortable. It was a single cabin with a comfortable bed, a simple but attractive dresser and a very serviceable wing chair.

We boarded in the morning and launched in the early afternoon. Everyone gathered on deck to wave goodbye to friends and family. There were, of course, a large number of Americans among the log of about 300 passengers. They were lined up at the railing, waving at the crowd below. There was a great deal of noise and laughter.

This parting had a double impact upon me. On the one hand, I was deeply gratified that I had been selected to attend West Point. It was an honour, a challenge and an opportunity to learn about warfare. On the other hand, there was no one waving at me from down below. I felt alone, anonymous and isolated. At the same time, I was pleased and amused by the good feelings of the people around me. This fell short of being patronizing. It was a recognition that some people had a real and meaningful life.

I had been instructed to meet other passengers for drinks once the ship had left port. This was a special invitation; not everyone was invited to meet the Captain like this. It appeared that I was a special person. I was quite delighted, although I didn't know why I had been selected.

It didn't take long to find out why I was special. The Captain had been briefed on all the passenger's status. Most of them were quite rich; some few were very wealthy. Those had been invited to the Captain's table. Why was I among them? I had been designated a war hero, and that was enough to classify me as a celebrity.

Among the thirty or so individuals in the room were a number of young Jewish Americans who had been on a kibbutz for several months while on an Aliyah, or arranged visit. They were the children of members of the congregation of a Reform synagogue in Vermont. They had met a lot of soldiers on their stay, so that in itself didn't impress them. But I was a hero selected to attend West Point, and that peeked their interest.

Three of the six chose to corner me for conversation. I was flattered, but still a bit awkward, which is so often my way with people I don't know.

"You're a member of the regular army?" One earnest young man asked me. His name was Danny and he wore the khakis of the kibbutz and a concerned but honest smile.

I smiled as simply as I could. "That's true." I said.

"Is that because you like being a soldier, or because you want to defend Israel?"

It was an uncomfortable question. "All Israeli's want to defend Israel." I said. "Isn't that why they are there?"

"But not everyone is a regular soldier." Danny stated pointedly. "You are."

"Yes." I said carefully. "That is a choice. I chose to be a soldier because I believe in it, but also because it is the life I have come to know."

"Avrum, then you were a soldier before the war?"

BAR KOCHBA

I did not want to expose the controversial issue of the Irgun so I ducked the question. "I was a survivor of Auschwitz and other camps."

Danny frowned and looked downward. "I'm sure that was an ordeal impossible to describe."

A young woman, long dark hair tied in a bun, full-figured and bright spoke up. "When did you come to Israel?"

I smiled at her pleasantly. There was something about her I instantly liked. She reminded me of Miriam. "In '46. I lived on a kibbutz."

She looked around happily at her friends. "See!" she said. "He's one of us!"

We all laughed. She picked up the ball again. "So you don't have to go to West Point." She chided me. "You can go to the University of Vermont for agriculture. Come with us! We'll show you where it is!"

Danny joked further. "Sure Laurie!" he said. "He'll learn to defend Israel with oranges, lemons and limes."

Laurie responded in kind. "What's wrong with that?"

Everyone laughed. "No, I mean it. You stuff them with gunpowder, light the stem and throw them at the enemy. They explode, and poof, they're blinded by citrus juice."

I enjoyed this bit of play. It seemed just right to me. "That's right." I said. "You make bombs out of the oranges and lemons but save the grapefruits for officers in particular."

Laurie put on a serious look. "Danny." She said. "Next time you insult my family I'm going to came after you with an exploding turnip! Army issue."

The third member of their party, a girl named Sharon, spoke up. "Did any of your family make it to Israel?"

I shook my head. "No." There was a very brief moment of quiet before Sharon spoke again.

"How many were you?"

I answered simply but with a wan smile. "Nine, including me."

The three Americans looked at each other silently. Sharon said. "You know. I don't think we can fully understand that. I have a brother and sister. Danny has a sister and Laurie has two brothers. That's eight between us, not counting our parents. I believe it's impossible for me to imagine losing everyone."

I became uncharacteristically broad. Their candor touched me. "Even though you have lost your family, you are not necessarily alone. All of us lost mostly everyone. It's the scale of the thing that numbs your senses eventually. The personal loss is, of course, horrible. But, even though it's hard to say, you can get some kind of grief out of it that makes some absurd kind of sense."

Danny spoke up. "It's the scale of it, isn't it?"

I added, "The scale of it and the intent of genocide."

Laurie threw up her arms. "That's what it takes to create a nation of soldiers."

Sharon looked into my eyes. "I don't think I'll ever be an Israeli, even though I love Isreal."

Laurie concurred. "Go to West Point." She said. "A little American savvy will do good."

I liked these Americans. They were refreshingly candid, honest and approachable. I met many other Americans on the voyage. Of a kind, they all seemed to be confident. They seemed to express a fresh, even joyful demeanor which, I guessed, came out of both emerging from the war as victors and a feeling of safety that I had never known. I hung out with Danny, Laurie and Sharon quite a bit, since it was not a terribly big ship to get lost in. We had meals together, and I often shared a cigarette after with Danny.

BAR KOCHBA

Laurie and I became companions also. I liked her very much, but had no romantic inclination. She was like a little sister. Even though she was broadly funny when she wanted to be, she was also sensitive. And the fact that she reminded me of Miriam actually dimmed the light of romance since I could not imagine another love like that in my life. Still, there was a suggestion hanging invisibly in the air that Laurie and I were an item. I think perhaps, even in her mind, Laurie thought of me as a kind of on board companion.

On the fourth day out something I had not anticipated happened. Laurie and Danny were playing some games in another part of the ship. Sharon and I were talking in deckchairs outside the dining room. Sharon was a very sharp and independent woman, more mature in fact than her friends and more able to penetrate my awareness. More than the others, she was interested in my background. On this occasion she was pressing me on the war in Europe. The sea air and my affection for her American freshness made me more open than usual.

"So you were a student when your father was taken to the Russian front?" she asked.

"Yes. What we call a *'yeshiva* boy'."

"Well, how does a *'yehiva* boy' take over the role of the father of seven children?"

I answered honestly. "Well, you're a Jew and you're not allowed to hold a job so it's difficult."

Sharon asked seriously. "Did you turn to crime?"

I laughed and leaned conspiratorially toward her. "Yes. As a matter of fact, that's what I did."

"No!" Seriously?"

I sat back in my deck chair. "Yes. I went on the Black Market, buying food in my town, transporting it to Budapest by train, selling it there, bringing the money back home to buy more food for our family."

Sharon was silent for a moment. "Desperate measures for desperate times."

"Yes."

Then she asked a pointed question. She knew me well enough to perceive good timing. "Was there a girl in Budapest?"

I was quite stunned by this. "Uh, well no. I was working illegally and I was a *Yeshiva* boy. *Yeshiva* boys don't have girls in Budapest!"

She was persistent, nonetheless. "Avrum, I don't know you very well, but I know you a lot better than you think. Tell me. There was a girl. I know there was a girl. You've been in love. I know it."

I considered what to disclose, then I spoke. "Sharon, I will tell you something. I have never told anyone else, but I too know you and I think you are sincere."

She cupped one hand to her face. "Go on. You can trust me with your heart."

I continued. "On the train. We didn't know where it was going, maybe to a work camp, maybe much worse. There were many of crowded into one car. There was a girl. I was fifteen."

Sharon looked deeply into my eyes as if to burn out the truth. "What happened."

I went on. "In the stench and the dirt on the floor of that car, we fell in love."

She pressed deeper. "...and did you...?"

I sat back decisively in my deckchair. "That's a matter of presidential privilege."

Sharon looked at me with an unusual emotion. It was a combination of certainty and comprehension. Without warning she reached out her hand and placed it tenderly on mine. "Tell me your state room number"

Surprised by the sheer sureness of her request I stated my room number.

She lifted her hand from mine and instead of holding it she poked it lightly with her index finger. "Go to your room and wait there."

I was perplexed. "But why?"

She continued. "Go there and wait."

I countered again. "But why, Sharon"

Her expression changed from one of persuasion to one of kind exasperation. "Because I'll be there soon."

I was stunned, but I didn't need any more incentive. Still, before I stumbled away I managed to say. "But Laurie?"

"Laurie is a big girl and she had no intentions of hurting you like I do. Go."

Sharon came to my state room 10 minutes after I arrived. Her shirt hit the floor within a few seconds and her slacks shortly after. She had the sharpest kiss I had ever experienced and her skin was brown and sensitive from the Middle-eastern sun and crème meant to keep it supple and radiant from an American firm.

We met like that in my state room twice more after that. Although we tried to be discrete, in such a limited environment secrecy was difficult. Laurie knew after the second time. Her reaction was to become sullen and distant from me. It was clear she was hurt and even confused. It didn't seem to be the case that she was exactly jealous. Rather, it appeared that the purely sexual nature of Sharon and my relationship was incomprehensible to her. My approach to her surprised me. I was concerned that she was hurt, but more concerned about my own pleasure.

It was uncharacteristic of me to be insensitive to another person's feelings, most especially someone I liked as much as Laurie. I took the high road on her sensibilities; I felt it was her problem, not mine. The day before we reached New York we happened to be left alone together as we were standing by the rail facing the ocean. The spray was just teasing our skin.

"Look!" she said in her characteristically buoyant way. "I think I can see land."

I wanted to make things better for her but didn't know how. "You'll be home tomorrow."

She regarded me with a penetrating stare. "That must be a disappointment for you."

I failed to meet her stare but held my own. "You know, Sharon and I have nothing to do with our friendship." I knew as soon as I said it that it was wrong.

"Doesn't it?" Laurie said plainly. "I thought you liked me. It appears you like her instead."

"I like you both the same."

That was also the wrong thing to say. "Well thanks a lot, Avrum, you really know how to make a girl feel special."

"You are special."

"Don't give me that line, Avrum. You don't have to patronize me just because I didn't throw myself at your feet in your stateroom."

I wanted to make amends. "You think I care about you less because of Sharon?"

She scowled. "Don't be ridiculous. Obviously either you don't care who you have sex with or you care more about her." She broke off abruptly. "It's too tacky to talk about."

"My friendship with Sharon is different, that's all."

Laurie looked out over the water and gestured broadly in her particular way, like her hands were small birds. "You think I want to be in Sharon's position? I hardly know you, Avrum. But I thought you cared about our friendship more than that. And you disappointed me, and so did Sharon. I know this kind of thing goes on but it hurts when it's under your nose, in your face, with someone I..." She paused on this sentence. "Someone I thought special thoughts about."

I tried to take this premise up. "My thoughts about you are very special."

She became sober. She looked into my face sincerely but without any hint of intimacy. "I thought we were having fun, Avrum. I believed you were a person with a lot of integrity and I thought Sharon knew that, even respected it. It's not only that you broke my trust, a trust that was, it's true, based on flimsy circumstantial evidence. It's that you broke the promise of a healthy but innocent infatuation that could possibly have been important to us for a sleazy affair that could only last a few days. You disappointed me, even though in some perverse way I deserved it, if for no other reason than that I was tragically naive."

My own illusions were broken. "I didn't think it would hurt you."

Laurie expressed quiet exasperation. "But why didn't you think, Avrum? Didn't you know I thought you were special? Didn't you know I liked you? Now, I'm not going back home with happy memories and a promise. I could have ended this wonderful trip to an incredible miracle that is Israel thinking high and lofty thoughts. Now, I'm going home thinking about a soldier I thought was special who turned out to be just another selfish jerk."

I arrived at West Point with high expectations which were not ruined by experience. I was going to be there for a year in a special program that focused on military strategy, personal fitness, combat readiness and weapons. The program was rigorous and demanding in every way. I was housed in a barracks with other cadets. There was a certain amount of camaraderie among us reflecting our institution, especially among the American cadets who were here for four years of training. This was not a strong factor for me since I was in some way a guest who would be going back to Israel after a year. But the program was fiercely competitive both on the field and in the classroom. It was a different approach that I wasn't entirely used to. In the Irgun and in the Israeli Defense Force the impetus was on cooperation rather more than competition. I was aware that the U.S. personality encouraged and promoted a distinct individualism that was more extreme than I was used to.

It didn't disturb me, but it didn't strike me as being absolutely the only way to be either. After a few weeks I became swept up in the momentum. I was friendly to some, indifferent to others. I perspired over every detail of my studies, focused on doing better than my peers rather than being better than my own abilities on the field. I learned a kind of discipline that was never to leave me which I believe is a very good thing.

The intense atmosphere of West Point was in counterpoint to the lavish social life I had access to off campus. We were near enough to New York City to be accessible, and here the Israeli command played a distinctive role by linking me up to Jewish communities. I was a minor celebrity since I was regarded not only as a 'hero' in my own right but also as the promise of a new and defensible Israel.

The community had something I had never experienced. A great deal of money, more so than had ever been a factor in my life up to this point. It may not have been evident to my Jewish hosts, but I had lived in almost desperate poverty, war and combat my whole life. I wasn't overwhelmed by the lavish dinners or the high fashion in clothes in themselves; I was simply impressed by the absolute sureness of it all, the underlying truth that it would never end.

It was these two diverse worlds that consumed me during my one year stay in America at West Point. On the one hand the precise discipline and competition of the academy, and on the other hand the lavish economic continuum that seemed destined never to end.

Amidst these two distinct communities there were two personal elements for me. At the academy there was conflict and some anti-Semitism. In the Jewish community there was sex. In fact, these two were consistent with American cultural life as I was able to experience it.

At the academy I ran into rivalry. I am not the best mixer. I hold my own based on my abilities more than my sparkling personality. Not surprisingly, I was a bit of a loner in the barracks and on the field. I stood out on account of my athletic and academic accomplishment, but this was not appreciated by everyone. One man in particular centered me out.

He was a young cadet from the mid-West. His name was Cam. His father had been a graduate of West Point. His ancestors had played a role in the American War of Independence. He was perfectly built physically, adept at every task. He struggled with his studies dutifully but they were a trial for him. He was, however, a natural leader and a devoted band of followers surrounded him at all times. I had no sense about him other than that I thought he would make an outstanding soldier. He was also deeply anti-Semitic.

In the first months at West Point Cam didn't pay any attention to me. Then, in one week, I rated third in physical training, second in combat arts and second in advanced math. That was too much for Cam. He couldn't stand to see a Jewish name so high on the lists.

He began by dropping insults in the change room; things like 'there seems to be a distinct odor in here' and 'I think you better go shower again. Your skin looks dirty.' I was used to this and I just let it go. But when it had no effect he began to confront me personally. I let it all ride. I wasn't interested in the conflict. Cam had no idea of my experience and background. I believed he would eventually lose this aggressive habit as he experienced more.

Meanwhile away from the academy I was being introduced as something completely different. I was in good shape physically, I had the glow of someone immersed in study and hard discipline doing something important that he liked. There was something else. I was a young man coming into his own. I had the power that accomplishment can give. And I was so young. Of course, I didn't think of myself as young.

I had developed a quality that I was actually unaware of at the time. I was strong, quite confident, aloof. I was, in fact, a detached individual with hope and power all around him. And, I had all the force and prestige of the Israeli Defense Forces behind me. I was their man in New York. This made me decidedly attractive to some young women.

Of course, I couldn't become romantically involved with anyone and certainly not any young, wealthy Jewish women attached to the social circuit. It was 1953. A woman's reputation was mandatory. But there were some exceptional women who were immune to the visible conventions for a variety of reasons. They were independent spirits. They were willing to take chances. They were married or divorced.

After Orly's death, my understanding of love changed. My whole understanding of faith and the virtue of obedience changed also. So much death, so much war, so much pain had pushed me over a precipice. There was no spiritual truth for me, everything seemed to be strictly empirical.

BAR KOCHBA

If your loved ones could die, one and all, then what use was love and attachment? What good, believing in a G-d who was inexplicable? What good was marriage if G-d could break any trust you might engage?

I participated in the sexual side of my life at West Point almost as if I were another person. I see myself at this time as bearing a kind of smirk about it; I was amused. It wouldn't be true to say I didn't care about my partners. I had no wish to hurt them or even confuse them, but they were so willing. They weren't great in number. I had brief affairs with three in the course of that year. The affairs were discrete, they were pleasant and uncommitted, they were mutual.

It would be unnecessary to provide details, because they were seamless. Characteristically, these affairs were a lesson to me and an experience. This is not so because of the promiscuity. It is so because I was a stranger passing through and that is what made me attractive. It is also significant to me because it represented a choice I made at that time. I could have declined these encounters, chosen instead to pursue a more moral approach. I could have waited to find the right girl, but I didn't choose to do that. Instead of accepting the religious mandate to choose enduring values I accepted the existential philosophy that G-d is dead. I believed, at the time, in my own existence.

While this reality was playing out in the city, a contingent reality was unraveling at West Point. In December, Cam's antagonism towards me as a Jew overcame him. I came in high on the list too many times, and the fact that I never responded to his taunts enraged him even more. In the showers he pointed out that I was circumcised. I responded that it was a issue of cleanliness and added that it was just as effective as his own in the act of procreation.

He exploded in anger. He called me an 'upstart, Jew, pig'. Later, he sent another cadet to challenge me to a battle at 11:00 pm behind the barracks. I accepted.

At 11:00 I approached the designated spot. I was wearing fatigues as was Cam. One of his associates acted as referee. Cam was angry, energetic. He was bouncing up and down, ready to defeat me.

He didn't know my history; he only knew that he had to teach me a lesson. When his friend indicated that we should start, Cam came at me right away. He was a good fighter who knew how to draw out his adversary's moves. So did I. I didn't want this to be a quick fight. I wanted Cam to show his abilities, to show his feelings, to enact his anger and outrage.

He was a strong fighter, well trained and persistent. Sometimes I let him hit me and sometimes he struck despite my efforts to prevent it. He fell three times; I fell twice. He was bleeding from the eye; I had a cut on my forehead. He was exhausted, I appeared exhausted.

What Cam didn't know is that I had been trained by three armies in hand-to-hand combat. He didn't know that I had seen a great deal of fighting. What he didn't know was that I had killed men who were more highly trained and skilled than him. What he didn't know was that I was a trained murderer.

After twenty minutes of fighting we were both worn out. Cam was a good opponent, there was no need to patronize him physically or in any other way. I knew he couldn't beat me because he didn't have the experience. But he had the potential. That was what I wanted him to learn as well as, of course, that a Jew can fight back too.

When the fight was almost worn down I wanted it to end. I waited for the right lunge, flipped his tired body over my own, placed my foot in his armpit and twisted his arm powerfully with my arms. This was a move we had been taught at the point, so I didn't give away the fact that I simply knew more about combat than Cam. The fight was over. I had won. But, in a civilized sense, Cam had not lost. He had not lost face, and that was my only objective. I actually liked Cam. I thought he had potential. His anti-Semitism was wrong and I very much wanted him to realize that in the only way I believed he ever could. By seeing us as equals. That had been my only real battle all my life.

When he got up, Cam looked tired but intact. He dusted himself off with some deliberation.

"That last move was a good one." He said soberly. "You got me on that one."

"I'm glad you didn't connect with that left hook." I said in return.

He looked surprised, and then made a quick, feint swipe in the air. "Yah!" he said. "You're lucky I missed."

We looked at each other warily and then we both broke into a quiet laugh. "You'll always be a Jew." He said. "But you proved you can fight for that right."

"You don't know how true that is." I replied.

Under his breath, but loud enough to that everyone could hear, he said. "Well, that may be true too."

As I turned to go he called out my name. "Avrum!."

I turned around. He stretched out his arm. "It's traditional to shake hands after a fair fight."

America, I discovered, is a land of enormous contradictions. Fiercely nationalistic, it is just a s ferociously individualistic. It is a country of strong moral character and at the same time a country of extreme moral divergence. It is a young country with enormous potential and at the same time a reactionary establishment with repressive tendencies. But the people of the United States are remarkable for bearing these contradictions heroically and making them, somehow, not only livable but progressive.

The existential stage I was experiencing during that period at West Point lasted much longer because it ran deeply into the heart of what I was. I was to continue to be promiscuous instead of devoted in my relationships and I was to continue to question G-d's will. But I learned during that time to accept myself in a way I had never learned before. That is the magic and the power of the American experience for me. Like so many others, I had to learn to trust myself.

My training was now quite strong. I knew I would have to reintegrate into the IDF. The odd thing was that even after this period at West Point, I still felt very much like an Israeli and had felt homesick many times. Strangely, in the last weeks before leaving America and heading home to Israel, Miriam came to mind more than a few times. All the encounters in New York had rather poisoned my mind about love, and the brutal loss of Orly was still so painful that I could only think about it in abstract ways, as if it were a story that had happened to someone else. Miriam remained the heart of true love even through this. I could think about her without regret. She was my invisible friend; ever true, somehow more real in my mind than anyone.

CHAPTER 37
The Suez Crisis

Such a new country, such an ancient land. After New York, Israel seemed to be an ironically peaceful place. The difference, physically, was startling. New York, with its fast streets and tall buildings, might have been an entirely different dimension, while Tel Aviv was, by contrast, slow and dusty. Still, there were striking similarities, and it was these that impressed me more than the differences.

Although the pace was slower, the people in Israel shared certain qualities with the Americans. Chief among these were the fierce spirit of progress and ambition as well as the strong ribbon of independence that appeared to stream out of the citizens like the water Moses called forth from the rock in the desert. In both nations individuals were bent upon building a country out of what had only recently been wilderness. In each country there seemed to be a effort in unison. In the U.S. this effort was economic and cultural. In Israel, it was political and spiritual. The Israelis, in a fashion somewhat similar to the Americans, were directed towards creating a civilization.

I no longer had a permanent place at the kibbutz, but the council put up a place for me on those occasions when I needed to stay there for a short stay, and for this I was very grateful. Immediately after I returned from West Point I returned there. It was the home in Israel that welcomed me and a place to renew my spirit and begin again. Most significantly to me, it was a chance to visit Orly's grave. After arriving and having a coffee with the director it was the first place I went.

I do not think I am a terribly sentimental person. I've seen a great deal of death and I have learned to mostly accept it. Orly's death was an exception to the rule since she was my wife and since her death had been so early and so uncalled for. I stood at her grave at first without speaking, but words were going through my head. These words were not in sentences; nor were they incoherent. They were an expression of grief certainly, but also they were a message of disbelief. Disbelief in the reasons for faith, disbelief in the justice of G-d. Eventually, I knelt down beside the marker that stood above her grave. I said the only words I could: "You will not have died for no reason. There will be a reason, and I will find it."

When I got back to the kibbutz Dov was waiting in the mess hall. He looked a little different than I remembered. There was a kind of glow around him and he wore a beard. We both expressed words of welcome and clasped each other to our chests. There was no awkwardness or hesitation. The distance had actually drawn us closer.

"Did you teach them a thing or two at West Point?" Dov asked.

"When I finished with them they were speaking Hebrew and latkes were on the menu." I said.

Dov laughed. "Are they tough?" he asked.

"Yes, well their discipline is tough. Their course in strategy is brilliant. The cadets are mostly farm boys, like you, with a powerful ambition to make the world safe for democracy. They're what they sometimes call 'wide-eyed optimists'. I'm not sure that I would call them 'battle-hardened veterans'."

Dov scowled in mock surprise. "And you? You are not a 'wide-eyed optimist'?"

I laughed in good nature. "Perhaps I am what you might call a 'battle-hardened optimist'." I turned the conversation around 180 degrees. "You look terrific. It's been a good three years?"

Dov let his expression drop a little, then picked it up quickly with a broad but unusually large smile. "The years have treated me kindly."

"How so?" I pressed.

He spoke slowly and clearly. "The fields ripened beautifully and in good time. We are a wealthy kibbutz and full of hope. Our members are strong, our purpose is strong. We are generally happy and our members are content. We are very aware of immanent dangers, but we have had a few years of relative peace and it shows."

I enquired cautiously. "Is there also romance?"

Dov laughed heartily. "In another kibbutz, a few dozen miles from here, there is a very pretty woman who waits for me each week with a welcoming smile and kind words."

"And you?" I asked. "You also have a smile in your heart for this woman?"

Dov laughed once again. "What do you think, Avrum? Do you think I want to spend my whole life as a lonesome, footloose bachelor?"

I shook my head gravely. "No. I never thought that. I always knew you were waiting for the right person."

For a brief moment, without realizing that we were doing so, we just looked into each other's eyes with broad smiles on our faces. Quickly, Dov broke the silence. "For you, Avrum? Was there any romance to soften the hard reality of military training?"

"There was romance." I said curtly. "There was distraction and there was sex. A Jewish soldier in New York makes an attractive object for rich Manhattan daughters."

"Avrum?" Dov spoke lowly. "You finally decided to play your cards straight? I wondered when that was going to happen?"

I was a bit baffled. "What do you mean?"

Dov scoffed. "You don't know what an attractive figure you are, do you?"

I was honestly at a loss. "I know enough, I think. I know that in New York, for the first time, I let girls think what they want. For the first time, I took what they gave without feeling any unwieldy moral obligation."

"You mean you knew you weren't going to marry them?"

"I mean they knew I wasn't going to marry them. They wanted something that I could give them. Maybe a bit of a thrill. Maybe a moment of illusion, but they knew it was only a moment and they knew it was only an illusion."

Dov looked at me with a serious attention. "For you, Avrum, was it illusion?"

I laughed almost cruelly. "What difference does it make, Dov? Does anybody care? Was there any injustice? We all got what we wanted? Does anything else matter?"

Dov countered my assessment. "Perhaps not, Avrum. It's not my place to judge. But there is a Judge and whatever we do we have to make our peace with H-m."

I felt anger and disgust, not at Dov but at myself. "Dov, I'm a killer by profession. Can I ever make peace with that?"

He paused briefly then said with purpose. "Have you ever read the 'Bagavad Gita'?"

I was stunned. "No."

"It's an important Hindu parable. A warrior named Arjuna asks his G-d why he has to kill. His G-d replies that it is his destiny to be a warrior and he must fulfill it."

I was not interested in parables. "That's nice, but I don't care Dov. I don't know what G-d wants. He's stripped my conscience of what I loved and what I wanted. He stripped me of trust and faith. More than this I don't know and can't figure out. If I am doing H-s work, that's fine. I don't ask anymore and I don't question H-m about it like your man in the parable. What comes to me I take, what I have to do I do. I believe in Israel because it is what is left to believe in. If I die believing in it fine, if not, fine."

Dov placed his hand over my forearm. "Avrum, you are telling me you no longer believe in G-d?"

I replied honestly. "I don't think about it any longer, Dov."

Dov let out a quiet sigh. "It's no wonder." He said. Then he added as almost an aside. "I'm going to a *Yeshiva* in a few months. I'm going to be a Rabbi."

I was immediately sorry for all I had said. "Dov! That's tremendous! That's a good decision."

He shook his head. "It's easy now. During the next war it will not be so easy."

I wanted to show support. "Israel needs spiritual guidance as much as it needs soldiers."

"That's what G-d also tells Arjuna in the 'Bagavad Gita'." Dov laughed. "G-d says the same things in any language."

I only stayed a few short days at the kibbutz. Dov and I chummed around quite a bit, the warrior and the rabbi. Could I believe that both were doing G-d's work?

When I arrived back at my barracks I was instructed to report to the Camp Director for briefing. I was told that I would be re-integrated into the commando unit, Group Zero, I had left a year before.

"You will be expected to use the training you received in America to assist your unit." He had said. "When things begin to mesh, your training and our operations, it is intended that you will take a greater leadership role."

Integration was not a great problem. The other men in my unit appreciated the training I had received without resentment or resistance and they were mostly eager to share it. They were not jealous of West point: they considered it a prep-school compared to their experience. I picked up quickly on the basic nature of our missions.

Abdul Nasser had wrested power in Egypt by a military coup and had called upon all other Arab states to wage a war of annihilation against Israel. The Egyptian Foreign Minister said,

"The Arab people will not be embarrassed to declare: We shall not be satisfied except by the final obliteration of Israel from the map of the Middle East."

In 1955 Nasser announced:

"Egypt has decided to dispatch her heroes, the disciples of Pharaoh and the sons of Islam and they will cleanse the land of Palestine...There will be no peace on Israel's border because we demand vengeance and vengeance is Israel's death."

Our role, as a commando unit, was to retaliate against the attacks of these heroes, who were called the Fedayeen. Most of this took place along the border with Jordan. It was not the most pleasing work. It was necessary to be swift and brutal and it was necessary also to inflict heavy casualties upon the enemy, many or whom were often civilians. We had no choice because the Fadayeen targeted our civilians in their attacks.

Eventually there was a cry for the Israeli forces to let up upon this type of retaliatory operation. It came both from within and outside Israel. I was satisfied with this outcome, personally, and so were my comrades. I believed that there had to be a more effective and strategic way of dealing with the mess the Fedayeen made of our country. In a short time, their zeal to purge Palestine came to a critical point. From a tactical point of view, this afforded us an improvement.

When it came to killing civilians I was more stoical than I expected I would actually be. In principal I despised it, but I kept my emotions focused on both our purpose in building a nation and the loss of those I had loved. It helped ease the issue but it didn't eliminate it. More than at any other time in my career, I acted purely as a soldier with a job to carry out. I protected myself by not thinking very much, although I know that is a very lame rationale.

The tensions between Egypt, the other Arab nations and Israel intensified through the winter of 1956 and the actions of that period led to a situation that became known as the Suez Crisis or the 100 hour war. In April Nasser took a step that placed the entire Middle East in jeopardy. Although restricted to shipping to and from Israel, the Suez Canal, an essential link for shipping to Africa and India, had been partially owned by both European and Egyptian interests. Political changes had left Britain with a 44% share. After 1952, when King Farouk of Egypt, who was an ally of the British, was deposed by the Generals and Nasser took control tensions between Britain and France intensified. Specifically, this related to their reluctance to help finance the Aswan Dam.

There were 3 elements that contributed to the crisis centered on the Suez Canal. One element was the militarization and contingent arming of Egypt, Syria and Jordan. Another element was the Fedayeen attacks on Israel. Finally, in October of 1956, Nasser nationalized the Suez Canal. Two weeks after the nationalization, on October 25, Egypt signed a tripartite agreement with Syria and Jordan placing Nasser in command of all three armies. He made his intent clear, both towards Israel and Britain and France:

"I am not solely fighting against Israel myself. My task is to deliver the Arab world from destruction through Israel's intrigue, which has its roots abroad. Our hatred is very strong. There is no sense of talking about peace with Israel. There is not even the smallest place for negotiations."

The time had come for Israel to defend itself militarily once again from attack. Our leaders were compelled to seek backing from Britain and France in lieu of this coming crisis. We were preparing for a major defense, and my group was awaiting orders intensely. We did not know this at the time since it was secret diplomacy, but Britain France and Israel had concluded an agreement called the Protocol of Sevres.

This agreement was complex. Israel would invade the Sinai. Britain and France would then intervene, instructing that both armies withdraw their forces to a distance of 16 km. from either side of the canal. The Europeans would then argue that the canal be placed under Anglo-French management.

The military plan, called Operation Kadesh, was made known to select officers, myself among them. Our planning for the conquest of the Sinai hinged on four main military objectives; Sharm el-Sheikh, al-Arish, Abu Uwayulah and the Gaza Strip.

The Egyptian blockade of the Tiran Straits was based at Sharm el-Sheikh, and by capturing the town Israel would have access to the Red Sea for the first time since 1953, which would allow us to restore the trade benefits of secure passage to the Indian Ocean.

The Gaza strip was chosen as another military objective because we wished to remove the training grounds for Fedayeen groups and because we recognized that Egypt could use the territory as a staging ground against the advancing Israeli troops.

Al-Arish and Abu Awayulah were important hubs for soldiers, equipment and command of the Egyptian army in the Sinai.

The capture of these four objectives was hoped to be the means by which the entire Egyptian Army would rout, and fall back into Egypt proper, which British and French forces would then be able to push up against an Israeli advance, and crush in a decisive encounter.

My specific action was directed at a strategically significant location called the Mitla Pass. Our commando unit had specific orders. The overall plan of attack was for the entire 1st Battalion, 202 Paratroop Brigade, under the command of Colonel Rafael Etyan, to drop near one section of the Pass. Our group was to drop first to reconnoiter and prepare for the main action. But things did not go as planned.

Although we landed well, we were inside enemy lines, just behind a flank of Egyptian troops who were placed on watch. We could see, as soon as we landed, that we would have to fight our way out and we knew that we would have to do that without attracting attention. This was what we were trained for, but it would put the best of our training to the test. We would have to approach three separate outposts undetected, kill all the men there without arousing suspicion, and leave without having been detected. There were 10 of us. We would be approaching from what was the outpost's rear.

We broke up into three groups of three commando's each, with one as a lookout. Each of the posts that we were attacking was well dug in, but they were not prepared for an approach from the rear. This was not an operation that relied on coordination as much as it relied on utterly effective execution. We had to kill several men each without making a sound, and we had to reach them silently.

My two comrades and I decided to use our approach as a means to surprise the enemy. I knew how to step without sound; we had practiced the technique over and over. We each had two knives. Our commander pointed out which man each of us would take as we came close to the rear of this post. There were five soldiers, each one sitting with their back to us. On his mark, we each threw a knife at the back of a soldier, each of us striking our mark cleanly. This happened in an instant. There were two men left. They didn't have time to speak. As each of them turned around to see what had happened, we were upon them. I had one. I killed him instantly with a pass of a knife. It was not easy. He was strong, he was well trained, and he didn't want to die. But I was too quick and he fell, as did the other one by my comrade's hand.

That was done so that we could escape from a situation that we had not planed on. To make matters worse the 2002 Paratroop Brigade was blown off course and landed several miles from the target. They were forced to waste several hours and a great deal of energy to reach the original drop point. Energy was extremely important since everything had to happen, and succeed, in a very small window of opportunity. When we linked up with the Paratroops we dug in to receive weapons from another airlift and to await the rest of the Brigade, under the command of Ariel Sharon, who were supposed to join us coming over ground.

While we were waiting there was not a lot of conversation. My commando group was dispersed to other units as combat leaders. When

I arrived at my group I was surprised that they were so young. I gave them my name and told them why I was there. One soldier, who looked about 19, asked me:

"Do you think we can do it?"

He was innocent of fear. He was excited and energetic. "We have a chance, if you do what's needed."

He had a determined smile. "You bet! I've never seen action, but I've had basic training. I'm in good shape. I work out after work."

I took an interest in this young soldier because he was so eager. "You want to kill that badly?" I asked.

He shook his head energetically. "No, I don't want to kill at all. I want to help put an

end to that. I want to be some help. Two of my friends were killed by the Fedayeen and my father was killed in '48."

"You want revenge?" I asked, wondering why this boy was so excited.

"Revenge, shemenge." He said. "I want to be a part of a miracle."

I was a well trained executioner. I didn't believe anymore in miracles. But I did have something similar to faith left in me. I believed that if we all did our part, including soldiers like this young man, success would always be possible.

"Rest assured." I said to him, "Do your part and that will bring good luck."

"Right. That's what I want!"

After a few hours Sharon arrived with the rest of the Battalion. Everything happened very quickly. We went up against Egyptian forces immediately and we defeated them fairly swiftly. The battle was fierce but controlled and our casualties were within expectation.

But Sharon saw a window of opportunity in attacking *Jebel Heitan*, an important Arab stronghold that promised open shipping to Israeli ships.

He wanted to send his lightly armed paratroopers against dug-in Egyptians supported by air and heavy artillery as well as tanks. I was put in charge of a new group. Our attack was brilliant, from a military perspective, but it verged on being reckless as well.

At a mid-point in the fighting, something happened that would have an effect upon the rest of my life. My group was facing a gap in the pass which was guarded by a soldier with a machine gun. Behind us were several other battle groups snagged at this particular spot.

I saw a chance to break through this snag, but it would take a tactical and military action that was not only difficult but dangerous. These soldiers did not know me and they did not know I had been at West Point for a year. Although I had never admitted it to anyone since I had left West Point I had secretly wanted to use some of what I learned. This seemed to be the right time.

The key to progress for our troops was to break through that machine gun. The Egyptians were dug in well and there was one chance: to overrun the position, secure the artillery and make use of it for our own protection. The necessary operation was to distract the gunner and allow one man to take him out hand to hand.

First, I split up my men and sent half of them to different location still in the sights of that gun. They were to distract him. The other's maintained their position but let up their fire. When they could see that the other half were in position they were to fire and alternate with the other group in distracting the machine gunner. Meanwhile, I instructed two soldiers to climb forward, although in positions that would attract attention but could not be hit.

I circled out to the flank and advanced carefully as the gunner was distracted. There were three other soldiers in the Egyptian position.

When I was situated correctly I shot each one separately with a hand gun. The machine gunner was now alone, but he couldn't see me and I couldn't shoot him.

When the moment of possibility arrived, I leapt at the gunner with a knife. We struggled, a struggle that was visible to all of my troops. It was a struggle I nearly didn't win. He pinned my arm, the one that held the knife, to his chest and he was very strong, but I had more moves and was not clumsy. I dropped the knife from the one hand, caught it in the other and had a clear path to his chest before he was able to respond. The knife pierced his chest below the heart and he fell. My men silently advanced over the position, took control of the offending gun, and allowed the other troops to move forward as well. If we hadn't taken that pass at that particular time the entire effort on *Jebel Heitan* might have failed.

This operation, undertaken by Sharon, proved to be very controversial. Israeli casualties were exceptionally high, although strategically it was a significant accomplishment.

The Military element of the crisis was virtually over by the next day. The operation was highly successful from a military point of view, but was a political disaster. This was due to a miscalculation by the French and the British over what support they could expect from the U.S. At the exact time the Suez Crisis was occurring the Russians were intervening in Hungary. The U.S. could not appear to condemn the Russian incursion into Hungary while condoning the French and British in Egypt. Moreover, at the U.N., the Russians under Khrushchev threatened to support Egypt in any wider battle and launch attacks "of all kinds of weapons of destruction" on London and Paris.

Thus, the Eisenhower administration forced a cease-fire on Britain and France which it had previously told the Allies he would not do. A resolution was passed at the U.N. General Assembly and Britain and France withdrew in a week. This was partly accomplished in response to a U.S. threat to sell reserves of the British pound and thereby cause a collapse of the British currency. To further encourage a withdrawal, Saudi Arabia started an oil embargo against Britain and France and the U.S. refused to fill in the gap until these powers withdrew.

But the most significant result of this conflict for Israel was security for its borders and advances in shipping availability. Under the encouragement of Lester Pearson, the Canadian Foreign Affairs Minister, a force deployed by the U.N. and composed of units from various countries was created to secure the peace between Egypt and Israel. These forces were called 'Peacekeepers' and they have been employed by the U.N many times since Suez to help settle international disputes. This measure meant some security for Isreal and, importantly, an end to the horrible physical and mental destructiveness of the Fedeyeen.

For my part, the Suez Crisis turned out to be a watershed in my career as well as my life overall. I had attained some recognition as a soldier previous to the conflict, but it had been somewhat private and localized to other member's of the forces. My name had been associated with skill in combat among a few. But the maneuver at *Jebel Heitan* had been carried out with and in front of a battery of relatively inexperienced and impressionable soldiers who saw an officer engineer a strategy and carry out hand to hand combat with an enemy that proved key to saving dozens of lives and possibly directly helped to win the war. The story got told over and over again down the line.

I was embarrassed by this, if not only because I nearly lost and because it was my job to do it and because it had involved killing a man who had the misfortune of being the enemy. Still, I had to bear it, even more so after the conflict ended and word of it reached the press. People wanted interviews. They wanted profiles. They wanted to use me as the symbol of Israeli military ability. I wanted desperately to avoid this. I am not only a private person, but I detest the romanticism that makes my necessary actions as a soldier special. I know that they are not special and I know that I am not special for doing them. I am trained and educated in warfare because fate has made it that way.

Even so, my superiors were strongly in favor of press coverage and so was the government that directed them. Israel needed heroes, the insight ran, and I was identified as appropriate for that role. I was interviewed for a national newspaper and also for television. A short time after the crisis had ended virtually everyone in the nation knew my name, my face and my story. I was a survivor from Hungary who had worked with the Irgun. I had lived on a kibbutz. I was a regular in the IDF who had distinguished himself in combat, I was a member of the Group Zero Commando Unit and I had been educated at West Point. Although this was all true, it sounded too good in print and over the air. Commentators remarked that I was polite, modest and articulate in person. The fact that I was single made an enormous impression in some quarters. I received unsolicited mail that I could not honestly respond to.

I hated all this, but accepted that I could not easily duck out of it. Once it had begun it took on a life of its own. Luckily, for the next few years Israel was not drawn into another crisis and the attention I was unhappily receiving soon died down. Still, I was a celebrity and for a while I laid low. My social life included one woman who I dated exclusively. She was a good friend and she never agreed to any interviews. I received a promotion to the rank of Commander. I trained troops in combat and strategy. The intermediate result of the Suez Crisis, for me personally, was the advent of a kind of normalcy. Being known as a soldier was almost an act of grace because it prevented me from hiding away in depression and angst. I didn't question my role in Israeli society; rather, I adapted to it.

I had been recognized for what I did and despite my misgivings it gave me a reason to go on. I don't know what might have happened if I had not received such note, but it possibly would have been less dramatic and uplifting. I did not feel like a fake because of it. I felt, ironically, more authentic. The future looked more solid and even more real. Perhaps this was the reward I had unconsciously wanted from G-d. I didn't think of it that way exactly. I thought of Arjuna, the warrior Dov had told me about from the Bagavad Gita. I accepted my destiny. I hoped that G-d would forgive me for it.

CHAPTER 38
Sarah Schenirer

Leah had become a serious young girl. At eighteen, she wasn't giddy or frivolous, but she wasn't a wallflower either. She was entirely visible although blithely ignorant of her quiet fame or reputation. She didn't think she was beautiful even though others did. When she looked at her reflection in the mirror, which she did as rarely as she could, she saw a face that was plain and unremarkable. That wasn't the face others saw. Her nose was supple, her eyes were uncharacteristically green and clear. They reflected a pensive, nearly vulnerable curiosity. Her skin was light, like Rivka's, and her face was a soft oval. Her lips were her unique feature. They projected just a slight, endearing pout, setting off an impression of humour which was, in fact, her secret weapon among the arsenal of qualities available to her personality.

It wasn't the features of her face that made her attractive, although those features were put together very well. It wasn't her slim, tidy figure that appeared utterly natural and uninhibited. It wasn't her thick chestnut hair that she wore often in a pony tail, often loose around her shoulders. It was, rather, that intangible quality that makes some people noticeable; an indefatigable spirit, a curiosity that is unselfconscious, an intellect that lacks inhibition. More than most adolescents, she followed her own path.

It wasn't so much that she was unique. It was that she possessed a passionate ambition to know what was true about things. She was impatient for knowledge, cautious about wisdom.

In 1963, as she started college at eighteen, she had three separate interests that consumed her time. The study of science, particularly physics, was her academic calling. She was one of very few females in her classes. Most of the students wanted to be engineers. Not Leah. She wasn't sure what she wanted as a profession related to science, she had contemplated teaching. But she loved the pure study. She was also strong in biology, but it was not her main focus. The pragmatics of the physical universe reminded her of G-d. The lawfulness, the precise symmetry, the unfailing certainty.

She was also drawn powerfully to journalism and had joined the College paper shortly after enrollment as a junior reporter covering campus clubs. Why did this interest her? Once again, it was the connection to a search for truth. Just as physics involved a quest for what is real in the universe, so journalism held out a search for truth also. Leah was a clear, solid writer with a keen eye for detail.

A lot of her time, especially in the evenings, was devoted to a local chapter of B'nai Brith, a Jewish youth organization. There were two interconnected streams, one for men and the other for women. Her chapter was called, "Sarah Shrenirer." Their namesake was a woman living in early 20th century Poland. After centuries of pogroms, persecution, and poverty, Jewish learning had drastically declined. Young women from traditional homes attended nonreligious schools and were led away from Judaism. She was known to say, "My sisters! When will you understand that our main purpose for being on this earth is to serve God?" Sarah Schenirer understood that those who left Judaism did so out of ignorance. opened her first school with 25 girls in 1918. Today, Bias Yackov is the largest Jewish women's educational system in the world.

The B'nai Brith was largely social, and Leah was at the upper end of the age range for members. Her only rivalry within the group was that she was the most religious girl, all of whom ranged from secular to conservative. This was not normally a conflict. Leah was used to being with all kinds of people, and her practice was not so much visible as it was internal. Her practice influenced others around her and their lifestyle, in turn, was an influence on her. As she entered college, two events began to shape her life in ways she wasn't entirely able to control. She was elected president of 'Sarah Shrenirer'. And she started to date.

The election had been a surprise. At the election meeting Leah, who had previously declined any nomination to the executive, was called on to make a speech summing up the past year. This was a feature of her experience on the B'nai Brith newspaper. At the end of the speech, which was funny and inspiring, she said:

"Our values, which have lit the way for civilizations for thousands of years, turn in our grasp. Judiasm is a living thing and it gets it's life from you and I, nowhere else. We make a difference. Our faith in G-d, our devotion to goodness and justice and equality give weight to the progress of every civilization. We are the daughters of a hope that has not died in Jewish hearts and will not die in ours."

Surprising to Leah, there was great applause and a standing ovation from the small group She took her seat next to her friend Wendy, who patted her gently on the back. "Well done!" she whispered.

Leah looked around in surprise. "What did I do?', she laughed.

"You made us happy." Wendy was smiling at her.

Leah shook her head in disbelief. "That's nice.", she said.

The nominations followed. They were very controlled but an element of excitement ran through them. First the lower positions, then president. The past president stood up. She had been a good leader and the members liked her. In a clear, firm voice she nominated Leah.

There was loud applause and cheers.

Leah looked at the ground. Uncharacteristically, her thoughts and feelings were confused. Wendy put her arm around her. "Why not?"

An idea broke in Leah's mind like a beacon. This was not wrong. She could do this. This was her last year. She should do what she could.

She looked up at Wendy's beaming face. She smiled a wistful smile.

Wendy's hand shot straight up in the air. "I second that nomination!" She cried.

Leah won the election as president soon after. When the congratulations and celebrations had ended a few hours later, Wendy and Leah went out for coffee on their own to a diner just outside of town. Chuck Berry was singing 'Maybeline'.

"We're a good chapter." Wendy mused.

"Are we?" Leah was stirring her coffee steadily, like it were a beaker of soluble material.

"You have doubts?"

Leah was quietly distracted. "We're a very average chapter, Wendy. Don't you think so? What is there about 'Sarah Shenirer' that makes us special?"

"I don't know?" Wendy said with some exasperation. "I think we're good dressers."

Big guffaw. "Oh, sure! Our clothes! That makes us special? We're a suburban chapter, we dress conservatively. That's special? That's worth bragging about?"

Wendy looked crestfallen. "Come on, Leah. Give me a break. You dress well."

Leah reacted strongly. "But I don't expect a prize for it. I do it because it's expected."

The temperature was rising. "So who's talking about wining prizes here? All of a sudden we're talking about winning prizes? You've been president less than two ours and you already want a prize?"

They both leaned forward in their booth. Leah said. "We have to do something good to be a good chapter. We have to serve the community in some way, not just look good at dances."

"Look," Wendy said. "Community service is important. I agree, yes, we should do community service. All the girls will agree. But we're a good chapter anyway, Leah, the way I see it. We follow the rules and we have good intentions."

"Yes, well, we have to act on that."

Wendy made a soft salute. "Right, Captain. We do."

Leah demurred a little. "Yeah. That's right. We do."

The gleam in Wendy's eye was sparkling. "And we have to be well dressed when we do it."

A year later, Leah and Wendy were at the diner again, after an election in the chapter for a new executive. It had been a year of community action by 'Sarah Shenirer", an intense, exciting year with worthwhile memories for everyone. No one had been untouched.

"How do you feel, Leah? Relieved? Excited?"

Leah was characteristically thoughtful. "I think it was a good year."

"The Fashion Show at the hospital was the highlight, I think."

"The community newsletter is more important."

Wendy laughed. "I still have ink on my windbreaker."

Leah laughed. "She's going to make a good president, isn't she?"

A positive gesture. "Oh, yeah. She's going to get her name in lights. Except I hate the way she does her hair with those foolish bangs."

Leah winced. Despite her protests over looks not being important, she readily participated in discussing them "Wouldn't she look better with a sort of wave, you know, cascading over her brow?"

Wendy agreed. They were silent for a brief moment. Wendy said, "The world will never be same, will it?"

Leah looked up. "You mean President Kennedy?" Wendy nodded. "It'll get better again. We're a strong country." Then a shadow passed across Leah's face. "I'm concerned about Israel even more." She said. "Everything is so threatening."

Wendy asked with a suggestion of seriousness, "Do you consider it your homeland?"

"Well, I consider it to be my homeland in the sense that I think my heart is there. But I consider America to be my country."

"You know what I think?" Wendy asked sincerely.

"What"

"I think there have been some changes in you and I over this past year. Actually, in you more than in me."

Leah appeared interested. "Really?"

"You've come out of yourself. You take responsibility for your decisions more. You're serious, but when you laugh you really laugh. You allow yourself that, from time to time."

Leah laughed, as if to show that it was true. "You mean like that?"

"Yes, yes!' She settled in her seat. "You work for the newspaper. You did well in all your courses. And you have a boyfriend."

Leah's lips dropped wide in an expression of outrage. "Oh, Wendy! I do not have a boyfriend!"

"You do." Wendy persisted. "But you don't know it yet."

"Wendy." Leah looked at her with her head on a slant. "Don't you think I would know."

"Actually, I'm not sure you would."

Leah wrapped an invisible veil of indifference around her shoulders. "You're referring to Stephen. We are friends, that's true. And I like him, as a friend. But he's going to medical school in a year and I'm going to graduate school and we're not serious yet."

Wendy steadied her approach. "You like him because he's serious, don't you?"

"I like him because he believes in things."

"It's over for you." Wendy intoned. "You're outta the game. You're taken, girl, and I mean it."

In her secret heart, Leah wished that what Wendy said was true. She hadn't done any serious dating before she met Stephen. She was a religious girl and felt that God would bring the right person to her at the right time. This kind of faith was girlish, but it cushioned the insecurities of adolescence. Leah, though caught up in the swirl of romance more common to her friends, had kept her sights firmly on a family life. When she met Stephen, she believed there was a possible future for her. At first she resisted the possibility, but in time that resistance started to break down.

The first time she met him was at a B'nai Brith Youth Organization regional event. She was on a panel discussing the future role of women in Jewish society. Socialism, as it was understood in Israel, was a popular model for Jewish youth, and as a girl Leah had spent some time on a kibbutz. Marriage had become a broader forum for women than it had been before the sixties and in the corridors of BBYO it was not entirely common to find young people rushing towards it. Leah, who was a thoughtful person in everything she did, believed marriage was a goal she wished to reach, but she was aware that she it was not the destiny it had been for women before. Her mother and father, who had survived the war in Europe, were actually more worldly than the parents of most of Leah's friends. Some, of course, had served as soldiers. Still, that seemed to be a very personal and non-political experience compared to the world shattering devastation of the Holocaust. Her mother, especially, did not encourage Leah to marry young. She was very concerned that Leah take her time and deepen.

The moderator of the panel was a woman, but two of the members were young men. One of them was a very lithe boy with longish dark hair and almost transparent complexion. His eyes were deep brown but his smile was lively. He was serious, but he had an engaging sense of humour. He had the lovely quality of making people laugh. He was one of only a few boys who wore a skull cap.

At a certain point, after discussing Jewish traditions for women and the emerging possibilities, Leah and Stephen got into a debate.

"If Jews are to play a role in society, women have to be leaders not followers." Leah stated. "It doesn't matter if they are wives and mother's as well. They can be doctors, teachers, anything."

"Yes, definitely, they can be all or any of these things. But all at the same time?"

The audience laughed. Leah said. "Why not? Men are."

The group laughed again, including Stephen. "In Judaism, we believe that women are superior to men."

Leah responded steadily. "That's right. They are considered closer to God. But even so, they have to obey their husband."

"We all have to obey someone, somehow. And this is not law. It's convention. It's politics of the home."

Leah bristled visibly. "Can I get a divorce?"

Stephen smiled. "Please, Leah." He whispered, "We're not married."

Leah crossed her arms in mock protest. "And we never will be, at this rate."

Everyone felt very lighthearted over this. They bantered on. Leah defended the role of marriage in Jewish life. Stephen revealed that he was more radical than that. He believed women should be completely equal to men. He believed they could have children outside of marriage and that society should adapt to this reality.

It was strange that Stephen should feel this way, since it appeared he was somewhat observant. When the event was over, later, when they were at the social closing hour, he approached Leah while she was sitting at a round party table talking with a Wendy.

"You have a very good chapter." He wore a bright, engaging smile.

Leah looked at him cautiously. "Thanks. But why do you say so?"

"I've talked to a few of them and they are all sparkling personalities."

Leah leered knowingly. "I think you exaggerate. You're just impressed because they're as bright as you are."

Stephen scratched his head. "I guess they are. They seem to love their president."

"I'm only a representative of their desires. I'm an organizer."

"I think that's modesty."

Leah shot back, "Do you?"

Stephen recovered. "Not false modesty, mind you. Look, I talk a good shtick, but in reality I'm not a mover at all. I love women…"

Leah jumped in. "I'm sure you do!"

"No, no. I mean I love them politically. I'm in favour of them."

Again. "I believe you're making it worse." Wendy was laughing out loud.

"Let me start again, okay?"

Leah made a face like she were debating it. "Okay." She said.

Stephen took a breath. "I'm really very shy and I don't do this to girls as a rule. I think you are nice and intelligent and I wonder…if you would mind giving me your phone number?"

Leah shook her head slowly. "I'm sorry, but I don't date boys I don't know."

Stephen appeared shaken. "But I'm not asking for a date."

"Then what are you asking for?'

Stephen was serious. "A conversation."

Wendy covered her mouth and looked at the floor. Leah said. "You want to talk to me?"

Stephen threw his arms in the air. "What else?"

Leah looked at Wendy in mock disbelief. "You want to talk about religion?"

He shook his head in assent. "Definitely. My favorite topic."

"You want to talk about the role of women in Jewish society?"

"Yes!"

She looked at him squarely. "And you want my phone number?"

Stephen looked on the verge of collapse. "Yes! Can I have it?"

They held a pose, looking squarely at each other, for a few seconds. "Yes." She said.

"Oh thank God!" said Stephen. "I thought you were going to say you didn't have a phone."

In late December, three month's after she had been elected president of her chapter, Leah went out with Stephen for their first conversation. He didn't pick her up; they met at a café on the university campus. It was during Hanukah and Stephen brought a gift for her. It wasn't wrapped. It was a book by Erich Fromm called *The Art of Loving*. He didn't give it to her right away. He sat down across for her at the small table.

"I thought you'd be early." He said almost triumphantly.

"I was on campus anyway. I wasn't very early."

"I was here too. I had a meeting with the Israel Council."

Leah looked surprised. "The Israel Council? Aren't they a socialist organization?"

Stephen shook his head. "Not exactly socialist. They believe in freedom and dignity for all people."

"Isn't that what the *Torah* believes in, too?"

"That's just the point. The *Torah* isn't only spiritual. It's political as well. It gives law, it encourages and guides civilization. Modern Israel is based on it."

"It's not based on dictatorship, state ownership and oppression."

Stephen didn't flinch. "Neither is socialism."

It wasn't a subtle discussion. It was a contest, really. But it set the scene for the relationship that was to follow. Leah was innately defensive with Stephen because it was her nature to strong. In this event, the first time she had seriously considered seeing someone, it was natural for her to be wary. And Stephen encouraged that because he was also strong, although less focused than Leah. His forceful intellect both challenged and attracted her and his funny, sometimes clumsy manner endeared her. After discussing politics for half an hour, Stephen made a short gesture of surprise.

"Oh, gosh!" he said. "I forgot! I brought something for you." He reached into his worn leather satchel and awkwardly pulled out the book. "You might like this." he said, and he handed it to her over the table.

Disguising her disappointment that he was giving her a book on their first meeting, thinking maybe it would be something a little more genuine, she took it carefully from his hand. "*The Art of Loving.*" She looked at Stephen accusingly. "Is this a sex book!" she demanded.

Stephen was vividly apologetic. " No, no. Not even a bit. It's about our capacity to love one another."

This didn't help. "Oh!" Leah slapped the book on the table. "You're assuming that I don't know how to love?"

Stephen was waving his arms in the air in front of him. "No, Leah, no! I would never assume that. It's about they psychology of love. The deeper meaning of love!"

Leah relaxed slightly into her seat. "Isn't love a rather controversial topic for our first conversation?"

Stephen reached out across the table for the slim book. "I'm sorry. That's not what I meant. I just meant that love is something we all have in common and the more we know about it the better off we are. Here. Give it to me."

Leah pulled the volume back. "No, it's okay. I'm interested in the book but I'm not interested in making a statement about love."

Stephen smiled a sly smile. "It's written by a Jewish doctor."

Leah slapped the book hard on his hand. "Maybe I should date him."

Stephen was stunned. "We're dating?"

Leah's face changed to a knowing leer. "Just a common expression. We're still having a conversation."

It took several more conversations at several different places on several more occasions before either of them we're in any way comfortable with the concept that they were anything more than friends. Leah, especially, wanted to delay that moment for as long as she could. But the more she saw of Stephen, the more she began to like him in a way that slowly seemed very special. She didn't always agree with his politics, and he was very political. But his interests in religious issues stimulated her. Stephen was controversial, by her standards, but he was honest and simple at the same time. Her parents liked him but thought he was scattered. They didn't disapprove of the relationship because Leah seemed so balanced within it.

By the end of her term as president of Sarah Schenirer, most of the people she knew thought they were a pair. It was actually them who were to be the last to know.

CHAPTER 39
Science and Arts

At the end of her first year at college Leah was sponsored by her father to take a six week trip, first to Europe for three weeks and then to Israel. Asher wanted her to see the places he had been and Rivka had lived in Hungary, Poland and Germany. He tutored her in the history of the war and he and his wife's personal history. He and Rivka had not talked about the war very much before this since they felt Leah was too young to understand and they thought it would only frighten her. Still, Leah new her father had been a Chaplin and she had an idea, although not in any detail, that her mother had been in the camps.

"Your mother was in Auschwitz for a while. It was the first camp she was in."

Leah looked deeply at his hands as he spoke. "That's the most famous of the camps, isn't it?"

"Yes. Because it was one of the biggest. Because it was an extermination camp and because the Americans liberated it."

Through the whole discussion, Leah held a look of some confusion and concern. "Daddy, how did she survive."

"She was lucky and she had friends. Aunty Wanda was her friend."

"I knew that, but I didn't know that they were friends in Auschwitz."

"Did they escape?"

Asher let a cool breath escape. "Almost no one escaped, Leah. You couldn't escape. They managed to survive and they were liberated by the Russians."

"Oh!" Leah looked confused. "That's funny. I guess I thought the Russians were the enemy."

Asher's eyes softened. "Not during the war. They were the allies."

"But now they're an enemy, right."

"Don't you know anything about the war from school?"

Leah looked baffled. "Not from High School, really. I know about the Nazis. I know about the Holocaust from Hebrew school and B'nai Brith. People have come to talk to us about it. But I didn't know that Russia was an ally during the war. I only know that they are communists and that they hate America."

Asher looked at his daughter with a gentle smile. "The Russians were communists during the war too. But they were against Germany. There's an expression, 'the enemy of my enemy is my friend.'."

Leah grimaced. "That sounds awfully…I don't know…calculating."

Asher laughed out loud. "Oh, the end of the war was a political quagmire. The Russians and the Americans raced to reach Berlin. In the end, they each occupied a different half of Germany and Berlin. That's when the Berlin Wall went up and the Iron Curtain came down."

"How did mom get out?"

"Oh, that's another story for another time. She made it to the American side. That's where I met her."

Leah looked puzzled. "I think I sort of knew that." Then she looked at Asher directly but without intent. "Daddy, did Mom have any family that she lost at Auschwitz?"

Asher's eyes went misty, but he didn't show surprise. "She had a sister. She lost her in the war."

Leah became thoughtful. "She would be my aunt." She looked again, this time more seriously, at Asher. "What was her name?"

"Miriam."

She paused just for a moment, as though trying out the name. "Aunt Miriam. Hmm."

Asher offered a bit more information to her. "You lost your grandfather too. Your grandmother died before the war began."

"I guess I just get so much love from Bubbie and Zaide that I don't think about momma's side." She gave a little shrug. "I never think of myself as the child of a Holocaust survivor. Isn't that funny? I just think of myself as an American."

"No. You lost family. That's why I want you to visit Auschwitz. You should know about your history."

Leah's trip through Europe was with a one Jewish youth group, and her trip to Israel was with B'nai Brith. She had a two day stopover in Berlin. Before she left she had the most serious conversation she had ever had with Stephen.

He was political on the Left. He was the only person Leah knew who wasn't totally wrapped up in the future of Israel. In the time that Leah knew him he became less and less observant of Jewish ways.

"Israel is surviving by the skin of it's teeth, you know." He said.

"Yes." Leah agreed. "It is. But I believe in Israel."

"I believe in Israel too. But not like you do."

Leah was shocked. "What do you mean?"

He waved his hand in the air like a flag. "You believe in the soft, cuddly Israel only a brutal animal would hurt."

Leah was surprised by this. "No I don't. I believe in the Israel that has to struggle to survive, just like you do."

Stephen shook his head. "Your Israel is innocent. My Israel is not."

Leah reacted to this. "So, you're Israel is guilty of something?"

Stephen didn't want to conflict with Leah, he only wanted to inform her. "Alright, not exactly guilty, but not exactly innocent either. We occupy land that was occupied by another only a few years ago."

"That's true but we deserve that land and it was given to us by the United Nations."

Stephen wanted to make his point. "I just want you to know that it's a very political situation and there are different sides to it."

"You want me to take a different side? Maybe support Egypt's intention to wipe Israel and all of the Jews into the sea? Is that what you want?"

"No. Of course not."

"Would you have sympathized with the Nazi's because they had a point of view?"

"No. This is different."

Leah was angry now. "No, this is the same. The Nazi's were evil murderers who wanted to annihilate the Jews and dominate the world. Isn't that true? You couldn't sympathize with them, that would be unthinkable. The Arabs want the same thing. Alright, maybe they don't want to dominate the world, but they state, unequivocally, that they want to destroy Israel and kill all Jews. The Russians want to dominate the world. You know what the Torah says: In every generation they rise up against us, but the Lord protects us'. That's what I believe. What do you believe?"

Stephen rallied. "I believe in the equality of all people. I believe in justice for all. I believe in liberty and freedom from oppression. But I don't believe in fairytales about countries."

Leah was thinking about her conversation with Asher. "You think the Holocaust was a fairytale?"

Stephen became vivid. "That's what I mean. The Holocaust gave a rationale for the State of Israel. Now we have to defend ourselves, it's true. No one believes in that more than me. But, believe it or not, the world doesn't revolve around the Jews. That's the fairytale."

Leah responded with energy. She had never been so far in a political discussion. "We have to fight for Israel because the rest of the world will not. And, yes, the Jews are at the centre of the world, if you must know. Just like any nation will put itself there. And we, America, are at the centre too, because we are American. It's our values that make the world safe and sound, not the values of the Arabs and the Russians who only want to destroy and dominate. We stand for freedom, and if you are trying to convince me that we don't or that we shouldn't you should go and join them."

Stephen took a moment to look at Leah in a different way. "Look. I'm proud to be a Jew and I'm proud to be an American. I just don't think we own every truth."

"Why shouldn't we?"

"Well, if you give me a minute we will!" It was the first time his voice had risen. "Do you think there is no inequality in the rest of the world? Do you think there is only hunger or poverty or oppression anywhere but Israel? If Israel were threatened seriously I would go there to help in a minute. That's because I do believe, like you do, that our right to survive is necessary. But I have some conscience about it, too. It's not the only fight. It's the fight that I happen to be responsible to."

This conversation stayed with Leah long after it occurred. But instead of making her less conscious of being a Jew, it made her more conscious of it. It became, in her mind, not a matter of truth or even justice to support Israel. It became a matter of absolute necessity and realism. What stuck in her mind, as she visited the horrors of Auschwitz and the cities of Europe, was that this was her legacy directly, her persecution to redress. The existence of Israel became even more vital as her trip went on, until by the time she actually arrived in Haifa she was rippling with anxiety and concern. She felt, as she had not felt before, that this was her place, even, perhaps, her destiny. Her Hebrew was fluent. When she descended from the plane and Wanda's warm arms wrapped around her she hugged her like a patriot, not like a friend from a far away land. She had become political, in a very specific way.

While on the trip, Leah had been keeping a journal to appear in her college newspaper. A first, it was hard and she had to force herself to put words on paper, as writing can sometimes be. But after Auschwitz it became easier and by the time she reached Amsterdam the prose was simply flowing. She attacked each entry with passion and energy. At first, her writing was most like a travelogue. By Israel, it had become a personal column with acute insights and perceptive commentary.

When she returned to Rochester Leah was a changed person. Her devotion to the ideals of Judaism was charged and shot through with purpose. It was more now than an identity and a faithfulness. It was a cause and a passion.

Also, she had become politicized. Whereas before the trip she had only vague insights into the importance of being a Jew, when she arrived back home she was aware of the rationale for persistence and action. The state of Israel had become a statement for a cause; a reference to the whole world of the necessity of resistance, hope and justice.

Two days after her return she met Stephen in their favorite coffee shop. Leah was a few minutes late. She was unsure about what their meeting might bring, since she had undergone a kind of transformation. She was not sure what he would mean to her now that she felt more focused, more independent. She saw him at a table near the rear of the shop. She noticed right away; he was not wearing a skull cap.

She walked to the round table and sat down immediately. She said 'Hi' brightly. "I didn't recognize you without a kepha."

He grimaced. "I've been thinking."

"About Judaism?"

His face fell into an expression of concern. "About Judaism, yes. And about hypocrisy."

Wanting to be even. "Are they somehow connected?"

Stephen shook his head in a measured gesture. "No. Not implicitly. But for me, to portray devotion when I am unsure is not right."

The idea that Stephen was unsure didn't seem solid. "Are you unsure that you are Jewish?"

"No. I'm unsure that religion is the best way to relate to the rest of the world."

Leah rested on that thought for a moment while they both took a sip of coffee. "This is a considered opinion."

Stephen had a brief answer. "It's been coming since I was 10 years old, if that's important. I observed for my family, not for myself. Now I'm 21. I have to live my life according my own ideals. I think of it as a moment of self expression that has been coming for a long time."

"So it's not a statement?"

Stephen winced. "You know, I never hated being a Jew. I have always embraced it. I have learned Jewish ideals and I have projected a Jewish identity. But in my heart I have always felt that this was a vehicle that carried me to a greater maturity, maybe even a greater purpose."

Leah wanted to be critical. She didn't want to move him but she wanted to shake his reasons. "This vehicle has taken you somewhere where it is no longer necessary to be a Jew?"

"Just because I am not fully observant doesn't mean I'm not a Jew."

"Yes, but it changes what it means to be a Jew."

Stephen felt his emotions bristle. "What does it mean to be a Jew, Leah? Does it mean being separate to the rest of the world? You wear a kappa, so you are distinct? You prepare your food in a distinct way so you are necessarily better?"

Leah rallied around these points. "Yes, it means you are distinct, but it's not the fact of distinction that makes you a Jew, it's the belief in God and civilization and a better world."

Stephen responded with both reason and passion. "Leah, you know this, I can't eat with other people. I can't go into their homes and join them in their own cultures. I can't visit in other countries because of this distinction. The kosher laws are not a statement of any kind of faith. They're a symbol that I reject the entire world that is not precisely the same as mine."

"You can visit. You can't reject your own laws."

"Yes, well. Who made the laws and for what reasons."

Leah's face became briefly incongruent. "You forget the most fundamental purpose of the law, which is to worship God and carry His covenant through all time."

Stephen looked at the floor. "This is an issue of faith, Leah, not reason."

She bent over very slightly to see his face. "But faith is everything,

Stephen. It's faith that has brought us through two millennium. It's faith that has brought us to the State of Israel."

He looked up again and into her concerned eyes. "Maybe faith, Leah. Maybe sound political thinking. I don't know which one is more real."

"You've neglected God in your plan, Stephen. You've neglected the very most essential element of who we are. Jews are not anything if they are not the nation that received the Torah, and we are nothing if we neglect or abandon that responsibility."

Stephen withdrew into himself slightly while addressing Leah's point. "I'd be a hypocrite if I used Judaism to rationalize my approach to life. There is no doubt that I am a Jew and I will always be a Jew. But I can't let outdated traditions and superstitions and mythology itself make me useless."

"And God?" Leah queried.

"God will judge me, Leah. No one else."

They paused, took sips of coffee in the silence. Stephen said, "I know this ruins us."

Leah looked away. "Do you want a divorce?"

Stephen laughed. "You will always remain remarkable to me."

Leah smiled crookedly. She held up her coffee cup. "To the rest of the world!"

He raised his cup too. "To the rest of the world! Let's make it work!"

In September, Leah resumed her studies. Two weeks into the term the editor of the college paper confronted her in the science lounge. She was a senior with a reputation for innovation.

Leah was working through a physics problem. The editor, Janice, stood in front of her and flicked Leah's book. "Hey!" She said. "If a newspaper is falling with a velocity of 4,500 copies per issue, does it land in refuse bin or the pub?"

Leah looked up and smiled. "It depends upon the direction of the wind."

Janice smiled genially. "I have a proposition for you."

"For me?"

"Yes. We need someone to cover college clubs, but I want it to be more than just the tired old boring reports. I want commentary and I want some humour. That's not an easy mix when you're dealing with the sensitive issues of racial and cultural identities. I want it as a column each week and I want you to do it. Is that a problem?"

Leah thought of her priorities briefly. "No. It's not a problem."

This was good news. "Come by the office later and I'll fill you in on the details."

Leah said okay.

As Janice left, walking with her characteristic sway down the hall, Leah thought about her time. This would be a challenge. A flicker of concern crossed her mind. She had to wonder where things were going with her. There was a major conflict developing in her mind.

In the middle of October that conflict had become strongly disruptive and presented a major obstacle looming over her existence. When she was helping Rivka in the kitchen one day, shelling peas, she let it out.

"Mom?" she said lightly but with an open questioning inflection.

"Yes?"

"I have a lot to do on the newspaper."

Knowingly. "I know. You're a good writer. I think you are a writer who always seems to have something interesting to say."

"You know, I think that's quite a compliment, Mom. I like writing."

"Hm-hm." Absently, Rivka was focused on cooking.

"I like writing and I like studying politics."

Again. "That's good, sweet. That's very good."

Leah said pointedly. "I like sciences too."

Rivka immediately sensed something was going on. Not from what Leah had said but from the emphasis she had used in saying it."

"So?" she said emphatically. "You like both writing and science. You're well rounded."

Leah hesitantly tried to express herself. "I think about what I'm doing, mom. What I want to do. Science is good. I could maybe be a teacher."

"Or a doctor."

There was a pause. "I don't want to be a doctor, mom. It's not the job I want."

Rivka paused too. "And why not?"

"I like working on the newspaper. I like being involved in the process of putting it together. I like following stories. I enjoy being a part of the world politically."

Rivka sat down beside her daughter. She had always wanted Leah to be her own person and make her own decisions. She didn't want to influence her by expressing a bias. But for Rivka, politics was only an excuse for one group to dominate another. The war had been politics. Rivka wanted Leah to be religious, because she believed that alone was enduring. She preferred that Leah become a physician for many reasons. Personal independence was one.

"What are you telling me, Leah? Medicine is not meaningful enough."

"I would not be happy, momma. I like being analytical and funny and a part of something dynamic. Like a newspaper."

Rivka put her hands on Leah's hands. "This is your decision. Journalism, politics these are not as necessary to life as medicine. And it's much harder to make a living and be successful. A journalist may have to travel a great deal. Is this very good for a Jewish girl?"

"Even Jewish girls want to know the truth."

Rivka almost smirked. "There are all kinds of truth, Leah. Sometimes it's so that we have to choose a truth and stick to it no matter what. Maybe not everyone agrees with your truth, you still have to keep it."

"But a journalist tells the truth from every perspective."

"No. They tell the truth from the perspective of their newspaper."

There was a still, but not unfriendly, moment. "Mom, I think it's in my blood. For the first time, for me, I really believe I know what I want, not only what I'm interested in."

Rivka looked at her daughter's face. She was not happy with the choice at all, but she was happy with her daughter for knowing what he wanted. Even though it was wrong in her eyes. "So, what do you want to do?"

"I want to change my major from science to arts."

Rivka looked into her own heart for a moment. "No." she said. "Stay with science, but stay also with the newspaper. You can do both. Then, when you graduate, you will have a choice. If you want to be a journalist, your science background won't prevent you. And if you want to study medicine, maybe that will be possible too."

Leah looked at her hands. In her mind, she had lost, but at least not completely. She wouldn't contradict her mother. "Okay, mom. I'll stay with science."

Rivka made a strong gesture, a maternal gesture. She took her sister's daughter's down turned chin in her hand and looked into her eyes. "You are a bright and talented girl, Leah. But I want you to promise me something. Promise me that whatever road your future might hold, you will always be observant of your Jewish role. This is the only safety, this is the only constant that you need to know. From this will come every meaning, from this will come happiness. All the rest is only dressing for the part."

Although she was not unhappy, a small tear rolled down Leah's right cheek, much more from tension than emotion. "Of course, mama. You don't have to tell me that."

By the new year Leah's column in the college paper was so popular mail praising her work was pouring in. Janice also had her do feature articles every few weeks. Her studies were fine. Her academic focus on science subjects gave a refreshing, objective slant to the writing

At the beginning of her third year Janice, who was wrapping up her tenure and moving on, again approached her with a proposition. They were in the newspaper office, organizing some equipment when they sat down together for a break.

"So who's the new editor?" Janice asked provocatively.

Leah looked sincerely curious. "I don't know? Who?"

"I don't know. We need someone with experience."

"That's for sure."

"Someone who can lead and someone who can meet deadlines."

"Right."

"At the same time, someone who's creative."

"Definitely."

Janice looked convinced. "I know someone!"

"Who."

Janice pointed at Leah. "You."

Leah could have reacted with surprise, but she didn't. She said, quietly, "Me?"

"Yeah."

Leah looked around as if collecting her thoughts. But she didn't equivocate. She knew that she was sound in this decision. "Okay. Okay."

This meant an escalation of activity and commitment for Leah. There was one thing she was sure of as she began. Being a journalist and being a Jew would not prove incompatible. As many times as there would be problems, she would find renewal in her religion. As many men as might press her for attention and intimacy she would hold out for the one whose soul was pure and deep. There would be a jest around the newspaper. They would call her 'The Virgin Queen." She didn't mind too much. She had faith, and that was stronger than anything on earth.

CHAPTER 40
The Six-Day War

We knew, early in the 1960's, that a major war was imminent and we knew that it would be decisive for our survival. The rhetoric of the Arab states steadily increased during that time. As Nasser, the President of Egypt told the United Arab Republic National assembly in March of 1964, "The danger of Israel lies in the very existence of Israel as it is in the present and in what she represents." More than words alone signalled this great offensive. Egypt, Syria, Jordan and the other Arab nations were preparing military operations in unison and their cooperation was unsettling.

As early as 1965 preparations were being made to face this inevitable confrontation. No one knew when it would happen or what the specific circumstances would be, but we knew we had to be ready for whatever they might be. Strategies were laid out and personnel were being trained.

My commander called me to see him in January of 1965. He greeted me formally but immediately encouraged me to be more relaxed.

"Avrum, your unit is in good shape, is that right?"

I considered my response carefully. "It's been a while since they have been tested by battle, Sir. We are on constant manoeuvres, but we lack that sharp edge which comes from a real fight. Individually we are all in good shape. We work well as a team. If we were put into an operation today our morale would be strong, but the powerful trust and assurance that gives a unit like ours a practical edge would probably be lacking."

My commander knew what he was looking for. I did not. "It's no secret that a conflict is on it's way?"

"No, Sir. Everyone is aware we are going to have to fight for our existence."

He offered me a cup of tea from a pot on his desk. "How do you think we should prepare?"

I took the delicate cup from his hand. My hand was steady. It did not shake. "I would think that two things are necessary, overall: morale and good strategic planning. As a people, we need to feel very much that we are close members of one army. No one will have the luxury of living only for themselves. They have to live for each other."

His gaze fell upon my eyes. "And strategically?"

My heart was in this answer. I had given it quite a bit of thought. "We are a small force most likely to be vastly outnumbered. We will have a hard time beating them on the ground. We have to strike effectively at the heart of their operations, like a sharp knife, and kill their command."

The commander placed his teacup on his desk. "You are speaking now as the leader of a special operations unit?"

"As a soldier, sir. I'm only a soldier. I am not an expert in strategy."

A wry smile crossed his features. "Very good, Bar Kochba, but you are actually well versed in strategy in fact. I want to make use of that as well as your field experience."

I also placed my cup back on his desk. "Yes, Sir."

He stood straight up from his position of leaning back upon the edge of the desk. "We want to plan a quick, highly effective and dangerous operation in Jerusalem. We don't know the exact details yet, they will be contingent on specific circumstances. It will most likely involve extremely covert measures. You will be behind enemy lines. Your operatives will be disguised. They will need to be fluent in the language and manner of the enemy. They will need to be utterly sure of the precise details of their mission and they will have to be uniquely sensitive to their role as a team. I believe your experience in covert operations is essential to the success of this kind of strategic operation, Avrum. You are going to lead it."

I nodded slightly. "Thank you, Sir."

He continued. "I want your unit to train with extreme vigour in Arab language and military culture. They are to be in top physical strength, ready to entirely act by reflex to any contingency. They must master every form of combat, especially with weapons that are silent. They must be able to appear to be Arab soldiers in every way."

I took a brief moment to respond. I didn't want to seem unappreciative of what he had said. "Sir. Our unit has carried out covert operations before, so we will not be entirely unfamiliar with these elements."

"Yes, I know. But you will need to start training right away. There are officers who will assist with this. You will personally help train your personnel and you will also be trained along with them."

I was pleased with that. "Yes, Sir." I relied. I stood up.

He glanced at my standing form. "This will be rigorous." He said. "We don't know when the actual aggressions will begin. Please God, you will be ready when it does."

We began training almost immediately. My commander had not lied; it was vigorous and prolonged. It began in January of 1965. We did not know our specific mission until the Spring of 1967.

BAR KOCHBA

On May 15, Israel's Independence Day, Egyptian troops began moving into the Sinai and massing near the Israeli border. By May 18, Syrian troops were prepared for battle along the Golan Heights.

Nasser ordered the UN. Emergency Force, stationed in the Sinai since 1956 as a buffer between Israeli and Egyptian forces after Israel's withdrawal following the Sinai Campaign, to withdraw on May 16. Without bringing the matter to the attention of the General Assembly (as his predecessor had promised), Secretary-General U Thant complied with the demand. After the withdrawal of the UNEF, the Voice of the Arabs radio station proclaimed on May 18, 1967:

"As of today, there no longer exists an international emergency force to protect Israel. We shall exercise patience no more. We shall not complain any more to the UN about Israel. The sole method we shall apply against Israel is total war, which will result in the extermination of Zionist existence."

An enthusiastic echo was heard May 20 from Syrian Defense Minister Hafez Assad:

"Our forces are now entirely ready not only to repulse the aggression, but to initiate the act of liberation itself, and to explode the Zionist presence in the Arab homeland. The Syrian army, with its finger on the trigger, is united... I, as a military man, believe that the time has come to enter into a battle of annihilation"

These threats and actions were specific and clear, but the most crucial event occurred immediately following. On May 22, Egypt closed the Straits of Tiran to all Israeli shipping and all ships bound for Eilat. This blockade cut off Israel's only supply route with Asia and stopped the flow of oil from its main supplier, Iran.

This closing of the Straits of Tiran were effectively a declaration of war.

Nasser was aware of the pressure he was exerting to force Israel's hand. The day after the blockade was set up, he said defiantly: "The Jews threaten to make war. I reply: Welcome! We are ready for war."

Nasser's deliberate challenge to Israel was to initiate the fight. On May 27 he stated, "Our basic objective will be the destruction of Israel. The Arab people want to fight," The following day, he added: "We will not accept any…coexistence with Israel…Today the issue is not the establishment of peace between the Arab states and Israel…The war with Israel is in effect since 1948."

Clearly, these words, coupled with the immediate military build up, were a direct threat. On May 30. Nasser announced:

"The armies of Egypt, Jordan, Syria and Lebanon are poised on the borders of Israel…to face the challenge, while standing behind us are the armies of Iraq, Algeria, Kuwait, Sudan and the whole Arab nation. This act will astound the world. Today they will know that the Arabs are arranged for battle, the critical hour has arrived. We have reached the stage of serious action and not declarations."

His statement was supported by the mobilization of Arab forces. Approximately 465,000 troops, more than 2,800 tanks, and 800 aircraft ringed Israel. At that time,. Israeli forces had been on alert for three weeks. We could not remain fully mobilized indefinitely, and we could not withstand the sea lane through the Gulf of Aqaba to be cut off for very long.

In response to this dire situation, the Israeli commanders took what turned out to be a decisive step in what became known as the Six Day

War. Realizing that they had to strike very hard and very quick at the key element of the enemies intent, they decided to pre-empt the expected Arab attack. On June 5, Prime Minister Eshkol gave the order to attack Egypt. To do this successfully, Israel needed the element of surprise. Had it waited for an Arab invasion, Israel would have been at a potentially catastrophic disadvantage.

The attack was precise and unexpected. In a unified and immediate attack almost the entire Israeli air force, consisting of approximately 200 planes, took to the air, leaving only 12 planes behind for potential defence. Their objective was to attack the Egyptian air force at their fields. They were airborne at 7:45 A.M.

The Egyptians were unprepared for this pre-emptive manoeuvre. Our planes came in beneath the radar cover and while most pilots were at breakfast. We used a mixed attack strategy, both bombing and strafing planes and ruining runways so that planes that were operational could not leave the ground. Because the Israeli Air Force had steadily drilled it's ground crews on effective and very quick refitting of returning aircraft they were able to create several successive wave of attack. During that first day, we were ourselves attacked by Jordanian, Syrian and Iraqi planes, and we also attacked their air forces.

The Egyptian Air Force consisted of approximately 400 air craft. Israel claimed that they destroyed approximately 300 of them. In turn, we lost 19 or our planes. At this point, and until the end of the war, Israel maintained air superiority.

Both Egypt and Israel first announced they had been attacked. Prime Minister Levi Eshkol sent a Message to King Hussein on June 5 saying Israel would not attack Jordan unless he initiated hostilities. In a mistaken moment, when Jordanian radar picked up a cluster of planes flying from

Egypt to Israel, and the Egyptians convinced Hussein the planes were theirs, he ordered the shelling of West Jerusalem. It turned out that the planes were Israel's and were returning from destroying the Egyptian air force on the ground.

As the engagement began, our special unit was in preparation for an operation. Although we had been ready for weeks, we didn't know the exact details of what we would be instructed to do. Even as our war planes flew over Egypt, our unit was awaiting specific instructions. Our readiness to perform, however was very high. It included:

Careful knowledge of Arabic and the protocol of Jordanian soldiers, including the designation of specific ranks for each of our 20 men.

Full capability in close combat techniques, including small arms, use of bayonet and knife, martial arts techniques, and field first aid.

The inclusion in our group of a professional actor, entirely fluent in Arabic, to impersonate a Jordanian officer.

By the morning of June 6, as battles were being fought on every front, we received orders. Just after dawn we were assembled in a field tent near the outskirts of Jerusalem. All of my men were calm and attentive. We were dressed in standard fatigues. It was to be the last time we were to bare any sign of belonging to the Israeli Defense Forces.

It was my own Commander who stood before us in front of a large scale map of the area in and around the Old City of Jerusalem. None of us had ever been there.

"We don't know how things will go in Jerusalem." He began. "We do not expect to enter the Old City unless or until we can do so without endangering the Temple Mount and the Western Wall. The Jordanians will not let that go easily, and they have a decided advantage. Precisely, they maintain guns in strategic positions above the city." He pointed to five places on the map, saying "Here. Here. Here. Here. Here."

He looked at us with a concerned visage. "If we move, they have us in their sights. In order to take Old Jerusalem, we have to eliminate these positions. We can't do that with artillery. Paratroops are not possible. We need to surprise the enemy."

His tone became almost confidential. "We need to disable those guns without the knowledge of the command or they will simply replace them immediately. It is not only a matter of destroying the guns themselves. It is necessary to eliminate the personnel. Without alerting the command itself. Only then will our troops be able to occupy Jerusalem. We need to pierce the defenses encircling the Old City, reach these guns, and eliminate the personnel so quickly, so effectively, so covertly that the Jordanian command will not even know they are gone until we are in the city."

"Your officers will have specific objectives. There are several elements each of you must keep in mind. Your success depends not only on the effectiveness of your deployment. It depends upon the complete seamlessness of your deception. You must not think of yourselves as Israeli soldiers disguised as Jordanians. You must think of yourselves as Jordanian soldiers. You must carry your purpose within you, to arise at the right time. This is essential."

He stooped slightly forward as he said this, perhaps burdened be the necessity of his message. "You must eliminate every enemy soldier with the utmost prejudice and covertness. No man must remain to alert any other personnel. You need to act with impeccable speed and effectiveness. You will take their positions and you will hold them until our troops are in place. You will return when Jerusalem is secure."

This was as much an inspirational speech as a briefing. Earlier in the morning I had been given more specific details. We were as ready for our assignment as we could be, not only physically but emotionally also. Each one of us recognized the import of our goal. It was the re-taking of the Old City of Jerusalem, the Western Wall and the Temple Mount. These were the ornaments of our existence as Jews. The strategic worth of our task was clear, but it was the psychological aspect that beat in all our hearts. We were ready. But even more, we were on fire with the meaning of this.

That day we prepared. We donned our Jordanian uniforms and fitted them not only with standard weapons but also with some hidden on our bodies. We practiced retrieving and using every piece. We spoke only Arabic. In our five command groups we rehearsed the roles we would enact. By evening, we were ready at the side of our cars. There was a sense of calm. We were well trained troops, ready for our designated mission.

Each of our five units were directed to a specific enemy position. Although the nests operated separately, they were connected to a single command centre located at the centre of their span which was spread out, more or less equally, over a field of about 3 kilometers. Each unit had its own leader, who was not necessarily the soldier with the highest Jordanian rank. My unit was the keystone. We would arrive at the command centre slightly before the others arrived at their designated sites.

The actor portraying a high ranking Jordanian officer rode with me. His role was to engage the personnel at the command centre and allow my two comrades and me to eliminate the enemy. He would then take over the radio and prevent the other four operators from having any suspicions about the soldiers who would be arriving. Those units would carry out the operation and man the radio as if it were normal.

We left our posts in the night, around 1:00 A.M. We each came in at such a location that we were undetected until we were in Jordanian held territory. This was possible because clear lines of defense were not in place yet, made especially difficult due to the irregular nature of the city. But reaching our specific destinations was not easy. One of our armored vehicles was stopped for several minutes, but eventually was let past since one of our men seemingly outranked theirs. My vehicle was stopped about a kilometer before our destination by three Jordanian soldiers. They wanted to radio our papers to headquarters. This would be entirely disastrous. I was disguised a Lieutenant, sitting in the back of the Jeep. As my 'superior' argued, I got out of the vehicle as if to stretch my legs. Without drawing attention I killed the three quickly and silently. We dragged their bodies to safe hiding place. It wasn't the best outcome, but we had anticipated that something like this would happen. We continued on our way.

The plan was for our group to achieve its objective and, once accomplished, for me and the false officer to travel to the other sites to ensure that our program was effective. When we arrived at the command centre there were 12 Jordanians manning the site. They were very busy, in preparation for battle. The radio was housed in a small building behind the guns. Our imposter identified himself. The sergeant accepted his papers and he went into the building. When he had done that, my men and I had to begin. There were seven of us. There were 9 Jordanians spread about the guns, three more of whom were with the radio. We had to eliminate each of them without making a sound.

One of my associates got the attention of two of the soldiers and they stood around the vehicle talking. The other commando stood behind them discussing something with another. I stood behind the other two as if taking a smoking break. Without giving a sign we all moved at the same time. I had each hand on a knife hidden on my lower back. I drew than quickly and without hesitating I struck each of the men before me, but I missed my mark with the one on the left and although he staggered he didn't fall. He was a strong man and a good soldier. He drew his weapon before I could stop him, wheeled around and fired. The shot caught me in the shoulder, but before it struck I had thrown my knife and caught him in the chest. He dropped to the ground and I was hurled backwards. That was bad enough, but worse was that a shot had been fired.

The operative in the car took out his two men and the other comrade did the same. There were still three of the enemy in the building. Many years of training were commanding my reactions now. I rose immediately to my feet and threw myself at the remaining Jordanians. One of my men was soon beside me. I was acting almost instinctively. I cut the throat quickly of one man and immediately struck another in the heart with the same weapon. My partner took out the third Jordanian and our actor, who was a very brave and competent man, was at the radio. At first, he was unsure whether or not any of the other sites had been alerted to any danger. But soon he received a leading question from one of the sites. He was able to deflect it, but it was not a good sign. He informed the operator that a car would be arriving shortly. We hoped that would be enough cover, but we had to do something.

The other location was less than a kilometer away. My wound was not at issue; the fact that it was visible was. We had to get to the other site immediately. I jumped into the rear of the armored vehicle and one of my men took the wheel. We took off. As we went, I draped a tarpaulin over myself so that I was not visible. We drove fast. There were no obstacles.

When we reached the site our men were sitting in the vehicle talking animatedly to the four Jordanian soldiers who were there. The situation was very tense. As we approached, another soldier appeared and signed for us to stop. My driver started to explain that we were here to see if something was wrong. But the circumstances were shifting out of our control.

It was necessary to make a snap decision. It was possible that the other three units would all be secured by now, since we were late at this one. The command centre was already secure. I decided to act strategically and hope for the best result.

I could see the Jordanian through a fold in the tarp. Without warning I threw off the cover and shot him in the chest. As he fell, the other soldiers turned to see. I shot two of them before they could reach for their arms and then I shot the radio operator. My men shot the other two. This was not good.

One of my men went immediately to the radio. Our other operatives had secured their objectives, but there was trouble. Even if our presence was not known, something unusual was most likely suspected.

There would be some kind of inspection to follow. Within thirty minutes a car approached our gun site. We engaged them in conversation at first, but it was clear that they were suspicious. I was hidden behind the small bunker that protected the radio. It was clear this was no longer a covert operation. We had no choice but to confront the enemy. One of their soldiers was quicker than the others. He drew his gun and waved it at my men, ordering then out of the car. They responded as if casually, then the firing from the machine gun on the armored car began. Two of my men were hit before the rest of us killed the others. Except the smart one. He leaped in the direction of the radio and caught a glimpse of me behind it. I shot him, but not before he himself fired as well. I was hit in the leg.

Now, we were fighting a defensive war. It was only an hour before dawn. Our commando group had to hold these positions, otherwise our troops would not be able to take the Old City of Jerusalem. This was such an essential goal that instead of being disheartened, we experienced an unimpeachable determination. We would hold these guns silent and we were readily prepared to die for it.

We had radio contact with the other sites through the command centre. We knew that three of the sites had not yet been checked. We dug in, with weapons and cover that we needed to protect us with the machine gun on the armored vehicle. The Jordanians could not bomb us, because they wouldn't want to destroy their guns. There were ten of us at this location. Six of us were wounded. In a radio message, I was able to communicate in a kind of encrypted message to the other sites: "Hold tight. Fight fire with fire". I maintained a form of communication with them through the early hours of that morning. They held their posts without as much resistance as there was at ours. Our guns were aimed at the Temple Mount and the Western Wall.

Just before dawn the Jordanian army came down on us, but they had themselves created an almost impossible to access strategic position for their guns. The only way to approach the guns was from the road, and the Jordanians didn't have time to create a more effective strategy. We were outnumbered, but we had the tactical advantage.

They came in waves. A few soldiers at a time, at first. We took them down with our machine gun. Then more at once. We used our rifles and grenades as well. They came in larger numbers. We had one other light machine gun in our car. For almost an hour this went on. And then the morning broke.

As the sun came up over the city, The battle for Jerusalem finally began. The Jordanians kept at us, but they were deploying precious troops and loosing many and their men were needed elsewhere. The Jordanian forces were being driven back. We saw Israeli paratroopers landing in the city.

The Israeli military had only commenced action after Jordanian forces made thrusts in the area of Jerusalem. By the evening of that day, the Jerusalem infantry brigade had moved south of Jerusalem, while the mechanized troops and paratroopers had encircled it from the north. Moishe Dayan had ordered his troops not to enter Jerusalem; however, upon hearing that the U.N. was about to declare a ceasefire, he had changed his mind, and without cabinet clearance, decided to take the city. Paratroopers entered the Old City of Jerusalem via the Lion's Gate, and captured the Western Wall and the Temple Mount. The Jerusalem brigade then reinforced them.

By the evening, having held our position in open combat for 15 hours, we were free of attack. Israeli soldiers appeared approaching on the road. The scene was dreadful. Many bodies, much blood. I had been wounded twice more, once in the hip and once more in the chest. All of my men were wounded, but surprisingly only three others were dead at this location. Seven had been killed in the other locations. Our imposter, who was a civilian, was hurt but alive. Most of all, the sacred sites of Jerusalem were safe. The city was now in our hands.

In all, it took only three days for Israeli forces to defeat the Jordanian legion. On the morning of June 7, the order had been given to recapture the Old City. Israeli paratroopers stormed the city and secured it. Defense Minister Moishe Dayan arrived with Chief of Staff Yitzhak Rabin to formally mark the Jews' return to their historic capital and their holiest site. At the Weatern Wall, the IDF's chaplain performed a sacred rite. He blew a shofar. It had not been heard at that site in a long time.

The victory came at a very high cost. In storming the Golan Heights, Israel suffered 115 dead-roughly the number of Americans killed during

Operation Desert Storm. Altogether, Israel lost twice as many men—777 dead and 2,586 wounded—as would be in proportion to her total population as the U.S. lost in eight years of fighting in Vietnam. Also, despite the incredible success of the air campaign, the Israeli Air Force lost 46 of its 200 fighters. The death toll on the Arab side was 15,000 Egyptians, 2,500 Syrians, and 800 Jordanians.

Our specific mission was effective, however the war itself went well for us. From the start, we created an advantage in the air and we deployed our forces well in the ensuing days. This war, which had been calculated to utterly destroy us, was unsuccessful. After only six days we emerged the clear victors. For my part, my wounds were not life threatening, although I lost the full use of my right leg and partial capacity of one lung. That, I could take in stride, so to speak. Much harder to deal with was the celebrity attention I received from the media. I was a hero again. That was worse than my limp and my occasional shortness of breath.

There were, of course, plenty of heroes that the media could have chosen. My particular appeal was in the seemingly colorful details. I was a special forces, commando leader. Our mission had been covert, but we were forced to defend ourselves against overpowering odds. We had killed a great many of the enemy in direct combat.

These issues seem to attract attention, though they are not elements I am particularly proud of, for clear reasons. There were two other reasons that made my case more romantic than some others, and the military had no reluctance to release them. I was a career soldier, and they like to feel pride in their soldiers.

First, our mission permitted the Israeli forces to take the Old City including the Western Wall and the Temple Mount. They definitely wanted a person to symbolize that event, and they chose me to be it.

BAR KOCHBA

Secondly, I am a Holocaust survivor and a former member of the Irgun. It is ironic to me that something which had at one time been so unpopular could at another time appear to have been an asset. The portrait of a death camp survivor eventually becoming a Jewish warrior and finally being instrumental in the repossession of the Western Wall is a symbolism too great to ignore, if you are part of the media. I couldn't deny the seeming 'facts'. I could only maintain that they were not heroic. That, it seems, make me even more of a celebrity.

I was in hospital for several weeks before having to deal with any kind of future. I was probably severely injured enough to permanently prevent me from further field duty. I was not entirely ambivalent about that. Hopefully, there would be no more war. That would be a feature of an optimistic mind. I was 37 years old. I did not expect to simply retire.

CHAPTER 41
Romance

I received many requests for all kinds of interviews after I came out of the hospital. I turned almost all of then down, although I was pressured by my superiors to talk to the media. I had learned after the Suez Crisis that the media said what they wanted no matter what information I gave them. They painted me as some kind of hero in almost every case, even though I was careful to point out that I was in no way special, that far better men than I had fallen and that there was nothing romantic in being a trained soldier.

One request for an interview caught my attention. It was from a journalist writing for a weekly Jewish paper in New York. What attracted me was that the orientation of the story was not on heroism. The paper itself had a spiritual slant. The proposed title was, "The will to fight: The journey of a Jewish warrior." The writer of the proposal was a young woman by the name of Leah Teperman. I agreed to meet with her to discuss the proposed story at a discrete café I knew of close to the Old City.

She was there when I arrived. I picked her out immediately even though the café was small and not crowded. She had light hair that hung slightly over her shoulder, cut with bangs in front which was a popular style. Although she was slight she did not appear small or petite. She was dressed casually but with conservative good taste. These were details that registered with me right away. Most important, though, was her face. It was simply the most pleasing face I had ever seen. It was symmetrical, lively, in order. There was something in it that conveyed confidence, but most importantly it had humility. That was something rarely seen in journalists.

When she saw me standing outside the perimeter of the outdoor café she raised her hand in a gesture of greeting and smiled. That smile somehow moved me. It was beautiful, as some smiles can be, but it was more. It was genuine and without a hint of deceit. I raised my own hand to return the gesture. It felt like my arm was floating in a sea of joy. When I introduced myself and shook her hand, that smile flashed again. Before I had even sat down I was entranced. This is not normal for me. It caught me off guard.

"Major Bar Kochba?" Her voice was a bit throaty.

"Miss Teperman?" I replied simply.

"I'm so glad to meet you. I know you have a busy schedule."

I sat down with some grace; more than I am used to. "Actually, I'm not so busy, Miss Teperman. The IDF has given me some free time."

The corners of her mouth turned down slightly. "Would you mind calling me Leah. I would feel more comfortable."

She was candid. "Definitely. I will call you Leah. Why don't you address me as Avrum. So we can dismiss that formality."

This relaxed her somewhat, though she maintained a suitably professional approach. "You may have something to say about the nature of this article. The story is not intended to be about what you did in the Six Day War, Avrum. Everyone knows of your heroism and the wounds you suffered and it's truly remarkable. The story is not about how you fought, but why you fought. Is that a foolish question?"

Her blue eyes appeared almost apologetic. It was the first time I realized how young she must be. Early twenties, not more. "No, Leah. It's not foolish. It's the most important question that a soldier has to ask."

"You survived the camps. How much of a factor was that in your decision to be a soldier?"

I found myself in a curious state. On the one hand, I didn't want to patronize this bright young woman. On the other hand, I sensed that she was delicate and that I had to treat her sensitively. "It wasn't the actual place where I decided to be a soldier. It was the place where I decided to be a Jew. Everything else came from that."

She took a notebook out of her bag. "Do you mind if I take notes, Avrum?" she asked.

I said I didn't mind.

"When did you decide to be a soldier?"

"I don't know that I ever actually made that decision in itself. What I decided was that I could be a dead Jew or I could be a Jew who will fight for survival. I knew I had nothing on earth to do but help to establish Israel. That was my choice."

"You were with the Irgun before the War for Independence. Why did you choose that route?"

These were questions I could easily answer, but they were somewhat more relevant than the questions asked by most of the other journalists. While they wanted sensational elements, this young girl seemed more interested in motives and history. "I accepted their strategy. I believed we were at war with the British army."

We talked for over an hour. I was impressed with the way she led her questions out of my answers rather than leading me with her questions.

But most of all, it was her face that interested me. It was so young, and yet it had the marks of a serious personality. At the end of the hour she asked the first serious question.

"How does being a soldier fit into your spiritual life?"

I had to stop there. "You know, Leah, if you want to discuss spiritual matters I am very interested. I wonder if it's relevant, but it's something I would like to talk about. But, perhaps, not right now. I have an appointment for one thing, but more importantly I'd like to think about my answer. Can we meet again, say, day after tomorrow, same place and the same time?"

Her face fell into a small state of confusion. "You want to meet again?"

"Yes, if it's possible."

She smiled awkwardly. "Well, yes, definitely. Day after tomorrow, same time and place. That's fine."

I stood up. She stood up too. "Until then?"

"Take care." She said. She shook my hand. I left.

There were secret motives for making another date with this young woman. I did want to think about her questions, that was true. An article in an American Jewish paper in which a Major in the IDF discusses the spiritual aspects of war was a piece I would want to see. Too much had been made of the military victory in this past war. Too much had been made of our 'brilliant' effort. Not enough focus had been given to the fact that we did not achieve statehood for its own sake. We achieved it so that we could be Jews in our own place. Not politically. Not militarily. Spiritually. My efforts had always been to worship God, uncanny and ironic as that may seem. I wanted to express this view and downplay the heroics.

There was another reason. I liked her. I liked her spirit. I liked her manner. She was an observant woman, so I knew I couldn't casually date her. She attracted me. Something eerie was at work here that I couldn't shake. She reminded me of someone. I couldn't quite be sure of who.

When we met the second time our interview started out, surprisingly for me, a bit formal. Perhaps she was nervous because she sensed my interest. The first questions were about my military background. She was particularly interested in West Point since her readers were American. It was on that point that she loosened up a bit.

"You grew up in Europe." She said. "Were there any surprises in America?"

I laughed, more to help loosen the discussion than for the humour. "Everything in America was surprising! The Europe I knew was at war, and before it was at war I was so poor I was not very aware of culture. I'm a rural boy, not a city boy."

She was curious. "You were poor?"

I was actually thrown off by her astonishment. "Desperately. Most Jews were poor in the countryside. Before the war it was very hard to make a living and we were a family of seven. When the war began my father was sent to slave labour. Our businesses were taken away. But in fairness, almost everybody was poor in my part of Hungary."

"When you got to Israel, how old were you?"

"Seventeen."

"It must have been very different." She commented.

"Until I came to Israel I wasn't really a person because I had no real identity. In my town, I was a Jew. I had a personality, I had Jewish friends, so to speak. But survival was such a struggle in itself it was almost all you had time for. When the war came, it allowed the deep rooted anti-

Semitism to become public. There were good people, no doubt about it. And they were precious and highly regarded. But mostly I experienced open hatred. If you were a Jew, that's what you lived with."

Leah was very interested in this. "You were poor and you were hated."

I wanted to convey this aspect of being a Jew to her in a surprising way. Not as journalist, but as a Jewish woman. I wanted her to understand what it meant and why it was so much a part of the Six Day War. "It was very hard for a Jew to find a place in the world. That was why we fought for Israel. It was to have a place in the world. When I got to Israel, I was no longer a person without a place. I had a people and I had a goal. You have to understand, I never fought out of hatred. I fought only to take back what is mine...no, even more than that. I fought for the ability to stand up straight, like any human being should be able to do."

Leah was keen on these points. "You fought for survival."

I responded with more emotion than I would normally express. "We fought for an identity. To be people in the world. That's what any repressed people fight for, I think. That's an understanding that is sometimes lacking in the rest of the world; the fact that the repressed will rise, not out of hatred but out of a need to be acknowledged and out of a desire for identity. This latest war? What do you think it was fought for?"

Leah looked confused for a moment, to be asked a question rather than to ask one. "Well, certainly to survive as a nation. The Arab's threatened to push us into the sea."

"Yes. They threatened to wipe us out, as the Nazi's did. But we stood up for ourselves, which we weren't able to do as a people in Europe less that a generation ago. We were able to do that against this threat because only now are we a people. That's what we fought for. Not only survival; survival is always a personal problem. We fought for an identity. As a people. For the first time in two thousand years we acted as a people. That's the meaning of this last war. That's what I learned when I came here 21 years ago and that's what this war has given us. We can stand on our own footing, we can survive as a nation and we have our own identity as a people."

Leah was very clever. "You're saying this was more than a military victory."

"Exactly. This is a cultural victory. And do you know who understands this better than anyone else?"

She looked interested and that made her seem even more attractive. "No. Who?"

I gestured towards her gently. "The Americans. You understand this victory more deeply than any other nation because your nation is partially founded on this notion of identity. I think, even more than any specific sympathy for the Jews, Americans recognize our right to be a people."

Leah responded from her experience. "I can say that as an American Jew, I have always believed that Israel was as important to who I am as America, but in a different way. I didn't grow up poor, though."

She was a good journalist but an inexperienced one. From this point on, the conversation began to focus on her as much as on me. I learned that she was the daughter of an American Rabbi and a war survivor, that she had been a journalist since college and something about her status as a Jew. This information she gave without misrepresentation.

"I am what some people call observant. I was brought up that way, but I don't think that's the reason for it exactly. I live a very good life, and I believe that is no accident. I mean, I know anyone can suffer; I know that I will suffer like anyone else in my life to come. But God has given me so many blessings, I feel I have to give something back. My parents. My country. My beliefs. It's no accident that I was born a Jew, and I don't allow for the accident that I should not show faith as well.

"But mostly, I have to admit, it's my belief in God that makes me observant. I do fear God, because I know enough to know He is strong. But my love for God, because he has allowed me to be as I am and because he has made a beautiful creation is what motivates me most. I'm observant out of gratitude and because by being observant I live a very good life. That's it."

She looked like a woman who had just been deeply flattered. "I hope it doesn't change."

As I listened to this young Jewish woman and heard her simple but strong words a feeling grew inside of me. It was a feeling almost of recognition. I had not felt anything like this since I had known Orly. In fact, I had not felt anything like this except for what I had felt with Miriam.

At the end of our conversation I led into a more personal approach.

"You are staying at a hotel?" I asked.

"No." she said. "I'm staying with a friend of the family's."

I was a bit coy with my next question. "I'm alone in the city tomorrow night. Can I take you out to dinner?"

Leah looked at the ground briefly and then looked up. "What time?"

It was as respectable an answer as I could have expected. We arranged to meet at a nice restaurant that would give us some privacy. My recent popularity in the press had made it necessary to be selective about where I chose to dine.

We met the next night in more informal circumstances. Leah was more relaxed and the conversation was more far ranging. I learned we shared a love of history and historical figures. Both of us admired Albert Einstein.

"Did you know he was asked to be the first Prime Minister of Israel?" She asked brightly.

"No." I said. "That I didn't know."

"He said 'Who wants to be Prime Minister of six million Prime ministers,'."

We both laughed. She went on. "He said that if he had thought his ideas would lead to a terrible weapon, he would have been a shoemaker."

"And who wouldn't have wanted to walk in his shoes?" I quipped. "He didn't believe in a personal God. He said he didn't believe in a God that answered prayers or intervened in individual destiny."

Leah was especially astute for a young person on this point, I thought. "He couldn't. As a scientist he believed in the infinite order of the universe, so a God that might disturb that was not possible."

I looked quizzically at Leah. "You believe in a personal God?" I said.

She was quick to answer. "I do, of course. I believe in an infinite God that can order the universe as well as deal with our personal prayers and destinies." She looked up at the sky as if in defeat. "Of course, I'm not a scientist."

"But…" I added. "a sometimes philosopher."

Leah demurred on this. "I'm not a philosopher, Avrum. I don't know why things are or what they mean. I believe in the Torah because that's where all the answers seem to be. That's not philosophy."

"Oh." I pressed her more than I would normally press an acquaintance. "If it's not philosophy, Leah, what is it?"

She hesitated just for a moment and then replied, as if to herself, "It's practice. It's the practice of doing what's right."

I looked at her lovely face, down turned in thought. "I've heard that before in various context, most of them political. I don't think I ever believed it from anyone until now."

Leah looked at me directly. "Oh, Avrum! You're only patronizing me. What do you believe about the Torah, then?"

I caught her gaze but decided not to meet it. "I believe it's necessity. It's a handbook of necessity."

She looked curious and her face became soft. "I've never thought of it that way. It seems unusual."

"I'm a soldier. I don't know what's right. That's not my place. I do what's necessary."

Her mouth became a little slack and her eyes grew wider. "But you must think that what you are doing is right?"

I debated in my mind how to answer. I decided to avoid details. "No. I don't always think it's right. But I also, like you, believe in an infinite God. Perhaps I even think he guides and protects me. Perhaps I even think He guides and protects Israel."

"You say 'perhaps'. You should say, 'certainly'."

She was like a cool breeze to me. "Well, you see Leah, my faith, unlike yours, is not perfect. If it was, I'm sure I would be observant like you."

Her idealism spilled over. "You don't have to be observant to know what's right."

"No." I replied simply. "But you have to believe in it completely."

She reached out to me with her hand for the first time. She touched my wrist. "You seem to me to be one of the most religious persons I have ever met. There's a glow about you."

"Well, that's interesting because I could say the same thing about you."

I actually hadn't expected this: that there would be a bond between us. But from that moment, my interest in Leah altered. I had seen her as a fresh young woman with whom to spend a casual evening. That simple evening made a difference. I enjoyed myself completely, but there was more. Leah appeared to actually like me, too.

Perhaps it was because the Six Day War was recently over. Perhaps it was because I was still recovering from my wounds. Perhaps it was because I knew my action in the military was over. I responded very strongly to someone I sincerely liked showing the same for me. A soldier cannot respond very honestly to affection. We are not used to being 'liked'. Now, at this point in my life, I was vulnerable.

But it was Leah, herself, too. She was so bright and so forthright. She was the best woman I had ever met in terms of personal honesty, the quality of having both humility and insight. There was something authentic about her that, more and more, I couldn't resist.

We saw each other a few days after that evening, and then a few times a few days after that. We became friends over the next few weeks while she was posted in Jerusalem. Her article on me came out in her newspaper. The angle was that I was a 'spiritual warrior' of deep conviction as well as a hero. It was more than flattering. It showed a window into my deeper nature as no article ever had.

I didn't realize that there was anything romantic in our relationship. After all, she was more than ten years younger than I and she was observant, which I was not. Somehow, over the several months we saw each other often, she became more of a figure of focus for me. The truth was, I was becoming infatuated. I believed I was falling in love with her. She seemed to be, somehow, a part of my life I just had to have.

We met many more times over the following weeks. At each encounter we became more easy and casual. Was it her youth, her optimism, her fresh approach to every issue that moved me? I loved hearing her thoughts. Or was it her sincere smile, her still girlish but full

BAR KOCHBA

figure that trapped me? For the first time in my life I felt emotions that had never before reached their peak. I anticipated each scheduled meeting with a mixture of doubt and expectancy. Each time I saw her, after a few days apart, it was as if I was seeing her for the first time. Every day I attempted to put her to the back of my mind, and each day the idea of her would push out of the shadows into the light of affections I actually didn't know I had. I knew I loved Orly, but that love had been slow and grounded. This love was giddy and light. I knew I had loved Hannah, but that love had been sensual and rough. The only person I could compare Leah to, in her affection for me, was Miriam. Some of the same feelings were there for her. She reminded me of Miriam, not because she was like her as much as that she effected my feelings in a similar way. It was like 'first love' all over again, but in the ripeness of my life experience it seemed even more strong and compelling.

I began loosing sleep. There began to be a new feature to my daily tasks. I approached people with a lightness that was uncharacteristic, as though I were under the influence of wine or brandy. This young woman was becoming the reason for a transformation in my way of knowing the world. I did not relate to the world, at this time, much like a soldier.

Still, I didn't know her feelings for me. In the middle of the third month after we met I invited Leah to come with me on a picnic to Dafna, the Kibbutz I had lived on when I came Israel. It was a long drive and on the way we talked about current events and odd topics as people do on long drives. There were periods of silence, too, just watching the scenery.

When we arrived at the Kibbutz there were greetings and informal introductions. People remembered me, but there was no one left there I had been close to. They had all moved or been killed. We went to the grounds where Orly was buried and I said *Kadish*. Leah knew I had almost been married, but not more than that.

We went into the orchard for our picnic. Both of us were in a somewhat heightened mood, because of the travel, the setting and the history. Leah didn't know about the battles here or anywhere else. I didn't talk about any of that to her, for obvious reasons. We sat on the grass, with the fruit trees above and surrounding us. And I probed her feelings.

"Are there indications that you'll be staying longer in Israel?" I asked.

"Yes, as a matter of fact, there are. My editor wants me to stay as a correspondent for at least a few months."

"That's good." I said. "I would miss you if you left now."

Leah smiled. brightly. "Yes. I would miss you, too."

I'm really very clumsy when it comes to feelings. "Would you miss me a great deal?"

Leah looked a bit bewildered, but she said sincerely, "Yes, Avrum. I would miss you a great deal."

I pushed a bit. "Like, as a friend?"

She shook her head back and forth indicating a bit of pressure. "Avrum, how should I miss you? You are my good friend, even my true friend, if the truth be known. You mean the world to me."

I could see that she was responding honestly. I pushed even further, into possibly dangerous territory. "My feelings for you are very strong, Leah. I'm not someone who is very free with feelings, but you are very important to me, so I want you to know."

Leah's lips were tight but her face was clear. "Know what, Avrum?"

I spoke as gently as possible, as if the very words were dangerous weapons that could cause enormous hurt… "I'm more fond of you, perhaps, Leah, than you are of me. I believe I love you."

We paused on this for a moment silently. Leah broke the silence. "Well, that's interesting Avrum. You know that I am a religious woman?"

"I know." And then I stumbled and said, "But a woman, nonetheless." I had been reduced to the emotions of a schoolboy.

"Avrum, you are the only man I have ever met who really respects me both for who I am as a person and also as a religious individual."

"What does that mean, Leah?'

She let her face fall into a million pieces. "Oh, Avrum!" she said. "Don't you know, I love you too? But what should that mean? You're not about to marry me."

This was as if a divine purpose had touched my heart. "Oh, but you're wrong, Leah. I would never compromise your most beautiful faith. I do want to marry you. I have a ring, right here, that I brought for you."

I brought a silver ring out of my shirt pocket and held it out to her like a sacred artifact. I really felt so awkward and tentative. "Is this the time to give it to you, Leah. Will you say 'yes'? Will you marry me?"

Leah looked at the ring with a smile on her face. "You planned for this?"

"I only, in my fondest dreams, thought it would ever happen."

Leah laughed a happy nervous laugh. She snatched the ring out of my fingers and held it in front of my eyes. "Avrum, I was taught to want marriage more than almost anything in life. I haven't given it much thought in the last few years, but inside I think it was a great hope. This is fine! I'll marry you, Avrum, but you have to meet one condition."

"And what is that?" I asked.

"You have to become observant."

I nodded my head. "That's not a problem. I started out that way and can go back to it."

"And you have to get permission from my parents."

That seemed possible. My hopes had been realized in this brief moment. I felt an almost awkward gratitude, sitting in the orchard, on the kibbutz, with a woman more than ten years younger than myself. I had a feeling like somehow being at school, in the playground, playing at romance. My feelings for Leah were real, but something seemed wrong at the same time. I dismissed this idea. I kissed Leah's cheek. She threw her arms around my neck and kissed my cheek. We smiled at each other. What more could we do?

CHAPTER 42
Relationships

The next 10 days flew by. Leah and I decided not to announce our engagement until I had met her parents who were scheduled to arrive at that time. I was in an emotional state that was just somewhat shy of euphoria. Leah and I saw each other for a least a brief period almost every day. This was unique for me. The old warrior, despite his wounds, was in love.

When Leah's parent's did arrive I was very tense. Leah met them at the airport and I was expected to join them for dinner at a good restaurant. When I first saw them, I knew I liked them. I don't know why. Rivka, her mother, was almost stately, but with a suggestion of humour that also showed in her smile. Asher, her father, was a man with soft but masculine features. What struck me about them was two-fold. Leah looked more like her mother. And her parent's looked about the same age as I.

The introductions were formal. I introduced myself as Avrum Bar Kochba and shook both their hands. Everyone nodded and smiled and we sat down.

Asher said. "Can I call you Avrum? Or Major Bar Kochba?"

I laughed. "Please call me Avrum. I don't consider this to be a military matter. Do you?"

Asher blushed very slightly. "No. Not at all. It's strictly pleasure."

Rivka spoke up. She had a slight Hungarian accent. "We know a lot about you from the article Leah wrote."

"I think Leah flattered me. I'm really just a soldier."

Asher broke in. "In the article it said you once wanted to be a rabbi."

I thought to respond lightly. I was, in fact, embarrassed that I had such a brutal past. "I still do, Rabbi. Do you think I am passed the mark for the *Yeshiva?*"

He and Rivka both laughed. Leah was, at this point, not yet really a part of the conversation. She was more like the dutiful daughter among her elders. Because of the situation we were all anxious. Leah's parents were doing their best not to make the meeting like an interrogation.

"Do you like fish, Avrum?" Rivka asked.

"I'm old fashioned." I replied. "I like baked carp."

"Me too." She said almost meaningfully. "It's a European favorite. It's so rare that I get the chance to enjoy it."

Asher jumped in. "Where in Europe are you from?"

"Hungary." I replied.

Rivka coughed suddenly. She brought her hand to her mouth. "Sorry. I swallowed down the wrong pipe."

When she had cleared her throat she said, "What part of Hungary are you from?"

I told her. The blood drained from her face. "Excuse me a moment. I need to leave the table."

Asher and I rose as she left. Leah finally spoke. "Daddy, Avrum will be on leave for a few more weeks."

Asher smiled. "That's nice. Well deserved, I'm sure."

"Leah told me that you were a Chaplin in the war. So you are also a military man."

BAR KOCHBA

Asher made a sad face. "No, Avrum, I wouldn't say that. I was just one of so many who served. But it is where I met Leah's mother. She was born in Germany."

I was surprised. "I didn't know that. But I did know that your wife is a survivor, like myself."

"Yes, that's true."

Leah spoke up. "She lost her sister."

I was interested. "Really?" What more could one say. So many were lost.

At that moment Rivka came back. She seemed shaken. She addressed her family. "Would you mind if Avrum and I talked Hungarian for a while. I have a few questions to ask him. In fact," she said, "would you excuse us while we go to the balcony? It won't take long."

Leah and Asher agreed, and Rivka accompanied me to the restaurant balcony. She was visibly focused and determined in her approach. She spoke to me in Hungarian and sometimes in Yiddish, which we both spoke somewhat better.

"Your name hasn't always been Bar Kochba?"

"No." I replied.

"What was it originally?"

I told her, "Benjamin."

"In the war, were you transported to Auschwitz on a cattle train. In the Fall of 1944."

This question was a complete surprise. How could she know such a thing? "Yes. I was transported on a train to Auschwitz. How could you possibly know this?"

"You used your name 'Avrum'?"

That was the train I traveled on with Miriam. I began to sweat. "Yes. That was my only name."

Rivka grabbed my wrist, so hard I couldn't believe it. "You knew a girl named Miram? Miriam Spitz? On that train?"

For the first time in my life I felt so much emotion that I actually became dizzy with it. "You know her?" I almost shouted.

"She's my sister!" Rivka cried out. Tears began to fall from her trembling eyes.

I held her arm to steady her. "Rivka, please. Where is she?"

Through her tears of both sorrow and joy she said simply. "No. You don't understand, Avrum she's dead."

I couldn't say a word. More a sound. A mournful cry. I had always somehow hoped she was alive somewhere. I didn't realize how much I still mourned for her, how much my love for her was still the greatest love in my life.

Rivka regained her bearings, but she didn't let go of my arm. "But there's more. With that young girl, Miriam…did you have sexual relations?"

I was stunned. I stammered. "Yes, but no one could know that except her and I."

"Avrum." Rivka said. "You must listen, unbelievable as it may sound."

I didn't know what to expect.

"From that encounter my sister Miriam conceived. She was pregnant. While an inmate. In the camps."

I stood in stunned awe. She was talking about my beloved being pregnant. "She died while carrying our child?"

"No!" Rivka exclaimed. "She carried the child until liberation by the Russians and then she gave birth to a baby girl."

I actually fell to my knees on that balcony. "A girl!" I cried. I had carried this with me all my life. "A girl."

"But Miriam was very weakened and no one could help her."

"Oh G-d!" I cried out. I couldn't bear it. And then I realized what the truth might actually be.

"The daughter?!" I said. "What happened to the daughter."

Rivka knelt down beside me. "She lived, Avrum. She's a beautiful woman. She was adopted and brought up by Asher and I. She's named Leah."

I broke into massive sobs that shook my whole body. I was bathed in tears. So long I had waited for a sign that Miriam had lived. And now, I had found this wonderful young person who was our little girl. It was as if G-d had touched me with a forgiving finger for all that I had done. "Our little girl." I sobbed. I was lost for several minutes.

When I lifted up my head, Rivka was looking into my face. "You really loved my sister, didn't you?"

"Yes. More than all the world." My voice was soft and hoarse.

"She loved you. But you can't marry your daughter. Can you?"

"Of course not."

"She doesn't know any of this: who her mother really is, that she isn't our child, who you are."

I pulled myself together quickly. In all my years of fighting I had never broken like this. "That's quite clear."

"I think Asher and I have to tell her, Avrum. She needs to know now."

"Of course." I said simply. "I think perhaps I should go. I'll leave from here."

Rivka nodded assent. "That's good. I'll take care of the rest. I'll contact you when the time is right."

There wasn't much I could say. "Rivka, nothing embarrassing went on. She's a wonderful girl. True to her heart."

Rivka smiled. "Like her mother." She said.

I left the balcony, went out of the restaurant by a side entrance and breathed, as if for the first time, the night air.

Three weeks later I received a phone call from Leah. "I think we should talk.", she said. We arranged to meet at a small café the next afternoon. I was nervous. I can only imagine how she felt.

She was already there when I arrived, wearing a casual skirt and blouse in light colours. It was the first time I saw her as my daughter. Bright. Pretty. Young. She didn't smile as I said 'Shalom' and sat down. It would be inadequate to say I didn't know how to speak.

"I don't know how to regard you. As my father or as my former fiancé?" Her face was set hard. There was tension in her neck and forehead.

"You can regard me as someone who loved you at first sight." Her face relaxed a bit.

"I think it was more spiritual than physical, Avrum." She paused. "Should I call you Avrum?"

I looked at the concern that was still reflected on her face. "We're both adults, no matter what, Leah. I don't believe we have to ignore that."

She looked down pensively. "I've thought about you a lot over the past few weeks. I feel a little ashamed that I fell in love with my father, but my mother, Rivka…I've started calling her by that name…tells me that it's nothing to be ashamed of, that I couldn't know. Asher tells me that I wouldn't be the first girl to fall in love with her father."

I laughed gently, partly to ease the tension for her. "You didn't fall in love with your father. You fell in love with a soldier in an unfamiliar land."

A small smile broke over her lips. "It was very romantic wasn't it?"

For the first time I spoke to her as a father might. "It was for me. A beautiful young woman was giving me a lot of attention. I was flattered. And, I admit, I'm a little ashamed too."

Leah spoke as if to herself as she lightly bit her lower lip. "I can get over this."

"We can both get over this, Leah." I wanted her to understand that the romantic relationship was not going to be an obstacle for us. "If anything, we know each other better as human beings and that can only give us insight and knowledge. Not grief." I expected that was too mature a point of view for her to fully understand at that point, but her tension eased and she looked more congruent.

We paused briefly, then she looked up with a serious expression. "Tell me about my mother."

I was glad she asked. "She was the only woman I have ever loved so deeply that everything else in the world seemed unimportant. We were only together for a few days, but in those few days she transformed my life. She was smart far beyond her years. She was brave, but Rivka can tell you more about that. She was funny and bright but not at all frivolous. It was my love for her that caused me to survive. Not just the camps, but after, here in Israel, as well."

"Mama…Rivka…says she was 16 when she died."

I was silent. Leah started to weep.

"My poor little mother!" she said. And through her tears, "I'm so sad."

For a moment, I thought I was looking at Miriam, crying in that stinking cattle car, heading towards oblivion. To soothe her, "So am I. So am I."

"I want to see you again, Avrum. But I need time to understand my emotions. I don't think I have to think of you as anything but the father I am just getting to know, but learning that I am not who I thought I was all my life is too hard right now. I'll see you again, maybe in a few weeks. Now I want to go. You understand, don't you?"

My voice was gentle and calm. "Perfectly, Leah. You go. Take all the time you need. I promise I will always be your father, nothing else. When we see each other again, perhaps it will be easier?"

And it was easier. Step by step, it got easier for both of us, so that now, years later, I can look back with interest. Leah went back to the U.S. after a few months, months in which our relationship became steady and in perspective. She looked into herself and as a result, went back to college to study medicine shortly after returning to Rochester. Rivka wrote to me often and, with that and all else, my own life became more full. A few years after I met her Leah, graduated and soon after married in New York. I have two grandchildren. I've seen them and they are both precious.

I retired from the IDF shortly after Leah, Rivka and Asher left Israel. I went back to the university and now I teach history there. I still walk with a slight limp in my gait, I cough after some exertion but there are many soldiers who do.

Can a life of combat, war, persecution lead to a love of G-d? It would be ironic. Reality is both a harsh backdrop for faith and, I think, a necessary one. Once a *yeshiva* boy, then a warrior, I think that is what G-d decreed. You have to fight for something to know the value of anything. In the end I have found that this struggle, this war of person or even country, is almost entirely spiritual rather than physical in the end. Having lived long enough to know this, I have, not pride, but resolution. The old wounds heal. G-d both forgives and redeems.

Manufactured By: RR Donnelley
Breinigsville, PA USA
January, 2011